PENG

THE PURSUIT ~~OF THE WELL-B~~ELOVED
and THE WELL-BELOVED

THOMAS HARDY was born in a cottage in Higher Bockhampton, near Dorchester, on 2 June, 1840. He was educated locally and at sixteen was articled to a Dorchester architect, John Hicks. In 1862 he moved to London and found employment with another architect, Arthur Blomfield. He now began to write poetry and published an essay. By 1867 he had returned to Dorset to work as Hicks's assistant and began his first (unpublished) novel, *The Poor Man and the Lady*.

On an architectural visit to St Juliot in Cornwall in 1870 he met his first wife, Emma Gifford. Before their marriage in 1874 he had published four novels and was earning his living as a writer. More novels followed and in 1878 the Hardys moved from Dorset to the London literary scene. But in 1885, after building his house at Max Gate near Dorchester, Hardy again returned to Dorset. He then produced most of his major novels: *The Mayor of Casterbridge* (1886), *The Woodlanders* (1887), *Tess of the D'Urbervilles* (1891), *The Pursuit of the Well-Beloved* (1892) and *Jude the Obscure* (1895). Amidst the controversy caused by *Jude the Obscure*, he turned to the poetry he had been writing all his life. In the next thirty years he published over nine hundred poems and his epic drama in verse, *The Dynasts*.

After a long and bitter estrangement, Emma Hardy died at Max Gate in 1912. Paradoxically, the event triggered some of Hardy's finest love poetry. In 1914, however, he married Florence Dugdale, a close friend for several years. In 1910 he had been awarded the Order of Merit and was recognized, even revered, as the major literary figure of the time. He died on 11 January 1928. His ashes were buried in Westminster Abbey and his heart at Stinsford in Dorset.

PATRICIA INGHAM is General Editor of all Hardy's fiction in the Penguin Classics Edition. She is a Fellow in English at St Anne's College, Oxford, and *The Times* Lecturer in English Language, University of Oxford. She has written extensively on the Victorian novel and on Hardy in particular. Her most recent publications include *Dickens, Women and Language* (1992) and *The Language of Gender and Class: Transformation in the Victorian Novel* (1996). She has also edited Hardy's *The Woodlanders* and Elizabeth Gaskell's *North and South* for Penguin Classics.

THOMAS HARDY

The Pursuit of the Well-Beloved

&

The Well-Beloved

Edited with an Introduction and Notes by
PATRICIA INGHAM

PENGUIN BOOKS

PENGUIN BOOKS

Published by the Penguin Group
Penguin Books Ltd, 27 Wrights Lane, London w8 5tz, England
Penguin Putnam Inc., 375 Hudson Street, New York, New York 10014, USA
Penguin Books Australia Ltd, Ringwood, Victoria, Australia
Penguin Books Canada Ltd, 10 Alcorn Avenue, Toronto, Ontario, Canada m4v 3b2
Penguin Books (NZ) Ltd, Private Bag 102902, NSMC, Auckland, New Zealand

Penguin Books Ltd, Registered Offices: Harmondsworth, Middlesex, England

The Pursuit of the Well-Beloved first published in serial form 1892
The Well-Beloved first published in book form 1897
This edition published in Penguin Classics 1997
3 5 7 9 10 8 6 4 2

Editorial matter copyright © Patricia Ingham, 1997
All rights reserved

The moral right of the editor has been asserted

Set in 10/12.5pt Monotype Baskerville
Typeset by RefineCatch Limited, Bungay, Suffolk
Printed in England by Clays Ltd, St Ives plc

CONTENTS

Acknowledgements   vii
General Editor's Preface   viii
Chronology: Hardy's Life and Works   xi
Map: The Wessex of the Novels   xv
Bibliographical Note   xvi
Introduction   xvii
Further Reading   xxxiv
A Note on the History of the Texts   xxxvi

THE PURSUIT OF THE WELL-BELOVED   I

Contents   3
Map: The Isle   5
Part First: A Young Man of Twenty   7
Part Second: A Young Man of Forty   63
Part Third: A Young Man of Fifty-Nine   III

THE WELL-BELOVED   169

Map: The Isle of Slingers   170
1897 Preface   171
1912 Preface   173
Contents   175
Part First: A Young Man of Twenty   177
Part Second: A Young Man of Forty   215
Part Third: A Young Man Turned Sixty   281

Notes to The Pursuit of the Well-Beloved   339
Notes to The Well-Beloved   353
Appendix: A Note on the Illustrations to The Pursuit of the
    Well-Beloved   366
Glossary   372

ACKNOWLEDGEMENTS

I am indebted to Jenny Harrington and Shannon Russell for all their help
and advice; and to Rosemary Kelly, Peter Ghosh, Margaret Howatson
and Hazel Rossotti for specific information. To all these I am most
grateful.

This edition uses, with one exception, the first edition in *volume* form of each of Hardy's novels and therefore offers something not generally available. Their dates range from 1871 to 1897. The purpose behind this choice is to present each novel as the creation of its own period and without revisions of later times, since these versions have an integrity and value of their own. The outline of textual history that follows is designed to expand on this statement.

All of Hardy's fourteen novels, except *Jude the Obscure* (1895) which first appeared as a volume in the Wessex Novels, were published individually as he wrote them (from 1871 onwards). Apart from *Desperate Remedies* (1871) and *Under the Greenwood Tree* (1872), all were published first as serials in periodicals, where they were subjected to varying degrees of editorial interference and censorship. *Desperate Remedies* and *Under the Greenwood Tree* appeared directly in volume form from Tinsley Brothers. By 1895 ten more novels had been published in volumes by six different publishers.

By 1895 Hardy was sufficiently well-established to negotiate with Osgood, McIlvaine a collected edition of all earlier novels and short story collections plus the volume edition of *Jude the Obscure*. *The Well-Beloved* (radically changed from its serialized version) was added in 1897, completing the appearance of all Hardy's novels in volume form. Significantly this collection was called the 'Wessex Novels' and contained a map of 'The Wessex of the Novels' and authorial prefaces, as well as frontispieces by Macbeth-Raeburn of a scene from the novel sketched 'on the spot'. The texts were heavily revised by Hardy, amongst other things, in relation to topography, to strengthen the 'Wessex' element so as to suggest that this half-real half-imagined location had been coherently conceived from the beginning, though of course he knew that this was not so. In practice 'Wessex' had an uncertain and ambiguous development in the earlier editions. To trace the growth of Wessex in the novels as they appeared it is necessary to read them in their original pre-1895 form. For the 1895 edition represents a substantial layer of reworking.

Similarly, in the last fully revised and collected edition of 1912–13, the Wessex Edition, further alterations were made to topographical detail and photographs of Dorset were included. In the more open climate of opinion then prevailing, sexual and religious references were sometimes (though not always) made bolder. In both collected editions there were also many changes of other kinds. In addition, novels and short story volumes were grouped thematically as 'Novels of Character and Environment', 'Romances and Fantasies' and 'Novels of Ingenuity' in a way suggesting a unifying master plan underlying all texts. A few revisions were made for the Mellstock Edition of 1919–20, but to only some texts.

It is various versions of the 1912–13 edition which are generally available today, incorporating these layers of alteration and shaped in part by the critical climate when the alterations were made. Therefore the present edition offers the texts as Hardy's readers first encountered them, in a form of which he in general approved, the version that his early critics reacted to. It reveals Hardy as he first dawned upon the public and shows how his writing (including the creation of Wessex) developed, partly in response to differing climates of opinion in the 1870s, 1880s and early 1890s. In keeping with these general aims, the edition will reproduce all contemporary illustrations where the originals were line drawings. In addition, for all texts which were illustrated, individual volumes will provide an appendix discussing the artist and the illustrations.

The exception to the use of the first volume editions is *Far from the Madding Crowd*, for which Hardy's holograph manuscript will be used. That edition will demonstrate in detail just how the text is 'the creation of its own period': by relating the manuscript to the serial version and to the first volume edition. The heavy editorial censoring by Leslie Stephen for the serial and the subsequent revision for the volume provide an extreme example of the processes that in many cases precede and produce the first book versions. In addition, the complete serial version (1892) of *The Well-Beloved* will be printed alongside the volume edition, since it is arguably a different novel from the latter.

To complete the picture of how the texts developed later, editors trace in their Notes on the History of the Text the major changes in 1895 and 1912–13. They quote significant alterations in their explanatory notes and include the authorial prefaces of 1895 and 1912–13. They also indicate something of the pre-history of the texts in manuscripts where these are available. The editing of the short stories will be separately dealt with in the two volumes containing them.

Patricia Ingham
St Anne's College, Oxford

1840 2 June: Thomas Hardy born, Higher Bockhampton, Dorset, eldest child of a builder, Thomas Hardy, and Jemima Hand, who had been married for less than six months. Younger siblings: Mary, Henry, Katharine (Kate), to whom he remained close.

1848–56 Schooling in Dorset.

1856 Hardy watched the hanging of Martha Browne for the murder of her husband. (Thought to be remembered in the death of Tess Durbeyfield.)

1856–60 Articled to Dorchester architect, John Hicks; later his assistant.

late 1850s Important friendship with Horace Moule (eight years older, middle-class and well-educated), who became his intellectual mentor and encouraged his self-education.

1862 London architect, Arthur Blomfield, employed him as a draughts-man. Self-education continued.

1867 Returned to Dorset as a jobbing architect. He worked for Hicks on church restoration.

1868 Completed his first novel *The Poor Man and the Lady* but it was rejected for publication (see 1878).

1869 Worked for the architect Crickmay in Weymouth, again on church restoration.

1870 After many youthful infatuations thought to be referred to in early poems, met his first wife, Emma Lavinia Gifford, on a professional visit to St Juliot in north Cornwall.

1871 *Desperate Remedies* published in volume form by Tinsley Brothers.

1872 *Under the Greenwood Tree* published in volume form by Tinsley Brothers.

1873 *A Pair of Blue Eyes* (previously serialized in *Tinsleys' Magazine*). Horace Moule committed suicide.

1874 *Far from the Madding Crowd* (previously serialized in the *Cornhill Magazine*). Hardy married Emma and set up house in London

(Surbiton). They had no children, to Hardy's regret; and she never got on with his family.

1875　The Hardys returned to Dorset (Swanage).

1876　*The Hand of Ethelberta* (previously serialized in the *Cornhill Magazine*).

1878　*The Return of the Native* (previously serialized in *Belgravia*). The Hardys moved back to London (Tooting). Serialized version of part of first unpublished novel appeared in *Harper's Weekly* in New York as *An Indiscretion in the Life of an Heiress*. It was never included in his collected works.

1880　*The Trumpet-Major* (previously serialized in *Good Words*). Hardy ill for many months.

1881　*A Laodicean* (previously serialized in *Harper's New Monthly Magazine*). The Hardys returned to Dorset.

1882　*Two on a Tower* (previously serialized in the *Atlantic Monthly*).

1885　The Hardys moved for the last time to a house, Max Gate, outside Dorchester, designed by Hardy and built by his brother.

1886　*The Mayor of Casterbridge* (previously serialized in the *Graphic*).

1887　*The Woodlanders* (previously serialized in *Macmillan's Magazine*).

1888　*Wessex Tales*.

1891　*A Group of Noble Dames* (tales). *Tess of the D'Urbervilles* (previously serialized in censored form in the *Graphic*). It simultaneously enhanced his reputation as a novelist and caused a scandal because of its advanced views on sexual conduct.

1892　Hardy's father, Thomas, died. Serialized version of *The Well-Beloved*, entitled *The Pursuit of the Well-Beloved*, in the *Illustrated London News*. Growing estrangement from Emma.

1892–3　*Our Exploits at West Poley*, a long tale for boys, published in an American periodical, the *Household*.

1893　Met Florence Henniker, one of several society women with whom he had intense friendships. Collaborated with her on *The Spectre of the Real* (published 1894).

1894　*Life's Little Ironies* (tales).

1895　*Jude the Obscure*, a savage attack on marriage which worsened relations with Emma. Serialized previously in *Harper's New Monthly Magazine*. It received both eulogistic and vitriolic reviews. The latter were a factor in his ceasing to write novels.

1895–6 First Collected Edition of novels: Wessex Novels (16 volumes), published by Osgood, McIlvaine. This included the first book edition of *Jude the Obscure*.

1897 *The Well-Beloved* (rewritten) published as a book; added to the Wessex Novels as vol. XVII. From now on he published only the poetry he had been writing since the 1860s. **No more novels**.

1898 *Wessex Poems and Other Verses*. Hardy and Emma continued to live at Max Gate but were now estranged and 'kept separate'.

1901 *Poems of the Past and the Present*.

1902 Macmillan became his publishers.

1904 Part 1 of *The Dynasts* (epic-drama in verse on Napoleon). Hardy's mother, Jemima, 'the single most important influence in his life', died.

1905 Met Florence Emily Dugdale, his future second wife, then aged 26. Soon a friend and secretary.

1906 Part 2 of *The Dynasts*.

1908 Part 3 of *The Dynasts*.

1909 *Time's Laughingstocks and Other Verses*.

1910 Awarded Order of Merit, having previously refused a knighthood.

1912–13 Major collected edition of novels and verse, revised by Hardy: The Wessex Edition (24 volumes). 27 November: Emma died still estranged. This triggered the writing of Hardy's finest love-lyrics about their early time in Cornwall.

1913 *A Changed Man and Other Tales*.

1914 10 February: married Florence Dugdale (already hurt by his poetic reaction to Emma's death). *Satires of Circumstance*. *The Dynasts: Prologue and Epilogue*.

1915 Mary, Hardy's sister, died. His distant young cousin, Frank, killed at Gallipoli.

1916 *Selected Poems*.

1917 *Moments of Vision and Miscellaneous Verses*.

1919–20 Mellstock Edition of novels and verse (37 volumes).

1922 *Late Lyrics and Earlier with Many Other Verses*.

1923 *The Famous Tragedy of the Queen of Cornwall* (drama).

1924 Dramatized *Tess* performed at Dorchester. Hardy infatuated with the local woman, Gertrude Bugler, who played Tess.

1925 *Human Shows, Far Phantasies, Songs and Trifles.*

1928 Hardy died on 11 January. His heart was buried in Emma's grave at Stinsford, his ashes in Westminster Abbey. *Winter Words in Various Moods and Metres* published posthumously. Hardy's brother, Henry, died.

1928–30 Hardy's autobiography published (on his instructions) under his second wife's name.

1937 Florence Hardy (his second wife) died.

1940 Hardy's last sibling, Kate, died.

This map is from the Wessex Novels Edition, 1895–6

BIBLIOGRAPHICAL NOTE

The following abbreviations are used for texts frequently cited throughout the edition.

Biography: M. Millgate, *Thomas Hardy: A Biography* (Oxford: Oxford University Press, 1982)

Collected Letters: R. L. Purdy and M. Millgate (eds.), *The Collected Letters of Thomas Hardy*, 7 vols. (Oxford: Clarendon Press, 1978–88)

Life: Thomas Hardy, *The Life and Work of Thomas Hardy*, ed. M. Millgate (London: Macmillan, 1984)

Literary Notebooks: L. Björk (ed.), *The Literary Notebooks of Thomas Hardy*, 2 vols. (London: Macmillan, 1985)

Personal Notebooks: R. Taylor (ed.), *The Personal Notebooks of Thomas Hardy* (London: Macmillan, 1978)

Poems: S. Hynes (ed.), *The Complete Poetical Works of Thomas Hardy*, 5 vols. (Oxford: Clarendon Press, 1982–95)

The Pursuit of the Well-Beloved and *The Well-Beloved*

The Well-Beloved is and is not Hardy's last novel. No manuscript exists but the serial version, *The Pursuit of the Well-Beloved. A Sketch of a Temperament* was printed in the *Illustrated London News* from 1 October to 17 December 1892 (hereafter *The Pursuit* always refers to this 1892 version). It has never since been reprinted in full. In volume form there was published, in March 1897, *The Well-Beloved. A Sketch of a Temperament*, a text usually re-garded as definitive and yet simultaneously as a variant of the 1892 ver-sion (hereafter *The Well-Beloved* always refers to the 1897 version). By this sleight of hand a date of 1892 is attributed to the work and *Jude the Obscure* (volume edition 1895) is somewhat confusedly assigned the status of the last novel that Hardy wrote. There are, however, good reasons for giving equal status to the texts of 1892 and 1897, and treating the latter as his final novel. Chief among these reasons are major differences in plot be-tween the two versions: Pearston (the name for the central figure in 1892) in *The Pursuit* marries twice, once bigamously; Pierston (the name for the central figure in 1897) only once in *The Well-Beloved* as a belated act of kindness to an ageing former mistress; Pearston attempts seduction and suicide, Pierston neither.

Such changes are enough to turn the two texts into different novels. Hence the printing of both versions in full in this edition. Five years elapsed between the publication of the two and Hardy spoke during that time of the work as 'short and slight and written entirely with a view to serial publication' only.[1] In fact during the revision for book publication more was changed than the plot. The alterations to that already removed much sexual reference along with Pearston's two marriages. And there were other changes too, to be discussed later, which are also detailed in the explanatory Notes.

The central core shared (with individual variations) by the two texts is the story of a sculptor, Jocelyn Pearston (1892)/Pierston (1897), who pursues throughout his life a migrating 'Well-Beloved' whom he finds embodied serially under many names: 'To his intrinsic Well-Beloved he had always been faithful; but she had had many embodiments. Each individuality known as Lucy, Jane, Florence, Evangeline, or what-not, had been merely a transient condition of her' (1892 pp. 16–17; 1897 p. 184).[2] The physical approximations to the ideal have varied too: 'She was a blonde, a brunette, tall, *petite*, *svelte*, straight-featured, full, curvilinear. Only one quality remained unalterable in her: her instability of tenure' (1892 pp. 43–4; 1897 p. 212). In the main story-line she is incarnate under the name Avice Caro, borne by three generations of women in the same family, all of whom are loved by Pearston/Pierston: the first a romantic ingenue, the second a knowing coquette and the third a shy, well-educated and virginal creature. In the serial, Pearston, at the age of nearly sixty, marries the unwilling third Avice; in the book version she elopes with a man of her own age on the eve of the intended wedding with Pierston.

Interwoven with these affairs is the story of another temporary incarnation, Marcia Bencomb, a figure like Arabella in *Jude the Obscure*, whom he marries in *The Pursuit* but with whom he has only a brief liaison in *The Well-Beloved*. She re-enters his life in the final scenes of both works, more extensively in the 1897 text as the stepmother of the third Avice's lover Henri Leverre. Pearston's/Pierston's artistic life runs parallel to all this since his sculpture consists in endlessly trying to capture Aphrodite, the goddess of love, in stone from the Isle of Slingers (Portland), whence all these characters somewhat incestuously derive, as the reader is constantly reminded. I shall therefore treat *The Pursuit* and *The Well-Beloved* as a further development of that openness already seen occasionally in the *endings* of Victorian novels: as a double form with not merely alternative *endings* but alternative *texts*, an either/or structure. This syntactically co-ordinated branching is completely innovatory and characteristic of Hardy's increasing insistence on the provisionality of his later novels such as *Jude*, which he described as 'a series of seemings'. As I shall show later, it is Hardy's way of interrogating in a striking way any conventional gender power-hierarchy.

The Well-Beloved, by which was meant the text of 1897 (and its 1912 modifications), has always been regarded as in some way exceptional. The hostile critic in *The World* in 1897, who saw it as an illustration of Hardy's 'sex-mania', still ironically recognized its uniqueness: 'It may be fairly admitted that in the whole range of fiction from the days of the Greek author of *The Wonders of Thule* down to Mr Hardy himself, there is nothing at all approximating to the plot of *The Well-Beloved*'.[3] Hardy himself, at least in the Preface to the volume in the 1912 edition, claimed to think the story different 'from all or most others of the series in that the interest aimed at is of an ideal or subjective nature' (*The Well-Beloved*, pp. 173-4). The extreme contrivance of plot, with its repetition of incident suggestive at once of mathematical progression and of a fairy tale, draws attention to its own fictiveness. This struck that most self-referential of novelists, Proust, who makes his hero Marcel describe *The Well-Beloved* as an outstanding example of the 'stonemason's geometry' that is the summation of Hardy's artistry.[4] Often its extraordinariness has been strikingly displayed by its absence from general critical studies of Hardy's fiction such as Ian Gregor's *The Great Web* (1974). It is not only a double text but often an absent one too.

It is perhaps, then, a relatively recent interest in linguistic absence combining with a concern with self-referentiality that has reinstated the 1897 version as a (conveniently empty) centre of the canon. Two explicit accounts of the reinstatement are John Fowles's 'Hardy and the Hag' and J. Hillis Miller's 'The Well-Beloved: The Compulsion to Stop Repeating'. Fowles sees the work as expressive of 'a nausea at the fictionality of fiction . . . or as a dread of once more entering an always ultimately defeating labyrinth'.[5] Hillis Miller develops the same idea of self-reference differently:

> As with many great writers, a central theme of Hardy's writing is literature itself, its nature and powers. More or less hidden in the earlier novels, this theme surfaces in . . . the form of an interrogation of the relation between erotic fascination, creativity, and Platonic metaphysics which makes *The Well-Beloved* one of a group of important nineteenth-century novels about art.[6]

Certainly this text is self-referential, not only locally but in relation to the whole 'Great Web' that is Hardy's fiction. Many connections, transpositions or alternative working out of incidents can be seen amongst earlier novels. And I have demonstrated elsewhere the interconnectedness of Hardy's 'final trilogy' of 'provisional narratives', *The Pursuit, Jude* and *The Well-Beloved*.[7] Other critics have argued for links between texts or groups of texts, but, as I shall show, *The Pursuit* and *The Well-Beloved* are two linked novels making up a unique metatext which reflects on all Hardy's preceding novels. Despite Hillis Miller's account, the earlier novels are not capable of being summarized under the heading of texts which pose the question 'Why is it that most human beings go through life somnambulistically, compelled to repeat the same mistakes in love, so inflicting on themselves and on others the same suffering, again and again?'[8] More certainly the 'covert structure and meaning of Hardy's earlier novels' which are in this novel 'brought more fully into the open'[9] are operative at a level on which feminine and masculine are *not* subsumed into the category of human beings (which seems in the end, like many such subsumings, to be masculine). On the contrary, they develop a dialectical structure as the patriarchal voice of the narrator falters before the women that Hardy creates. For an alternative discourse develops alongside Hardy's original misogyny even in the early novels, and more fully from *The Woodlanders* onwards. What both texts of these novels do is to reflect upon this artistic process of an attempt at a misogynistic perspective and Hardy's own lapses from it: the alternative plots of the double text of *The Pursuit / The Well-Beloved* figure plainly that breakdown of the conventional gender power-hierarchy which fuels this dialectic.

One specificity that is overlooked by Hillis Miller is the high self-esteem of this particular artist-figure, so different from the sense of social inferiority his prototypes experience in the early novels. With Jocelyn (the first name will be used when the reference is to both texts) the sympathetic bond of perceived social inferiority which formerly in Hardy bound together narrator and artist is no longer in place. He is viewed with a cold eye in both texts. For him class is an absence rather than a state of mind, a fact to which the narrator ironically draws attention. Early on the point is cynically made that the sculptor condescends to receive money from his quarrier father who 'had never stinted his son' (1892 p. 44). This is elaborated in 1897 into the statement that Jocelyn receives from his father, 'an inartistic man of trade and commerce merely', a yearly allowance 'pending the famous days to come' (p. 181).

The compromises of the artistic market place are also plainly in evidence in Jocelyn's friend and mentor Somers who, once married, devotes himself to the production of consumer goods, 'executing . . . many pleasing aspects of nature addressed to the furnishing householder through the middling critic' (1892 p. 131; 1897 p. 301). By this means Somers affords a sumptuous style of living and the education of a family of daughters. Jocelyn assumes himself to be quite different but the text throws this into question. When he wonders idly whether, like Somers, to play the 'jackal to this lion of a family and house and studio and social reputation' (1892 p. 131; 1897 p. 301) he returns no answer. But his musing raises the question of why already he has been so successful financially and 'prospered without effort', while believing himself to be indifferent to 'the popular reception of his dream-figures' (1892 p. 42; 1897 p. 211). Such a belief begins to look like an example of his expedient double-think, in the light of the narrator's further gloss: 'these dreams he translated into marble, and found that by them he was hitting a public taste he had never deliberately aimed at, and mostly despised' (1892 p. 44; 1897 p. 212). Significantly it is Somers, the enthusiastic entrepreneur, who, to dissuade Jocelyn from not attending an 'Academy night', dubs him 'our only in-spired sculptor . . . our Praxiteles' (1892 p. 59) and adds in 1897 'or rather our Lysippus' (p. 233). Since neither Praxiteles, a famous sculptor of Aphrodite figures, nor Lysippus, a realistic artist, is an appropriate analogy, Somers's artistic judgement is effectively undercut. The artist has become a dubious figure, possibly ungifted and commercially driven, probably venal, certainly comic, rather than a suffering representative of the human race.

Obviously *The Well-Beloved* is a work about, not just involving, art; but the art that Jocelyn is engaged in is always and only the representation of women. The novel may have implications about art in general, but they must derive from what it has to say about women-focused art such as Jocelyn's obsessive attempts to capture in stone a unitary 'essence' of Aphrodite. For all his public profit there is talk from him of failure in his task. His vaunted sculpture is represented to the reader as so much dusty lumber when he lures the domesticated second Avice to his London flat with the suggestion that it will give her the chance to 'dust casts of hands and heads and feet' (1892 p. 94; 1897 p. 264 'dust all my Venus failures').

The literary appropriation of women, first attempted in *Desperate Remedies* when the heroine is endowed with the astonishing name, Cytherea, a variant of Aphrodite, is now subjected to scrutiny as Jocelyn boldly but unavailingly imposes a single descriptive label, 'the Well-Beloved', on many women in an attempt to impose on them an identity that will gratify his desire. The 1897 epigraph for the whole novel, 'One shape of many names', taken from Shelley's 'The Revolt of Islam' (where it is used to describe the spirit of evil), describes not only Jocelyn's behaviour, but that of the narrators in Hardy's early novels who try to impose a single ideal of womanliness on all heroines through their Ruskin-ian generalizations. Like Jocelyn, the narrators fail and, presumably like him also, are perceived by 1892 as inimical to the supposed adored object.

For women identity is evidently a gift bestowed by men's words only.

Not surprisingly, women's own words which might claim individual identity are revealed, in the kinds of texts represented by Jocelyn's life and works, as deliberately unheard. Listening to the second Avice through a wall, he is interested only in those cadences of her voice that she shares with her mother, the 'real' Avice: 'The subject of her discourse he cared nothing about... He took special pains that in catching her voice he might not comprehend her words. To the tones he had a right, none to the articulations' (1892 p. 77; 1897 p. 248). The girl is literally not allowed to mean anything but instead has extracted from her speech only what confirms the Avice/Aphrodite formula. The episode becomes, like others in the text, an account of the entrapment of women in the web of men's language, which is a metonymy for the erasure of women's individual identity. Jocelyn characteristically carries out this process by the use of a high-flown philosophical term:

He could not read her individual character, owing to the confusing effect of her likeness to a woman whom he had valued too late. He could not help seeing in her all that he knew of another, and veiling in her all that did not harmonise with his sense of metempsychosis (1892 p. 73; 1897 p. 244).

But just as his attempts to capture Aphrodite are 'dusty failures', so too the Caro women are resistant to the imposition of a uniform signification. Their individuality spills out into the corners of the text. In particular the working-class second Avice reveals an idiosyncratic attitude to lovers, paralleling Jocelyn's own:

I get tired o' my lovers as soon as I get to know them well. What I see in one young man for a while soon leaves him and goes into another yonder, and I follow, and then what I adore fades out of him and springs up somewhere else; and so I follow on, and never fix to one. I have loved *fifteen* already! (1892 p. 83; 1897 p. 253).

This is, of course, disallowable in a woman and explained away quickly as an inheritance from a common (and presumably male) ancestor. Jocelyn overlooks it as he does her involvement and, as it turns out, marriage, with another man. Similarly in imposing his tarnished signifier on the third Avice he averts his eyes from the real individual. In *The Pursuit*, in spite of her evident reluctance and the fact that she has a secret lover already, he manages to marry her and to avoid for some time the recognition that her obvious unhappiness is his fault. The marriage is achieved by using Avice's affection for her dying mother who wishes the match. This imposition of inherited tribal identity on an unwilling woman through an appeal to her sense of duty is another exposure of the tyranny of literature (such as Hardy's own early novels) that tries to do the same.

In both texts the nature of this masculine artistic process and its inadequacy are highlighted by the extremes to which it is carried: women are categorized only as being or not being Jocelyn's Well-Beloved. And though the three Avices are linked by a common name, they are particularly distinct from each other in intelligence, temperament and education. This is very plain with the second Avice whom Jocelyn, none the less, insists on seeing only as a 'perfect copy' or, ironically transposed into dialect, a 'daps' (1892 p. 74; 1897 p. 244) of her mother. The terms suitable for a sculptor of the period, such as 'reproducing' and 'copying', are singularly inept for uncloned human beings; but they serve well as metaphors for the artifice of the process adopted by Hardy's early narrators when they attempt to assimilate a range of different individuals to a standard image of the ideal woman.

Such an analysis by Hardy of the literary processing of 'uncomplementary' women is amplified by a detailed picture of the artist at work on an individual woman. The second Avice is forced to earn her living as a washerwoman, and this seems to be her description until Jocelyn sets to work. The narrator satirically translates Jocelyn's creative process into words:

But, after all, it was not the washerwoman that he saw now. In front of her, on the surface of her, was shining out that more real, more penetrating being whom he knew so well! The occupation of the subserving woman, the blemishes of the temporary creature who formed the background, were of no more account in the presentation than the posts and framework which support a pyrotechnic display (1892 pp. 72–3; 1897 p. 243).

The process in reverse occurs when he ceases to regard Nichola Pine-Avon as his Well-Beloved and she becomes a non-person: 'she became a woman of his acquaintance with no distinctive traits; she seemed to grow material, a superficies of flesh and bone merely; she was a person of lines and surfaces.' Since he no longer writes her as Well-Beloved, she was here 'a language in living cypher – no more' (1892 p. 56; 1897 p. 229).

These mismatches between signifier and individual are a spelling out in figurative terms of the mismatch in earlier novels between Cytherea, El-fride, Bathsheba and the web of narratorial generalizations in which they are trapped. In *The Pursuit / The Well-Beloved* the conventional need to re-model individuals to fit the prototype is further ironized by Jocelyn's plans to dismantle and refurbish the ideal woman who has perversely deviated into washerwomanhood: 'He could pack her off to school for two or three years, marry her, enlarge her mind by a little travel, and take his chance of the rest' (1892 p. 84; 1897 p. 255). His attempt and failure to overcome this bit of recalcitrant material mirrors the dialectic latent in all Hardy's would-be patriarchal texts. From this dialectic emerges the idea that moulding women to a preconceived artistic ideal does not work, a conclusion evident to Hardy by 1892.

And despite Jocelyn's protestations about the spiritual nature of his ob-session, what he sees in all these women is their physical attraction. When the Well-Beloved is embodied in Marcia, the Junoesque, 'she filled every fibre and curve of this woman's form' (1892 p. 29; 1897 p. 197). He is struck with a temporary candidate for the role as object of his desire by 'a sky-blue dress, which had nothing between it and the fair skin of her neck, lending her an unusually soft and sylph-like aspect' (1892 p. 48; 1897 p. 220). With Nichola Pine-Avon he notices how her black velvets and silks 'finely set off the exceeding fairness of her neck and shoulders, which, though unwhitened artificially, were without a speck or blemish of the least degree'. This close scrutiny of her skin has a detail lacking in his subsequent assessment of her intellectual gifts: 'she held also sound rather than current opinions on the plastic arts, and was the first intel-lectual woman he had seen there that night' (1892 p. 50; 1897 p. 223). It is as usual the body not the brain that interests him.

Similarly, oblique references to sexual arousal comically underline the nature of the impulse about which he dissimulates even to himself. His arousal is also implicit in the scene where, after sheltering from a storm by huddling under a boat with Marcia, he recognizes strong feelings:

Somewhere about this time . . . he became distinctly conscious of a sensation which, in its incipient and unrecognised form, had lurked within him from some unnoticed moment when he was sitting close to her under the lerret. Though a young man, he was too old a hand not to know what this was, and felt considerably alarmed (1892 p. 26; 1897 p. 195).

Later he is disappointed at a lack of matching sexual 'consciousness' in the second Avice when alone at night with him in his London flat she ingenuously concentrates all her attention on a troublesome mouse. He wants her to recognize a 'danger in this propinquity' (1892 p. 102; 1897 p. 272). Since he is busy thinking 'how soft and warm she was in her fur covering, as he held her so tightly' the conclusion that this means 'a possible migration of the Well-Beloved' (1892 p. 26; 1897 p. 195) becomes an obvious euphemism. This is emphasized by the fact that it is a further reflection on her 'fine figure' and on the clothes she has discarded to be dried at the inn when they elope together that completes the migration and precipitates the affair or marriage (1892 p. 27; 1897 p. 195).

In this display of what is not made explicit about Jocelyn's passion in the two novels, the meaning of the Avices' surname plays a part. It has, like the epigraphs, more significance than at first appears. Caro is, according to Hardy's later gloss, 'an imitation of a local name . . . this particular modification having been adopted because of its resemblance to the Italian for "dear" '.[10] It is also, as he fails to point out, not the expected feminine but the masculine form in Italian and, more significantly, a Latin word meaning 'flesh'. As the hostile reviewer put it: '*Caro, carnis* is the noun with the declension of which Mr. Hardy is perpetually and everlastingly preoccupied.'[11]

Like earlier stories which deal with womanliness and which bypass sexuality, this one denies Jocelyn's sexual desire while in reality privileging it. It thus enacts the duplicitousness of some early Hardy novels. The connection between the statues of Aphrodite and the sculptor's real life pursuit of the Well-Beloved suggests from the start that the link between them is erotic love. Yet Jocelyn constantly dissociates his passion verbally from the flesh. This is sometimes done by a bizarre appeal to authority, as when he equates his plight with St Paul's: 'As flesh she dies daily, like the Apostle's material self; because when I grapple with the reality she's no longer in it, so that I cannot stick to one incarnation if I would' (1892 p. 44; 1897 p. 213).

Several times already in the serial version of 1892, Jocelyn reveals himself to be a literary artist in relation to his own tyrannical acts as he skilfully turns morally undesirable conduct into aesthetically pleasing forms. He is adept at translating his life into themes for literature: his intention of remaking the unsuitable second Avice by schooling and travel blossoms into a subject for a lyric, captured as the idea that she represents his youth which it is an innocent pleasure to recapture. In terms that might make a sonnet he sees himself as offering her not an injury but an 'enriching', which will make a balanced 'reparation' for casting off her mother (1892 p. 89; 1897 p. 259). With the third Avice he can erase a sensation of his being 'overmuch selfish' by over-writing it with transforming nostalgia for her grandmother: 'a redeeming quality in the substratum of old pathetic memory by which such love had been created' (1892 p. 129; 1897 p. 299). The 'genealogical passion' with which he justifies his hijacking of the unwilling girl forty years his junior is typical of his poeticizing. To liken it ingenuously to Hardy's own poetry on heredity is to miss the satirical point: what is described here is ruthless self-interest ironically seen as favourably glossed by its possessor. Such rewritings are not unexpected from a man like Jocelyn who even describes his domestic strife with Marcia as playing Romeo to her Juliet. And the texts draw attention to the role of the literary imagination in sustaining appropriating fictions by giving the reader a miniature version of how Jocelyn's coercive courtship of the third Avice might be told so as to make a romance:

Yet to everyone, except, perhaps, Avice herself, Pearston was the most romantic of lovers. Indeed, was there ever such a romance as that man embodied in his relations to her house? Rejecting the first Avice, the second had rejected him, and to decline upon the third with final achievement was an artistic and tender finish to which it was ungrateful in anybody to be blind (1892 p. 137; 1897 p. 315).

Given this exposure of Jocelyn's art as the rewriting of self-interest, self-deception and the desire for sexual gratification in romantic terms, it becomes impossible to see him as a tragic representative of humanity in whose 'experience of disillusionment the once-beloved becomes no longer the sign of a spiritual plenitude, but the sign of an absence'.[12] This very general post-structuralist reading repeats Jocelyn's own artistic practice by glossing the plot with the same transforming literary imagination that later applies to all his own actions. It is a view that repeats the compulsive practice of appropriating women (already carried on in the text) as mere reflections of the male psyche.

This interpretation overlooks the fact that both texts use high farce as the medium for the examination of the artist and his art, the lover and his love. The 1892 novel speaks ironically of Pearston's pursuit of the third Avice as 'This desultory courtship of a young girl by an old boy' (p. 130). Jocelyn is careful during his laborious courtship of her never to let her see him except by moonlight: 'Whatever Pearston's years might have made him look by day, in the dusk of evening he was fairly presentable as a pleasing man of no marked antiquity, his outline differing but little from what it had been when he was but half his years' (1892 p. 123; 1897 p. 293). Before he finally allows her to see him in full light he has qualms:

there flashed across his mind the recollection that Avice the youngest had never yet really seen him, had seen nothing more of him than an outline, which might have appertained as easily to a man thirty years his junior as to himself, and a countenance so renovated by faint moonlight as fairly to correspond (1892 p. 131; 1897 p. 302).

Small wonder that the twenty-year-old girl murmurs after his proposal, 'I thought Mr. Pearston was younger!' (1892 p. 133; 1897 p. 302). Nor that when told that he loved her mother and grandmother before her, she asks nervously whether he loved her great-grandmother too (1892 p. 142; 1897 p. 306). In the 1897 text the narrator refers satirically to the age gap by inserting the phrase 'like her granny' into the description of how at their first meeting she was 'too inexperienced to be reserved' (1892 p. 124; 1897 p. 294).

Hillis Miller, however, insists on a solemn reading of the (later version of the) novel in which the three Avices represent 'the displacement of the self's love of its own image in a changed sex'. He interprets Pierston's failure to appropriate the women as his '*refusal* [my emphasis] to mate with any of the Avices' in order to hold off the 'final revelation of his lack'.[13] This reading itself carries on the appropriation under discussion. It is not Pierston who 'refuses' to mate with the Caro women. The second Avice, who is attracted only by Pierston's money and status, turns out to be married already, unknown to him. Also, as she has told him earlier, she only thought she loved him 'for a week; when I first saw you' (p. 254). And her daughter, the third Avice, runs away with another younger lover after being coerced into a proposed marriage.

What this reading ignores is a larger significance which becomes apparent when the texts of 1892 and 1897 are recognized as different novels. In *The Pursuit* the main events of the plot, which can only be seen as a struggle for possession of four women, are initiated as the title suggests by Pearston. He presses Marcia Bencomb whom he barely knows into a rash and hasty marriage. He uses coercion and her mother's influence to bring about marriage forty years later to the reluctant third Avice who is already in love with Henri Leverre. In marrying her, he does not hesitate to commit bigamy: though a common law presumption of a spouse's death after seven years of absence remained until 1938, conditions were attached about determining each case on its own facts. Pearston's 'due enquiries' are desultory as befits a man 'whose pursuits had taught him to regard impressions and sentiments as more cogent than legal' (p. 146). His magisterial control of events is evident in his assumption that he can, in effect, annul his own marriage when he discovers Avice's love for Leverre:

My marriage with Avice is valid if I have a reasonable belief in my first wife's death. Now, what man's belief is fixed, and who shall enter into my mind and say what my belief is at any particular time? The moment I have a reasonable belief that Marcia lives Avice is not my wife . . . (p. 161).

Power lies, in this version, with the man.

By contrast, in the 'or' half of this *either/or* narrative structure, *The Well-Beloved* where, even in the title, women move centre stage, it is they who dominate the action. Without being asked to, the first Avice makes clear that she will not conform to the Island custom of a trial marriage. This put-down is emphasized rather than concealed by Jocelyn's face-saving pique 'at Avice and her mother's antiquated simplicity in supposing that to be still a grave and operating principle which was a bygone barbarism to himself' (p. 189). Likewise it is Marcia who, though socially and sexually 'ruined', decrees the end of their affair, preferring scandal to a life-long union 'on the strength of a two or three days' passion' (p. 209). The third Avice takes her life into her own hands and elopes before he can complete their marriage. (She later chooses to run away from her husband Leverre as well.) Pierston becomes the object acted upon, until in the last chapter out of pity he marries Marcia.

What this reversal of gender roles in the alternative plots provides is not an assertion of the superiority of women over men. With its either/or structure the double text offers an interrogation of the conventional gender power-structure, whether men treat women as objects, as in *The Pursuit*, or women treat men as objects, as in *The Well-Beloved*. This questioning was implicit in earlier brief transpositions of the sexes such as those in *Far from the Madding Crowd* which made Bathsheba the authority figure. The presentation of two equally possible, equally extreme, power-structures is a *reductio ad absurdum* of conventional assumptions about a 'natural' hierarchy, from which Hardy has moved away. The bold figure takes a stage further the dialectic that emerges in the other novels and gives it ludic form. From the dismantling of the conventional gender power-structure a further question follows: if neither sex is naturally superior to the other, then what are the differences between them, apart from biological ones? To biology, in these texts Hardy, as always, gave an over-emphasis, as a reason for women being at a disadvantage. It is said of Mrs Somers (once Nichola Pine-Avon):

She was another illustration of the sad fact that the succeeding generations of women are seldom marked by cumulative progressiveness, their advance as the girl being lost in their recession as the matron ... This, however, not by reason of their faults as individuals, but of their misfortune as child-rearers (1892 pp. 130–31; 1897 p. 301).

On the more general question, it is shown in 1897, with the production of an alternative novel to that of 1892, that he has arrived at an agnosticism which echoes John Stuart Mill on the subject:

Hence, in regard to that most difficult question, what are the natural differences between the two sexes ... however great and apparently ineradicable the moral and intellectual differences between men and women might be, the evidence of there being natural differences could only be negative. Those only could be inferred to be natural which could not possibly be artificial – the residuum, after deducting every characteristic of either sex which can admit of being explained from education or external circumstances.[14]

Such a position as this which Hardy shares with Mill is already enlightenment. If there is ultimately an absence in this text it is that of a definition conscientiously withheld.

But in 1897 there are other significant changes to Pierston along with his loss of power over events. His lack of agency is accompanied by a psychological weakness that shows itself in a desire to exculpate himself for both his obsession and his failure. It grows out of the casually arrogant 'literary' glosses of his behaviour found in 1892 and referred to above. Much of the new 'literariness' of *The Well-Beloved* is injected into the text by Pierston himself. In talking to his friend Somers or in his own mind, he attempts to rewrite himself as a figure to whom the newly added epigraphs from Richard Crashaw, Thomas Wyatt and Shakespeare, relating to desperate and worthy lovers, would be appropriate. Most of the additional classical references (which are pointed out in the

Notes to the 1897 text) come from him. So, contemplating his obsession with the Well-Beloved early in the text (when he is twenty) – 'Sometimes at night he dreamt that she was "the wile-weaving Daughter of high Zeus" in person, bent on tormenting him for his sins against her beauty in his art – the implacable Aphrodite herself indeed' (pp. 184–5). This translates his infatuation with a series of young girls into the divine working out of the revenge of the love goddess Aphrodite. He simultaneously claims heroic status for himself and explains away his own lack of agency.

Other similarly flattering (and sometimes contradictory) versions of his compulsion to pursue women and his lack of success are also found in the second part of *The Well-Beloved*. At the age of forty he makes the same claims to himself:

he was aware, however, that though it might be now, as heretofore, the Loved who danced before him, it was the Goddess behind her who pulled the string of that Jumping Jill. He had lately been trying his artistic hand again on the Dea's form in every conceivable phase and mood. He had become a one-part man – a presenter of her only. But his efforts had resulted in failures. In her implacable vanity she might be punishing him anew for presenting her so deplorably (p. 224).

Later in the same section he develops this simple explanation into a more complicated one. His obsession is not self-created nor a form of divine retribution. It is to do with the Avices' heredity and with his other obsession, the Isle:

He began to divine the truth. Avice, the departed one, though she had come short of inspiring a passion, had yet possessed a ground-quality absent from her rivals . . . Like his own, her family had been islanders for centuries – from Norman, Anglian, Roman, Balearic-British times. Hence in her nature, as in his, was some mysterious ingredient sucked from the isle; otherwise a racial instinct necessary to the absolute unison of a pair (p. 232).

With his usual ingenuity, he connects this idea of a common past and geography shared with the Caros to the idea of Venus/Aphrodite in a new way. Perhaps the Caros were of 'Roman lineage' since the Romans had long colonized the Isle:

Tradition urged that a temple to Venus once stood at the top of the Roman road leading up into the isle; and possibly one to the love-goddess of the

Slingers antedated this. What so natural as that the true star of his soul would be found nowhere but in one of the old island breed? (1897 p. 232).

This already gives an over-determined account of his incestuous obsession with three generations of women by relating it to two sorts of pagan goddess rather than one. But it is even further developed later into a pagan-Christian punishment in a yet more fanciful elaboration:

Pierston saw only the retreating Avice, and knew that he was helpless in her hands. The church of the island had risen near the foundations of the Pagan temple, and a Christian emanation from the former might be wrathfully torturing him through the very false gods to whom he had devoted himself both in his craft, like Demetrius of Ephesus, and in his heart. Perhaps Divine punishment for his idolatories had come (p. 261).

The heroic model for this self-image-making surfaces in the 1897 novel as the elderly hero sits beside the corpse of the second Avice, dead from shock at the elopement of her daughter, his bride-to-be, the twenty-year-old Avice the third. His thoughts in this extensive reverie are all of himself: he is an Aeneas (also pursued by the wrath of a goddess, Juno), picturing his past loves 'in sad array, like the pictured Trojan women . . . on the walls of Carthage' (p. 324). The 'sad array' is superimposed on the reality since some of them left him willingly or rejected him. What troubles him, however, is what view others will take of him since they will not recognize his as an Aeneas figure:

The probable ridicule that would result to him from the events of the day he did not mind in itself at all. But he would fain have removed the misapprehensions on which it would be based. That, however, was impossible . . . Nobody would guess the further sentiment – the cordial loving-kindness – which had lain behind what had seemed to him the enraptured fulfilment of a pleasing destiny postponed for forty years (pp. 324–5).

In *The Pursuit*, when at sixty he courts and marries the young third Avice, his age is only a matter of intermittent concern to him. In *The Well-Beloved* it becomes the central subject of two new closing chapters which gain emphasis from their final position. Age is translated from a mere number into physical facts. The illness through which the returned Marcia nurses him is no longer the after-effect of a gallant attempt to drown himself. Instead it is caused by a feebleness (mirroring his psychological weakness) under which he gives way after the second Avice's funeral: 'It was supposed that his exposure that day in the bleakest churchyard in Wessex, telling upon a distracted mental and bodily condition, had thrown Pierston into the chill and fever which held him swaying for weeks between life and death' (p. 329). The consequences of this fever are both mental and physical. They include the 'strange death of the sensuous side of Jocelyn's nature'; the loss of artistic sentiment which leaves him unable to 'attach a definite sentiment to images of beauty recalled from the past' (p. 330); and the onset of sciatica. He grows only 'as well as one of his age could expect to be after such a blasting illness' (p. 333).

His deterioration is reflected back at him by Marcia whom at first he takes to be still beautiful, 'a fair five-and-thirty' (p. 331). But when she discards all her cosmetic aids the relentlessness of ageing is impressed upon him: 'She stood the image and superscription of Age – an old woman, pale and shrivelled, her forehead ploughed, her cheek hollow, her hair white as snow' (p. 332). His sciatica is matched by her rheumatism, her wrinkles by his baldness. His first and only marriage in the 1897 novel is without a whiff of the romance that has coloured his life. He marries Marcia out of pity because she is living in a draughty, uncomfortable house. The fluttering sylphs of his past life are overwritten by the picture of Marcia, his bride, 'well wrapped up . . . wheeled into the church in a chair' (p. 335).

With his artistic inspiration also gone, he now occupies himself domestically with 'a scheme for the closing of the old natural fountains in the Street of Wells, because of their possible contamination' (p. 336). The drying up of erotic and artistic impulses comically imagined here as a mundane job of work has often been noticed: a double impotence concludes what is no longer *his* story: 'His life seemed no longer a professional man's experience, but a ghost story' (p. 325).

In his later novels Hardy is given to shadowing actual plots with 'ghost plots'[15] stressing how nearly things might have been otherwise. Actuality itself becomes provisional. In the double text of *The Pursuit of the Well-Beloved* and *The Well-Beloved* this sense of the nearness of contingency to reality is given emphatic form by the counterpointing of the male against the female plot as an alternative course that events might so easily take. *Jude the Obscure*, placed between them chronologically, amplifies this double text into a trilogy, 'realizing' events in yet another way.

Notes

1. A. C. Pilgrim, 'Hardy's Retroactive Self-Censorship: The Case of *The Well-Beloved*' in J. Kennedy (ed.), *Victorian Authors and their Works: Revision, Motivations and Modes* (Athens: Ohio University Press, 1991), p. 127.

2. While references are made to both 1892 and 1897, the quotation is in the wording of the 1892 text. Verbal differences from 1897 are not noted here.

3. 'Thomas Hardy, Humorist', *The World* 24 March 1897, 13–14.

4. C. K. Scott Moncrieff (transl.), Marcel Proust, *The Captive* (London: Chatto & Windus, 1968), Part 2, p. 235.

5. J. Fowles, 'Hardy and the Hag' in L. St J. Butler (ed.), *Thomas Hardy after Fifty Years* (London: Macmillan, 1978), p. 30.

6. J. Hillis Miller, *Fiction and Repetition: Seven English Novels* (Oxford: Basil Blackwell, 1982), p. 148.

7. P. Ingham, 'Provisional Narratives: Hardy's Final Trilogy' in L. St J. Butler (ed.), *Alternative Hardy* (London: Macmillan, 1989), pp. 49–73.

8. Hillis Miller, p. 150.

9. Hillis Miller, p. 151.

10. *Life*, p. 304.

11. *The World* 1897, 13.

12. Hillis Miller, p. 162.

13. Hillis Miller, p. 168.

14. J. S. Mill, *On the Subjection of Women* (London: Longmans, Green, Reader and Dyer, 1869), p. 41.

15. G. Beer, *Darwin's Plots: Evolutionary Narrative in Darwin, George Eliot and Nineteenth-Century Fiction* (London: Routledge & Kegan Paul, 1983), p. 239.

Biographical Material

M. Millgate, *Thomas Hardy: A Biography* (Oxford: Oxford University Press, 1982). The definitive biography and only reliable one.

M. Millgate (ed.), *The Life and Work of Thomas Hardy* (London: Macmillan, 1984). An edition of the work published by Hardy's second wife Florence but which is largely by Hardy himself.

Books on Hardy's Novels

P. Boumelha, *Thomas Hardy and Women: Sexual Ideology and Narrative Form* (Brighton: Harvester Press, 1982).

L. St J. Butler (ed.), *Alternative Hardy* (London: Macmillan, 1989).

J. C. Dave, *The Human Predicament in Hardy's Novels* (Atlantic Highlands, N. J.: Humanities Press, 1985).

J. Fisher, *The Hidden Hardy* (London: Macmillan, 1992).

J. Goode, *Thomas Hardy: The Offensive Truth* (Oxford: Basil Blackwell, 1988).

P. Ingham, *Thomas Hardy* (Hemel Hempstead: Harvester Wheatsheaf, 1989).

R. Morgan, *Women and Sexuality in the Novels of Thomas Hardy* (London and New York: Routledge, 1988).

P. Widdowson, *Hardy in History: A Study in Literary Sociology* (London: Routledge, 1989).

Articles or Chapters on The Well-Beloved

A. A. M. Bulaila, ' "The Clay but not the Potter": Love and Marriage in *The Well-Beloved*', *Thomas Hardy Journal* 9(2) (May 1993), 61–71.

J. Hillis Miller, 'The Well-Beloved: The Compulsion to Stop Repeating' in his *Fiction and Repetition: Seven English Novels* (Oxford: Basil Blackwell, 1982), pp. 147–75.

P. Ingham, 'Provisional Narratives: Hardy's Final Trilogy' in L. St J. Butler (ed.), *Alternative Hardy* (London: Macmillan, 1989), pp. 49–73.

B. O'Donoghue, 'The Well-Beloved and the Vita Nuova', *Notes and Queries* 34 (December 1987), 500–501.

T. O'Toole, 'Genealogy and Narrative Jamming in Hardy's *The Well-Beloved*', *Narrative* 1(3) (October 1993), 207–22.

A. C. Pilgrim, 'Hardy's Retroactive Self-Censorship: The Case of *The Well-Beloved*' in J. Kennedy (ed.), *Victorian Authors and their Works: Revision, Motivations and Modes* (Athens: Ohio University Press, 1991), pp. 125–39.

No manuscript of this novel exists but there were seven editions of *The Pursuit of the Well-Beloved/ The Well-Beloved* before Hardy's death in 1928. The two earliest represent two quite different texts. They are the version serialized in the *Illustrated London News* in 1892 and that which appeared as volume XVII of the first collected edition, the Wessex Novels, in 1897. There were five subsequent editions all from Macmillan, who became Hardy's publishers in 1902.

The two early versions are distinctive in that, amongst other things, they have been thought to show an outspoken serial and a self-censored volume edition. Usually it is the serial texts that are censored and bowdlerized under outside pressure and the volume editions that, at least in part, reverse this process. The circumstances of serial publication for this novel are of some interest, especially since it is being treated here as a separate novel from the volume edition for reasons discussed in the Introduction.

Hardy claimed later that though the serial was published in 1892, 'it was sketched many years before that date, when I was comparatively a young man' (*Life* pp. 303–4). However, it was in the aftermath of an unfortunate episode with Tillotson's that in February 1890 he agreed to write a 60,000 word serial capable of division into twelve parts. Tillotson's had set up in 1873 what came to be called the Newspaper Fiction Bureau[1] to sell on the serialized versions of popular authors' fiction to newspapers and magazines. In 1889, however, they had terminated an agreement to handle 'Too Late Beloved' (an earlier title for *Tess of the D'Urbervilles*) which Hardy had refused to cut and censor as they wished. But since they were willing to pay for the serial as arranged, Hardy remained on sufficiently good terms to supply his next work to them. In a vague synopsis evidently intended to be reassuring he claimed that 'There is not a word or scene in the tale which can offend the most fastidious taste; and it is equally suited for the reading of young people, and for that of persons of maturer years'.[2] The serial appeared in 1892 in the *Illustrated London News* from 1 October to 17 December with a headpiece and two illustrations by Walter Paget for each of twelve weekly instalments.

Hardy did not at this stage arrange for publication in volume form and did not seem anxious to do so. This is clear from his dealings with Harper and Brothers who had sought the right to publish the serial in America. In 1892 they told him, through their London agents, that they were willing to publish it in volume form after he had had time to revise it. In reply he equivocated, allowing them some prospect of publishing it as a volume but saying that 'the story being short and slight and written entirely with a view to serial publication, it may be found upon consideration to be inadvisable in the interest of future novels to issue this as a book at all; hence I reserve the right to withhold it in that form either altogether, or until the story can be re-written'.[3]

And despite Harper's offer Hardy did *not* immediately revise the story but went on to write *Jude the Obscure* (published in volume form in 1895) and to prepare revisions and new prefaces for the first collected edition of all his novels (the Wessex Novels 1895–6) published by Osgood, McIlvaine. It was only late in 1896 that he agreed (it is not known at whose suggestion) to revise *The Pursuit of the Well-Beloved*. This became the seventeenth volume of the Wessex Novels under the title *The Well-Beloved*. It had the usual kind of frontispiece by Henry Macbeth-Raeburn: a picture of 'The "Isle" of the story'.

Hardy's letters at this time indicate some kind of nervousness about the novel. He apologizes to certain friends for not sending them copies because the work was too slight to be worth it. And he tells Edmund Gosse, after a single vicious review in *The World*, that 'one of the reasons why I consented to the reprinting of such a bygone, wildly romantic fancy was that it would please Mrs. Grundy & her young Person, & her respected husband, by its absolutely "harmless" quality' (*Collected Letters* II p. 157).

In fact the 1897 version was by no means a 'reprinting' but a radical rewriting, related to both *The Pursuit of the Well-Beloved* and *Jude the Obscure*, that produced a new novel. It lacks the first chapter recounting the burning of love-letters from the hero Jocelyn's former loves. It cuts out his hasty marriage to another native of the Isle (Portland), Marcia Bencomb, who leaves him in the serial only after four years of cohabitation. It also omits his second bigamous marriage to the third Avice Caro forty years later, after successive attachments to her mother and grandmother. Instead it adds a late first marriage to Marcia at the age of sixty. It also replaces a dramatic attempt to drown himself in 1892 with the elopement and near-drowning of his fiancée Avice the third and Marcia's stepson. Many other changes in the plot are consequent upon these alterations.

In addition the 1897 version adds literary epigraphs to each of the three Parts and increases the number of classical and historical references. It also includes a new and romantic Preface about the 'Isle'.

From then on all further printed versions of the novel in Hardy's lifetime are based on the 1897 volume. The only significant one is that in the collected Wessex Edition of 1912 for which Hardy scrupulously revised detail, though there are no radical changes to the substance of the story. The last collected edition published in Hardy's lifetime in the Mellstock Edition was a resetting of 1912 and shows few changes. There is no evidence that the handful of changes made to *The Well-Beloved* (volume XXI, published in 1920) is Hardy's work. None of them is included in his handwritten list (now in the Dorset County Museum) of 'Corrections for the Mellstock Edition'.

The other editions of the novel used a set of plates of the 1897 volume bought from Osgood, McIlvaine by Macmillan before Hardy transferred to them as his publishers. These were the Colonial Library edition, 1898; the Wessex Novels edition, 1903; and the Wessex Novels Pocket edition, 1907. These remained virtually unchanged except that a 1911 reprinting of the 1903 edition included a new penultimate paragraph to the Preface.

The present edition, in line with the general policy of the Penguin Classics Hardy, prints the first volume edition. But since examination reveals the 1892 serial to be a separate lost novel in its own right, that too is reprinted in full for the first time. The Notes to 1892 draw attention in detail to passages omitted in 1897; the Notes to 1897 indicate additions there. Only obvious errors are silently emended; original punctuation and accidentals are retained. The main changes made in 1912 are cited in the 1897 Notes. The 1897 and 1912 Prefaces are also included.

Notes

1. R. L. Purdy, *Thomas Hardy: A Bibliographical Study* (Oxford: Clarendon Press, 1954), p. 340.
2. Purdy, p. 95.
3. A. C. Pilgrim, 'Hardy's Retroactive Self-Censorship: The Case of *The Well-Beloved*' in J. Kennedy (ed.), *Victorian Authors and their Works: Revision, Motivations and Modes* (Athens: Ohio University Press, 1991), p. 127.

The Pursuit of the Well-Beloved

1892

CONTENTS

The Pursuit of the Well-Beloved

PART FIRST: A YOUNG MAN OF TWENTY

I	*Relics*	9
II	*A Supposititious Presentment of Her*	10
III	*The Incarnation is Assumed to be a True One*	13
IV	*The Lonely Pedestrian*	19
V	*A Charge*	24
VI	*On the Brink*	29
VII	*Her Earlier Incarnations*	31
VIII	*A Miscalculation*	36
IX	*Familiar Phenomena in the Distance*	41
X	*The Old Phantom Becomes Distinct*	44
XI	*She Draws Close, and Satisfies*	51
XII	*She Becomes an Inaccessible Ghost*	56

PART SECOND: A YOUNG MAN OF FORTY

XIII	*She Threatens to Resume Corporeal Substance*	65
XIV	*The Resumption Takes Place*	68
XV	*The Past Shines in the Present*	71
XVI	*The New Becomes Established*	76
XVII	*His Own Soul Confronts Him*	81
XVIII	*Juxtapositions*	85
XIX	*She Fails to Vanish when Closely Confronted*	91
XX	*A Homely Medium does not Dull the Image*	95
XXI	*A Grille Descends Between the Vision and Him*	100
XXII	*She is Finally Enshrouded from Sight*	106

CONTENTS

PART THIRD: A YOUNG MAN OF FIFTY-NINE

XXIII	*She Returns for the New Season*	113
XXIV	*Misgivings on this Unexpected Re-embodiment*	120
XXV	*The Renewed Image Burns Itself In*	125
XXVI	*He Makes a Dash for the Last Incarnation*	130
XXVII	*He Desperately Clutches the Form*	136
XXVIII	*He Possesses it: He Possesses it Not*	141
XXIX	*The Elusiveness Continues*	145
XXX	*He Becomes Retrogressive*	150
XXXI	*The Magnanimous Thing*	155
XXXII	*The Pursuit Abandoned*	159
XXXIII	*He Becomes Aware of New Conditions*	165

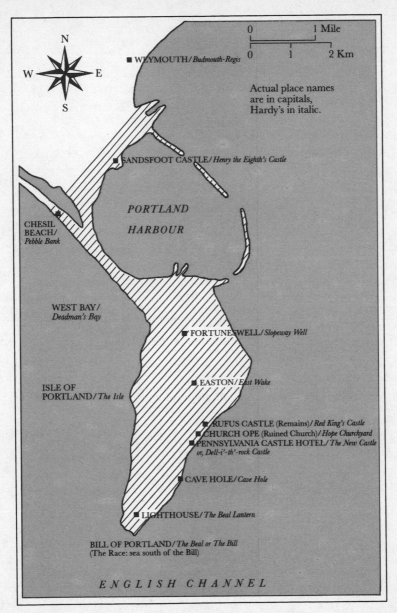

The Isle, as described in the 1892 version

PART FIRST

A Young Man of Twenty

CHAPTER I
Relics

Once – and that not long ago – there was a young sculptor who had not quite made a great name; and pending that event he lived on a small income allowed him by his father, an inartistic man of trade and commerce merely.

The sculptor was not engaged in his art on one particular midnight in the summer season, when, having packed up such luggage as he might require for a sojourn in the country, he sat down in his temporary rooms in a London square to destroy a mass of papers that he did not wish to carry with him and objected to leave behind.

Among them were several packets of love-letters, in sundry hands.

He took the first bundle, laid it in the grate, lit a match under it, and waited. The bundle of hard, close-lying note sheets would not burn.

He cut the string, loosened the letters, and kindled another match. The flames illuminated the handwriting, which sufficiently recalled to his knowledge her from whom that batch had come, and enabled him to read tender words and fragments of sentences addressed to him in his teens by the writer. Many of the sentiments, he was ashamed to think, he had availed himself of in some attempts at lyric verse, as having in them that living fire which no lucubration can reach. The edges of some of the sheets began to be browned by the flame; but they would not in this cold grate light up and consume as he had expected.

By this time he had begun to experience a sentimental feeling for the letters, though, till the present evening, he had not once thought of them for a twelvemonth. He had no longer heart to burn them. That packet, at least, he would preserve for the writer's sake, notwithstanding that the person of the writer, wherever she might be, was now but as an empty shell which had once contained his ideal for a transient time.[1] He drew the letters from the grate, shook them clean, and laid them aside.

The next package was in a contrasting hand – thick and rotund, generated by a scratching quill. A school-girl she: he had never much cared for her; and her effusions were unceremoniously tumbled in.

The young man repeated the match-lighting process, stirring the letters with the poker. Some flamed, but the majority remained clean and legible as when written. Her handwriting had been so large and inky that she had spread over a multitude of sheets a very small quantity of thought and affection; and the bundle, made up of only a short correspondence, was enormous. There was no destroying it in a hurry, unless a fiery furnace into which to thrust it could have been improvised.

Suddenly there arose a little fizzle in the dull flicker: something other than paper was burning. It was hair – *her* hair.

"Good heavens!" said the budding sculptor to himself. "How can I be such a brute? I am burning *her* – part of her form – many of whose curves as remembered by me I have worked into statuettes and tried to sell. I cannot do it – at any rate, to-night."

All that remained of the bundle – by far the greater part – he hastily withdrew from the grate, shook the feathery black scales of paper-ash from the pages, refastened them, and put them back for preservation also.

He looked at the other packages. One signed in round-hand, one in long-hand, one in square-hand, one in pointed-hand, crippled and pinched. She had been much older than he. They all showed affection which once had lived, though now it was past and gone. No, he could not burn them here and alone.

What could he do with them? He would take them with him, and re-consider their existence. But all his luggage was packed; in his portmanteaus and hand baggage not a square inch of room remained. At last he took his summer overcoat, which he would certainly not require to use till wet weather recommenced, rolled it hastily round the lumps of un-dying affection, strapped the whole compactly together, and, flinging it down beside his portmanteaus, went to bed.

CHAPTER II

A Supposititious Presentment of Her

About two o'clock the next day he was ascending the steep roadway which led from the village of Slopeway Well to the summit of the rocky peninsula, called an island;' that juts out like the head of a flamingo into the English Channel, and is connected with the mainland of Wessex by a long, thin beach of pebbles, representing the neck of the bird.

He recollected that it was two years and eight months since he had paid his last visit to his father at this, his birthplace, the intervening time having been spent amid many contrasting scenes at home and abroad. What had seemed natural in the isle when he left it now looked quaint and odd amid these later impressions. The houses above houses, one man's doorstep[2] rising behind his neighbour's chimney, the gardens hung up by one hedge to the sky, the unity of the whole island as a solid and single block of stone four miles long, were no longer familiar and commonplace ideas. All now stood dazzlingly clean and white against the blue sea, the sun flashing on the stratified façades of rock –

> The melancholy ruins
> Of cancelled cycles. . . . Prodigious shapes
> Huddled in grey annihilation.[3]

After a laborious clamber he reached the top, and walked along the plateau towards East Wake. The road was glaring and dusty as always, and drawing near to his father's house, he sat down in the sun.

He stretched out his hand upon the rock beside him. It felt warm. That was the island's personal temperature. He listened, and heard sounds: nick-nick, saw-saw-saw. Those were the island's voice – the noises of the quarrymen and stone-sawyers.

Opposite to the spot on which he sat was a roomy cottage or homestead. Like the island, it was all of stone, not only in walls but in window-frames, roof, chimneys, fence, stile, pig-sties and stable, almost door.

He remembered who had used to live there – and probably lived there now – the Caro[4] family, the roan-mare Caros,[5] as they were called to distinguish them from other branches of the same family, there being but half-a-dozen christian and surnames in the whole island. He crossed the road and looked in at the open doorway. Yes, there they were still.

Mrs. Caro, who had seen him from the window, met him in the entry, and there an old-fashioned greeting took place. A moment after a door leading from the back rooms was thrown open, and a young girl of about seventeen or eighteen came bounding in.

"Why, '*tis* dear Joce!" she burst out joyfully. And running up to him, she seized his hand and kissed him before he was aware of her intention.

The demonstration was sweet enough from the owner of such an affectionate pair of bright hazel eyes and brown tresses of hair. But it was so sudden, so unexpected, that he winced for a moment quite involuntarily; and there was some constraint in the manner in which he returned her kiss, and said, "My pretty little Avice, how do you do after so long?"

For a few seconds her impulsive innocence hardly noticed his start of surprise; but Mrs. Caro, the girl's mother, had observed it instantly. With a pained face she turned to her daughter severely –

"Avice[6] – my dear Avice! Why – what are you doing? Don't you know that you've grown up to be a woman since Jocelyn – Mr. Pearston – was last down here? Of course you mustn't do now as you used to do three or four years ago."

The awkwardness which had arisen was hardly removed by Pearston's assurance that he quite expected her to keep up the practice of her childhood, followed by several minutes of conversation on general subjects. He was vexed from his soul that his unaware movement should so have betrayed him. At his leaving he repeated that if Avice regarded him other than as she used to do, he would never forgive her; but though they parted good friends her regret at the incident was visible in her face. Jocelyn passed out into the road and onward to his father's house hard by. The mother and daughter were left alone.

"I was quite astonished at 'ee, my child!" exclaimed the elder. "A young man from London and the Continent, used now to the strictest company manners, and ladies who a'most think it vulgar to smile broad! How could ye do it, Avice?"

"I – I didn't think about how I was altered," said the conscience-stricken girl. "I used to kiss him, and he used to kiss me before he went away."

"But that was years ago, my dear!"

"O, yes, and for the moment I forgot! He seemed just the same to me as he used to be."

"Well, it can't be helped now. You must be careful in the future."

Meanwhile Jocelyn Pearston had gone onward to his father's; but the latter, having received no warning of his son's intended visit, was not at home to receive him. Jocelyn looked round the familiar premises, glanced across the way at the great yard within which eternal saws were going to and fro upon eternal blocks of stone – the very same saws and the very same blocks that he had seen there when last in the island, so it seemed to him – and then passed through the dwelling into the back garden.

Like all the gardens in the isle, it was surrounded by a wall of dry-jointed spawls, and at its further extremity it ran out into a corner, which adjoined the garden of the Caros. He had no sooner reached this spot than he became aware of a murmuring and sobbing on the other side of the wall. The voice he recognised in a moment as Avice's, and she seemed to be confiding her trouble to some young friend of her own sex.

"O, what shall I *do*! what *shall* I do!" she was saying bitterly. "So bold as it was – so shameless! How could I think of such a thing! He will never forgive me – never. Never like me again. He'll think me a forward hussy, and yet – and yet I quite forgot how much I had grown. But that he'll never believe." The accents were those of one who had for the first time become conscious of her womanhood as an unwonted possession which shamed and frightened her.

"Did he seem angry at it?" inquired the friend.

"O, no – not angry! Worse. Cold and haughty. O, he's such a fashionable person now – not at all an island man. But there's no use in talking of it. I wish I was dead!"

Pearston retreated as quickly as he could. The incident which had brought such pain to this innocent soul was now beginning to be a source of considerable pleasure to him. He returned to the house, and when his father had come back and they had shared a meal together Jocelyn again went out, full of an earnest desire to soothe his young neighbour's grief in a way she little expected; though, to tell the truth, his affection for her was rather that of a friend than of a lover, and he felt by no means sure that the migratory, elusive idealisation he called his Love was going to take up her abode in the body of Avice Caro.

CHAPTER III

The Incarnation is Assumed to be a True One

It was difficult to meet her again, even though on this lump of rock the difficulty lay as a rule rather in avoidance than in encountering. But Avice had been transformed into a very different kind of young woman by the self-consciousness engendered of her impulsive greeting, and, notwithstanding their propinquity, he could not meet her, try as he would. No sooner did he appear an inch beyond his father's door than she was to earth like a fox – that is, she bolted upstairs to her room.

Anxious to soothe her after his recent slight, he could not stand these evasions long. The manners of the isle were primitive and straightforward, even among the well-to-do, and noting her disappearance one day he followed her into the house and onward to the foot of the stairs.

"Avice!" he called.

"Yes, Mr. Pearston."

"Why do you run upstairs like that?"

"O – only because I wanted to come up for something."

"Well, if you've got it, can't you come down again?"

"No, I can't very well."

"Come, *dear* Avice. That's what you are, you know."

There was no response.

"Well, if you won't, you won't!" he continued. "I don't want to bother you." And Pearston went away.

He had hardly left the door when Mrs. Caro's servant ran out to ask him if he had left his coat behind him when he called on the day of his arrival. They had found it in the house, and had not been sure whose it was.

"O, yes, it is mine," said Jocelyn, hastily. "I forgot it."

The great coat was strapped up round the letters just as he had arranged it; but he wondered as he walked on whether Mrs. Caro or Avice had looked inside as a means of identification. Determining to run no further risks, he set about destroying the letters' there and then. To burn them in a grate was an endless task. He went into the garden, threw them down, made a loose heap of a portion, and put a match to the windy side.

By the help of a pitchfork to stir them about he was fairly successful, though as soon as he ceased to stir they ceased to burn. He was deeply occupied in the business of feeding the fire from the adjoining heap when he heard a voice behind him.

"Mr. Pearston – I wasn't angry with you just now. When you were gone I thought – you might mistake me, and I felt I could do no less than come and assure you of my friendship still."

Turning he saw the blushing face of Avice immediately behind him.

"You are a good, dear girl!" said he, impulsively, as he threw down the pitchfork, and seizing her hand, set upon her cheek the kiss that should have been the response to hers on the day of his coming.

"Darling Avice!" he said, "forgive me for the slight that day! Say you do. Come, now!"

She blushed, looked rather than spoke her forgiveness, and shrank away, sitting down upon a squared stone, around which the unburnt sheets of paper were strewn. With some embarrassment at her presence he withdrew another handful from the collection and threw it on the flames.

"What are you burning?" she asked.

"O, only some papers I hadn't time to destroy before I left town, and which I forgot till to-day that I had brought with me."

"Ah, that was the parcel you left at our house, perhaps?"

"Yes."

She scanned more closely the packets scattered round her. "They are letters, in different handwritings."

"Yes."

"O, Joce – Mr. Pearston – they are in women's hands; they are love-letters?"

He did not answer for a moment, during which interval a sudden sadness overspread her face, which had just before blushed so significantly under his caress. She bent her head and covered her eyes with her hands. "I see – I see now!" she whispered, "I am – only one – in a long, long row!"[2]

From the white sheets of paper round about her seemed to rise the ghosts of Isabella, Florence, Winifred, Lucy, Jane, and Evangeline – each writer from her own bundle respectively – and Maud and Dorothea from the flames. He hardly knew what to say to the new personality in the presence of the old. Then a sudden sense of what a good and sincere girl Avice was overpowered the spectres, and, rushing up to her and kneeling down upon the letters, he exclaimed, "Avice, dear Avice! – I say to you what I have never said to one of them, or to any other woman, living or dead, 'Will you have me as your husband?' "

"Ah! – I am only one of many!"

"You are not, dear. You knew me when I was young, and they didn't – at least, not many of them. Still, what does it matter? We must gain experience."

Somehow or other her objections were got over, and, though she did not give an immediate assent, she agreed to meet him later in the afternoon, when she walked with him to the southern point of the island called the Beal, or, by strangers, the Bill, pausing over the treacherous cavern known as Cave Hole, into which the sea roared and splashed now as it had done when they visited it together as children. To steady herself while looking in he offered her his arm, and she took it, for the first time, as a woman, for the hundredth time as his old companion.

They rambled on to the lighthouses, where they would have lingered longer if Avice had not suddenly remembered that she had to recite poetry from a platform that very evening at Slopeway Well, one of the villages on the island – the village that had advanced to be almost a town.

"Recite!" said he. "Who'd have thought anybody or anything could recite down here except the reciter we hear away there – the never silent sea."

"O, but we are quite intellectual now," she said. "In the winter particularly. But, Jocelyn – don't come to the recitation, will you? It would spoil my performance if you were there, and I want to be as good as the rest."

"I won't if you really wish me not to. But I shall meet you at the door and bring you home."

"Yes!" she said, looking up into his face; and they hastened back together. Avice was perfectly happy now; she could never have believed at the time of her despair on the day of his coming that she would ever be so happy. When they reached the east side of the isle they were compelled to part at once, that she might be soon enough to take her place on the platform. Pearston went home, and after dark, when he thought it would be about the hour for accompanying her back, he went along the middle road northward to Slopeway Well.

He was full of misgiving. He had known Avice Caro so well of old that his feeling for her now was rather one of friendship than love; and what he had said to her in a moment of impulse that morning rather appalled him in its consequences. Not that either of the women who had attracted him successively would be likely to rise inconveniently between them. For he had quite disabused his mind of the old-fashioned assumption that the idol of a man's fancy was an integral part of the personality in which it might be located for a long or a short while.

To his intrinsic Well-Beloved[3] he had always been faithful; but she had had many embodiments. Each individuality known as Lucy, Jane, Florence, Evangeline, or what-not, had been merely a transient condition of her. He did not recognise this as an excuse or as a defence, but as a fact simply. Essentially she was perhaps of no tangible substance; a spirit, a dream, a frenzy, a conception, an aroma, an epitomised sex, a light of the eye, a parting of the lips. God only knew what she really was; Pearston did not. He knew that he loved the Protean creature[4] wherever he found her, whether with blue eyes, black eyes, or brown; whether presenting herself as tall, fragile, or plump. She was never in two places at once; but hitherto she had never been in one place long. She was indescribable, unless by saying she was a mood of himself.

By making this clear to himself some time before this date, he had escaped a good deal of ugly reproach which he might otherwise have incurred from his own judgment, as being the very embodiment of fickleness. It was simply that she who always attracted him, and led him whither she would, as by a silken thread, had not remained the occupant of the same fleshly tabernacle[5] throughout her career so far. Whether she would ultimately settle down into one, he could not say.

Had he felt that she had now taken up her abode in Avice, he would have tried to believe that this was the terminal spot of her migrations, and have been content to abide by his words. But did he love Avice – see the Well-Beloved made manifest in Avice at all? The question was somewhat disturbing.

He had reached the brow of the hill, and descended towards Slopeway, where in the long straight street he soon found the lighted hall. The performance was not yet over; and by going round to the side of the building and standing on a slope he could see the interior as far down as the platform level. Avice's turn, or second turn, came on almost immediately. Her pretty embarrassment on facing the audience rather won him away from his doubts. She was, in truth, what is called a "nice" girl; pretty, certainly, but above all things nice – one of the class with whom the risks of matrimony approximate most nearly to nil.[6] Her intelligent eyes, her broad forehead, her thoughtful carriage, ensured one thing, that of all the girls he had known he had never met one with more charming and solid qualities than Avice Caro's. This was not a mere conjecture – he had known her long and thoroughly, her every mood and temper.

A heavy wagon passing without drowned her small, soft voice for him; but the audience were pleased, and she blushed at their applause. He now took his station at the door, and when the people had done pouring out he found her within awaiting him.

They climbed homeward slowly by the Old Road, Pearston dragging himself up the steep by the iron hand-rail, and pulling Avice after him upon his arm. Reaching the top, they turned and stood still. To the left of them the sky was streaked like a fan with the lighthouse rays, and in their front, at periods of a quarter of a minute, there arose a deep, hollow stroke, like the single beat of a drum, the intervals being filled with a long-drawn rattling, as of bones between huge canine jaws. It was Deadman's Bay, rising and falling against the pebble bank.

The kiss that evening was not on Avice's initiative. Her former demonstrativeness seemed to have increased her present reserve. However, to-day was the beginning of a pleasant month passed mainly in each other's society by the pair. He found that she could not only recite poetry at intellectual gatherings, but play the piano fairly, and sing to her own accompaniment.

He observed that every aim of those who had brought her up had been to get her away mentally as far as possible from her natural and individual life as an inhabitant of a peculiar isle; to make her an exact copy of tens of thousands of other people, in whose circumstances there was nothing special, distinctive, or picturesque; to teach her to forget all the experiences of her ancestors; to drown the local ballads by songs purchased at the Budmouth fashionable music-sellers', and the local vocabulary by a governess-tongue of no country at all. She lived in a house that would have been the fortune of an artist, and learned to draw London suburban villas from printed copies.

Avice had seen all this before he pointed it out, but, with a girl's tractability, had acquiesced. By constitution she was local to the bone, but she could not escape the tendency of the age.

The time for Jocelyn's departure drew near, and she looked forward to it sadly, but serenely, their engagement being now a settled thing. Pearston thought of the local custom[7] on such occasions, which had prevailed in both his and her family for centuries, both being of the old stock of the isle. The influx of "kimberlins," or "foreigners" (as strangers were called), had led in a large measure to its discontinuance; but underneath the veneer of Avice's education many an old-fashioned idea lay slumbering, and he wondered if, in her natural melancholy at his leaving, she expected any such ceremony as a formal ratification of their betrothal, according to the precedent of their sires and grandsires.

To scent her views on the point he asked her to meet him in the old Hope churchyard one evening at seven o'clock.

CHAPTER IV

The Lonely Pedestrian

The Hope churchyard lay in a dell formed by a landslip ages ago, and the church had long been a ruin. At the hour appointed she descended the rocks and found him waiting at the foot of them.

They wandered hither and thither in the shades, and the solemnity of the spot and the absence of daylight assisted him in sounding her mind on a subject which could not be approached with levity.

He found that, in common with all the islanders born, she knew of the observance. But it was obvious that, in view of herself as a modern young woman, she had never expected it to arise as a practical question between him and her. Some of the working quarriers kept it up, but nobody else, she said. Jocelyn hastened to inform her that he only wished to consult her desires as to the terms of their engagement, and not knowing how far she respected the island's history, felt bound to mention it; though urge it he did not.

"Well," said he; "here we are, arrived at the fag-end of my holiday. What a pleasant surprise my old home, which I have thought not worth coming to see for more than two years, had in store for me!"

"You must go to-morrow?" she said uneasily.

"Yes." He reflected, and decided that instead of leaving in the daytime he would defer his departure till the night mail-train from Budmouth. He had hardly looked into his father's quarries, and this would give him time to do so, and enable her, if she chose, to accompany him a little way. If she would agree, he purposed to send on his luggage to the aforesaid watering-place, and ask her to walk with him along the beach as far as to Henry the Eighth's Castle above the sands, where they could stay and see the moon rise over the sea. He would see her nearly all the way back, and there would be ample time after that for him to catch the last train.

"You can reserve your answer till to-morrow," he added.

She hesitated. "I understand you to mean, dear Jocelyn," she said, "that my accompanying you to the castle would signify that I conform to the custom of working the spell?"

"Well, yes," he answered.

"I will think it over to-morrow, and ask mother if I ought to, and decide," said she. "I fear it is heathen and ungodly."

After spending the next day with his father in the quarries, Jocelyn prepared to leave, and at the time appointed set out from the stone house of his birth in this stone isle to walk to Budmouth-Regis by the path along the beach, Avice having some time earlier gone down to see some friends at Slopeway Well, which was halfway towards the spot of their proposed tryst. The descent soon brought him to the pebble bank, and leaving behind him the last houses of the isle, and the ruins of the village destroyed by the November gale of 1824, he struck out along the narrow thread of land. When he had walked a hundred yards he stopped, turned aside to the pebble ridge which walled out the sea, and sat down to wait for her.

Between him and the lights of the ships riding at anchor in the roadstead two men passed slowly in the direction he intended to pursue. One of them recognised Jocelyn, and bade him good-night, adding, "Wish you joy, Sir, of your choice, and hope the wedding will be soon?"

"Thank you, Seaborn. Well – we shall see what Christmas will do towards bringing it about."

"My wife opened upon it this mornen: 'Please God, I'll up and see that there wedden,' says she, 'knowing 'em both from their crawling days.'"

The men moved on, and when they were out of Pearston's hearing the one who had not spoken said to his friend, "Who was that young kimberlin? He don't seem an islander."

"O, he is, though, every inch o' en. He's Mr. Jocelyn Pearston, the stone-merchant's only son up at East Wake. He's to be married to a stylish young body, whose mother, a widow, carries on the same business as well as she can; but their trade is not a twentieth part of Pearston's. He's worth thousands and thousands, they say, though 'a do live on in the same wold way up in the same wold house. His son is doing great things in London as a image-carver; and I can mind when, as a boy, 'a first took to carving soldiers out o' bits o' stone from the soft bed of his father's quarries; and then 'a made a set o' stonen chess-men, and so 'a got on. He's quite the gent in London, they tell me; and the wonder is that 'a cared to come back here and pick up little Avice Caro – nice maid as she is notwithstanding. . . . Hullo! there's to be a change in the weather soon."

Meanwhile, the subject of their remarks waited at the appointed place till seven o'clock, the hour named between himself and his affianced, had struck. Almost at the moment he saw a figure coming forward from the last lamp at the bottom of the hill. She meant, then, to conform to the custom.[1] But the figure speedily resolved itself into that of a boy, who, advancing to Jocelyn, inquired if he were Mr. Pearston, and handed him a note.

(*To be continued.*)

When the boy had gone Jocelyn retraced his steps to the last lamp, and read, in Avice's hand –

"My Dearest, – I shall be sorry if I grieve you at all, but I have thought over your inquiry, and cannot agree[2] to conform to the old pagan custom (or whatever it is) of the isle. I did not expect you to ask me so suddenly, or I should have been more positive at the time it was mentioned. As I am quite aware that you merely asked, and did not press me, I know that this decision will not disturb you for long, that you will understand my feelings, and, above all, think the better of me in time to come.

"And if we were unfortunate in the trial of it we could never marry, could we, honourably? This is an objection which I am sure you have not thought of, and will, I know, share with me.

"I am sorry that the custom, uncivilised as it is, which has prevailed in our families on both sides for so many centuries should thus be brought to an end by me, and I am the more sorry in that it prevents my bidding you farewell. However, you will come again soon, will you not, dear Jocelyn? and then the time will soon draw on when no more farewells will be required. – Always and ever yours,

"*Avice.*"

Jocelyn, having read the letter, pondered awhile: and then, finding that the evening seemed louring, yet feeling indisposed to go back and hire a vehicle, he went on quickly alone. In such an exposed spot the night wind was gusty, and the sea behind the pebble barrier kicked and flounced in complex rhythms, which could be translated equally well as shocks of battle or shouts of thanksgiving.

Presently on the pale road before him he discerned a figure, the figure of a woman. He remembered that a woman passed him while he was reading Avice's letter by the last lamp, and now he was overtaking her.

He did hope for a moment that it might be Avice, with a changed mind. But it was not she, nor anybody like her. It was a taller, squarer form than that of his betrothed, and, although the season was only autumn, she was wrapped in furs, or in thick and heavy clothing of some kind.

He soon advanced abreast of her, and could get glimpses of her profile against the roadstead lights. It was dignified, arresting, that of a very Juno.[3] Nothing more classical had he ever seen. She walked at a swinging pace, yet with such ease and power that there was but little difference in their rate of speed for several minutes; and during this time he regarded and conjectured. However, he was about to pass her by when she suddenly turned and addressed him.

"Mr. Pearston, I think, of East Wake?"

He assented, and could just discern what a handsome, commanding, imperious face it was – quite of a piece with the proud tones of her voice. She was a new type altogether in his experience; and her accent was not so local as Avice's.

"Can you tell me the time, please?"

He looked at his watch by the aid of a light, and in telling her that it was a quarter past seven observed, by the momentary gleam of his match, that her eyes looked a little red and chafed, as if with weeping.

"Mr. Pearston, will you forgive what will appear very strange to you, I dare say? That is, may I ask you to lend me some money for a day or two? I have been so foolish as to leave my purse on the dressing-table at home."

It did appear strange: and yet there were features in the young lady's personality which assured him in a moment that she was not an impostor. He yielded to her request, and put his hand in his pocket. Here it remained for a moment. How much did she mean by the words "some money." The Junonian quality of her form and manner made him throw himself by an impulse into harmony with her, and he responded regally. He scented a romance. He handed her five pounds.

His munificence caused her no apparent surprise. "It is quite enough, thank you," she remarked quietly, as he announced the sum, lest she should be unable to see it for herself.

While overtaking and conversing with her he had not observed that the rising wind, which had proceeded from puffing to growling, and from growling to screeching, with the accustomed suddenness of its changes here, had at length brought what it promised by these vagaries – rain. The drops, which at first hit their left cheeks like the pellets of a pop-gun, soon assumed the character of a raking fusillade from the bank adjoining, one shot of which was sufficiently smart to go through Jocelyn's sleeve. The tall girl turned, and seemed to be somewhat concerned at an onset which she had plainly not foreseen before her starting.

"We must take shelter," said Jocelyn.

"But where?" said she.

To windward was the long, monotonous bank, too obtusely piled to afford a screen, over which they could hear the canine crunching of pebbles by the sea without; on their right stretched the inner bay or roadstead, the distant riding lights now dim and glimmering; behind them a faint spark here and there in the lower sky showed where the island rose; before there was nothing definite, and could be nothing, till they reached a house by the bridge, a mile farther on, Henry the Eighth's Castle being a little farther still.

But just within the summit of the bank, whither it had apparently been hauled to be out of the way of the waves, was one of the local boats called lerrets, bottom upwards. As soon as they saw it the pair ran up the pebbly slope towards it by a simultaneous impulse. They then perceived that it had lain there a long time, and were comforted to find it capable of affording more protection than anybody would have expected in a distant view. It formed a shelter or store for the fishermen, the bottom of the lerret being tarred as a roof. By creeping under the bows, which overhung the bank to leeward, they made their way within, where, upon some thwarts, oars, and other fragmentary woodwork, lay a mass of dry netting – a whole seine. Upon this they scrambled and sat down, through inability to stand upright.

CHAPTER V

A Charge

The rain fell upon the keel of the old lerret like corn thrown in handfuls by some colossal sower, and darkness set in to its full shade.

They sat so close to each other that he could feel her furs against him. Neither had spoken since they left the roadway till she said, with attempted unconcern: "This is unfortunate."

He admitted that it was, and found, after a few further remarks had passed, that she certainly had been weeping, there being a suppressed gasp of passionateness in her utterance now and then.

"It is more unfortunate for you, perhaps, than for me," he said, "and I am very sorry that it should be so."

She replied nothing to this, and he added that it was rather a desolate place for a woman, alone and afoot. . . . He hoped nothing serious had happened to drag her out at such an untoward time.

At first she seemed not at all disposed to show any candour on her own affairs, and he was left to conjecture as to her history and name and how she could possibly have known him. But, as the rain gave not the least sign of cessation, he observed: "I think we shall have to return."

"Never!" said she, and the firmness with which she closed her lips was audible in the word.

"Why not?" he inquired.

"There are good reasons."

"I cannot understand how you should know me, while I have no knowledge of you."

"Oh, you know me – about me, at least."

"Indeed, I don't. How should I? You are a kimberlin."

"I am not. I am an islander – or was, rather . . . Haven't you heard of the Best-Bed Stone Company?"

"I should think so! They tried to ruin my father by getting away his trade – or, at least, the founder of the company did – old Bencomb."

"He's my father!"

"Indeed. I am sorry I should have spoken so disrespectfully of him, for

I never knew him personally. After making over his large business to the company, he retired, I believe, to London?"

"Yes. Our house, or rather his, not mine, is at South Kensington. We have lived there for years. But we have been tenants of the New Castle, on the island here, this season. We took it for a month or two of the owner, who is away."

"Then I have been staying quite near you, Miss Bencomb. My father's is a comparatively humble residence hard by."

"But he could afford a much bigger one if he chose."

"You have heard so? I don't know. He doesn't tell me much of his affairs."

"My father," she burst out suddenly, "is always scolding me for my extravagance! And he has been doing it to-day more than ever. He said I go shopping to simply a diabolical extent, and exceed my allowance!"

"Was that this evening?"

"Yes. And then it reached such a storm of passion between us that I pretended to retire to my room for the rest of the evening, but I slipped out; and I am never going back home again."

"What will you do?"

"I shall go first to my aunt in London; and if she won't have me, I'll work for a living. I have left my father for ever! What I should have done if I had not met you I cannot tell – I must have walked all the way to London, I suppose. Now I shall take the train as soon as I reach the mainland."

"If you ever do in this hurricane."

"I must sit here till it ceases."

And there on the nets they sat. Pearston knew of old Bencomb as his father's bitterest enemy, who had made a great fortune by swallowing up the small stone-merchants, but had found Jocelyn's sire a trifle too big to digest – the latter being, in fact, the chief rival of the Best-Bed Company to that day. Jocelyn thought it strange that he should be thrown by fate into a position to play the son of the Montagues to this daughter of the Capulets.[1]

As they talked there was a mutual instinct to drop their voices, and on this account the roar of the storm necessitated their drawing quite close to each other. Something tender came into their tones as time went on, and they forgot the lapse of time. It was quite late when she started up, alarmed at her position.

"Rain or no rain, I stay no longer," she said.

"Do come back," said he, taking her hand. "I'll return with you. My train has gone."

"No; I shall go on, and get a lodging in Budmouth town, if ever I reach it."

"It is so late that there will be no house open, except a little place near the station where you won't care to stay. However, if you are determined I will show you the way. I cannot leave you. It would be too awkward for you to go there alone."

She persisted, and they started through the twanging and spinning storm. The sea rolled and rose so high on their left, and was so near them on their right, that it seemed as if they were traversing its bottom like the children of Israel.[2] Nothing but the frail bank of pebbles divided them from the raging gulf without, and at every bang of the tide against it the ground shook, the shingle clashed, the spray rose vertically, and was blown over their heads. Quantities of sea-water trickled through the pebble wall, and ran in rivulets across their path to join the sea within.

They had not realised the force of the elements till now. Pedestrians had often been blown into the sea hereabout and drowned, owing to a sudden breach in the bank, which, however, had something of a spectral quality in being able to close up and join itself together again after any disruption. Her clothing offered more resistance to the wind than his, and she was consequently in the greater danger.

It was impossible to refuse his proffered aid. First he gave his arm, but the wind tore them apart as easily as coupled cherries. He steadied her bodily by encircling her waist with his arm; and she made no objection.

Somewhere about this time – it might have been sooner, it might have been later – he became distinctly conscious of a sensation which, in its incipient and unrecognised form, had lurked within him from some unnoticed moment when he was sitting close to her under the lerret. Though a young man, he was too old a hand not to know what this was, and felt considerably alarmed. It meant a possible migration of the Well-Beloved. It had not, however, taken place; and he went on thinking how soft and warm she was in her fur covering, as he held her so tightly; the only dry spots in the clothing of either being her left side and his right, where they excluded the rain by their mutual pressure.

As soon as they had crossed the ferry-bridge there was a little more shelter, but he did not relinquish his hold till she requested him. They passed the ruined castle, and having left the island far behind them drew near to the outskirts of the neighbouring watering-place. Into it they plodded without pause, crossing the harbour bridge about midnight, wet to the skin.

He pitied her, and, while he wondered at it, admired her determination. The houses facing the bay now sheltered them completely, and they reached the vicinity of the railway terminus (which it was at this date) without difficulty. As he had said, there was only one house open hereabout, a little temperance hotel, where the people stayed up for the arrival of the morning mail and passengers from the Channel boat. Their application for admission led to the withdrawal of a bolt, and they stood within the gaslight of the modern world.

He could see now that though she was such a fine figure, quite as tall as himself, she was not much more than a schoolgirl in years. Her face was certainly striking, though rather by its imperiousness than its beauty; and the beating of the wind and rain and spray had inflamed her cheeks to peony hues.

She persisted in the determination to go on to London by an early morning train, and he therefore offered advice on lesser matters only. "In that case," he said, "you must go on to your room and send down your things, that they may be dried by the fire immediately, or they will not be ready. I will tell the servant to do this, and send you up something to eat."

She assented to his proposal, without, however, showing any marks of gratitude, and when she had gone Pearston dispatched her the light supper promised by the sleepy girl who was "night porter" at this establishment. He felt ravenously hungry himself, and set about drying his clothes as well as he could, and eating at the same time.

At first he was in doubt what to do, but soon decided to stay where he was till the morrow. By the aid of some temporary wraps and some slippers from the cupboard, he was contriving to make himself comfortable when the maid-servant came downstairs with a damp armful of woman's raiment.

Pearston withdrew from the fire. The maid-servant knelt down before the blaze and held up with extended arms one of the habiliments of the Juno upstairs, from which a cloud of steam began to rise. As she knelt, the girl nodded forward, recovered herself, and nodded again.

"You are sleepy, my girl," said Pearston.

"Yes, Sir; I have been up a long time. When nobody comes I lie down on the couch in the other room."

"Then I'll relieve you of that; go and lie down in the other room, just as if we were not here. I'll dry the clothing and put the articles here in a heap, which you can take up to the young lady in the morning."

The "night porter" thanked him and left the room, and he soon heard her snoring from the adjoining apartment. Then Jocelyn opened proceedings, overhauling the mystic robes and extending them one by one. As the steam went up he fell into a delicious reverie, and regarded the fair white linen[3] that screened his face from the fire with a curious interest. His eyes traced the pattern of the wondrous flowers and leaves in the delicate lace-work, the wheels, rockets, quatrefoils, and spirals of the embroidery, all the while that their owner above was little thinking of the care he was taking that she should not get cold. The fabrics seemed almost part and parcel of her queenly person. He again became conscious of the germ with which he had been impregnated. The Well-Beloved was moving house – had gone over to the wearer of this attire.

He kissed each of the articles of apparel, and in the course of ten minutes adored her.

And how about little Avice Caro? He did not think of her as before.

He was not sure that he had ever seen the Well-Beloved in that friend of his youth, solicitous as he was for her welfare. But, loving her or not, he perceived that the spirit, emanation, idealism, which called itself his Love was flitting stealthily from some remoter figure to the near one in the chamber overhead.

But he must carry out his engagement to marry Avice. True, she had not kept her engagement to meet him this evening, and the irrevocable ratification of their betrothal had not been reached. Still, he was bound to marry her.

CHAPTER VI

On the Brink

Miss Bencomb was leaving the hotel for the station, which was quite near at hand. At Jocelyn's suggestion she wrote a telegram to inform her father that she had gone to her aunt's, with a view to allaying anxiety and deterring pursuit. They walked together to the platform and bade each other good-bye; each obtained a ticket independently, and Jocelyn got his luggage from the cloak-room.

On the platform they encountered each other again, and there was a light in their glances at each other which said, as by a flash telegraph: "We are bound for the same town, why not enter the same compartment?"

They did.

She took a corner seat, with her back to the engine; he sat opposite. The guard looked in, thought they were lovers, and did not show other travellers into that compartment. They talked on strictly ordinary matters; what she thought he did not know, but at every stopping station he dreaded intrusion. Before they were halfway to London the event he had just begun to realise was a patent fact. The Beloved was again embodied; she filled every fibre and curve of this woman's form. His heart had clean gone out to her.

Drawing near Waterloo Bridge Station was like drawing near Doomsday. How should he leave her in the turmoil of a London street? She seemed quite unprepared for the rattle of the scene. He asked her where her aunt lived.

"Bayswater," said Miss Bencomb.

He called a cab, and proposed that she should share it till they arrived at her aunt's, whose residence lay not much out of the way to his own. Try as he would he could not ascertain if she understood his feelings, but she assented to his offer and entered the vehicle.

"We are old friends," he said, as they drove onward.

"Indeed, we are," she answered, without smiling.

"But hereditarily we are mortal enemies, dear Juliet."[1]

"Yes— What did you say?"

"I said Juliet."[1]

She laughed in a half-proud way, and murmured: "Your father is my father's enemy, and my father is mine. Yes, it is so." And then their eyes caught each other's glance. "My queenly darling!" he burst out; "instead of going to your aunt's, will you come and marry me?"

A flush covered her over, which seemed akin to a flush of rage. It was not exactly that, but she was excited. She did not answer, and he feared he had mortally offended her dignity. Perhaps she had only made use of him as a convenient aid to her intentions. However, he went on –

"Your father would not be able to reclaim you, then? After all, this is not so precipitate as it seems. You know all about me, my history, my prospects. I know all about you. Our families have been neighbours on that isle for hundreds of years, though you are now such a London product."

"Will you ever be a Royal Academician?"[2] she asked musingly, her excitement having calmed down.

"I hope to be – I *will* be, if you will be my wife."

She looked at him long.

"Think what a short way out of your difficulty this would be," he replied. "No bother about aunts, no fetching home by an angry father."

It seemed to decide her. She yielded to his embrace.

"How long will it take to marry?" Miss Bencomb asked, with obvious self-repression.

"We could do it to-morrow. I could get to Doctors' Commons[3] by noon to-day, and the license would be ready by to-morrow morning."

"I won't go to my aunt's; I will be an independent woman. I have been reprimanded as if I were a child of six. I'll be your wife if it is as easy as you say."

They stopped the cab while they held a consultation. Pearston had rooms and a studio in the neighbourhood of Campden Hill; but it would be hardly desirable to take her thither till they were married. They decided to go to an hotel.

Changing their direction, therefore, they went back to the Strand, and soon ensconced themselves as Mr. and Miss Pearston in one of the establishments off that thoroughfare. Jocelyn then left her and proceeded on his errand eastward.

It was about three o'clock when, having arranged all preliminaries necessitated by this sudden change of front, he began strolling slowly back; he felt bewildered, and to walk was a relief. Gazing occasionally into this shop window and that, he called a hansom as by an inspiration, and directed the driver to "Mellstock Gardens." Arrived here, he rang the bell of a studio, and in a minute or two it was answered by a young man in shirt-sleeves, about his own age, with a great square palette on his left thumb.

"Oh, you, Pearston! I thought you were in the country. Come in. I'm awfully glad to see you. I am here in town finishing off a painting for an American customer, who wants to take it back with him."

Pearston followed his friend into the painting-room, where a pretty young woman was sitting sewing. At a signal from the painter she disappeared without speaking.

"I can see from your face you have something to say; so we'll have it all to ourselves. What'll you drink?"

"Oh! it doesn't matter what, so that it is alcohol in some shape or form. . . . Now, Somers, you must just listen to me, for I *have* something to tell."

Pearston had sat down in an armchair, and Somers had resumed his painting. When a servant had brought in brandy to soothe Pearston's nerves, and soda to take off the injurious effects of the brandy, and milk to take off the depleting effects of the soda, Jocelyn began his narrative, addressing it rather to Somers' chimney-piece, and Somers' antique clock, and Somers' Persian rugs, than to Somers himself, who stood at his picture a little behind his friend.

"Before I tell you what has happened to me," Pearston said, "I want to let you know the manner of man I am."

"Lord – I know already."

"No, you don't. This is to be a sort of *Apologia pro vitâ meâ.*"[4]

"Very well. Fire away!"

CHAPTER VII
Her Earlier Incarnations

"You, Somers, are not, I know, one of those who continue in bondage to the gigantic cosmopolitan superstition that the Beloved One of any man always, or even usually, remains in one corporeal nook or shell for any great length of time. If I am wrong, and you do still hold to that ancient error – well, my story will seem rather queer."

"Suppose you say some men, not any man."

"All right – I'll say one man, this man only, if you are so particular. The Beloved of this one man, then, has had many incarnations – too many to describe in detail. Each shape, or embodiment, has been a temporary residence only, into which she has entered, lived in a while, and made her exit from, leaving the substance, so far as I have been concerned, a corpse. Now, there is no spiritualistic nonsense in this – it is simple fact, put in the plain form that the correct and conventional public are afraid of. So much for the principle."

"Good. Go on."

"Well; the first embodiment of her occurred, so nearly as I can recollect, when I was about the age of nine. Her vehicle was a little blue-eyed girl of eight or so, one of a family of eleven, with flaxen hair about her shoulders, which attempted to curl, but ignominiously failed, hanging like chimney-crooks only. This defect used rather to trouble me; and, in short, was, I believe, one of the main reasons of my Beloved's departure from that tenement. I cannot remember with any exactness when the departure occurred. I know it was after I had kissed my little friend in a garden-seat on a hot noontide, under a Chinese umbrella, which we had opened over us as we sat, that passers through East Wake might not observe our marks of affection, forgetting that our screen must attract more attention than our persons.

"When the whole dream came to an end through her father leaving the island, I thought my Well-Beloved had gone for ever (being then in the unpractised condition of Adam[1] at sight of the first sunset). But she had not. Laura had gone for ever, but not my Best-Beloved.

"For some months after I had done crying for the flaxen-haired edition of her, my Love did not reappear. Then she came suddenly, unexpectedly, in a situation I should never have predicted. I was standing on the kerb-stone of the pavement in Budmouth-Regis, outside the Preparatory School, looking across towards the sea, when a middle-aged gentleman on horseback, and beside him a young lady, also mounted, passed down the street. The girl turned her head, and – possibly because I was gaping at her in awkward admiration, or smiling myself – smiled at me. Having ridden a few paces, she looked round again and smiled.

"It was enough, more than enough, to set me on fire. I understood in a moment the information conveyed to me by my emotion – the Well-Beloved had reappeared. This second form in which it had pleased her to take up her abode was quite a young woman's, darker in complexion than the first. Her hair, also worn in a knot, was of an ordinary brown, and so, I think, were her eyes, but the niceties of her features were not to be gathered so cursorily. However, there sat my coveted one, re-embodied; and, bidding my schoolmates a hasty farewell as soon as I could do so without suspicion, I hurried along the Esplanade in the direction she and her father had ridden. But they had put their horses to a canter, and I could not see which way they had gone. In the greatest misery I turned down a side street, but was soon elevated to a state of excitement by seeing the same pair galloping towards me. Flushing up to my hair, I stopped and heroically faced her as she passed. She smiled again, but, alas! upon my Love's cheek there was no blush of passion for me."

Pearston paused, and drank from his glass, as he lived for a brief moment in the scene he had conjured up.

(*To be continued.*)

Somers was in a mood to reserve his comments, and Jocelyn continued –

"That afternoon I idled about the streets, looking for her in vain. When I next saw one of the boys who had been with me at her first passing I stealthily reminded him of the incident, and asked if he knew the riders.

"'O yes,' he said. 'That was Colonel Targe and his daughter Elsie.'

"'How old do you think she is?' said I, a sense of disparity in our ages disturbing my mind.

"'O – nineteen. I think they say. She's going to be married the day after to-morrow to Captain Popp, of the 501st, and they are ordered off to India at once.'

"The grief which I experienced at this intelligence was such that at dusk I went away to the edge of the harbour, intending to put an end to myself there and then. But I had been told that crabs had been found clinging[2] to the dead faces of persons who had fallen in thereabout, leisurely eating them, and the idea of such an unpleasant contingency deterred me. I should state that the marriage of my Beloved concerned me little; it was her departure that broke my heart. I never saw her again.

"Though I had already learnt that the absence of the corporeal matter did not involve the absence of the informing spirit, I could scarce bring myself to believe that in this case it was possible for her to return to my view without the form she had last inhabited.

"But she did.

"It was not, however, till after a space of time during which I passed through that bearish age in boys, their early teens, when girls are their especial contempt. I was about seventeen, and was sitting one evening over a cup of tea in a restaurant of the aforesaid watering-place, when opposite me a lady took her seat with a little girl. We looked at each other awhile, the child made advances, till I said: 'She's a good little thing.'

"The lady assented, and made a further remark.

"'She has the soft dark eyes of her mother,' said I.

"'Do you think her eyes are good?' asks the lady, as if she had not heard what she had heard most – the last three words of my opinion.

"'Yes – for copies,' said I, regarding her.

"After this we got on very well. She informed me that her husband had gone out in a yacht, and I said it was a pity he didn't take her with him for the airing. She gradually disclosed herself in the character of a deserted young wife, and later on I met her in the street without the child. She was going to the landing-stage to meet her husband, so she told me; but she did not know the way.

"I offered to show her, and did so. I will not go into particulars, but I afterwards saw her several times, and soon discovered that the Beloved (as to whose whereabouts I had been at fault so long) lurked here. Though why she had chosen this tantalising situation of an inaccessible matron's form when so many others offered, it was beyond me to discover. The whole affair ended innocently enough, when the lady left the town with her husband and child: she seemed to regard our acquaintance as a flirtation; yet it was anything but a flirtation for me!

"After this, the Well-Beloved put herself in evidence with greater and greater frequency, and it would be impossible for me to give you details of her various incarnations. She came nine times in the course of the two or three ensuing years. Four times she masqueraded as a brunette, twice as a pale-haired creature, and two or three times under a complexion neither light nor dark. Sometimes she was a tall, fine girl. More often, I think, she preferred to slip into the skin of a lithe airy being, of no great stature. I grew so accustomed to these exits and entrances that I resigned myself to them quite passively, talked to her, kissed her, corresponded with her, ached for her, in each of her several guises. So it went on until a month ago. And then for the first time I was puzzled. She either had, or she had not, entered the person of Avice Caro, a young girl I had known from infancy. Upon the whole, I have decided that, after all, she did not enter the form of Avice Caro, because I retain so great a respect for her still."

Pearston here gave in brief the history of his revived comradeship with Avice, the verge of the engagement to which they had reached, and its unexpected rupture by him, merely through his meeting with a woman into whom the Well-Beloved unmistakably moved under his very eyes – by name Miss Marcia Bencomb. He described their spontaneous decision to marry offhand; and then he put it to Somers whether he ought to marry or not – her or anybody else – in such circumstances.

"Certainly not," said Somers. "Though, if anybody, little Avice. But not even her. You are like other men, only rather worse. Essentially, all men are fickle, like you; but not with such activity, such open-eyed perceptiveness."

"My dear Somers, fickle is not the word. Fickleness means getting weary of a thing while the thing remains the same. But I am faithful to what I fancy each woman to be till I come to close quarters with her. I have ever been faithful to the elusive ideal creature whom I have never been able to get a firm hold of, unless I have done so now. And let me tell you that her flitting from each to each individual has been anything but a pleasure for me – certainly not a wanton game of my instigation. Somers, to see the creature whom you have thought perfect, divine, lose under your very gaze the divinity which has informed her, grow commonplace, turn from flame to ashes, from a radiant vitality to a corpse, is anything but a pleasure for any man, and has been nothing less than a racking spectacle for me. Each mournful emptied shape stands ever after like the nest of some beautiful bird from which the inhabitant has departed and left it to fill with snow.[3] I have been ready to weep when I have looked in a face for Her I used to see there, and can see Her there no more."

"You ought not to marry," repeated Somers.

"Then no man ought."

"No man ought – there you've hit it," replied the painter.

Pearston soon after took his leave. A friend's advice not to embark on matrimony is just the feather-weight required to turn the scale and make a man do it. He quickly returned to Miss Bencomb.

She was different now. Anxiety had visibly brought her down a notch or two, undone a few degrees of that haughty curl which her lip could occasionally assume. "How long have you been away!" she moaned tearfully, leaning her face against his shoulder.

"Never mind, darling. It is all arranged,"[4] said he.

CHAPTER VIII

A Miscalculation

The pair had been married[1] two months, and had just returned from a Continental trip to Pearston's house in Hintock Road, Kensington. They were getting through the heavy task of opening a heap of letters and papers which had accumulated since the last batch had been forwarded.

Pearston was filled with zest for availing himself to the utmost of the artistic stimulus afforded by London – that great and enlightened city, which dedicates its squares, streets, and parks to figure-heads and *fainéants*, and a lane at the East-End to Shakespeare; and, with a view to showing its sympathy with a more rapid form of mental elevation than results from the tedious process of picture-gazing, makes its taverns the Sunday resort by closing its museums. Nevertheless, for them it was London or nowhere, and here they were going to make the best of their recent matrimonial plunge.

Marcia's parents, finding from the newspapers what had happened, put as hopeful a face as they could on the matter, but did not communicate with the truants. In birth the pair were about equal, but Marcia's family had gained a start in the accumulation of wealth and in the initiation of social distinction, which lent a colour to the feeling that the advantages of the match had been mainly on one side. Nevertheless, Pearston was a sculptor rising to fame by fairly rapid strides; and potentially the marriage was not a bad one for a woman who, beyond being the probable successor to a stone-merchant's considerable fortune, had no exceptional opportunities.

Among their letters was one for her, in which she was informed that her father and mother had gone to spend the winter in the Riviera and

Italy. On this particular morning, as on most mornings, the London atmosphere was of a neat drab with the twenty-ninth fog of the season, and Marcia looked out of the window as far as she could see, which was two feet, and sighed. She had been eight weeks Pearston's wife.

"I should have been in the City of Flowers[2] by this time if"—

"You hadn't been so foolish as to marry me," laughed Jocelyn.

She opened another letter.

"Good gracious!" she exclaimed, and burst into laughter.

"What is it?" asked her husband.

Marcia began to read the letter aloud. It came from an old lover of hers, an army man, who stated that he was on his way home to claim his darling, according to her plighted word.

She was half risible – half concerned. "What shall I do?" she said.

"Do? It seems to me that there is only one thing to do, and that a very obvious thing. Tell him as soon as possible that you are already married."

She accordingly wrote out a reply to that effect, Jocelyn helping her to make the phrases as gentle as possible.

"I repeat" (the letter concluded) "that I had quite forgotten! I am deeply sorry; but that is the truth. I have told my husband everything, and he is looking over my shoulder as I write."

Said Jocelyn, when he saw this set down: "You might leave out the last stab at the poor fellow."

"Stab, indeed! It isn't such a thing. Why does he come bothering me? Jocelyn, you ought to be very proud that I have put it in. You said the other day I was conceited in declaring I might have married that science-man I spoke of; but now you see there was yet another available."

He, impatiently, "Well, no more about that. To my mind this is a decidedly unpleasant degrading business, though you treat it so lightly. Making a fool of a man! You ought to have remembered."

"H'm – or ought to have married him?"

"Yes. I wonder if I should have suffered much in that alternative?"

"I only did half what you did."

"What was that?"

"I only proved false through forgetfulness, but you were false deliberately."

"To whom?"

"Avice Caro."

"Don't vex me about her, or I shall regret the falseness, as you call it – for more reasons than one."

By degrees Pearston fell into his customary round of existence; his profession occupied him to the exclusion of domestic affairs; but with Marcia life began to be rather dull. Her parents were not resentful or bitter, but they were not very warm. They had returned to London, and, while willing to receive Marcia at their house, refrained from calling on the young couple. Pearston was a little sarcastic at their obvious estimate of him, and Marcia took umbrage at his sarcasm.

"I am one deserving of satire, if anybody! What a foolish girl I was to run away from a father for such a trumpery reason as a little scolding because I had exceeded my allowance!"

"I advised you to go back."

"In a sort of way; not in the right tone. You spoke most contemptuously of my father as a merchant."

"I couldn't speak otherwise of such a man."

"Such a man! What have you to say against him?"

"A very great deal, if it comes to that. I know that at one time he made it the business of his life to ruin my father."

"It is not true, Sir! That narrow, grovelling miser be ruined by an open-handed man like my father! It is like your misrepresentations to say that!"

"By God! Marcia, you do exasperate me! I could give you every step of the proceeding in detail – the getting the quarries, the underhand"—

"It is untrue! There was no such proceeding!"

Pearston, without replying for a moment, gazed at the fine picture of scorn that his Juno-wife's face[3] and dark eyes presented.

"I ought to have known it," he murmured.

"What?"

"That such a face as that meant temper."

She left the room. Some days after the subject was renewed by their seeing in a local paper an announcement of the marriage of Avice Caro with her cousin. Jocelyn remembered him, though but indistinctly. He had been the manager of her mother's quarries since her father's death, and had recently been thrown much in her company.

Jocelyn sat in a reverie.

"You spoke of my temper the other day," said she. "Do you think temper had nothing to do with your dear Avice's quick marriage?"

"She was not 'dear,' not dear enough, at any rate, to me."

"Unfortunately for me."

"Well, yes, I ought to have married her, because she was the only woman I never loved. But instead of wedding Rosaline,[4] Romeo must needs go marrying Juliet; and that's where he made the mistake. A fortunate thing for the affections of those two that they died. In a month or two the enmity of their families would have proved a fruitful source of dissension; Juliet would have lived with her people, he with his; the subject would have split them as much as it has split us."

Thus it began and continued in the home of these hastily wedded ones. Sometimes it was worse, far worse, than a hot quarrel. There was a calm, cold reasoning in their discussions, and they talked in complete accord of the curse of matrimony. In their ill-matched junction on the strength of a two or three days' passion they felt the full irksomeness of a formal tie which, as so many have discovered, did not become necessary till it was a cruelty to them.

A legal marriage it was,[5] but not a true marriage. In the night they heard sardonic voices and laughter in the wind at the ludicrous facility afforded them by events for taking a step in two days which they could not retrace in a lifetime, despite their mutual desire as the two persons solely concerned.

Marcia's haughty temper unfolded in the direction of irascibility when she beheld clearly in what a trap she had been ensnared. She was her husband's property, like one of his statues that he could not sell. "Was there ever anything more absurd in history," she said bitterly to him one day, "than that grey-headed legislators from time immemorial should have gravely based inflexible laws upon the ridiculous dream of young people that a transient mutual desire for each other was going to last for ever!"

Jocelyn saw that the slow and mournful departure of the Well-Beloved from the form at his side was hastened, to one of his unfortunate temperament, by the tie that was supposed to hinder it. He thought sometimes that if the law had ordained separate residences, with periodical visitations strictly limited to Sundays and holidays as the rigorous matrimonial condition, he might have got on with Marcia, despite her *Quos egos*[6] and high-handed rulings; indeed, in such circumstances those traits would not have been unattractive to him. But love's dewy freshness could not live under a vertical sun, and that gradual substitution of friendship, which is indispensable and, perhaps, usual in marriage, was not possible with natures so jarring as these.

There followed a long period of dreary calm, and then the storm which had been gathering under its silence burst forth with unmitigated fury.

The Well-Beloved had quite vanished away. What had become of her Pearston knew not, but not a line of her was any longer discoverable in Marcia's contours, not a sound of her in Marcia's accents. Having entered into a signed and sealed contract to do no such thing, he would not in honour look about to discover the other's lurking-place; but he sometimes trembled at the thought of what would become of that solemn covenant if she were suddenly to disclose herself and confront him before he was aware. Once or twice he fancied that he saw her in the distance – at the end of a street, on the far sands of a shore, in a window, or at the opposite side of a railway station; but he always religiously turned on his heel and walked the other way (especially if Marcia was with him).

There came a day when she returned from visiting her mother at Kensington, bringing the news that, travel having benefited her father's health so markedly on the last occasion, her parents had decided on a tour round the world, and a possible stay with her uncle, who was a banker in San Francisco. Since retiring from his large business, old Mr. Bencomb had not known what to do with his leisure. They were going to let their house on a lease or sell it outright, rating London life as dreary by comparison with cosmopolitan freedom and an absence of responsibility in the conduct of the world's affairs.

"And here am I chained to London!" Marcia added. "You said you were going to revisit Rome and Athens, but you don't. I wish I could go with them."

"Go, in Heaven's name! I don't hinder you," said he. "You are always, it seems to me, dwelling upon the inconveniences I have caused you by marrying you, and thereby interfering with your natural life. Why doesn't your father come and talk over his project like a man, and perhaps I could arrange to go with them."

"That would be treachery to your own dear parent, so cruelly robbed by my wicked one."

"Now, no more of that, Marcia! . . . Though it is true enough."

"It is not!"

"It is. I have the papers to prove it."

"I tell you it is not so, Sir!" she cried. "It was an honest trade rivalry. Don't you be so fond of your insinuations! A miserly, grasping skin-flint"—

"Upon my soul, Marcia, I won't hear you, or anybody else, call my father names! Why, you mean woman, we are partly living, aren't we, at this very moment, upon what he allows me; and you can put your tongue to such an expression as that!"

"And you can put your tongue to call me a mean hussy!"

"I didn't."

"You did!"

Jocelyn sprang up to leave the room, and her anger being culminative, she caught up the first thing she could seize, which happened to be one of his statuettes, and flung it at his head. The figure missed him, but struck the wall, and fell broken to atoms. The sight of his darling little work irretrievably ruined so exasperated Pearston that he rushed back, took her by the shoulders, and shook her: after which he went out of the room, put on his hat, and departed for his club.

CHAPTER IX

Familiar Phenomena in the Distance

After four years of common residence, diversified by drawing-room incidents of this lively character, these two irreconcilables parted by common consent. The voyage of Marcia's parents had implanted in them a zest for the New World, already the home of some relatives; Marcia's father, a man still in full vigour of life except at intervals, found occupation for the leisure which the sale of his business afforded him in investing capital in undertakings commensurate with the scale of the country wherein they were to be carried out; and when in the development of these schemes he again rejoined his brother in the Western States Marcia accompanied him.

The separation was quite of an informal kind, each merely promising the other never to intrude into that other's life again, by written word or personal presence: its object being to undo, as far as lay in their power, the mischief that misapprehension of each other's characters had effected during the past few years.

Marcia declared she would never return to England, but would make her home with her uncle on the Pacific shore. "And for my part," she added in this her last letter to him, "I fail to see why, in making each our own home, we should not make our own matrimonial laws[1] if we choose. This may seem an advanced view, but I am not ashamed of advanced views. If I strictly confine myself to one hemisphere, and you, as I expect you to do, confine yourself to the other, any new tie we may form can affect nobody but ourselves. As I shall feel myself at liberty to form such, I accord the same liberty to you."

Whether the advanced idea were a Parthian fling[2] of defiance, which she had no intention whatever of acting on, or whether it were written coolly, as a possible contingency, with an eye on the jilted Indian captain, Pearston had no means of knowing.

A long period of outward stagnation followed the break-up of his house and home. During the interval Jocelyn threw into creations that ever-bubbling spring of emotion which, without some conduit into space, will surge upwards and ruin a man. It was probably owing to this, certainly not on account of any care or anxiety for such a result, that he was successful in his art, successful by a seemingly sudden spurt, which carried him at one bound over the hindrances of years.

He prospered without effort. He was an A.R.A.[3]

But recognitions of this sort, social distinctions, which he had once coveted so keenly, seemed to have no utility for him now. Pearston, now practically a bachelor, was floating in society without any soul anchorage or spot that he could call his own; and, for want of a domestic centre, round which honours might crystallize,[4] they dispersed in impalpable vapour without accumulating or adding specific gravity to his material position.

He would have gone on working with his chisel with just as much zest if his creations had been doomed to be seen by no mortal eye but his own. By reason of this indifference to the popular reception of his dream-figures he acquired a curious artistic *aplomb* that carried him through the gusts of opinion without suffering them to disturb his inherent bias.

The study of beauty was his only joy.[5] In the streets he would observe a face, or a fraction of a face, which seemed to express to a hair's-breadth in mutable flesh what he was at that moment wishing to express in durable shape. He would dodge and follow the owner like a detective; in omnibus, in cab, in steam-boat, through crowds, into shops, churches, theatres, public-houses, and slums – mostly, when at close quarters, to be disappointed for his pains.

In these beauty-chases he sometimes cast his eye across the Thames to the wharves on the south side, and to that particular one whereat his father's tons of freestone were daily landed from the ketches of the south coast. He could occasionally discern lying there those white blocks, persistently nibbled by his parent from that island rock in the English Channel all familiar to Jocelyn, so persistently as if in time his father would nibble it all away.

One thing it passed him to understand: on what field of observation the poets and philosophers based their assumption that the passion of love was intensest in youth and burnt lower as the years advanced. It was possibly because of his utter domestic loneliness, but it was certainly the fact, that during the years which followed his wife's departure, when he was drifting along from five-and-twenty to five-and-thirty years of age, Pearston occasionally loved with an ardour – though, it is true, also with a self-control – unknown to him when he was green in judgment.[6]

The Well-Beloved – now again on earth – was always existing somewhere near him. For months he would find her on the stage of a theatre: then she would flit away, leaving the poor, empty carcase that had lodged her to mumm on as best it could without her – a sorry lay figure to his eyes, heaped with imperfections and sullied with commonplace. She would reappear, it might be, in an at first unnoticed lady, met at some fashionable "crush," exhibition, bazaar, or dinner: to flit from her, in turn, after a few months, and stand as a graceful shop-girl at some large drapery establishment or other into which he had strayed on an unaccustomed errand. Then she would forsake this figure and redisclose herself in the guise of some popular authoress, *pianiste*, or fiddleress, at whose shrine he would worship for perhaps a twelvemonth. Once she was a dancing-girl at the Royal Moorish Palace[7] of Varieties, though during her whole continuance at that establishment he never once exchanged a word with his Beloved, nor did she while there ever dream of his existence. He knew that a ten-minutes' conversation in the wings with the substance would send the elusive phantom scurrying fearfully away into some other even less accessible mask-figure.

She was a blonde, a brunette, tall, *petite*, *svelte*, straight-featured, full, curvilinear. Only one quality remained unalterable in her: her instability of tenure. In Börne's phrase,[8] nothing was permanent in her but change.

"It is odd," he said to himself, "that this experience of mine, or idiosyncrasy, or whatever it is, which would be sheer waste of time for other men, creates sober business for me." For all these dreams he translated into marble, and found that by them he was hitting a public taste he had never deliberately aimed at, and mostly despised. He was, in short, in danger of drifting away from a solid artistic reputation to a popularity which might possibly be as brief as it would be brilliant and exciting.

"You will be caught some day, my friend," Somers would occasionally observe to him. "I don't mean to say entangled in anything discreditable, for I admit that you are in practice a moral man; I mean the process will be reversed. Some woman, whose Well-Beloved flits about as yours does now, will catch your eye, and you'll stick to her like a limpet, while she follows her phantom and leaves you to ache as you will."

"You may be right, but I think you are wrong," said Pearston. "As flesh she dies daily,[9] like the Apostle's material self; because when I grapple with the reality she's no longer in it, so that I cannot stick to one incarnation if I would."

"Wait till you are older," said Somers.

But Pearston's artistic emotions were abruptly suspended by the news of his father's sudden death at Sandbourne, whither the merchant had lately gone for a change of air by the advice of his physician.

CHAPTER X

The Old Phantom Becomes Distinct

Mr. Pearston, senior, it must be admitted, had been something miserly in his home life. But he had never stinted his son. He had been rather a hard taskmaster, though, as a paymaster, trustworthy; a ready-money man, just and ungenerous. To everyone's surprise, the capital he had accumulated in the stone trade was of large amount for a business so unostentatiously carried on – much larger than Jocelyn had ever regarded as possible.

While the son had been modelling and chipping his ephemeral fancies into perennial shape, the father had been persistently chiselling for half a century at the original matter of those shapes, the stern, isolated rock in the Channel; and by the aid of his cranes and pulleys, his trolleys and his boats, had sent off his spoil to all parts of Great Britain. When Jocelyn had wound up everything and disposed of the business, as recommended by his father's will, he found himself enabled to add about eighty thousand pounds to the twelve thousand which he already possessed from professional and other sources.

After arranging for the sale of some freehold properties in the island other than quarries – for he did not intend to reside there – he returned to town. He had promised his wife never to trouble her again; nor for a whole dozen years had he done so; but in this access of means he considered that it behoved him to make inquiries, so as to ascertain if she wished for an allowance.

Neither letters nor advertisements brought any tidings. Nothing more could be done without personal search; and that he resolved to make the year following, if he heard nothing of her earlier. Her parents were, he believed, dead; possibly she had formed the new tie of which she had spoken, and had no wish to be recognised by her old name.

A reposeful time ensued. His first entry into society after his father's death occurred one evening, when, for want of knowing what better to do, he responded to a card of invitation sent by one of the few ladies of rank whom he numbered among his friends, and set out in a cab for the square wherein she lived during three or four months of the year.

The hansom turned the corner, and he obtained a raking view of the houses along the north side, of which hers was one, with the familiar linkman at the door. There were Chinese lanterns, too, on the balcony. He perceived in a moment that the customary "small and early"[1] reception had resolved itself on this occasion into something very like large and late. He remembered that there had just been a political crisis, which accounted for the enlargement of the Countess of Channelcliffe's assembly;[2] for hers was one of the neutral or non-political houses at which more politics are agitated than at the professedly party gatherings.

There was such a string of carriages that Pearston did not wait to take his turn at the door, but alighted some yards off and walked forward. He had to stay a moment behind the wall of spectators which barred his way, and as he paused some ladies in white cloaks crossed from their carriages to the door on the carpet laid for the purpose. He had not seen their faces, nothing of them but vague forms, and yet he was suddenly seized with a presentiment. Its gist was that he might be going to re-encounter the Well-Beloved that night: after her long, long hiding she meant to re-appear and intoxicate him. That liquid sparkle of the eye, that lingual music, that turn of the head, how well he knew it all, despite the many superficial changes, and how instantly he would recognise it under whatever complexion, contour, accent, height, or carriage that it might choose to masquerade!

Pearston's other conjecture, that the night was to be a lively one, received confirmation as soon as he reached the hall, where a simmer of excitement was perceptible as the surplus or overflow from above down the staircase – a feature which he had always noticed to be present when any climax or sensation had been reached in the political world.

"And where have you been keeping yourself so long, young man?" said his hostess, archly, when he had shaken hands with her. Pearston was always regarded as a young man. "Oh, yes, of course, I remember," she added, looking serious in a moment at thought of his loss. The Countess was a woman with a good-natured manner, verging on that oft-claimed feminine quality, humour, and was quickly sympathetic. She then began to tell him of a scandal in the political side to which she nominally belonged, that had come out of the present crisis, and that, having sworn to abjure politics for ever on account of it, he was to regard her as a neutral house-holder forthwith. By this time some more people had surged upstairs, and Pearston prepared to move on.

"You are looking for somebody – I can see that," said she.

"Yes – a lady," said Pearston.

"Tell me her name, and I'll try to think if she's here."

"I cannot; I don't know it," he said.

"What is she like?"

"I cannot describe her, not even her dress."

Lady Channelcliffe looked a pout, as if she thought he were teasing her, and he moved on in the current. The fact was that, for a moment, Pearston fancied he had discovered her he was in search of lurking in the person of the very hostess he had conversed with, who was charming always, and particularly charming to-night; he was just feeling an incipient consternation at the possibility of such a jade's trick in his Well-Beloved, who had once before chosen to embody herself as a married woman, though, happily, at that time with no serious results. However, he felt that he had been mistaken, and that the fancy had been solely owing to the highly charged electric condition in which he had arrived by reason of his recent isolation.

The whole set of rooms formed one great utterance of the opinions of the hour. The high gods of party were present, and the brilliancy of style and form in their handling of public questions was only less conspicuous than the paucity of their original ideas. But Jocelyn's mind did not run in this stream: he was like a stone in a brook, waiting for some peculiar floating object to be brought towards him and to stick upon his surface.

He was looking for the next new version of the fair one, and he did not consider at the moment, though he had done so at other times, that this presentiment of meeting her was, of all presentiments, just the sort of one to work out its own fulfilment.

He looked for her in the knot of persons gathered round an ex-Cabinet Minister of very high rank indeed, who was standing in the middle of the largest room discoursing in the genial, almost jovial, manner natural to him at these times. The two or three ladies forming his audience had been joined by another, and it was on her that Pearston's attention was directed, as well as the great statesman's, whose first sheer gaze at her, expressing "Who are you?" almost audibly, changed into an interested, listening look as the few words she spoke were uttered – for the ex-Minister differed from many of his standing in being extremely careful not to interrupt a timid speaker, giving way in an instant if anybody else began with him. Nobody knew better than himself his own limitations, and his manner was that of a man who could catch an idea readily, even if he could not create one.

The lady told her little story – whatever it was Jocelyn could not hear it – the ex-Cabinet Minister laughed: "Haugh-haugh-haugh!"

The lady blushed. Jocelyn, wrought up to a high tension by the aforesaid presentiment that his Shelleyan "One-shape-of-many-names"[3] was about to reappear, paid little heed to the man of State, watching for a full view of the lady who had won his attention.

(*To be continued.*)

That lady remained for the present partially screened by her neighbours. A diversion was caused by Lady Channelcliffe bringing up somebody to present to the political Jove; the ladies got mixed, and Jocelyn lost sight of the one whom he was beginning to suspect as the stealthily returned absentee.

He looked for her in the young lady of the house,[4] his hostess's younger sister, who appeared to more advantage that night than she had ever done before – in a sky-blue dress, which had nothing between it and the fair skin of her neck, lending her an unusually soft and sylph-like aspect. She saw him, and they converged. Her look of "What do you think of me now?" was suggested, he knew, by the thought that the last time they met she had appeared under the disadvantage of mourning costume, on a wet day in a country-house, where everybody was cross.

"I have some new photographs, and I want you to tell me whether they are good," she said. "Mind, you are to tell me truly, and no favour."

She produced the pictures from an adjoining drawer, and they sat down together upon an ottoman for the purpose of examination. The portraits, taken by the last fashionable photographer, were very good, and he told her so; but as he spoke and compared them his mind was fixed on something else than the mere judgment. He wondered whether the elusive one were indeed in the frame of this girl.

He looked up at her. To his surprise, her mind, too, was on other things bent than on the pictures. Her eyes were glancing away to distant people, she was visibly considering the effect she was producing upon them by this cosy tête-à-tête with Pearston, and upon one in particular, a man of 'thirty, of military appearance, whom Pearston did not know. Quite convinced now that no phantom belonging to him was contained in the outlines of the present young lady, he could coolly criticise her as he talked. They were both doing the same thing – each was pretending to be deeply interested in what the other was talking about, the attention of the two alike flitting away to other corners of the room when the very point of the discourse was pending.

No, he had not seen Her yet. He was not going to see Her, apparently, to-night; she was scared away by the twanging political atmosphere. But he still moved on searchingly, speaking to those he knew. Under the white hair of that ribanded old man was a forehead grown wrinkled over treaties that had swayed the fortunes of Europe; under the forehead spoke a voice which had numbered sovereigns and heirs-apparent among its listeners; under the voice was a heart that would go inside a hazel-nut shell. Beneath those white ropes of pearls was the pink bosom; beneath the pink bosom the half-lung which had, by hook or by crook, to sustain its possessor above ground till the wedding-day.

At that moment he encountered his amiable host, and almost simultaneously caught sight of the lady who had at first attracted him and then had disappeared. Their eyes met, far off as they were from each other. Pearston laughed inwardly: it was only in ticklish excitement as to whether this was to prove a true *trouvaille*, and with no instinct to mirth, for when under the eyes of his Jill-o'-the-Wisp[5] he ever palpitated like a sheep in a fair.

However, for the minute he had to converse with his host, Lord Channelcliffe, and almost the first thing the Earl said to him was: "Who is that pretty woman in the black dress with the white fluff about it and the pearl necklace?"

"I don't know," said Jocelyn, with incipient jealousy; "I was just going to ask the same thing."

"O, we shall find out presently, I suppose. I daresay my wife knows." They had parted, when a hand came upon his shoulder. Lord Channelcliffe had turned back for an instant: "I find she is the granddaughter of my father's old friend, the last Lord Hengistbury. Her name is Mrs. – Mrs. Pine-Avon;[6] she lost her husband two or three years ago, very shortly after their marriage."

Lord Channelcliffe became absorbed into some adjoining dignitary of the Church, and Pearston was left to pursue his quest alone. A young friend of his – the Lady Mabella Buttermead,[7] who appeared in a cloud of muslin and was going on to a ball – had been brought against him by the tide. A warm-hearted, emotional girl was Lady Mabella, who laughed at the humorousness of being alive; she asked him whither he was bent, and he told her.

"O yes, I know her very well!" said Lady Mabella, eagerly. "She told me one day that she particularly wished to meet you. Poor thing – so sad – she lost her husband. Well, it was a long time ago now, certainly. Women ought not to marry and lay themselves open to such catastrophes, ought they, Mr. Pearston? *I* never shall. I am determined never to run such a risk! Now, do you think I shall?"

"Marry? O no; never," said Pearston, drily.

"That's very comforting. But sometimes I think I may, just for the fun of it. . . Now we'll steer across to her, and catch her, and I'll introduce you. But we shall never get to her at this rate!"

"Never, unless we adopt 'the ugly rush,' like the citizens who follow the Lord Mayor's Show."

They talked, and inched towards the desired one, who, as she talked to a neighbour, seemed one of those –

Female forms, whose gestures beam with mind,[8]

seen by the poet in his Vision of the Golden City of Islam.

Their progress was continually checked. Pearston was, as he had sometimes seemed to be in a dream, unable to advance towards the object of pursuit unless he could have gathered up his feet into the air. After ten minutes given to a preoccupied study of shoulder-blades, back hair, glittering headgear, napes of necks, moles, hairpins, pearl-powder,[9] pimples, strange minerals cut into facets of all colours and rays, necklace-clasps, fans, stays, the seven styles of elbow and arm, the thirteen varieties of ear; and by using the toes of his dress-boots as coulters with which he ploughed his way and that of Lady Mabella in the direction they were aiming at, he drew near to Mrs. Pine-Avon, who was drinking a cup of tea in the back drawing-room.

"My dear Nichola, we thought we should never get to you, because it is worse to-night, owing to these dreadful politics! But we've done it." And she proceeded to tell her friend of Pearston's existence hard by.

It seemed that the widow really did wish to know him, and that Lady Mabella Buttermead had not indulged in one of the too-frequent inventions in that kind. When the youngest of the trio had made them acquainted with each other, she left them to talk to a younger man than the sculptor.

Mrs. Pine-Avon's black velvets and silks, with their white accompaniments, finely set off the exceeding fairness of her neck and shoulders, which, though unwhitened artificially, were without a speck or blemish of the least degree. The gentle, thoughtful creature she had looked from a distance she now proved herself to be; she held also sound rather than current opinions on the plastic arts, and was the first intellectual woman he had seen there that night, except the poetess aforesaid.

They soon became well acquainted, and at a pause in their conversation noticed the new excitement caused by the arrival of some late comers with more news. The latter had been brought by a rippling, bright-eyed lady in black, who made the men listen to her, whether they would or no.

"I am glad I am an outsider," said Jocelyn's acquaintance, now seated on a sofa beside which he was standing. "I wouldn't be like my cousin, over there, for the world. She thinks her husband will be turned out at the next election, and she's quite wild."

"Yes; it is mostly the women who are the gamesters; the men only the cards. The pity is that politics are looked on as being a game for politicians, just as cricket is a game for cricketers; not as the serious duties of political trustees."

"How few of us ever think or feel that 'the nation of every country dwells in the cottage,'¹⁰ as somebody says!"

"Yes. Though I wonder to hear you quote that."

"O – I am of no party, though my relations are. There can be only one best course, and the wisdom of the nation should be directed to find it."

Having started thus, they found no difficulty in agreeing on many points. When Pearston went downstairs from that assembly at a quarter to one, and passed under the steaming nostrils of an ambassador's horses to a hansom which waited for him against the railing of the square, he had an impression that the Beloved had re-emerged from the shadows, without any hint or initiative from him – to whom, indeed, such re-emergence was an unquestionably awkward thing.

CHAPTER XI

She Draws Close, and Satisfies

He could not forget her eyes, though he remembered nothing of her general facial detail. They were round, inquiring, luminous.¹ How that chestnut hair of hers had shone: it required no tiara to set it off, like that of the dowager he had seen there, who had put ten thousand pounds upon her head to make herself look worse than she would have appeared with the ninepenny muslin cap of a servant woman.

Now the question was, ought he to see her again? He had his doubts.

But, unfortunately for discretion, just when he was coming out of the rooms he had encountered an old lady of seventy, his friend Mrs. Bright-walton – the Honourable Mrs. Brightwalton – and she had hastily asked him to dinner for the day after the morrow, stating in the honest way he knew so well that she had heard he was out of town, or she would have asked him two or three weeks ago. Now, of all social things that Pearston liked it was to be asked to dinner off-hand, as a stopgap in place of some bishop, duke, or Secretary of State who couldn't come, and when the invitation was supplemented by the information that the lady who had so impressed him was to be one of the guests, he had promised instantly.

At the dinner, he took Mrs. Pine-Avon down upon his arm, and talked to nobody else during the meal. Afterwards they kept apart awhile in the drawing-room for form's sake; but eventually gravitated together again, and finished the evening in each other's company. When, shortly after eleven, he came away, he felt almost certain that within those luminous grey eyes his Aphrodite[2] had verily taken lodgings – and for a long lease. But this was not all. At parting, he had, almost involuntarily, given her hand a pressure of a peculiar and indescribable kind; a little response from her, like a mere pulsation, of the same sort told him that the impression she had made upon him was reciprocated. She was, in a word, willing to go on.

But was he able?

There had not been much harm in the flirtation thus far; but did she know his history, and that of his wife,[3] and of the separation a dozen years ago, and his ignorance of whether Marcia were dead or alive? He was now a man over forty, she was probably thirty; and he dared not make meaningless love with the carelessness of a younger man. It was impossible to go further without telling her, even though, hitherto, such explicitness had not been absolutely demanded. Yet, for himself, he had a strong conviction that Marcia had ceased to be.

He determined to call immediately on the New Incarnation.

She lived not far from the long, fashionable Hamptonshire Square, and he went thither with expectations of having a highly emotional time at least. But somehow the very bell-pull seemed cold, although she had so earnestly asked him to come.

As the house spoke, so spoke the occupant, much to the astonishment of the sculptor. The doors he passed through seemed as if they had not been opened for a month; and, entering the drawing-room, he beheld, in an easy-chair in the far distance, a lady whom he journeyed to reach, and ultimately did reach. To be sure it was Mrs. Nichola Pine-Avon, but frosted over indescribably. Raising her eyes in a slightly inquiring manner from the book she was reading, she leant back in the chair, as if soaking herself in luxurious sensations which had nothing to do with him, and replied to his greeting with a few commonplace words.

Now, the unfortunate Jocelyn, though recuperative to a degree, was at first terribly upset by this reception. He had distinctly begun to love Nichola, and he felt sick and almost tearful. But happily his affection was incipient as yet, and a sense of the ridiculous which suddenly appeared in his own position carried him to the verge of risibility during the scene. She signified a chair, and began the critical study of some rings she wore.

They talked over the day's news, and then an organ began to grind outside. The tune was a rollicking air he had heard at some music-hall; and, by way of a diversion, he asked her if she knew the composition.

"No, I don't!" she replied.

"Now, I'll tell you all about it," said he, gravely. "It is based on a sound old melody and song called 'Calder Fair.'[4] Just as they turn Madeira into port in the space of a single night, so this old air has been taken and doctored, and twisted about, and brought out as a new popular ditty."

"Indeed!"

"If you are in the habit of going much to the music-halls or the burlesque theatres"—

"Yes?"

"You would find this is often done, with excellent effect."

She thawed a little, and then they went on to talk about her house, which had been newly painted, and decorated with greenish-blue satin up to the height of a person's head – an arrangement that somewhat improved her slightly faded, though still pretty, face, and was helped by the awnings over the windows.

"Yes; I have had my house five years," she observed complacently, "and I like it better every year."

"You have only had it two years, if you deduct the three years you let it to some friends of mine, whom I have often called on in this very room, my darling," he said to himself – but not to her.

However, before he rose she grew friendly to some degree, and when he left, just after the arrival of three opportune young ladies, he thought she seemed regretful. She asked him to come again; and he thought he would tell the truth. "No; I shall not come again," he answered, in a tone inaudible to the young ladies.

She followed him to the door. "What an uncivil thing to say!" she murmured, in surprise.

"It is rather uncivil. Good-bye," said Pearston.

As a punishment she did not ring the bell, but left him to find his way out as he could. "What this means I cannot tell," he said to himself. And yet the meaning was staring him in the face.

Meanwhile one of the three young ladies had said, "What interesting man was that, with his lovely head of hair? I saw him at Lady Channelcliffe's the other night."

"Jocelyn Pearston."

"Oh, Nichola, that *is* too bad! To let him go in that shabby way, when I would have given anything to know him! I have wanted to know him ever since I found out how much his experiences had dictated his statuary, and I discovered them by seeing in an American paper of the death of a person supposed to be his wife, who left him many years ago, don't you know, and had been living with somebody under another name, according to some novel social principles she had invented for herself."

"O! is she dead?" said Mrs. Pine-Avon, with a start. "Why, I heard only yesterday that it was probable she was alive."

"She is believed to have died two or three years ago," said the young lady. "How I wish I could run after him!"

But Jocelyn was receding from the pretty widow's house with long strides. He went out very little during the next few days, but about a week later he kept an engagement to dine with Lady Iris Speedwell, whom he never neglected, because she was the brightest hostess in London.

By some accident he arrived rather early. Lady Iris had left the drawing-room for a moment to see that all was right in the dining-room, and when he was shown in there stood alone in the lamplight Nichola Pine-Avon. She had been the first arrival. He had not in the least expected to meet her there, further than that, in a general sense, at Lady Iris's you expected to meet everybody.

She had just come out of the cloak-room, and was so tender and even apologetic that he had not the heart to be other than friendly. As the other guests dropped in, the pair retreated into a shady corner, and she talked beside him till all moved off for the eating and drinking.

He had not been appointed to take her across to the dining-room, but at the table found her exactly opposite to him. She looked very charming between the candles, and then suddenly it dawned upon him that her previous manner must have originated in some false report about his late wife, of whose death he had been credibly, though not absolutely, assured a couple of years before this time. Anyhow, he was not disposed to resent an inexplicability in womankind, having found that it usually arose independently of fact, reason, probability, or his own deserts.

So he dined on, catching her eyes and the few pretty words she made opportunity to project across the table to him now and then. He was courteously responsive only, but Mrs. Pine-Avon herself distinctly made advances. He readmired her, while at the same time her conduct in her own house had been enough to check his confidence – enough even to make him doubt if the Well-Beloved really resided within those contours or had ever been more than the most transitory passenger through that interesting and accomplished soul.

He was pondering this question, yet growing decidedly moved by the playful pathos of her attitude, when, by chance, searching his pocket for his handkerchief, something crackled, and he felt there an unopened letter, which had arrived at the moment he was leaving his house, and he had slipped into his coat to read in the cab as he drove along. Pearston drew it sufficiently forth to observe by the post-mark that it came from his natal isle. Having hardly a correspondent in that part of the world now, he began to conjecture on the possible sender.

The lady on his right, whom he had brought in, was a leading actress[5] of the town – indeed, of the United Kingdom and America, for that matter – a creature in airy clothing, translucent, like a balsam or sea-anemone, without shadows, and in movement as responsive as some highly lubricated many-wired machine, which, if one presses a particular spring, flies open and reveals its works. The spring in the present case was the artistic commendation she deserved. At this particular moment she was engaged with the man on her own right, a representative of Family, who talked positively and hollowly, as if shouting down a vista of five hundred years from the Feudal past. The lady on Jocelyn's left, wife of a Lord Justice of Appeal, was in like manner talking to her companion on the outer side; so that, for the time, he was left to himself. He took advantage of the opportunity, drew out his letter, and read it as it lay upon his napkin, nobody observing him, so far as he was aware.

It came from the wife of one of his father's former workmen, and was concerning her son, whom she begged Jocelyn to recommend as candidate for some post in town she wished him to fill. But the end of the letter was what arrested him –

"You will be sorry to hear, Sir, that dear little Avice Caro, as we used to call her in her maiden days, is dead. She married her cousin, if you do mind, and went away from here for some years, but was left a widow, and came back a twelvemonth ago; since when she began to falter, and now is gone."

CHAPTER XII

She Becomes an Inaccessible Ghost

By imperceptible and slow degrees the scene at the dinner-table seemed to recede into the background behind the more distinct presentment of Avice Caro and the old, old scenes on the stone island which were inseparable from her personality. The handsome Marchioness in geranium-red and diamonds, who was visible to him on his host's right hand opposite, became as one of the misty vermilion sunsets that he had watched so many times over the West Bay, with the form of Avice in the foreground. Between his eyes and the judge who sat next to Nichola, with a chin so raw that he must have shaved every quarter of an hour during the day, intruded the face of Avice, as she had glanced at him in their last parting. The old society lady, who, if she had been a few years older, would have been as old-fashioned as her daughter, suggested the powdery, dusty quarries of his and Avice's parents, down which he had clambered with Avice hundreds of times. The ivy trailing about the table-cloth, the lights in the tall silver candle-sticks, and the bunches of flowers, mixed in with the ivies and the flower-beds of the castle on the isle and the lighthouses down at the Beal.

More than all, Nichola Pine-Avon gradually lost the radiance which she had latterly acquired; she became a woman of his acquaintance with no distinctive traits; she seemed to grow material, a superficies of flesh and bone merely; she was a person of lines and surfaces, a language in living cypher – no more.

When the ladies had withdrawn it was just the same. The soul of Avice – the only woman he had *never* loved (of those who had loved him) – surrounded him like a firmament. Art drew near to him in the person of one of the most distinguished of portrait-painters; but there was only one painter for Jocelyn – his own memory. All that was eminent in European surgery addressed him in the person of that harmless and unassuming fogey whose hands had been inside the bodies of hundreds of living men; but the lily-white corpse of an obscure country girl chilled the interest of discourse with such a king of operators.

Reaching the drawing-room he talked to his hostess: Though she had entertained twenty guests at her table that night she had known not only what every one of them was saying and doing throughout the repast, but what every one was thinking. So, being an old friend, she said quietly, "What has been troubling you? Something has, I know."

Nothing could less express the meaning his recent information had for him than a statement of its facts. He told of the opening of the letter and the discovery of the death of an old acquaintance.

"The only woman whom I never loved, I may almost say!" he added, smiling; "and therefore the only one I shall ever regret!"

Whether she considered it a sufficient explanation or not, the woman of the world accepted it as such. She was the single lady of his circle whom nothing erratic in his doings could surprise, and he often gave her stray ends of his confidence thus with perfect safety.

He did not go near Mrs. Pine-Avon again; he could not: and on leaving the house walked abstractedly along the streets till he found himself at his own door. In his own room he sat down, and placing his hands behind his head thought his thoughts anew.

At one side of the room stood an escritoire, and presently going to a lower drawer of the same he took out a small box tightly nailed down. He forced the cover with the poker. The box contained a multifarious variety of odds and ends, which Pearston had thrown into it from time to time in years gone by for future sorting – an intention that he had never carried out. From the melancholy mass of papers, faded photographs, seals, diaries, withered flowers, and such like, Jocelyn drew a little portrait, one taken on glass in the more primitive days' of photography, and framed with tinsel in the commonest way.

It was Avice Caro, as she had appeared during the summer month or two which he had spent with her on the island twenty years before that time, her young lips pursed up, her hands meekly folded. The effect of the glass was to lend to the picture much of the softness characteristic of the original. He remembered when it was taken – during one afternoon they had spent together at the neighbouring watering-place, when he had suggested her sitting to a touting artist on the sands, there being nothing else for them to do. A long contemplation of the likeness completed in his emotions what the letter had begun. He loved the woman dead and inaccessible as he had never loved her in life. He had unceremoniously forsaken her on the eve of what would have become an irrevocable engagement, because he did not love her; and it had been, in one view, the kindest thing he could have done, though the harshest, no spark of passion existing. He had thought of her but at distant intervals during the whole nineteen years since that parting occurred, and only as somebody he could have wedded. Yet now the years of youthful friendship with her, in which he had learnt every fibre of her innocent nature, flamed up into a yearning and passionate attachment, embittered by regret beyond words.

That kiss which had offended his dignity, which she had so childishly given him before her consciousness of womanhood had been awakened, what he would have given to have a quarter of it now!

Pearston was almost angry with himself for his feelings of this night, so unreasonably, motivelessly strong were they towards that lost young playmate. "How senseless of me!" he said, as he lay in his lonely bed. She had been another man's wife almost the whole time since he had been estranged from her, and now she was a corpse. Yet the absurdity did not make his grief the less: and the consciousness of the intrinsic, almost radiant, purity of this new-sprung affection for a flown spirit forbade him to check it. The flesh was absent altogether; it was love rarefied and refined to its highest attar. He had felt nothing like it before.

The next afternoon he went down to his club; not his large club, where the men hardly spoke to each other, but the smaller one, where they told stories of an afternoon, and were not ashamed to confess among themselves to the most extraordinary personal weaknesses and follies, knowing well that such secrets would go no further. But he could not tell this; so volatile and intangible was the story, that to convey it in words would have been as hard as to cage a perfume.

They observed his altered manner, and said he was in love. Pearston admitted that he was; and there it ended. When he reached home he looked out of his bed-room window, and began to consider in what direction from where he stood that darling little figure lay. It was straight across there, under that young pale moon. The symbol signified well. The divinity of the silver bow was not more excellently pure than she, the lost, had been. Under that moon was an island of stone, and on the island a house, framed from mullions to ridge-tile like the isle itself, of stone. Inside the window, the moonlight irradiating her winding-sheet, lay Avice, reached only by the faint noises inherent in the isle; the tink-tink of the chisels in the quarries, the surging of the sea in the Bay, and the muffled grumbling of the waves in the never-pacified Race.

After dinner his old friend Somers came in to smoke, and when they had talked a little while Somers alluded casually to some place at which they would meet on the morrow.

"I sha'n't be there," said Pearston.

"But you promised."

"Yes. But I shall be at the island – looking at a dead woman's grave." As he spoke his eyes turned, and remained fixed on a table near. Somers followed the direction of his glance to a photograph on a stand.

"Is that she?" he asked.

"Yes."

"Rather a bygone affair, then?"

Pearston acknowledged it. "She's the only sweetheart I never loved, Alfred," he said. "Because she's the only one I ought to have loved. That's just the fool I have always been."

"But if she's dead and buried, you can go to her grave at any time as well as now, to keep up the sentiment."

"I don't know that she's buried."

"But to-morrow – the Academy night! Of all days why go then?"

"I don't care about the Academy."

"Pearston – you are our only inspired sculptor. You are our Praxiteles.[2] You are almost the only man of this generation who has been able to mould and chisel forms living enough to draw the idle public away from the popular *genre* paintings into the usually deserted lecture-room, and people who have seen your last piece of stuff say there has been nothing like it since sixteen hundred and — since the sculptors 'of the great race' lived and died. Well, then, for the sake of others you ought not to rush off to that God-forgotten island just when you are wanted in town, all for a woman you last saw a hundred years ago."

"No – it was only nineteen," replied his friend, with abstracted literalness. He went the next morning.

Since the days of his youth a railway had been constructed along the pebble bank, so that, except when the rails were washed away by the tides, which was rather often, the peninsula was directly accessible. At two o'clock in the afternoon he was rattled along under the familiar monotonous line of bran-coloured stones, and emerged from the station among the black lerrets and the white cubes of ashlar.

In entering upon the pebble beach the train had passed close to the ruins of Henry the Eighth's castle, whither Avice was to have accompanied him on the night of his departure. Had she appeared the betrothal would have taken place; and as no islander had ever been known to break that compact,[3] she would have become his wife.

Ascending the steep incline to where the quarrymen were chipping just as they had formerly done, and within sound of the great stone saws, he looked southward towards the Beal.

The level line of the sea horizon rose above the surface of the isle; and against the stretch of water, where a school of mackerel twinkled in the afternoon light, was defined, in addition to the distant lighthouse, a church with its tower, standing about a quarter of a mile off, near the edge of the cliff. The churchyard gravestones could be seen in profile against the same vast spread of watery babble and unrest.

Among the graves moved the form of a man clad in a white sheet, which the wind blew aside every now and then, revealing dark trousers under. Near him moved six men bearing a long box, and two or three persons in black followed. The coffin, with its twelve legs, looked like a large insect crawling across the isle, under whose belly the flashing lights from the sea and school of mackerel were reflected; a fishing-boat, far out in the Channel, being momentarily discernible through the opening.

The procession wandered round to a particular corner, and halted, and stood there a long while in the wind, the sea behind them, the surplice of the priest still blowing. Jocelyn stood with his hat off: he was present, though he was a quarter of a mile off; and he seemed to hear the words that were being said, though nothing but the wind was audible.

He instinctively knew that it was none other than Avice whom he was seeing interred; *his* Avice, as he now began presumptuously to call her. Presently the little group withdrew from before the sea, and disappeared.

He felt himself unable to go farther in that direction, and turning aside went aimlessly across the open land, visiting the various spots that he had formerly visited with her. But, as if tethered to the churchyard by a cord, he was still conscious of being at the end of a radius whose pivot was the grave of Avice Caro; and as the dusk thickened he closed upon his centre and entered the churchyard gate.

Not a soul was now within the precincts. The grave, newly shaped, was easily discoverable behind the church, and when the same young moon arose which he had observed the previous evening from his window in London he could see the yet fresh foot-marks of the mourners and bearers. The breeze had fallen to a calm with the setting of the sun: the lighthouse had opened its glaring eye, and, disinclined to leave a spot sublimed both by early association and present regret, he moved back to the church wall, warm from the afternoon sun, and sat down upon a window-sill facing the grave.

END OF PART FIRST

PART SECOND

A Young Man of Forty

CHAPTER XIII

She Threatens to Resume Corporeal Substance

The lispings of the sea beneath the cliffs were all the sounds that reached him, for the quarries were silent now. How long he sat here leaning and thinking he did not know. Neither did he know, though he felt drowsy, whether inexpectant sadness – that gentle soporific – lulled him into a short sleep, so that he lost count of time and consciousness of realities. But all of a sudden he seemed to see Avice Caro herself, standing beside her own grave in the light of the moon.

She seemed not a year older, not a digit less slender, not a line more angular than when he had parted from her, twenty years earlier, in the lane hard by. A dim renascent reasoning on the impossibility of such a phenomenon as this being more than a dream-fancy roused him with a start from his heaviness.

"I must have been asleep!" he said.

The outline of the grave was as distinct as before he had dozed, but nobody stood there. Yet she had seemed so real. Pearston resolutely dismissed the strange impression, arguing that even if the information sent him of Avice's death should have been false – a thing incredible – that sweet friend of his youth, despite the transfiguring effects of moonlight, would not have looked the same as she had appeared nineteen or twenty years ago.

Having satisfied his sentiment by coming to the graveside, there was nothing more for him to do in the island, and he decided to return to London that night. But, some time remaining still on his hands, as soon as he arrived at the junction of roads Jocelyn, by a natural instinct, turned his feet in the direction of East Wake, the village of his birth and of hers. Passing the market-square he pursued the arm of road to Dell-i'-th'-rock Castle, a private mansion of comparatively modern date, in whose grounds stood the single plantation of trees of which the isle could boast. The cottages extended close to the walls of the enclosure, and one of the last of these dwellings had been Avice's, in which, as it was her freehold, she possibly had died.

To reach it he passed the gates of Dell-i'-th'-rock, and observed above

65

the lawn-wall a board announcing that the house was to be let furnished. A few steps farther revealed the cottage which, with its quaint and massive stone features of two or three centuries' antiquity, was capable even now of longer resistance to the rasp of Time than ordinary new erections. His attention was drawn to the window, which was unblinded, though a lamp lit the room within. He stepped back against the wall opposite, and gazed intently.

At a table covered with a white cloth a young woman stood putting tea-things away into a corner-cupboard. She was in all respects the Avice he had lost, the girl he had seen in the churchyard and had fancied to be the illusion of a dream. And though there was this time no doubt about her reality, the isolation of her position in the silent room lent her a curiously startling aspect. Divining the explanation, he waited for footsteps, and in a few moments a quarryman passed him on his journey homeward. Pearston inquired of him concerning the spectacle.

"O yes, Sir; that's poor Mr. Caro's only daughter, and it must be lonely for her there to-night, poor maid! Yes, good-now; she's the very daps of her mother – that's what everybody says."

"But how does she come to be so lonely? They were quarryowners at one time."

The quarryman "pitched his nitch,"[1] and explained to the supposed stranger that there had been three families thereabouts in the stone trade, who had got much involved with each other in the last generation. They were the Bencombs, the Pearstons, and the Caros. The Bencombs strained their utmost to outlift the other two, and partially succeeded. They grew enormously rich, sold out, and retired to London. The Pearstons kept a dogged middle course, throve without show or noise, and also retired in their turn. The Caros were pulled completely down in the competition with the other two, and when Widow Caro's daughter married her cousin Jim Caro he tried to regain for the family its original place in the three-cornered struggle. He took contracts at less than he could profit from, speculated more and more, till at last the crash came and he was sold up, went away, and later on came back to live in this little cottage, which was his wife's by inheritance. There he remained till his death, and now his widow was gone. Hardships had helped on her end.

The quarryman proceeded on his way, and Pearston, deeply remorseful, knocked at the door of the minute freehold. The girl herself opened it, lamp in hand.

"Avice!" he said tenderly, "Avice Caro!" even now unable to get over the strange feeling that he was twenty years younger, addressing Avice the First.

"Yes, Sir," said she.

"Ah, your name is the same as your mother's!"

"Yes. Both my names.[2] Poor mother married her cousin."

"And you have lost her now?"

"I have, Sir."

She spoke in the very same sweet voice that he had listened to a score of years before, and bent eyes of the same familiar hazel inquiringly upon him.

"I knew your mother at one time," he said: "and learning of her death and burial I took the liberty of calling upon you. You will forgive a stranger doing that?"

"Yes," she said dispassionately, and glancing round the room: "this was mother's own house, and now it is mine. I am sorry not to be in mourning on the night of her funeral, but I have just been to put some flowers on her grave, and I took it off afore going that the damp mid not spoil the crape. You see, she was bad a long time, and I have to be careful, and do washing and ironing for a living. She hurt her side with wringing up the large sheets she had to wash for the Castle folks here."

"I hope you won't hurt yourself doing it, my dear."

"O no, that I sha'n't! There's Charl Woollat, and Sammy Wayes, and Ted Gibscy, and lots o' young chaps; they'll wring anything for me if they happen to come along. But I can hardly trust 'em. Sam Wayes t'other day twisted a linen tablecloth into two pieces, for all the world as if it had been a pipe-light. They never know when to stop in their wringing."

The voice truly was his Avice's; but Avice the Second was more matter-of-fact, unreflecting, less cultivated than her mother had been. This Avice would never recite poetry from any platform, local or other, with enthusiastic appreciation of its fire. There was a little disappointment in recognising this; yet she touched him as few had done: he could not bear to go away. "How old are you?" he asked.

"Going in nineteen."

It was about the age of her double, Avice the First, when he and she had strolled together over the cliffs during the engagement. But he was now forty, if a day. She before him was an uneducated laundress, and he was a sculptor with a fortune and a reputation. Yet why was it an un-pleasant sensation to him just then to recollect that he was two score?

He could find no further excuse for remaining, and having still half-an-hour to spare he went round by the road to the west side of the modern castle, and came to the last house out there on the cliff. It was his early home. Used in the summer as a lodging-house for visitors, it now stood empty and silent, the evening wind swaying the euonymus and tamarisk boughs in the front – the only evergreen shrubs that could weather the salt sea gales which raked past the walls. Opposite the house, far out at sea, the familiar light-ship winked from the sand-bank, and all at once there came to him a wild wish – that, instead of having an artist's reputa-tion, he could be living here an illiterate and unknown man, wooing, and in a fair way of winning, the pretty laundress in the cottage hard by.

CHAPTER XIV

The Resumption Takes Place

Having returned to London, he mechanically resumed his customary life; but he was not really living there. The phantom of Avice, now grown to be warm flesh and blood, held his mind afar. He thought of nothing but the isle, and Avice the Second dwelling therein. The very defects in the country girl became charms as viewed from town.

Nothing now pleased him so much as to spend that portion of the afternoon which he devoted to out-door exercise in haunting the purlieus of the wharves along the Thames, where the stone of his native isle was unshipped from the coasting-craft that had brought it thither. He would pass inside the great gates of these landing-places on the right or left bank, and contemplate the white cubes and oblongs, imbibe their associ-ations, call up the *genius loci* whence they came, and almost forgot that he was in London.

One afternoon he was walking away from the mud-splashed entrance to one of the wharves, when his attention was drawn to a female form on the opposite side of the way, going towards the spot he had just left. She was somewhat small, slight, and graceful; her attire alone would have been enough to attract him, being simple and countrified to picturesqueness; but he was more than attracted by her strong resemblance to Avice Caro.

Before she had receded a hundred yards he felt absolutely certain that it was Avice indeed; and his dreamy, fanciful mood of the afternoon was now so intense that the lost and the found Avice seemed essentially the same person. Their external likeness to each other – probably owing to the cousinship between the elder and her husband – went far to nourish the fantasy. He hastily turned, and rediscovered the girl among the pedestrians. She kept on her way to the wharf, where, looking inquiringly around her for a few seconds, with the manner of one unaccustomed to the locality, she opened the gate and disappeared.

Pearston also went up to the gate and entered. She had crossed to the landing-place, beyond which a lumpy craft lay moored. Drawing nearer, he discovered her to be engaged in conversation with the skipper and an elderly woman – both come straight from the oolitic isle, as was apparent in a moment from their accent. Pearston felt no hesitation in making himself known as a native, the ruptured engagement between Avice's mother and himself twenty years before having been known to few or none now living.

The present embodiment of Avice recognised him, and with the artless candour of her race and years explained the situation, though that was rather his duty as an intruder than hers.

"This is Cap'n Kibbs, a distant relation of poor father's," she said. "And this is Mrs. Kibbs. We've come up from the island wi' en just for a trip, and are going to sail back wi' en Wednesday."

"O, I see! And where are you staying?"

"Here – on board."

"What, you live on board entirely?"

"Yes."

"Lord, Sir," broke in Mrs. Kibbs, "I should be afeard o' my life to tine my eyes among these here kimberlins at night-time; and even by day, if so be I venture into the streets, I nowhen forget how many turnings to the right and to the left 'tis to get back to Ike's vessel – do I, Ike?"

The skipper nodded confirmation.

"You are safer ashore than afloat," said Pearston, "especially in the Channel, with these winds and those heavy blocks of stone."

"Well," said Cap'n Kibbs, after privately clearing something from his mouth, "as to the winds, there idden much danger in them at this time o' year. 'Tis the ocean-bound steamers that make the risk to craft like ours. If you happen to be in their course, under you go – cut clane in two pieces, and they never stopping to pick up your carcases, and nobody to tell the tale."

Pearston turned to Avice, wanting to say much to her, yet not knowing what to say. He lamely remarked at last: "You go back the same way, Avice?"

"Yes, Sir."

"Well, take care of yourself afloat."

"O yes."

"I hope – I may see you again soon – and talk to you."

"I hope so, Sir."

He could not get further, and after a while Pearston left them, and went away thinking of Avice more than ever.

The next day he mentally timed them down the river, allowing for the pause to take in ballast, and on the Wednesday pictured the sail down the open sea. That night he thought of the little craft under the bows of the huge steam-vessels, powerless to make itself seen or heard, and Avice, now growing inexpressively dear, sleeping in her little berth at the mercy of a thousand chance catastrophes.

Honest perception had told him that this Avice, fairer than her mother in face and form, was her inferior in soul and understanding. Yet the fervour which the first could never kindle in him was, almost to his alarm, burning up now. He began to have misgivings as to some queer trick that his migratory Well-Beloved was about to play him.

A gigantic satire upon the mutations of his nympholepsy[1] during the past twenty years seemed looming in the distance. A forsaking of the accomplished and well-connected Mrs. Pine-Avon for the little laundress, under the traction of some mystic magnet which had nothing to do with reason – surely that was the form of the satire.

But it was recklessly pleasant to leave this suspicion unrecognised as yet and follow the lead.

In thinking how best to do this Pearston recollected that, as was customary when the summer-time approached, Dell-i'-th'-rock Castle had been advertised for letting furnished. A solitary dreamer like himself, whose wants all lay in an artistic and ideal direction, did not require such gaunt accommodation as the aforesaid residence offered; but the spot was all, and the expenses of a few months of tenancy therein he could well afford. A letter to the agent was dispatched that night, and in a few days Jocelyn found himself the temporary possessor of a place which he had never seen the inside of since his childhood, and had then deemed the abode of unpleasant ghosts.

CHAPTER XV

The Past Shines in the Present

It was the evening of Pearston's arrival at Dell-i'-th'-rock Castle, an ordinary manor-house on the brink of the sea; and he had walked through the rooms, about the lawn, and into the surrounding plantation of elms, which on this island of treeless rock lent a unique character to the enclosure. To find other trees thereon, it was necessary to recede a little in time—to dig down to a loose stratum of the underlying stone-beds, where a forest of conifers lay as petrifactions, their heads all in one direction, as blown down by a gale in the secondary geologic epoch.

Dusk had closed in, and he now proceeded with what was, after all, the real business of his sojourn. The two servants who had been left to take care of the house were in their own quarters, and he went out unobserved. Crossing a hollow overhung by the budding boughs he approached an empty garden-house of Elizabethan design, which stood on the outer wall of the grounds, and commanded by a window the fronts of the nearest cottages. Among them was the home of the resuscitated Avice.

· He had chosen this moment for his outlook through knowing that the inhabitants of the village were in no hurry to pull down their blinds at nightfall. And, as he had divined, the interior of the young woman's living-room was distinctly visible to him as illuminated by the rays of its own lamp.

A subdued thumping came every now and then from the apartment. She was ironing linen on a flannel table-cloth, a row of such articles hanging on a clothes-horse by the fire. Her face had been pale when he formerly encountered her, but now it was warm and pink with her exertions and the heat of the stove. Yet it was in perfect and passionless repose, which imparted a Minerva[1] cast to the profile. When she glanced up her lineaments seemed to have all the soul and heart that had characterised her mother's, and had been with her a true index of the spirit within. Could it be possible that in this case the manifestation was fictitious? He had met with many such examples of hereditary persistence without the qualities signified by the traits. He unconsciously hoped that it was at least not entirely so here.

The room was less furnished than when he had last beheld it. The "bo-fet," or double corner-cupboard, where the china was formerly kept, had disappeared, its place being taken by a plain board. The tall old clock, with its ancient oak carcase, arched brow, and humorous mouth, was also not to be seen, a cheap, white-dialled specimen doing its work. What these displacements betokened saddened his humanity less than it cheered his primitive instinct in pointing out how her necessity for aid might bring them together.

Having fixed himself near her for some lengthy time he felt in no hurry to obtrude his presence, and went indoors. That this girl's frame was doomed to be a real embodiment of that olden, seductive one[2] – that Protean dream-creature, who had never seen fit to irradiate the mother's image till it became a mere memory after dissolution – he doubted less every moment.

There was still an uneasiness in recognising this. There was something abnormal in his present proclivity. A certain sanity had, after all, accompanied his former passions: the Beloved had seldom informed a personality which, while enrapturing his soul, simultaneously shocked his intellect. A change, perhaps, had come.

It was a fine morning on the morrow. Walking in the grounds towards the gate he saw Avice entering to the house with a broad oval wickerbasket covered with a white cloth; and she bore her burden round to the back door. Of course, she washed for his own household: he had not thought of that. In the morning sunlight she appeared rather as a sylph than as a washerwoman; and he could not but think that the slightness of her figure was as ill adapted to this occupation as her mother's had been.

But, after all, it was not the washerwoman that he saw now. In front of her, on the surface of her, was shining out that more real, more penetrating being whom he knew so well! The occupation of the subserving woman, the blemishes of the temporary creature who formed the background, were of no more account in the presentation than the posts and framework which support a pyrotechnic display.

She left the house and went homeward by a path of which he was not aware, having probably changed her route because she had seen him standing there. It meant nothing, for she had hardly become acquainted with him; yet that she should have avoided him was a new experience. He found no opportunity for a further study of her by distant observation, and hit upon a pretext for bringing her face to face with him. He found fault with his linen, and directed that the laundress should be sent for.

"She is rather young, poor little thing," said the housemaid, apologetically. "But since her mother's death she has enough to do to keep above water, and we make shift with her. But I'll tell her, Sir."

"I will see her myself. Send her in when she comes," said Pearston.

One morning, accordingly, when he was answering a spiteful criticism of a late work of his, he was told that she waited his pleasure in the hall. He went out.

"About the washing," said the sculptor, stiffly. "I am a very particular person, and I wish no preparation of lime to be used."

"I didn't know folks used it," replied the maiden, in a shy and reserved tone, without looking at him.

"That's all right. And then, the mangling smashes the buttons."

"I haven't got a mangle, Sir," she murmured.

"Ah! that's satisfactory. And I object to so much borax in the starch."

"I never put any – never heard o't," Avice returned in the same close way.

"O I see."

All this time Pearston was thinking of the girl – that is to say, Nature was working her plans for producing the next generation under the cloak of a dialogue on linen. He could not read her individual character owing to the confusing effect of her likeness to a woman whom he had valued too late. He could not help seeing in her all that he knew of another, and veiling in her all that did not harmonise with his sense of metempsychosis.

The girl seemed to think of nothing but the business in hand. She answered to the point, and was not aware of his sex or of his shape.

"I knew your mother, Avice," he said. "You remember my telling you so?"

"Yes."

"Well – I have taken this house for two or three months, and you will be very useful to me. You still live just outside the wall?"

"Yes, Sir," said the self-contained girl.

Demurely and dispassionately she turned to leave – this pretty creature with features so still. There was something strange in seeing that form which he knew passing well move off thus, she who was in past years so throbbingly alive to his presence that, not many yards from this spot, she had flung her arms tenderly round him and given him a kiss which, despised in its freshness, had revived in him latterly as the dearest kiss of all his life. And now this "daps" of her mother, this perfect copy, why did she turn away?

"Your mother was a refined and well-informed woman, I think I remember?"

"She was, Sir; everybody says so."

"I hope you resemble her."

She archly shook her head, and drew warily away.

"O! one thing more, Avice. I have not brought much linen, so you must come to the house every day."

"Very good, Sir."

"You won't forget that?"

"O no."

Then he let her go. He was a town man, and she an artless islander, yet he had opened himself out without disturbing the epiderm of her nature. It was monstrous that a maiden who had literally assumed the personality of the woman he loved with such tender memory should be so impervious. Perhaps it was he who was wanting. She might be Venus masking as Minerva,[3] because he was so many years older in outward show.

This brought him to the root of it. In his heart he was not a day older than when he had wooed the mother at the daughter's present age. His record moved on with the years, his sentiments stood still.

When he beheld the class of his fellow-subjects defined as buffers and fogeys – imperturbable, matter-of-fact, slightly ridiculous beings, past masters in the art of populating homes, schools, and colleges, and present adepts in the science of giving away brides – how he envied them, assuming them to feel as they appeared to feel, with their commerce and their politics, their glasses and their pipes. They had got past the distracting currents of passionateness,[4] and were in the calm waters of middle-aged philosophy. But he, their contemporary almost, was tossed like a cork hither and thither upon the crest of every fancy, precisely as he had been tossed when he was half his present age, with the added condition now of double pain to himself.

Avice had gone, and he saw her no more that day. Since he could not again call upon her, she was as inaccessible as if she had entered the military citadel on the hilltop beyond them.

In the evening he went out and paced down the lane to the Red King's castle, beside whose age the castle he occupied was but a thing of yesterday. Below the castle precipice lay enormous blocks, which had fallen from it, and several of them were carved over with names and initials. He knew the spot and the old trick well, and by searching in the faint moonrays he found a pair of such names which, as an ambitious boy, he himself had cut. They were "AVICE" and "JOCELYN" – Avice Caro's and his own. The letters were now nearly worn away by the weather and the brine. But close by, in quite fresh letters, stood another "AVICE," coupled with the name "GEORGE." They could not have been there more than two or three years, and the "Avice" was probably Avice the Second. Who was George? Some boy admirer of her child-time doubtless.

He retraced his steps, and passed the Caros' house towards his own. The revivified Avice animated the dwelling, and the light within the room fell upon the window. She was just inside that blind.

Whenever she unexpectedly came to the castle he started, and even trembled. It was not at her presence, but at the new condition, which seemed to have something sinister in it. On the other hand, the most abrupt encounter with him moved her to no emotion as it had moved her prototype in the old days. She was indifferent to, almost unconscious of, his propinquity. He was no more than a statue to her; she was a growing fire to him.

A sudden Sapphic terror of love[5] would ever and anon come upon the sculptor, when his matured reasoning powers would insist upon informing him of the fearful lapse from dignity that lay in this infatuation. It threw him into a sweat. What if now, at last, he were doomed to do penance for his past emotional wanderings (in a material sense), by being chained in fatal fidelity to an object that his intellect despised? Sometimes he thought he saw dimly visioned in that young face "the white, implacable Aphrodite."[6]

However, the Well-Beloved was alive again; had been lost and was found. He was amazed at the change in front of himself. She had worn the guise of strange women; she had been a woman of every class, from the dignified daughter of some ecclesiastic or peer to a Nubian Almeh[7] with her handkerchiefs undulating to the beat of the tom-tom; but all these embodiments had been endowed with a certain smartness, either of the flesh or spirit: some with wit, a few with talent, and even genius. But the new impersonation had apparently nothing beyond sex and pretti-ness. She knew not how to sport a fan or handkerchief, hardly how to pull on a glove.

But her limited life was innocent, and that went far. Poor little Avice! her mother's image: there it all lay. After all, her parentage was as good as his own; it was misfortune that had sent her down to this. Odd as it seemed to him, her limitations were largely what he loved her for. Her rejuvenating power over him had ineffable charm. He felt as he had felt when standing beside her predecessor; but, alas! he was twenty years further onward into the shade.

CHAPTER XVI

The New Becomes Established

A few mornings later he was looking through an upper back window over a screened part of the garden. The door beneath him opened, and a figure appeared tripping forth. She went round out of sight to where the gardener was at work, and presently returned with a bunch of green stuff fluttering in each hand. It was Avice, her dark hair now braided up snugly under a cap. She sailed on with a rapt and unconscious face, her thoughts a thousand removes from him.

How she had suddenly come to be an inmate of his own house he could not understand, till he recalled the fact that he had given the castle servants a whole holiday to attend a review of the yeomanry in the watering-place over the bay, on their stating that they could provide a temporary substitute to stay in the house. They had evidently called in

Avice. To his great pleasure he discovered their opinion of his require-
ments to be such a mean one that they had called in no one else.

The spirit, as she seemed to him, brought his lunch into the room
where he was writing, and he beheld her uncover it. She went to the
window to adjust a blind which had slipped, and he had a good view of
her profile. It was not unlike that of one of the three goddesses in
Rubens's "Judgment of Paris,"[1] and in contour was nigh perfection. But it
was in her full face that the vision of her mother was most apparent.

"Did you cook all this, Avice?" he asked, arousing himself.

She turned and smiled, merely murmuring, "Yes, Sir."

Well he knew the arrangement of those white teeth! In the junction of
two of the upper ones there was a slight irregularity; no stranger would
have noticed it, nor would he, but that he knew of the same mark in her
mother's mouth, and looked for it here. Till Avice the Second had revealed it this moment by her smile, he had never beheld that mark since
the parting from Avice the First, when she had smiled under his kiss as the
copy had done now.

Next morning, when dressing, he heard her through the ricketty floor
of the old building engaged in conversation with the other servants, who
had come back, though she had not gone.

By this time she had regularly installed herself in his heart as the new
exponent of the Well-Beloved – as one who, by no initiative of his own,
had been chosen as the vehicle of her next début. He was struck with the
exquisite cadences of her voice rather than by its tone; she would suddenly drop it to a rich whisper of roguishness, when the slight rural monotony of its narrative speech disappeared, and soul and heart – or what
seemed soul and heart – resounded. The charm lay in the intervals, using
that word in its musical sense. She would say a few syllables in one note,
and end her sentence in a soft modulation upwards, then downwards,
then into her own note again. The curve of sound was as artistic as any
line of beauty ever struck by the pencil – as satisfying as the curves of her
who was the world's desire.[2]

The subject of her discourse he cared nothing about[3] – it was no more
his interest than his concern. He took special pains that in catching her
voice he might not comprehend her words. To the tones he had a right,
none to the articulations. By degrees he could not exist long without this
sound.

On Sunday evening he found that she went to church. He followed behind her over the open road, keeping his eye on the little hat with its bunch of cock's feathers as on a star. When she had passed in Pearston observed her position and took a seat behind her.

Engaged in the study of her ear and the nape of her white neck, he suddenly became aware of the presence of a lady still farther ahead in the aisle, whose attire, though of black materials in the quietest form, was of a cut which rather suggested London than this *Ultima Thule*.[4] For the minute he forgot, in his curiosity, that Avice intervened. The lady turned her head somewhat, and, though she was veiled with unusual thickness for the season, he seemed to recognise Mrs. Pine-Avon in the form.

(*To be continued.*)

Why should Mrs. Pine-Avon be there? Pearston asked himself. If it should, indeed, be she, he could hardly assume that she had come on his account.

The end of the service found his attention again concentrated on Avice to such a degree that at the critical moment he overlooked the mysterious lady in front of her, and learnt that she had left the church by the side-door. Supposing it to have been Mrs. Pine-Avon, she would probably be discovered staying at one of the hotels at the watering-place over the bay, and to have come along the Pebble Bank, as so many did, for an evening drive. For the present, however, the explanation was not forthcoming; and he did not seek it.

When he emerged from the church the great placid eye of the light-house at the Beal Point was open, and he moved thitherward a few steps to escape Nichola Pine-Avon, or her double, and the rest of the congregation. Turning at length, he hastened homeward along the now deserted trackway, intending to overtake his revitalised Avice. But he could see nothing of her, and concluded that she had walked too fast for him. Arriving at his own gate, he paused a moment, and perceived that Avice's little freehold was still in darkness. She had not come.

He retraced his steps, but could not find her, the only persons on the road being a man and his wife, as he knew them to be, though he could not see them, from the words of the man –

"If you had not already married me, you would cut my acquaintance! That's a pretty thing for a wife to say!"

The remark reminded him unpleasantly of his own experiences, and presently he went back again. Avice's cottage was now lighted: she must have come round by the other road. Satisfied that she was safely domiciled for the night, he opened the gate of Dell-i'-th'-rock Castle, and retired to his room also.

Eastward from the grounds the cliffs were rugged and the view of the opposite coast picturesque in the extreme. A little door from the lawn gave him immediate access to the rocks and shore on this side. Without the door was a dip-well of pure water, which possibly had supplied the inmates of the adjoining and now ruinous Red King's Castle in the time of the Crusades. On a sunny morning he was meditating here, when he discerned a figure on the shore below spreading white linen upon the pebbly strand.

Jocelyn descended. It was Avice, as he had supposed, she having now returned to her own occupation. Her shapely pink arms, though slight, were plump enough to show dimples at the elbows, and were set off by her purple cotton print, which the shore-breeze licked and tantalised. He stood near, without speaking. The wind dragged a shirt-sleeve from the pebble which held it down. Pearston stooped and put a heavier one in its place.

"Thank you," she said quietly. She then turned up her hazel eyes, and seemed gratified to perceive that her assistant was Pearston. She had plainly been so wrapped in her own thoughts that she had not considered him till then.

The young girl continued to converse with him in friendly frankness, showing neither ardour nor shyness. As for love – it was evidently further from her thoughts than even death and dissolution.

When one of the sheets became intractable Jocelyn said, "Do you hold it down, and I'll put the pebbles."

She acquiesced, and in placing a pebble his hand touched hers.

It was a young hand, rather long and thin, a little damp and coddled from her slopping. In setting down the last stone, he laid it, by a pure accident, rather heavily on her fingers.

"I am very, very sorry!" Jocelyn exclaimed. "O, I have bruised the skin, Avice!" Saying which he seized her fingers to examine the damage done.

"No, Sir, you haven't!" she cried luminously, allowing him to retain her hand for examination without the least objection. "Why – that's where I scratched it this morning with a pin. You didn't hurt me a bit with the popple-stone."

Although her gown was purple, there was a little black crape bow upon each arm. He knew what it meant, and it saddened him. "Do you ever visit your mother's grave?" he asked.

"Yes, Sir, sometimes. I am going there to-night to water the daisies."

She had now finished here, and they parted. That evening, when the sky was red, he emerged by the garden-door and passed her house. The blinds were not down, and he could see her sewing within. While he paused she sprang up as if she had forgotten the hour, and tossed on her hat. Jocelyn strode ahead and round the corner, and was halfway up the straggling street before he discerned her little figure behind him.

He hastened past the lads and young women with clinking buckets who were drawing water from the fountains by the wayside, and took the direction of the church. With the disappearance of the sun the lighthouse had set up its star against the sky, the dark church rising in the foreground. Here he allowed her to overtake him.

"You loved your mother much?" said Jocelyn.

"I did, Sir; of course I did," said the girl, who tripped so lightly that it seemed he might have carried her on his hand.

Pearston wished to say, "So did I," but did not like to disclose events which she, apparently, did not guess. Avice fell into thought, and continued –

"Mother had a very sad life for some time when she was about as old as I. I should not like mine to be as hers. Her young man proved false to her because she wouldn't agree to island custom,[5] and it grieved mother almost all her life. I wouldn't ha' fretted about him, if I'd been she. She would never mention his name, but I think he was a wicked, cruel man; and I hate to think of him."

After this he could not go into the churchyard with her, and walked onward alone to the south of the isle. He was wretched all night. He would not have stood where he did stand in the ranks of an imaginative profession if he had not been at the mercy of every sentiment of fancy that can beset man. It was in his weaknesses as a citizen and a national unit that his strength lay as an artist, and he felt it childish to complain of susceptibilities not only innate but cultivated.

He saw a terrible vengeance ahead. What had he done to offend the cruel Aphrodite[6] that she should scheme this thing against him? The Well-Beloved, after flitting from the frame of Nichola Pine-Avon to the phantom of a dead woman whom he never adored in her lifetime, had taken up her abode in the living representative of that phantom with a permanence of hold which the absolute indifference of that little brown-eyed representative only seemed to intensify.

Did he really wish to proceed to marriage with this chit of a girl? He certainly did. It was true that as he studied her more closely he saw defects in addition to her social insufficiencies. His judgment, hoodwinked as it was, told him that she was colder in her nature, commoner in her character, than that well-read, bright little woman Avice the First. But twenty years make a difference in ideals, and the added demands of middle-age in physical form are more than balanced by its concessions as to the spiritual content. He looked at himself in the glass, and felt glad at those inner deficiencies in Avice which formerly would have impelled him to reject her.

There was a strange difference in his regard of his present folly and of his love in his youthful time. Now he could be mad with method,[7] knowing it to be madness: then he was compelled to make-believe his madness wisdom. In those days any flash of reason upon his loved one's imperfections was blurred over hastily and with fear. Such penetrative vision now did not cool him. He knew he was the creature of a tendency; and indulged himself in continuing the pleasant glide.

CHAPTER XVII

His Own Soul Confronts Him

From his castle and its grounds and the cliffs hard by he could command every move and aspect of her who was the rejuvenated Spirit of the Past to him – in the effulgence of whom all sordid details were disregarded.

Among other things, he observed that she was often anxious when it rained. If, after a wet day, a golden streak appeared in the sky over the West Bay, under a lid of cloud, her manner was joyous and her tread light.

This puzzled him; and he soon found that if he endeavoured to encounter her she shunned him – stealthily and subtly, but unmistakably. He determined to find out the meaning of this avoidance. One evening, accordingly, when she had left her cottage and tripped off in the direction of Slopeway Well, he set out by the same route, resolved to await her return along the high and level roadway which stretched between that place and East Wake.

He reached the top of the old road where it makes a sudden descent to the townlet, but she did not appear. Turning back, he sauntered along till he had nearly reached his own house again. Then he retraced his steps, and thus, in the still night, he walked backwards and forwards on the bare and lofty level; the stars above him, the two lighthouses on the distant point, the lightship winking from the sandbank, the combing of the pebble-beach by the tide audible from beneath, the church away south-westward, where the original Avice lay.

He walked till his legs ached, and still she did not come. It was more than foolish to wait, yet he could not help waiting. At length he discerned a dot of a figure, which he knew to be hers rather by its motion than by its shape.

How strange this prepossession was! How incomparably the imma-terial dream dwarfed the grandest of substantial things, when here, be-tween those three sublimities – the sky, the rock, and the sea – the minute personality of this washergirl filled his consciousness to its extremest boundary, and the stupendous inanimate scene shrank to a corner therein!

But all at once the approaching figure had disappeared. He looked about; she had certainly vanished. At one side of the road was a low wall, but she could not have gone behind that without considerable trouble and singular conduct. He looked behind him; she had reappeared farther on the road.

Jocelyn, desperate, ran after; and, discerning his movement, Avice stood still. When he came up, she was slily shaking with restrained laughter.

"Well, what does this mean, my dear girl?" he asked.

Her inner mirth bursting out in spite of her, she turned askance and said: "When you was following me to Slopeway Well, two hours ago, I looked round and saw 'ee, and hid behind a stone! You passed and brushed my frock without seeing me. And when, on my way backalong, I saw you waiting here about again, I slipped over the wall, and ran past you! If I had not stopped and looked round at 'ee, you would never have catched me!"

"What did you do that for, you elf!"

"That you shouldn't find me."

"That's not exactly a reason. Give another, dear Avice," he said, as he turned and walked beside her homeward.

She hesitated. "Come!" he urged again.

"'Twas because I thought you wanted to be my young man," she answered.

"What a wild thought of yours! Supposing I did, wouldn't you have me?"

"Not now. . . . And not for long, even if it had been sooner than now."

"Why?"

"If I tell you, you won't laugh at me or let anybody else know?"

"Never."

"Then I will tell you," she said quite seriously. "'Tis because I get tired o' my lovers as soon as I get to know them well. What I see in one young man for a while soon leaves him and goes into another yonder, and I follow, and then what I adore fades out of him and springs up somewhere else; and so I follow on, and never fix to one. I have loved *fifteen* already! Yes, fifteen, I am almost ashamed to say," she repeated laughing. "I can't help it, Sir, I assure you. Of course it is really, to *me*, the same one all through, only I can't catch him!" She added anxiously, "You won't tell anybody of this in me, will you, Sir? Because if it were known I am afraid nobody would marry me when I wish to marry."

Pearston was surprised into stillness. Here was this obscure and almost illiterate girl engaged in the pursuit of the impossible ideal, just as he had been himself doing for the last twenty years. She, like him, was doing it quite involuntarily, by sheer necessity of her organisation, puzzled all the while at her own instinct. He suddenly thought of its bearing upon himself, and said, with a sinking heart –

"Am I – one of them?"

She pondered critically.

"You was – for a week; when I first saw you."

"Only a week?"

"About that."

"What made the being of your fancy forsake my form and go elsewhere?"

"Well – though you seemed handsome and gentlemanly at first"—

"Yes?"

"I found you too old soon after."

"You are a candid young person."

"But you asked me, Sir!" she expostulated.

"I did; and, having been answered, I won't intrude upon you longer. So cut along home as fast as you can. It is getting late."

When she had passed out of earshot he also followed homewards. This pursuit of the Well-Beloved was, then, of the nature of a knife which could cut two ways. To be the pursuer was one thing: to be one of the corpses from which the ideal inhabitant had departed was another; and this was what he was now, in the mockery of fate.

Drawing near his own gate he smelt tobacco, and could just discern two figures in the side lane leading past Avice's door. They did not, however, enter her house, but strolled onward to the narrow pass conducting to Red King Castle and the sea. He was in momentary heart-sickness at the thought that they might be Avice with a lover, but a faintly argumentative tone from the man informed him that they were the same married couple going homeward whom he had encountered on a previous occasion.

The next day he gave one of the servants a half-holiday on purpose to get Avice into the castle again for a few hours, the better to observe her. While she was pulling down the blinds at sunset a whistle of peculiar quality came from some point on the cliffs outside the lawn. He observed that her colour rose slightly, though she bustled about as if she had noticed nothing.

Pearston suddenly suspected that she had not only fifteen past admirers but a current one. Still, he might be mistaken. Stimulated now by ancient memory and present passion to use every effort to make her his wife, despite her conventional unfitness, he strung himself up to sift this mystery. If he could only win her – and how could a country girl refuse such an opportunity? He could pack her off to school for two or three years, marry her, enlarge her mind by a little travel, and take his chance of the rest. As to her want of ardour for him – so sadly in contrast with her sainted mother's affection – a man twenty years older than his bride could expect no better, and he would be well content to put up with it in the pleasure of possessing one in whom seemed to linger as an aroma all the charm of his youth and his early home.

CHAPTER XVIII

Juxtapositions

It was a sad and leaden afternoon, and Pearston paced up the long, steep street of Slopeway Well. On both sides of the road young girls stood with pitchers at the fountains which bubbled up there, and behind the houses rose the massive summit of the isle – crowned with its enormous ramparts.

As you approach the upper end of the street all progress seems about to be prevented by the almost vertical face of the escarpment, into which your track apparently runs point-blank: a confronting mass which, if it were to slip down, would overwhelm the whole town. But in a moment you find that the road, the old Roman highway into the peninsula, turns at a sharp angle when it reaches the base of the scarp, and ascends in a stiff incline to the right. To the left there is also another ascending road, modern, as steep as the first, and perfectly straight. This is the road to the forts.

Pearston arrived at the forking of the ways, and paused for breath. Before turning to the right, his proper course, he looked up the left road to the fortifications. It was long, white, regular, tapering to a vanishing point, like a lesson in perspective. About a quarter of the way up a girl was resting beside a basket of white linen; and by the shape of her hat and the nature of her burden he recognised her to be Avice.

She did not see him, and abandoning the right-hand course he slowly ascended the incline she had taken. Drawing near, he observed that her attention was absorbed by something aloft. He followed the direction of her gaze. Above them towered the green-grey mountain of grassy stone, here levelled at the top by military art. The sky-line was broken every now and then by a little peg-like object – a sentry-box, and near one of these a small red spot kept creeping backwards and forwards monotonously against the heavy sky.

Then he divined that she had a soldier-lover.

She turned her head, saw him, and took up her clothes-basket to continue the ascent. The steepness was such that to climb it unencumbered was a breathless business; the linen made her task a cruelty to her. "You'll never get to the forts with that weight," he said. "Give it to me."

But she would not, and he stood still, watching her as she panted up the way; for the moment an irradiated being, the epitome of a whole sex: by the beams of his own infatuation –

> . . . robed in such exceeeding glory
> That he beheld her not;[1]

not, that is, as she really was, even to himself sometimes. But to the soldier what was she? Smaller and smaller she waned up the rigid mathematical road, still gazing up at the soldier aloft, as Pearston gazed up at her. He could just discern sentinels springing up at the different coigns of vantage[2] as she passed, but seeing who she was they did not intercept her; and presently she crossed the drawbridge over the enormous chasm surrounding the forts, passed the sentries there also, and disappeared through the arch into the interior. Pearston could not see the sentry now, and there occurred to him the hateful idea that this scarlet rival was meeting and talking freely to her; perhaps, relieved of duty, escorting her across the interior, carrying her basket, her tender body encircled by his arm.

"What the devil are you staring at, as if you were in a trance?"

Pearston turned his head; and there stood his old friend Somers – still looking the long-leased bachelor he was.

"I might say what the devil do you do here, if I weren't so glad to see you."

Somers said that he had come to see what was detaining his friend in such an out-of-the-way place at that time of year, and incidentally to get some fresh air into his own lungs. Pearston made him welcome, and they went towards Dell-i'-th'-rock Castle.

"You were staring, as far as I could see, at a pretty little washerwoman with a basket of clothes?" resumed the painter.

"Yes; it was that to you, but not to me. Behind the mere pretty island-girl (to the world) is, in my eye, the Idea, in Platonic phraseology – the essence and epitome of all that is desirable in this existence . . . I am under a curse, Somers. Yes, I am under a curse. To be always following a phantom which I saw in woman after woman while she was at a distance, but vanishing away on close approach, was bad enough;

but now the terrible thing is that the phantom does *not* vanish, but stays to tantalise me even when I am near enough to see that it is a phantom! That girl holds me, *though* my eyes are open and I see that I am a fool!"

Somers regarded the visionary look of his friend, which rather intensified than decreased as his years wore on, but made no further remark. When they reached the castle Somers gazed round upon the scenery, and Pearston, signifying the quaint little Elizabethan cottage, said, "That's where she lives."

"What a romantic place altogether! A man might love a scarecrow or turnip-lantern here."

"But a woman mightn't. Scenery doesn't impress them. This girl is as fickle as"—

"You once were."

"Exactly. She has told me so – candidly. And it hits me hard."

Somers stood still in sudden thought. "Well – that *is* a strange turning of the tables!" he said. "But you wouldn't really marry her, Pearston?"

"I would – to-morrow. Why shouldn't I? What are fame and name and society to me?"

"Then you'll win."

While they were sitting after dinner that evening their quiet discourse was interrupted by the long low whistle from the cliffs without. Somers took no notice, but Pearston started. That whistle always occurred at the same point of time in the evening: then she was helping again in the house. Aphrodite's own messenger in a kitchen – was there ever such satire to a man of art! He excused himself for a moment to his visitor and went out upon the dark lawn. A crunching of light feet upon the gravel mixed in with the articulation of the sea – steps light as if they were winged. And then he knew two minutes later that the mouth of some hulking fellow was upon hers, which he himself hardly ventured to look at, so touching was its young beauty.

Hearing people about – among others a couple quarrelling, for there were rough as well as gentle people here in the island – he returned to the house. Next day Somers roamed abroad to look for scenery for a marine painting, and, going out to seek him, Pearston met Avice.

"So you have a lover, my lady!" he said severely, to which she admitted that it was the fact. "You won't stick to him," he continued.

87

"I think I may this one," said she. "He deserted me once, but he won't again."

"I suppose he's a wonderful sort of fellow?"

"He's good enough for me."

"So handsome, no doubt."

"Handsome enough for me."

"So refined and respectable."

"Refined and respectable enough for me."

He could not disturb her equanimity, and let her pass. The next day was Sunday, and Somers having chosen his view at the other end of the island, Pearston determined to see Avice's lover. In the afternoon he found that she had left her cottage stronghold, and, divining the direction they would be likely to take, went on towards the lighthouses at the Beal. Turning when he had reached the nearest, he presently saw on the lonely road between the quarries a young man, evidently connected with the stone trade, with a girl upon his arm, in whom he soon recognised Avice the Second.

She looked prettily guilty and blushed a little under his glance. The man's was one of the typical island physiognomies – his features energetic and wary in their expression, and half covered with a close, crisp black beard. Pearston fancied that out of his keen dark eyes there glimmered a dry humour at the situation, as though he meant to say: "Isn't this a joke, Sir? I've got the pretty girl and you've got the blues!"

If so, Avice must have told him of Pearston's symptoms of tenderness. This girl, whom, for her dear mother's sake almost more than for her own attractiveness, he would have guarded as the apple of his eye, how could she estimate him so flippantly!

The overpowering sense of humiliation at having brought himself to this position with the antitype, by his early slight of her who was the type, blinded him for the moment to what struck him with sudden surprise a short time after. The man upon whose arm she hung was not a soldier. What, then, became of her entranced gaze at the sentinel? She could hardly have transferred her affections so promptly; or, to give her the benefit of his own theory, her Well-Beloved could scarcely have flitted from frame to frame in so very brief an interval. And which of them, then, had been he who whistled softly in the dusk to her?

On account of this puzzling incident he did not attempt to seek out

Alfred Somers, but walked homeward, moodily thinking that the strong desire to make reparation to the original woman by wedding and enriching the copy – which lent such an unprecedented permanence to his new love – was thwarted, as if by set intention of his destiny.

At the door of the grounds about the castle there stood a carriage. He observed that it was not one of the flys from Slopeway Well, but that it came apparently from the fashionable town across the bay. Wondering why the visitor had not driven in, he entered, to find in the drawing-room no other person than Nichola Pine-Avon.

At his first glance upon her, fashionably dressed and graceful in movement, she seemed beautiful; at the second, when he observed that her face was pale and agitated, she seemed pathetic likewise. Altogether, she was now a very different figure from her who, sitting in the chair with such finished composure, had snubbed him in her drawing-room in Hamptonshire Square.

"You are surprised at this? Of course you are!" she said in a low, pleading voice, as she languidly lifted her heavy eyelids while he was holding her hand. "But I couldn't help it! I know I have done something to offend you – have I not? Oh! what can it be, that you have come away to this outlandish rock to live with barbarians in the midst of the London season?"

"You have not offended me, my dear Mrs. Pine-Avon," he said. "How very sorry I am that you should have supposed it! Yet I am glad, too, that your supposition should have done me the good turn of bringing you here to see me."

"I am staying at Budmouth-Regis," she explained.

"Then I did see you at a church service here a little while back?"

She blushed faintly upon her pallor, and she sighed. Then their eyes met. "Well," she said at last, "I don't know why I shouldn't show the virtue of candour. You know what it means. I was the stronger once; now I am the weaker. Whatever pain I may have given you in the ups and downs of our acquaintance I am sorry for, and – would willingly repair all errors of the past by – being amenable to reason in the future."

It was impossible that Jocelyn should not feel a tender impulse towards this attractive and once independent woman, who from every worldly point of view was an excellent match for him – a superior match, indeed. He took her hand again and held it awhile, and a faint wave of gladness seemed to flow through her. But no – he could go no further.

That island girl, in her coquettish Sunday frock and little hat with its bunch of hen's feathers held him as by strands of Manilla rope. He dropped Nichola's hand.

"I am leaving Budmouth to-morrow," she said. "That was why I felt I must call. You did not know I had been there through the Whitsun holidays?"

"I did not, indeed; or I should have come to see you."

"I didn't like to write. I wish I had, now!"

"I wish you had, too, dear Mrs. Pine-Avon."

But it was "Nichola" that she wanted to be. As they reached the landau he told her that he should be back in town himself again soon, and would call immediately. At the moment of his words Avice Caro, now alone, passed close along by the carriage on the other side, towards her house hard at hand. She did not turn head or eye to the pair: they seemed to be in her view objects of absolute indifference.

Pearston became cold as a stone. The sudden chill towards Nichola that the presence of the girl, – sprite, witch, elf that she was – brought with it came well-nigh like a doom. In common speech, he knew what a fool he was. But he was utterly powerless in the grasp of this other passion. He cared more for Avice's finger-tips than for Mrs. Pine-Avon's whole personality.

Perhaps Nichola saw it, for she said mournfully: "Now I have done all I could! I felt that the only counterpoise to my cruelty to you in my drawing-room would be to come as a suppliant to yours."

"It is most handsome and noble of you," said he, with courtesy rather than enthusiasm.

Then adieux were spoken, and she drove away. But Pearston saw only the retreating Avice, and knew that his punishment for his erratic idolatries had come.

(*To be continued.*)

CHAPTER XIX

She Fails to Vanish when Closely Confronted

Pearston had not turned far back towards the castle when he was over-taken by Somers and the man who carried his painting lumber. They paced together to the door; the man deposited the articles and went away, and the two walked up and down before entering.

"I met an extremely interesting woman in the road out there," said the painter.

"Ah, she is! A sprite, a sylph – Psyche[1] indeed!"

"I was struck with her."

"It shows how beauty will out through the homeliest guise."

"Yes, it will; though not always. And this case doesn't prove it, for the lady's attire was in the latest and most approved taste."

"O! you mean the lady who was driving?"

"Of course. What! were you thinking of the little cottage girl outside here? I did meet her, but what's she? Very well for one's picture, though hardly for one's fireside. This lady"—

"Is Mrs. Pine-Avon. A kind, proud woman, who'll do what people with no pride would not condescend to think of. She is leaving Budmouth to-morrow, and she drove across to see me. You know how things seemed to be going with us at one time. But I am no good to any woman. She's been very generous towards me, which I've not been to her . . . She'll ulti-mately throw herself away upon some wretch unworthy of her, no doubt."

"Do you think so?" murmured Somers. After a while he said abruptly, "I'll marry her myself, if she'll have me. I like the look of her."

"I wish you would, Alfred, or rather could! She has long had an idea of slipping out of the world of fashion into the world of art. She is a woman of individuality and earnest instincts. I am in real trouble about her. I won't say she can be won – it would be ungenerous of me to say that. But try. I can bring you together easily."

"I'll marry her, if she's willing." With the phlegmatic dogmatism that was part of him, Somers added: "When you have decided to marry, take the first nice woman you meet. They are all alike."

"Well – you don't know her yet," replied Jocelyn, who could at least give praise where he could not give love.

"But you do, and I'll take her on the strength of your judgment. Is she really pretty? – I had but the merest glance. But I know she is, or she wouldn't have caught your discriminating eye."

"You may take my word for it; she looks as well at hand as afar."

"What colour are her eyes?"

"Her eyes? I don't go much into colour, being professionally sworn to form. But, let me see – grey; and her hair rather light than dark brown."

"I wanted something darker," said Somers, airily. "There are so many fair models among native Englishwomen. Still, blondes are useful property . . . Well, well; this is flippancy! But I liked the look of her."

Somers had gone back to town. It was a wet day on the little peninsula; but Pearston walked out as far as the garden-house of his hired castle, where he sat down and smoked. This erection being on the boundary-wall of his property, his ear could now and then catch the tones of Avice's voice from her open-doored cottage, a few yards off in the lane which skirted his fence; and he noticed that there were no modulations in it. He knew why that was. She wished to go out, and could not. He had observed before that when she was planning an outing a particular note would come into her voice during the preceding hours: a dove's round-ness of sound; no doubt the effect upon her voice of her thoughts of her lover, or lovers. Yet the latter it could not be. She was absolutely single-hearted: half an eye could see that. Whence, then, the two men? Possibly the quarrier was a relation?

There seemed reason in this, especially when, going out into the lane, he encountered one of the very red-jackets he had been thinking of. Soldiers were seldom seen in this outer part of the isle; their beat from the forts, when on pleasure bent, was usually in the opposite direction, and this man must have had a special reason for coming hither. Pearston surveyed him. He was a round-faced, beer-blown fellow, having two little pieces of moustache on his upper lip, like a pair of minnows rampant, and small black eyes, over which the Glengarry cap straddled flat. It was altogether a hateful idea that her tender cheek should be kissed by the lips of this thick and heavy young man, who had never been sublimed by a single battle, even with defenceless savages.

He went before her house, looked at the door, and passed on down the crooked way to the cliffs, where there was a path back to the forts. But he did not adopt it, returning by the way he had come. This showed his wish to pass the house anew. She gave no sign, however, and the soldier disappeared.

Pearston could not be satisfied that Avice was in the house, and in an uncontrollable impulse he crossed over to the front of her little freehold, and tapped at the door, which stood ajar.

Nobody came, and, hearing a slight movement within, he crossed the threshold. Avice was there alone, sitting on a low stool in a dark corner, as though she wished to be unobserved by any casual passer-by. She looked up at him without emotion or apparent surprise; but he could then see that she was crying. The view, for the first time, of distress in an unprotected young girl, towards whom he felt drawn by ties of extra-ordinary delicacy and tenderness, moved Pearston beyond measure. He entered without ceremony.

"Avice, my dear girl!" he said. "Something is the matter!"

She looked a passive assent, and he went on: "Now tell me all about it. Perhaps I can help you. Come, tell me."

"I can't!" she murmured. "Grammer Stockwool is upstairs, and she'll hear!" (Mrs. Stockwool was the old woman who had lived with the girl for company since her mother's death.)

"Then come into my garden opposite. There we shall be quite private."

In answer to this she rose, put on her hat, and accompanied him to the door. Here she asked him if the lane were empty, and on his looking up and down and assuring her that it was, she crossed over and entered with him through the garden-wall.

The place was a shady and secluded one, though through the boughs the sea could be seen quite near at hand, below the edge of the cliff, its moanings being distinctly audible. A water-drop from a tree fell here and there, but the rain was not enough to hurt them.

"Now let me hear it," he said soothingly. "You may tell me with the greatest freedom. I was a friend of your mother's, you know. That is, I knew her; and I'll be a friend of yours."

The statement was risky, since he wished her not to suspect him of being her mother's false one. But that lover's name appeared to be entirely unknown to the present Avice.

"I can't tell you, Sir," she replied unwillingly; "except that it has to do with my own changeableness – the failing I owned to you, if it is a failing. The rest is the secret of somebody else."

"I am sorry for that," said he.

"I am getting to care for one I ought not to think of. I wish I could get away!"

"You mean from the island?"

"Yes."

Pearston reflected. His presence in London had been desirable for some time; yet he had delayed going because this spot had latterly become endeared to him – partly by old memories revived, partly by their re-embodiment in the new form at his side. But to go and take her with him would afford him opportunity for watching over her, tending her mind, and developing it; while it might remove her from some looming danger. It was a somewhat awkward guardianship for him, as a lonely man, to carry out; still, it could be done. He asked her abruptly if she would like to go away for a while.

"I like best to stay here," she answered. "Still, I should not mind going somewhere, because I think I ought to."

"Would you like London?"

Avice's face lost its weeping shape. "How could that be?" she said.

"I have been thinking that you could come to my house and make yourself useful in some way. I rent just now one of those new places called flats,[2] which you may have heard of; and I have a studio at the back."

"I haven't heard of 'em," she said without interest.

"Well, I have two servants there, and you can help them for a month or two."

"Would polishing furniture be any good? I can do that."

"I haven't much furniture that requires polishing. But you can clear away plaster and clay messes in the studio, and chippings of stone, and help me in modelling, and dust casts of hands and heads and feet and bones, and other objects."

She was startled, yet attracted, almost fascinated by the novelty of the proposal.

"Only for a time?" she said.

"Only for a time. As short as you like, and as long."

The deliberate manner in which, after the first surprise, Avice discussed the arrangements that he suggested, might have told him how far any feeling for himself beyond friendship, and possibly gratitude, was from occupying her breast. But there was nothing really extravagant in the discrepancy between their ages, and he hoped, after shaping her to himself, to win her. What had grieved her to tears she would not more particularly tell.

There was naturally not much need of preparation for Avice, and she seemed willing, and even anxious, to start, making less preparation than, being a woman, he would have expected her to require. He could not quite understand why, if she were in love and had felt at first averse to leave the island, she should be so precipitate now. Above all, not a soul was to know of her departure.

Fancying her wishes on this point to be based on her fear of rumour, he took great care to compromise in no way a girl in whom his interest was as protective as it was passionate. Pearston accordingly left her to get out of the island alone, but he awaited her at a station a few miles up the railway, where, discovering himself to her through the carriage-window, he entered the next compartment, his frame pervaded by a glow which was almost joy at having for the first time in his charge one who inherited the flesh and bore the name so early associated with his own, and only not united to him through the merest trick of time.

A sense of putting things right which had been wrong through many years sustained Pearston in the face of this too obviously unusual step of bestowing so much attention upon one who, in a worldly view, would at the best be a clog upon his social and artistic activities, should these, which had now slept for some while, again awaken.

CHAPTER XX

A Homely Medium does not Dull the Image

It was dark when the four-wheeled cab wherein he had brought Avice from the station stood at the entrance-door to the pile of flats of which Pearston occupied one floor – then less common as residences in London than they are now. Leaving Avice to alight and get the luggage brought in with the assistance of the porter, Pearston went upstairs. To his surprise his floor was silent, and on entering with a latchkey the rooms were all in darkness. He descended to the hall, where Avice was standing helpless beside the luggage, while the porter was outside with the cabman.

"Do you know what has become of my servants?" asked Jocelyn.

"What – and ain't they there, Saur? Ah, then my belief is that what I suspected is thrue! You didn't leave your wine-cellar unlocked, did you, Saur, by no mistake?"

Pearston considered. He thought he might have left the key with his elder servant, whom he had believed he could trust, especially as the cellar was not well stocked.

"Ah, then it was so! She's been very queer, Saur, this last week or two. O, yes, sending messages down the spakin'-tube which were like madness itself, and ordering us this and that, till we would take no notice at all. I see the housemaid go out one morning, and possibly she went for good! Shure, if ye'd written, Saur, I'd ha' got the place ready, though it's not me duty at all!"

When Pearston got to his floor again he found that the cellar-door was open; some bottles were standing empty that had been full, and many abstracted altogether. All other articles in the house, however, appeared to be intact. His letter to his housekeeper lay in the box as the postman had left it.

By this time the luggage had been sent up in the lift; and Avice, like so much more luggage, stood at the door, the hall-porter behind offering his assistance.

"Come here, Avice," said the sculptor. "What shall we do now? Here's a pretty state of affairs!"

Avice could suggest nothing till she was struck with the bright thought that she should light a fire.

"Light a fire? – ah, yes! . . . I wonder if we could manage. This is an odd coincidence – and awkward!" he murmured. "Very well, light a fire."

"Is this the kitchen, Sir, all mixed up with the parlours?"

"Yes."

"Then I think I can do all that's wanted here for a bit; at any rate, till you can get help, Sir. At least, I could if I could find the fuel-house. 'Tis no such big place as I thought!"

"That's right: take courage!" said he with a tender smile. "Now, I'll dine out this evening, and leave the place for you to arrange as best you can with the help of the porter's wife downstairs."

This Pearston accordingly did, and so their common residence began.

Feeling more and more strongly that some danger awaited her in her native island he determined not to send her back till the lover or lovers who seemed to trouble her should have cooled off. He was quite willing to take the risk of his action thus far in his solicitous regard for her.

It was a dual solitude, indeed; for, though Pearston and Avice were the only two people in the flat, they did not keep each other company, the former being as scrupulously fearful of going near her now that he had the opportunity as he had been prompt to seek her when he had none. They lived in silence, his messages to her being frequently written on scraps of paper deposited where she could see them. It was not without a pang that he saw her unconsciousness of their isolated position – a position to which, had she experienced any reciprocity of sentiment, she would readily have been alive.

Considering that, though not profound, she was hardly a matter-of-fact girl, as that phrase is commonly understood, she was exasperating in the matter-of-fact quality of her responses to the occasional friendly remarks which would escape him in spite of himself, as well as in her general conduct. Whenever he formed some culinary excuse for walking across the two yards' width of passage which separated his room from the kitchen and spoke through the doorway to her, she answered, "Yes, Sir," or "No, Sir," without turning her eyes from the particular work that she was engaged in.

In the usual course he would have obtained a couple of properly qualified new servants immediately; but he lived on with the one, or rather the less than one, that the person of this cottage-girl afforded. It had been his almost invariable custom to dine at one of his clubs. Now he sat at home over the miserable chop or steak to which he limited himself in dread lest she should complain of there being too much work for one person, and demand to be sent home. A charwoman came every two or three days, effecting an extraordinary consumption of food and alcoholic liquids: Pearston dreaded her presence, lest in conversing with Avice she should open the girl's eyes to the oddity of her situation. Avice could see for herself that there must have been two or three servants in the flat during his former residence there; but his reasons for doing without them seemed never to strike her.

His original intention had been to keep her occupied exclusively at the studio, but accident had modified this. However, he sent her round one morning, and entering himself shortly after, found her engaged in wiping the layers of dust from the casts and models.

The colour of this dust never ceased to amaze her. "It is like the hold of a collier," she said, "and the beautiful faces of these clay people are quite spoilt by it."

"I suppose you'll marry some day, Avice?" remarked Pearston, without replying, as he regarded her thoughtfully.

"Some do and some don't," she said, with a reserved smile, still attending to the casts.

"You are very offhand," said he.

She archly weighed that remark without further speech. It was tantalising conduct in the face of his instinct to cherish her: especially when he regarded the charm of her bending profile; the well-characterised though softly lined nose, the round chin with, as it were, a second leap in its curve to the throat, and the sweep of the eyelashes over the cheek during the sedulously lowered glance. How futilely he had laboured to express the character of that face in clay, and, while catching it in substance, had yet lost something that was essential to it!

That evening at dusk, in the stress of writing letters, he sent her out for stamps. She had been absent some quarter of an hour, when, suddenly drawing himself up from over his writing-table, it flashed upon him that he had absolutely forgotten her total ignorance of London.

The head post-office, to which he had sent her, was two or three streets off, and he had made his request in the most general manner, which she had acceded to with alacrity enough. How could he have done such an unreflecting thing?

Pearston went to the window. It was about nine o'clock, and, owing to her absence, the blinds were not down. He opened it, and stepped out upon the balcony. The green shade of his lamp screened its rays from the gloom without. Over the opposite square a young moon hung, and to the right there stretched a long street, filled with a diminishing array of lamps, some single, some in clusters, among them an occasional blue or red one. From a corner came the notes of a piano-organ strumming out a stirring march of Donizetti's.[1] The shadowy black figures of pedestrians moved up, down, and across the embrowned roadway. Above the roofs was a bank of livid mist, and higher a greenish-blue sky, in which stars were visible, though its lower part was still pale with daylight, against which rose chimney-pots, in the form of elbows, prongs, and fists.

From the whole scene proceeded a ground rumble, miles in extent, amid which individual rattles, voices, a tin whistle, the bark of a dog, made themselves heard. The whole noise impressed him with the sense that no one in its enormous mass imagined rest to be ever required.

In this illimitable ocean of humanity there was a unit of existence, his Avice, wandering alone.

Pearston looked at his watch. She had been gone half an hour. It was impossible to distinguish her at this distance, even if she approached. He came inside, and putting on his hat, determined to go out and seek her. He reached the end of the street, and there was nothing of her to be seen. She had the option of two or three routes from this point to the post-office; yet he plunged at random into one, till he reached the office, to find it quite deserted. Almost distracted now by his anxiety for her, he retreated as rapidly as he had come, but regained home only to find that she had not returned.

He suddenly recollected telling her that if she should ever lose her way she must call a cab and drive home. It occurred to him that this was what she would do now. He again went out upon the balcony; the dignified street in which he lived was now almost vacated and silent, and the lamps stood like placed sentinels waiting for some procession to pass which did not arrive. At a point where the road was torn up there stood a red light, and at the corner two men were talking in leisurely repose, as if sunning themselves at noonday. Lovers of a feline disposition, who were never seen by daylight, joked and darted at each other as they passed.

His attention was fixed on the cabs, and he held his breath as the hollow clap-clap of each horse's hoofs drew near the front of the house, only to go onward into the square. The two lamps of each vehicle in the far distance dilated with its approach, and seemed to swerve towards him. It was she surely? No, it passed by.

Almost frantic, he again descended, and let himself out of the house, moving towards a more central part, where the roar still continued. Before emerging into the noisy thoroughfare he observed a small figure approaching leisurely along the opposite side, and hastened across to find it was she.

CHAPTER XXI

A Grille Descends Between the Vision and Him

"O, Avice!" he cried, with the tenderly subdued scolding of a mother. "What is this you have done to alarm me so!"

She seemed quite unconscious of having done anything, and was altogether surprised at his anxiety. In his relief he did not speak further for a while; then asked her suddenly if she would take his arm, since she must be tired.

"O no, Sir!" she assured him, "I am not a bit tired, and I don't require any help at all, thank you."

They went upstairs together without using the lift, and he let her and himself in with his latchkey. She entered the kitchen, and he, following, sat down in a chair there.

"Where have you been?" he said, renewing the subject with almost angered concern on his face. "You ought not to have been absent more than ten minutes."

"I knew there was nothing for me to do, and thought I should like to see a little of London," she replied naïvely. "So when I had got the stamps I went on into the fashionable streets, where folks are all walking about just as if it were daytime. 'Twas for all the world like coming home by night from Martinmas Fair¹ at Slopeway Well."

"O, Avice, Avice, you must not go out like this! Don't you know that I am responsible for your safety? I am your – well, guardian, in fact, and am bound by law and morals, and I don't know what-all, to deliver you up to your native island without a scratch or blemish. And yet you indulge in such a midnight vagary as this!"

"But I am sure, Sir, the people in the street were more respectable than they are at Slopeway Well! They were dressed in the latest fashion, and would have scorned to do me any harm; and as for their love-making to a body, I never heard anything so polite before."

"Well, you must not do it again. I'll tell you some day why. What's that you have in your hand?"

"A mouse-trap. There are lots of mice in this kitchen, and I thought I'd try to catch them. That was what I went so far to buy, as there were no shops open just about here. I'll set it now."

She proceeded at once to do so, and Pearston remained in his seat regarding the operation, which seemed entirely to engross her. It was extraordinary, indeed, to observe how she wilfully limited her interests; with what content she received the ordinary things that life offered, and persistently refused to behold what an infinitely extended life lay open to her through him. If she had only said the word, he would have got a license and married her the next morning. Was it possible that she did not perceive this tendency in him? She could hardly be a woman if she did not; and in her airy, elusive, offhand demeanour she was very much of a woman indeed.

"It only holds one mouse," he said absently.

"But I shall hear it throw in the night, and set it again."

He sighed, and left her to her own resources and retired to rest, though he felt no tendency to sleep. At some small hour of the darkness, owing, possibly, to some intervening door being left open, he heard the mouse-trap click. Another light sleeper must have heard it too, for almost immediately after the pit-pat of naked feet, accompanied by the brushing of drapery, was audible along the passage towards the kitchen. After an absence of the pit-patting figure in that department long enough to reset the trap, he was startled by a scream from the same quarter. Pearston sprang out of bed, jumped into his dressing-gown, and hastened in the direction of the cry.

Avice, barefooted and wrapped in a shawl, was standing in a chair; the mouse-trap lay on the floor, the mouse running round and round in its neighbourhood.

"I was trying to take him out," said she, excitedly, "and he got away from me!"

Pearston secured the mouse while she remained standing on the chair. Then, having set the trap anew, his feeling burst out petulantly –

"A girl like you to throw yourself away upon such a commonplace fellow as that quarryman! Why do you do it?"

Her mind was so intently fixed upon the matter in hand that it was some moments before she caught his irrelevant subject. "Because I am a foolish girl," she said quietly.

"What! Don't you love him?" said Jocelyn, with a surprised stare up at her as she stood, in her concern appearing the very Avice who had kissed him twenty years earlier.

"It is not much use to talk about that," said she.

"Then, is it the soldier?"

"Yes, though I have never spoken to him."

"Never spoken to the soldier?"

"Never."

"Has either one treated you badly – deceived you?"

"No. Certainly not."

"Well, I can't make you out; and I don't wish to know more than you choose to tell me. Come, Avice, why not tell me exactly how things are?"

"Not now, Sir!" she entreated, her pretty pink face and brown eyes turned in simple appeal to him. "I will tell you all to-morrow; indeed I will!"

He retreated to his own apartment and lay down meditating. Some quarter of an hour after she had retreated to hers the mouse-trap clicked again, and Pearston raised herself on his elbow to listen. The place was so still and the jerry-built door-panels so thin that he could hear the mouse jumping about inside the wires of the trap. But he heard no footstep this time. Disliking the idea of the little creature's misery, he again arose, proceeded to the kitchen with a light, and put the mouse to a merciful death. Returning, he listened once more. He could see in the far distance the door of Avice's room; but that thoughtful housewife had not heard the second capture. From the room came a soft breathing like that of an infant.

He entered his own chamber and reclined himself gloomily enough. Her freedom from all consciousness of him, the aspect of the deserted kitchen, the cold grate, impressed him with a deeper sense of loneliness than he had ever felt before.

Foolish he was, indeed, to be the slave of this young creature! Her defencelessness, her freedom from the least thought that there lurked any danger in this propinquity, were in fact secondary safeguards, not much less strong than that of her being her mother's image, against any risk to her from him. Yet it was out of this that his depression came.

At sight of her the next morning Pearston felt that he must put an end to such a state of things. He sent Avice off to the studio, wrote to an agent for a couple of servants, and then went round to his work. Avice was busy righting all that she was allowed to touch. It was the girl's delight to be occupied among the models and casts, which for the first time she regarded with the wistful interest of a soul struggling to receive ideas of the beautiful, vaguely discerned yet ever eluding her. That brightness in her mother's mind, which might have descended to the second Avice with the maternal face and form, had been dimmed by admixture with the mediocrity of her father's. By one who remembered like Pearston the dual organisation could be often seen wrestling internally.

They were alone in the studio, and his feelings found vent. Putting his arms round her, he said, "My darling, sweet little Avice! I want to ask you something – surely you guess what? I want to know this: will you be married to me, and live here with me always and ever?"

"O, Mr. Pearston, what nonsense!"

"Nonsense?" said he, shrinking somewhat.

"Yes, Sir."

"Well, why? Am I too old? Surely there's no serious difference?"

"O no – I should not mind that if it came to marrying. The difference is not much for husband and wife, though it is rather much for lovers keeping company."

She struggled to get free, and when in the movement she knocked down the Empress Faustina's head[2] he did not try to retain her. He saw that she was not only surprised but a little alarmed.

"You haven't said why it is nonsense!" he remarked tartly.

"Why, I didn't know you was thinking of me any longer like that! I hadn't any thought of it! And all alone here! What shall I do?"

"Say yes, my pretty Avice. We'll then go out and be married at once, and nobody be any the wiser."

She shook her head. "I couldn't, Sir."

"It would be well for you. You don't like me, perhaps?"

"Yes I do. But not in that sort of way – quite. Still, I might have got to do it in time, if"—

"Well, then, try," he said warmly. "Your mother did!"

No sooner had the words slipped out than Pearston would have recalled them. He had felt in a moment that they were hazardous.

(*To be continued.*)

"Mother loved you?" said Avice, incredulously gazing at him.

"Yes," he murmured.

"You were not her false young man, surely? That one who"—

"Yes, yes! Say no more about it."

"Who ran away from her?"

"Almost."

"Then I can *never, never* like you again! I didn't know it was a gentleman – I – I thought"—

"It wasn't a gentleman, then."

"O, Sir, please go away! I can't bear the sight of 'ee at this moment! Perhaps I shall get to – to like you as I did; but"—

"No; I'm d—d if I'll go away," said Pearston, thoroughly irritated. "I have been candid with you; you ought to be the same with me!"

"What do you want me to tell?"

"Enough to make it clear to me why you don't accept this offer. Everything you have said yet is a reason for the reverse. Now, my dear, I am not angry."

"Yes, you are."

"No, I'm not. Now what is your reason?"

"The name of it is Isaac Pearston, down home."

"How?"

"I mean he courted me, and led me on to island custom,[3] and then I went to chapel one morning and married him in secret, because mother didn't care about him; and I didn't either by that time. And then he quarrelled with me; and just before you and I came to London he went away to Australia. Then I saw a soldier; I never knew his name, but I fell in love with him because I am so quick at that! Still, as it was wrong, I tried not to think of him, and wouldn't look at him when he passed. But it made me cry very much that I mustn't. I was then very miserable, and you asked me to come to London. I didn't care what I did with myself, and I came."

"Heaven above us!" said Pearston, his pale and distressed face showing with what a shock this announcement had come. "Why have you done such extraordinary things? Or, rather, why didn't you tell me of this before? Then, at the present moment you are the wife of a man who is in Australia, whom you do not love at all; but instead of him love a soldier whom you have never spoken to; while I have nearly brought scandal upon us both by your letting me love you! Really, you are a very wicked young woman!"

"No, I am not!" she pouted.

Still, Avice looked pale and rather frightened, and did not lift her eyes from the floor. "I said it was nonsense in you to want to have me!" she went on, "and, even if I hadn't been married to that horrid Isaac

Pearston, I couldn't have married you after you told me that you were the man who ran away from my mother."

"I have paid the penalty!" he said sadly. "Men of my sort always get the worst of it in the end. Now, Avice – I'll call you dear Avice for your mother's sake and not for your own – I must see what I can do to help you out of the difficulty that unquestionably you are in. Why can't you love your husband now you have married him?"

Avice looked aside at the statuary as if the subtleties of her organisation were not very easy to define.

"Was he that black-bearded typical local character I saw you walking with one Sunday? The same surname as mine, though, of course, you don't notice that in a place where there are only half-a-dozen surnames?"

"Yes, that was Ike. It was that evening we disagreed. He scolded me again, and I answered him, and the next day he went away."

"Well, as I say, I must consider what it will be best to do for you in this. The first thing, it seems to me, will be to get your husband home."

She impatiently shrugged her shoulders. "I don't like him!"

"Then why did you marry him?"

"I was obliged to, according to the custom, after walking wi' 'en."

"Oh, it is only a tiff between you, I dare say. I'll start him in business if he'll come. . . . Is the cottage at home still in your hands?"

"Yes, it is my freehold. Grammer Stockwool is taking care o' it for me."

"Good. And back there you go straightway, my pretty Madam, and wait till your husband comes to make it up with you."

"I won't go! I don't want him to come!" she sobbed. "I want to stay here, or anywhere, except where he can come!"

"You'll get over that. Now, go indoors, there's a dear Avice, and be ready in one hour, waiting in the hall for me."

"I don't want to!"

"But I say you shall."

She found it was no use to disobey. Precisely at the moment appointed he met her there himself, burdened only with a valise and umbrella, she with a box and other things. Directing the porter to put Avice and her belongings into a four-wheeled cab for the railway station, he walked out of the door, and kept looking behind till he saw the cab approaching. He then entered beside the astonished girl, and onward they went together.

They sat opposite each other in an empty compartment, and the tedious railway journey began. Whenever he looked at her the girl's eyes filled with tears, and at last she wept outright. "I don't want to go to him!" she sobbed in a repressed voice.

Pearston was almost as much distressed as she. "Why did you put yourself and me in such a position?" he said bitterly. "It is no use to regret it now! And I can't say that I do. It affords me a way out of a trying position. Even if you had not been married to him you would not have married me!"

"Yes, I would, Sir."

"What! You would? You said you wouldn't not long ago."

"I like you better now! I like you more and more!"

Pearston sighed, for emotionally he was not much older than she. That hitch in his development, rendering him the most lopsided of God's creatures, was his standing misfortune. Little more passed between the twain on that wretched, never-to-be-forgotten day. Aphrodite was punishing him[4] sharply, as she knew but too well how to punish her votaries when they reverted from the ephemeral to the stable mood. This curse of his heart not aging while his frame moved naturally onward, when was it to end? Perhaps only with life.

His first act the day after depositing her in her own house was to go to the chapel where, by her statement, the marriage had been solemnised, and make sure of the fact. Perhaps he felt an illogical hope that she might be free, even then, in the tarnished condition which such freedom would have involved. However, there stood the words distinctly: Isaac Pearston, Avice Caro, son and daughter of So-and-so, married on such a day, signed by the contracting parties, the officiating minister, and the two witnesses.

CHAPTER XXII

She is Finally Enshrouded from Sight

One evening in early winter, when the air was dry and gusty, the dark little lane which divided the grounds of Dell-i'-th'-rock Castle from the cottage of Avice, and led down to the adjoining ruin of Red King Castle, was paced by a solitary man. The cottage was the centre of his beat; its western limit being the gates of the former residence, its eastern the drawbridge of the ruin. The few other cottages thereabout – all as if carved from the solid rock – were in darkness, but from the upper window of Avice's tiny freehold glimmered a light. Its rays were repeated from the far-distant sea by the lightship lying moored over the Shambles quicksand, which brought mysteriousness and domesticity into the position of balanced opposites.

The sea murmured – more than murmured – among the boulders below the ruins, a louder roll of its tide being timed at regular intervals. These sounds were accompanied by an equally periodic moan from the interior of the cottage chamber; so that the articulate heave of water and the articulate heave of life seemed but differing utterances of the self-same troubled Being – which in one sense they were.

Pearston – for the man in the lane was he – would look from lightship to cottage window; then back again. Soon an infant's wail of the very feeblest was also audible in the house. He started from his easy pacing, and went again westward, standing at the elbow of the lane a long time. Then the peace of the sleeping village which lay that way was broken by light wheels and the trot of a horse. Pearston went back to the cottage gate and awaited the arrival of the vehicle.

It was a light cart, and a man jumped down as it stopped. He was in a broad-brimmed hat, under which no more of him could be perceived than that he wore a black beard, clipped like a thorn fence – a typical aspect in the island.

"You are Avice's husband?" asked the sculptor, quickly.

The man replied that he was, in the local accent. "I've just come in by the last train," he added. "I couldn't get here avore."

"Well," said Pearston, "your coming means that you are willing to make it up with her?"

"Ay, I don't know but I be," said the man. "Mid so well do that as anything else!"

"If you do, thoroughly, a good business in your old line awaits you here in the island."

"Wi' all my heart, then," said the man. His voice was energetic, and, though slightly touchy, it showed, on the whole, a disposition to set things right.

The driver of the trap was paid off, and Jocelyn and Isaac Pearston, undoubtedly scions of a common stock in this isle of intermarriages –

entered the house. Nobody was in the ground-floor room, in the exact centre of which stood a square table, and in the exact centre of the table a lamp, the apartment having the appearance of being rigidly swept and set in order for an event of interest.

The woman who lived in the house with Avice now came downstairs, and to the inquiry of the comers she replied that matters were progressing favourably, but that nobody could be allowed to go upstairs just then. After placing chairs and viands for them she retreated, and they sat down, the candle between them – the lover of the sufferer above, who had no right to her, and the man who had every right to her, but did not love her. Engaging in desultory and fragmentary conversation, they listened to the trampling of feet on the floorboards overhead – Pearston full of anxiety and attentiveness, Ike awaiting the course of nature calmly.

Soon they heard the feeble bleats repeated, and then the local practitioner descended and entered the room.

"How is she now?" said Pearston, the more taciturn Ike looking up with him for the answer that he felt would serve for two as well as for one.

"Doing well, remarkably well," replied the professional gentleman, with a manner of having said it before; and his vehicle not being at the door he sat down and shared some refreshment with the others. When he had departed Mrs. Stockwool again stepped down, and informed them that Ike's presence had been made known to his wife.

The truant quarrier seemed rather inclined to stay where he was and finish the mug of ale, but Pearston quickened him, and he ascended the staircase. As soon as the room was empty Pearston leant with his elbows on the table, and covered his face with his hands.

Ike was absent no great time. Descending with a proprietary mien that had been lacking before, he invited Pearston to ascend likewise, since she had stated that she would like to see him. Pearston went up the crooked old steps, the husband remaining below.

Avice looked brighter and happier than he had expected to find her, and was apparently very much fortified by the pink little lump at her side. She held out her hand to him.

"I just wanted to tell 'ee – I thought it would be no harm to see you, though 'tis rather soon – to tell 'ee how very much I thank you for getting me settled again with Ike. He is very glad to come home again, too, he says. Yes, you've done a good many kind things for me, Sir."

Whether she were really glad, or whether the words were expressed as a matter of duty, Pearston did not attempt to learn.

He merely said that he valued her thanks. "Now, Avice," he added tenderly, "I resign my guardianship of you. I hope to see your husband in a sound little business here in a very short time."

"I hope so – for baby's sake," she said, with a bright sigh. "Would you – like to see her, Sir?"

"The baby? O, yes. . . . *your* baby! You must christen her Avice."

"Yes – so I will," she murmured readily, and disclosed the infant with some timidity. "I hope you forgive me, Sir, for concealing my marriage."

"If you forgive me for making love to you."

"Yes. How were you to know! I wish"—

Pearston bade her good-bye, kissing her hand; turned from her and the incipient being whom he was to meet again under very altered conditions, and left the bed-chamber with a tear in his eye.

"Here endeth that dream!" said he.

Hymen, in secret or overt guise, seemed to haunt Pearston just at this time with undignified mockery which savoured rather of Harlequin' than of the torch-bearer. Two days after parting in a lone island from the girl he so solicitously loved he met in Piccadilly his friend Somers, hastening along with a deeply preoccupied face.

"My dear fellow," said Somers, "what do you think! I was charged not to tell you yet, but, hang it! I may just as well make a clean breast of it now as later."

"What – you are not going to . . ." began Pearston, with a sort of divination.

"Yes. What I said on impulse I am about to carry out in cold blood. Nichola and I began in jest and ended in earnest. We are going to take one another next month for good and all."

END OF PART SECOND

PART THIRD

A Young Man of Fifty-Nine

CHAPTER XXIII

She Returns for the New Season

Nearly twenty years had closed over the events which came to a settlement with the reunion of the second Avice and her husband; and the peninsula called an island looked just the same as before; though many who had formerly projected their daily shadows over its unrelieved whiteness ceased now to disturb the colourless sunlight there.

The general change, nevertheless, was small. The silent ships came and went from the wharf, the chisels clinked in the quarries; file after file of whitey-brown horses, in strings of eight or ten, painfully dragged the square blocks of stone down the hill on the antediluvian wooden wheels just as usual. The lightship winked every night from the quicksands to the Beal Lantern, and the Beal Lantern glared through its eye-glass on the ship. The canine gnawing audible on the Pebble Bank had been repeated ever since at each tide, but the pebbles remained undevoured.

Men drank, smoked, and spat in the inns with only a few degrees more of adulteration in their refreshments and a trifle less dialect in their speech than of yore. One figure had never since been seen on the Channel rock, the form of Pearston, the sculptor, whose first use of the chisel that rock had instigated.

He had lived abroad a great deal, and, in fact, at this very date he was staying at an hotel in Rome. Though he had not once set eyes on Avice since parting from her in the room with her firstborn, he had managed to obtain tidings of her from time to time during the interval. In this way Pearston learnt that shortly after their resumption of a common life in her house Ike had ill-used her, till, the business to which the sculptor had assisted him chancing to prosper, he became immersed in its details, and allowed Avice to pursue her domestic courses without interference, initiating that kind of reconciliation which is so calm and durable, having as its chief ingredient neither hate nor love, but a dense, all-embracing indifference.

At first Pearston had sent her sums of money privately, fearing lest her husband should deny her material comforts; but he soon found, to his great relief, that such help was unnecessary, social ambition having prompted Ike to set up as quite a gentleman-islander, and to allow Avice a scope for show which he would never have allowed in mere kindness.

Being in Rome, as aforesaid, Pearston returned one evening to his hotel to dine, after spending the afternoon among the busts in the long gallery of the Vatican. The unconscious habit, common to so many people, of tracing likes in unlikes had often led him to discern, or to fancy he discerned, in the Roman atmosphere, in its lights and shades, and particularly in its reflected or secondary lights, something resembling the atmosphere of his native promontory. Perhaps it was that in each case the eye was mostly resting on stone – that here, in the Eternal City, there were quarries of ruins like the quarries of maiden rock at home.[1]

This being in his mind when he sat down to dinner at the common table, he was surprised to hear an American gentleman, who sat opposite, mention the name of Pearston's birthplace. The American was talking to a friend about a lady who had been a fellow-passenger with him in their voyage over. They were wondering whether she had been successful in her quest, which was for some near relation, who had lived in the before-mentioned isle, of which she also was a native.

Pearston was instantly struck with the perception that these facts, though general, were in accord with the history of his long-lost wife,[2] Marcia. To be sure they did not go far: and he hardly thought that she would be likely to hunt him up after more than thirty years of separation. Still, he was impressed enough to resolve to exchange a word with the strangers so soon as he could get opportunity.

He could not well attract their attention through the plants upon the wide table, and even if he had been able, to do so in public was not advisable. He waited on till dinner was over at the table d'hôte, and when the strangers withdrew Pearston withdrew in their rear.

They were not in the drawing-room, whither they had seemed to go. On inquiry, Pearston found that they had gone out. There was no chance of discovering them, but Pearston, stirred to restlessness by their remarks, wandered up and down the Piazza di Spagna, thinking they might return. The streets below were immersed in shade, the front of the church at the top was flooded with orange light, the gloom of evening gradually intensifying on the broad, long flight of steps, which foot-passengers incessantly ascended and descended with the insignificance of ants.

Getting back to the hotel he learnt that the Americans had only dropped in to dine, and were staying elsewhere. Briefly, he saw no more of them; but, on reflection, he was not deeply concerned at this, for by going straight back home he could easily ascertain on the isle itself if his wife had indeed arrived there. It seemed impossible: what earthly woman, going off in a freak as his wife had done, would have kept silence so long unless she had returned to dust; or, if indeed living, how should she bring herself to come back to him now?

Nevertheless, he felt it to be his duty to ascertain what truth might lie in this chance fancy; and about a week later he stood once more at the foot of the familiar steep whereon the houses of Slopeway Well were perched like pigeons on a roof-side.

He pursued his inquiries[3] as privately as possible, for his intention was to make himself known here no more. As he had ceased since his last residence here to wear his beard in the island fashion, nobody recognised him, though he had aged but little under the inactivity of twenty years. Nothing had been heard of any such lady, the nearest approach to a visit of the kind being that made by a woman whom a flyman had driven over the island in search of a family now dead. As this lady did not answer to the description, and the persons she sought were bearers of another name, Pearston concluded he had got to the bottom of the matter in considering it a casual correspondence only.

In returning to the town and station at eventide his attention was attracted by the busy doings around a quarry which lay at a distance on his left; he observed several men on the spot whom he might recognise. He was inclined to cross thither, feeling sure that the quarry was Ike Pearston's, and stood looking in that direction, where the numerous black hoisting-cranes scattered over the central plateau of the island had the appearance of a swarm of daddy-longlegs resting there. The way across was rugged, and nothing would be gained by making himself known. He proceeded on his way, having no real wish at present to encounter Avice's husband or friends.

At the station he found he had to wait a little while. Presently other people who had come from Top o' Hill (the summit of the rock was thus called) also entered the booking-office, and they were talking reflectively about an accident which had happened a week or two before. The name that caught his ear caused him to turn quickly to one of the quarrymen.

"Who do you say was killed?" Pearston asked.

"Mr. Isaac Pearston – Castleway Pearston as we did call 'n – 'cause there's so many Isaac Pearstons – was killed in his own quarry."

While Jocelyn stood silent at this intelligence the men went on conversing among themselves.

"I said to 'en that morning, 'Don't th' stand there, for Heaven's sake!' Born in a quarry a'most, you'd ha' thought he'd ha' known, if anybody would. But he was a man who'd never listen to argument – that one must say, though 'a's squatted. He went away shortly after, and we didn't expect to see 'en again that day. But 'a did come back, worse luck for 'n; and that was how it ended."

More details of the catastrophe and circumstances of the victim's life were given, from which Pearston gathered that though the Avice who had once been his Avice was now a widow, she had friends and sympathisers about her which would render any attention on his part at this juncture unnecessary. He therefore mechanically took his seat in the train and remained musing during the run along the Pebble Bank and round to the watering-place five miles off, at which he had taken up his quarters for a few days.

Here, as he stayed on, he heard further rumours of the accident; till Avice, who had been little in his mind of late, began to take up a somewhat distinct position there. He was fully aware that since his earlier manhood a change had come over his regard of woman. Once the individual had been nothing more to him than the temporary abiding-place of the typical or ideal; now his heart showed an extraordinary fidelity to the specimen, with all her pathetic flaws of detail; which, indeed, so far from sending him further, increased his tenderness. This maturer feeling, though more noble and generous, was less convenient, for the warmth of passion remained as in youth without the recuperative intervals which had accompanied evanescence.

The revived emotion detained him long and yet longer at this spot, where he could see the island that was Avice's home lying like a great snail upon the sea across the bay. It was the spring of the year; local steamers had begun to run, and he was never tired of standing on the thinly occupied deck of one of these as it skirted the island and revealed to him on the cliffs far up its height the ruins of Red King Castle, behind which the little village of East Wake lay.

Thus matters went on, if they did not rather stand still, for at least a month before Pearston had the courage of his romanticism, and ventured to seek out Avice. Even when he did go he was so afraid that he had intruded upon her too soon as to approach with unwonted diffidence. He need have shown no such concern.

The first surprise was to find that she had long ceased to live in the little freehold cottage she had occupied of old. In answer to his inquiries he was directed along the road to the west of the modern castle, past the entrance on that side, and onward to the very house that had once been his own home. There it stood as of yore, facing up the Channel, a comfortable roomy structure, the euonymus and other shrubs, which alone would stand in the teeth of the salt wind, living on at about the same stature in front of it: but the paint-work much renewed. A thriving man had resided there of late, evidently.

The widow in mourning who received him in the front parlour was, alas! but the sorry shadow of Avice the Second. How could he have fancied otherwise after twenty years? Yet he had been led to fancy otherwise, almost without knowing it, by feeling himself unaltered. Indeed, curiously enough, nearly the first words she said to him were: "Why – you are just the same!"

"Just the same. Yes, I am, Avice," he answered sadly; for this inability to ossify with the rest of his generation threw him out of proportion with the time. Moreover, while wearing the aspect of comedy, it was of the nature of tragedy.

"It is well to be you, sir," she went on. "I have had troubles to take the bloom off me!"

"Yes; I have been sorry for you."

She continued to regard him curiously, with humorous interest; and he knew what was passing in her mind: that this man, to whom she had formerly looked up as to a person far in advance of her along the lane of life, seemed now to be a well-adjusted contemporary, the pair of them observing the world with fairly level eyes.

He had come to her with warmth for a vision which, on reaching her, he found to have departed; and, though fairly weaned by the natural reality, he was so far staunch as to linger hankeringly. They talked of past days, his old attachment, which she had then despised, being now far more absorbing and present to her than to himself.

She unmistakably won upon him as he sat on. A curious closeness between them had been produced in his imagination by the discovery that she was passing her life within the house of his own childhood. Her similar surname meant little here; but it was also his, and, added to the identity of domicile, there was a strong suggestiveness about the accident.

"This is where I used to sit when my parents occupied the house," he said, placing himself beside that corner of the fireplace which commanded a view through the window. "I could see a bough of tamarisk wave outside at that time, and, beyond the bough, the same abrupt grassy waste towards the sea, and at night the same old lightship blinking far out there. Place yourself on the spot, to please me."

She set her chair where he indicated, and Pierston stood close beside her, directing her gaze to the familiar objects he had regarded thence as a boy. Her head and face – the latter thoughtful and worn enough, poor thing, to suggest a married life none too comfortable – were close to his breast, and, with a few inches further incline, would have touched it.

"And now you are the inhabitant; I the visitor," he said. "I am glad to see you here – so glad, Avice! You are fairly well provided for – I think I may assume that?" He looked round the room at the solid mahogany furniture, and at the modern piano and show bookcase.

"Yes, Ike left me comfortable. 'Twas he who thought of moving from my cottage to this larger house. He bought it, and I can live here as long as I choose to."

Apart from the decline of his adoration to friendship, there seemed to be a general convergence of positions which suggested that he might make amends for the original desertion by proposing to this Avice when a meet time should arrive. If he did not love her as he had done when she was a slim thing catching mice in his rooms in London, he could surely be content at his age with comradeship. After all she was only forty to his sixty. The feeling that he really could be thus content was so convincing that he almost believed the luxury of getting old and reposeful was coming to his restless, wandering heart at last.

"Now, Avice," he began archly, "I feel, of course, your situation at present, and Heaven forbid that I should say anything premature. But your life with your late husband has been such that I think it no harm to put an idea into your mind, as regards the future, for you to turn over – not too seriously – just for what it is worth. It originated, so far as it concerns you personally, with the sight of you in that cottage round the corner, nineteen or twenty years ago, when I became tenant of the castle opposite. But that was not the very beginning. The very beginning was a score of years before that, when I, a young fellow of nineteen, coming home here, from London, to see my father, encountered a tender woman as like you as your double; was much attracted by her as I saw her day after day flit past this window; till I made it my business to accompany her in her walks awhile. I, as you know, was not a staunch fellow, and it all ended badly. But better late than never . . ."

. "Ah! there she is!" suddenly exclaimed Avice, whose attention had wandered somewhat from his retrospective discourse. She was looking from the window towards the cliffs, where, upon the open ground quite near at hand, a slender female form was seen rambling along. "She is out for a walk," Avice continued. "I wonder if she is going to call here this afternoon? She is living at the castle, opposite, as governess."

"O, she's"—

"Yes. Her education was very thorough – better even than her grandmother's. I was the neglected one, and Isaac and myself both vowed that there should be no complaint on that score about her. We christened her Avice, to keep up the name, as you requested. I wish you could speak to her – I am sure you would like her."

"Is that the baby?" faltered Jocelyn.

"Yes, the baby."

The person signified, now much nearer, was a still more modernized, up-to-date edition of the two Avices of that blood with whom he had been involved more or less for the last forty years. A ladylike little creature was she – almost elegant. She wore a large-disked sun-hat, with a brim like a wheel whose spokes were radiating folds of muslin lining the brim, a black margin beyond the muslin being the felloe. Beneath this brim her hair was massed low upon her brow, the colour of the thick tresses being obviously, from her complexion, repeated in the irises of her large, deep eyes. Her rather nervous lips were thin and closed, so that they only appeared as a delicate red line. A changeable temperament was shown by that mouth – quick transitions from affection to aversion, from a pout to a smile.

It was Avice the Third.

(*To be continued.*)

CHAPTER XXIV

Misgivings on this Unexpected Re-embodiment

Jocelyn and the second Avice continued to gaze ardently at her.

"Ah! she is not coming in now; she hasn't time," said the mother, with some disappointment. "She means to run across in the evening."

The girl, in fact, went past and on till she was out of sight. Pearston stood as in a dream. It was the very girl, in all essential particulars, and without the absence of a single charm, who had kissed him forty years before. When he turned his head from the window his eyes fell again upon the old Avice at his side. Before but the relic of the Well-Beloved, she had now become its empty shrine. Warm friendship, indeed, he felt for her; but whatever that might have done towards the instauration of a former dream was now hopelessly barred by the rivalry of the thing itself in the guise of a lineal successor.

Pearston, who had been about to leave, sat down again on being timidly asked if he would stay and have a cup of tea. He hardly knew what he did for a moment; a dim thought that Avice – the renewed Avice – might come into the house after all made his reseating himself an act of spontaneity.

How he contrived to attenuate and disperse the subject he had opened up with the new Avice's mother, Pearston never exactly knew. Perhaps she saw more than he thought she saw – read something in his face – knew that about his nature which he gave her no credit for knowing. Anyhow, the conversation took the form of a friendly gossip from that minute, his remarks being often given while his mind was turned elsewhere.

It is hardly an exaggeration to say that a chill passed through Jocelyn when there had been time for reflection. The sedulous study of his art without any counterbalancing practical pursuit had nourished and developed his natural responsiveness to impressions; he now felt that his old trouble, his doom – his curse, indeed, he had sometimes called it – was come back again. Aphrodite[1] was not yet propitiated for that original sin against her image in the person of Avice the First, and now, at the age of nine-and-fifty, he was urged on and on like the Jew Ahasuerus[2] – or, in the phrase of the islanders themselves, like a blind ram.

The Goddess, an abstraction to the general,[3] was a very real personage indeed to Pearston. He had watched the marble image of her which stood in his working-room under all changes of light and shade – in the brightening of morning, in the blackening of eve, in moonlight, in lamp-light; every line and curve of her body none, naturally, knew better than he; and, though not quite a belief, it was a fancy, a superstition, that the three Avices were somehow interpenetrated with her essence.

"And the next Avice – your daughter," he said stumblingly; "she is, you say, a governess at the castle opposite."

Mrs. Pearston reaffirmed the fact, adding that the girl often slept at home because she (the speaker) was so lonely. She often thought she would like to keep her daughter at home altogether.

"She plays that instrument, I suppose?" said Pearston, regarding the piano.

"Yes, she plays beautifully; she had the best instruction that masters could give her. She was educated at Sandbourne."

"Which room does she sleep in when at home?" he asked curiously.

"The little one over this."

It had been his own. "Strange," he murmured.

He finished tea, and sat after tea, but the youthful Avice did not arrive. With the Avice present he conversed as the old friend – no more. At last it grew dusk, and Pearston could not possibly find an excuse for staying longer.

"I hope to make the acquaintance – of your daughter," he said in leaving, knowing that he might have said with equal truth, "of my new tenderly beloved."

"I hope you will," she said simply. "This evening she evidently has gone for a walk instead of coming here."

He went out of the house, but felt in no mood just then to get back to his lodgings, in the town on the mainland. He lingered about upon the undulating ground for a long while, thinking of the extraordinary repro-duction of the original girl in this new form he had seen, and of himself as of a foolish dreamer in being so suddenly fascinated by the renewed image in a personality not one-third his age. As a physical fact, no doubt, the preservation of the likeness was no uncommon thing here, but it helped the dream.

Passing round the walls of the new castle, he deviated from his home-ward track by turning down the familiar little lane which led to the ruined castle of the Red King. It took him past the cottage in which the new Avice was born, from whose precincts he had heard her first infantine cry. Pausing, he saw in the west behind him the new moon growing distinct upon the glow.

He was subject to gigantic superstitions. In spite of himself, the sight of the new moon, his chosen tutelary goddess, as representing, by her so-called inconstancy,[4] his own idea of a migratory Well-Beloved, made him start as if his sweetheart in the flesh had suddenly looked over the horizon at him. In a crowd secretly, or in solitude boldly, he ever bowed the knee three times to this divinity on her first appearance monthly, and directed a soft kiss towards her shining shape. He feared Aphrodite, but Selene he cherished.[5] All this did he, a man of fifty-nine! Truly the curse (if it were not a blessing) was far from having spent itself yet.

In the other direction the castle ruins rose against the sea. He went on towards these, around which he had played as a boy, and stood by the walls at the edge of the cliff pondering. There was no wind and but little tide, and he thought he could hear from years ago a voice that he knew. It certainly was a voice, but it came from the rocks beneath the castle ruin.

"Mrs. Atway!"

A silence followed, and nobody came. The voice spoke again; "John Bencomb!"

Neither was this summons attended to. The cry continued, with more entreaty: "William Scribben!"

The voice was that of a Pearston – there could be no doubt of it – Avice's, probably. Something or other seemed to be detaining her down there, against her will. A sloping path beneath the beetling cliff and the castle walls rising sheer from its summit led down to the lower level whence the voice proceeded. Pearston followed the pathway, and soon beheld a girl in light clothing – the same he had seen through the window – standing upon one of the rocks, apparently unable to move. Pearston hastened across to her.

"O, thank you for coming!" she murmured with some timidity. "I have met with an awkward mishap. I live near here, and am not frightened really. My foot has become jammed in a crevice of the rock, and I cannot get it out, try how I will. What *shall* I do!"

Pearston stooped and examined the cause of discomfiture. "I think if you can take your boot off," he said, "your foot might slip out, leaving the boot behind."

She tried to act upon this advice, but could not do so effectually. Pearston then experimented by slipping his hand into the crevice till he could just reach the buttons of her boot, which, however, he could not unfasten any more than she. Taking his penknife from his pocket, he tried again, and cut off the buttons one by one. The boot unfastened, and out slipped the foot.

"O, how glad I am!" she cried joyfully. "I was fearing I should have to stay here all night. How can I thank you enough?"

Pearston was tugging to withdraw the boot, but no force that he could exercise would move it. At last she said: "Don't try any longer. It is not far to the house. I can walk in my stocking."

"I'll assist you in," he said gallantly.

She said she did not want help, nevertheless allowed him to help her on the unshod side. As they moved on she explained that she had come out through the garden door, had been standing on the boulders to look at something out at sea just discernible in the evening light as assisted by the moon, and, in jumping down, had wedged her foot as he had found it.

Whatever Pearston's years might have made him look by day, in the dusk of evening he was fairly presentable as a pleasing man of no marked antiquity, his outline differing but little from what it had been when he was half his years. He was well preserved, still upright, trimly shaven, agile in movement; wore a tightly buttoned suit which set off a naturally slight figure; in brief, he might have been of any age as he appeared to her at this moment. She talked to him with the co-equality of one who assumed him to be not far ahead of her own generation; and, as the growing darkness obscured him more and more, he adopted her assumption of his age with increasing boldness of tone.

The flippant, harmless freedom of the watering-place Miss, which Avice had plainly acquired during her sojourn at the Sandbourne school, helped Pearston considerably in this rôle of *jeune premier*,[6] which he was only too ready to play at any time. Not a word did he say about being a native of the island; still more carefully did he conceal the fact of his having courted her grandmother, and engaged himself to marry that attractive lady.

He found that she had come out upon the rocks through the same little private door from the lawn of the modern castle which had frequently afforded him egress to the same spot in years long past. Pearston accompanied her across the grounds almost to the entrance of the mansion –

the place being now far better kept and planted than when he had rented it as a lonely tenant; almost, indeed, restored to the order and neatness which had characterised it when he was a boy.

She was too inexperienced to be reserved, and during this little climb, leaning upon his arm, there was time for a great deal of confidence. When he had bidden her farewell, and she had entered, leaving him in the dark, a rush of sadness through Pearston's soul swept down all the temporary pleasure he had found in the charming girl's company. Had Mephistopheles sprung from the ground there and then with an offer to Jocelyn of restoration to youth on the usual terms of his firm,[7] the sculptor certainly might have consented to sell that part of himself of which he felt less immediate need than of a ruddy lip and cheek and an unmarked brow.

But what could only have been treated as a folly by outsiders was almost a sorrow for him. Why was he born with such a temperament? And this concatenated interest could hardly have arisen, even with Pearston, but for a conflux of circumstances only possible here. The three Avices, the second much like the first, the third actually a double of the first, were the outcome of the immemorial island customs of intermarriage and of prenuptial union, under which conditions the type of feature was almost uniform from parent to child through generations; so that, till quite latterly, to have seen one native man and woman was to have seen the whole population of that isolated rock, so nearly cut off from the mainland. His own predisposition and the consciousness of his early faithlessness did all the rest.

He turned gloomily away, and let himself out of the precincts. Before walking along the couple of miles of road which would conduct him to the little station at Slopeway Well, he redescended to the rocks whereon he had found her, and searched about for the fissure which had made a prisoner of this belated edition of the Well-Beloved. Kneeling down beside the spot, he inserted his hand, and ultimately, by much wriggling, withdrew the little boot. He examined it thoughtfully – by touch rather than by sight – put it in his pocket, and followed the stony route to Slopeway Well.

CHAPTER XXV

The Renewed Image Burns Itself In

There was nothing to hinder Pearston in calling upon the new Avice's mother as often as he should choose, beyond the five miles of intervening railway, and two additional miles of clambering over the heights of the island. Two days later, therefore, Pearston repeated his journey and knocked about tea-time at the widow's door.

As he had expected, the daughter was not at home. He sat down beside the old sweetheart who, having eclipsed her mother in past days, had now eclipsed herself in her child. Jocelyn produced the girl's boot from his pocket.

"Then, 'tis *you* who helped Avice out of her predicament?" said Mrs. Pearston, with surprise.

"Yes, my dear friend; and perhaps I shall ask you to help me out of mine before I have done. But never mind that now. What did she tell you about the adventure?"

Mrs. Pearston was looking thoughtfully upon him. "Well 'tis rather strange it should have been you, Sir," she replied slowly. "She seemed to be a good deal interested. I thought it might have been a younger man – a much younger man."

"It might have been, as far as feelings were concerned¹ . . . Now, Avice, I'll to the point at once. Virtually I have known your daughter any number of years. When I talk to her I can anticipate every turn of her thought, every sentiment, every act, so long did I study those things in your mother and in you. Therefore I do not require to learn her; she was learnt by me in her previous existences. Now, don't be shocked: I am willing to marry her – I should be overjoyed to do it if there would be nothing preposterous about it, or that would seem like a man making himself too much of a fool, and so degrading her in consenting. I can make her comparatively rich, as you know, and I would indulge her every whim. There is the idea, bluntly put. It would set right something in my mind that has been wrong for forty years. After my death she would have plenty of freedom and plenty of means to enjoy it."

Mrs. Isaac Pearston seemed only a little surprised; certainly not shocked.

"Well, if I didn't think you might be a bit taken with her!" she murmured archly. "Knowing your sort of mind, from my little affair with 'ee years ago, nothing you could do in this way would astonish me."

"But you don't think badly of me for it?"

"Not at all; but, of course, it would depend upon what she felt. . . . I would rather have her marry a younger man."

"And suppose a satisfactory younger man should not appear?"

Mrs. Pearston showed in her face that she fully recognised the difference between a bird in hand and a better bird in the bush. She looked him curiously up and down.

"I know you would make anybody a very nice husband," she said presently. "I know that you would be nicer than many men half your age; and, though there is a great deal of difference between you and her, there have been more unequal marriages, that's true. Speaking as her mother, I can say that I shouldn't object to you, Sir, for her, provided she liked you. That is where the difficulty would lie."

"I wish you would help me to get over that difficulty," he said gently. "Remember, I brought back a truant husband to you twenty years ago."

"Yes, you did," she assented; "and, though I may say no great things as to happiness came of it, I've always seen that your intentions towards me were none the less noble on that account. I would do for you what I would do for no other man, and there is one reason in particular which would incline me to help you with Avice – that I should feel absolutely certain I was helping her to a kind husband."

"Well, that would remain to be seen. I would, at any rate, try to be worthy of your opinion. Come, Avice, for old times' sake, you must help me. You never felt anything but friendship in those days, you know, and that makes it easy and proper for you to do me a good turn now."

After a little more conversation his old friend was won to promise that she really would do everything that lay in her power. And, as if to show her good faith in this promise, she asked him to wait till later in the evening, when Avice might possibly run across to see her.

Pearston, who fancied he had won the younger Avice's interest, at least, by the part he had played upon the rocks the week before, had a dread of encountering her in full light till he should have advanced a little further in her regard. He accordingly was perplexed at this proposal, and, seeing his hesitation, Mrs. Pearston suggested that they should walk together in the direction whence Avice would come, if she came at all.

He welcomed this idea, and in a few minutes they started, strolling along under the now strong moonlight, and when they reached the gates of Dell-i'-th'-rock Castle, turning back again towards the house. After two or three such walks up and down, the gate of the castle grounds clicked, and a form came forth which proved to be Avice the younger.

As soon as they met the girl recognised in her mother's companion the gentleman who had helped her on the shore, and she seemed really glad to find that her chivalrous assistant was claimed by her parent as an old friend. She remembered hearing something about this worthy London man of talent and position, whose ancestry were people of her own isle, and possibly, from the name, of a common stock with her own.

"And you have actually lived in the castle yourself, Mr. Pearston?" asked Avice the daughter, presently, with her innocent young voice. "Was it long ago?"

"Yes, it was some time ago," replied the sculptor, with a sinking at his heart lest she should say how long.

"It must have been when I was away – or when I was very little?"

"I don't think you were away."

"But I don't think I could have been here?"

"No, perhaps you couldn't have been here."

"I think she was here, but too small to remember," said Avice's mother.

They talked in this general way till they reached Mrs. Pearston's house; but Jocelyn resisted both the widow's invitation and the desire of his own heart, and went away without entering. To risk, by visibly confronting her, the advantage that he had already gained, or fancied he had gained, with the re-incarnate Avice required more courage than he could claim in his present mood.

Such evening promenades as these were frequent during the waxing of that summer moon. On one occasion, as they were all good walkers, it was arranged that they should meet halfway between the island and the town in which Pearston had lodgings. It was impossible that by this time the pretty young governess should not have guessed the ultimate reason of these rambles to be a matrimonial intention; but she inclined to the belief that the widow rather than herself was the object of Pearston's regard; though why this educated and apparently wealthy man should be attracted by her mother – whose homeliness was apparent enough to the girl's more modern training – she could not comprehend.

They met accordingly in the middle of the Pebble Bank, Pearston coming from the mainland, and the women from the peninsular rock. Crossing the wooden bridge which connected the bank with the shore proper, they moved in the direction of Henry the Eighth's Castle, on the verge of the sand cliff. Like the Red King's Castle on the island, the interior was open to the sky, and when they entered and the full moon streamed down upon them over the edge of the enclosing masonry the whole present reality faded from Jocelyn's mind under the press of memories. Neither of his companions guessed what Pearston, that ancient youth, was thinking of. It was in this very spot that he was to have met the grandmother of the girl at his side, and in which he would have met her had she chosen to keep the appointment. The consequence of that meeting would have been the old-fashioned betrothal or island custom – discontinued in these days – from which he could not have receded. It might – nay, it must – have changed the whole current of his life.

Instead of that, forty years had passed – forty years of severance from Avice, till a secondly renewed copy of his sweetheart had arisen to fill her place. But he, alas, was not renewed. And of all this the pretty young face at his side, idealised by the moon's rays, knew nothing.

Taking advantage of the younger woman's retreat to view the sea through an opening of the walls, Pearston appealed to her mother in a whisper: "Have you ever given her a hint of what my meaning is? No? Then I think you might, if you really have no objection."

Mrs. Pearston, as the widow, was far from being so coldly disposed in her own person towards her friend as in the days when he wanted to marry her. Had she now been the object of his pursuit, he would not have needed to ask her twice. But like a good mother she stifled all this, and said she would sound Avice there and then.

"Avice, my dear," she said, when the girl returned from the window-gap, "what do you think of Mr. Pearston paying his addresses to you – coming courting, as *I* call it in my old-fashioned way. Supposing he were to, would you encourage him?"

"To *me*, mother?" said Avice, with an inquiring laugh. "I thought – he meant you!"

"O, no, he doesn't mean me," said her mother, hastily. "He is nothing more than my friend."

"I don't want any addresses," said the daughter.

"He is a man in society, and would take you to an elegant house in London suited to your education, instead of leaving you to mope here."

"I should like that well enough," replied Avice, carelessly.

"Then give him some encouragement."

"I don't care enough about him to do any encouraging. It is his business, I should think, to do all."

She spoke in her lightest vein; but the result was that when Pearston, who had discreetly withdrawn, returned to them, she walked docilely, though perhaps gloomily, beside him, her mother dropping to the rear. They came to a rugged descent, and Pearston took her hand to help her. She allowed him to retain it when they arrived on level ground.

Altogether it was not an unsuccessful evening for the man with the unanchored heart, though possibly initial success meant worse for him in the long run than initial failure. There was nothing marvellous in the fact of her tractability thus far. In his modern dress and style, under the rays of the moon, he looked a very presentable gentleman indeed, while his knowledge of art and his travelled manners were not without their attractions for a girl who with one hand touched the educated middle-class and with the other the rude and simple inhabitants of the isle. Her intensely modern sympathies were quickened by her peculiar outlook.

Pearston was almost ashamed of the brightness of his ardour for her. He would have been quite ashamed if there had not existed a redeeming quality in the substratum of old pathetic memory by which such love had been created – which still permeated it, rendering it the tenderest, most anxious, most protective instinct he had ever known. It may have had in its composition too much of the old boyish fervour that had characterised such affection when he was cherry-cheeked and slender in the waist as a girl; it was all this feeling of youth, and more.

He was not exactly old, he said to himself the next morning as he regarded his face in the glass.[2] And he looked considerably younger than he was. But there was history in his face – distinct chapters of it; his brow was not that blank page it once had been. He knew the origin of that line in his forehead; it had been ploughed in the course of a month or two by a crisis in his matrimonial trouble. He remembered the coming of this pale wiry hair; it had been brought by the illness in Rome, when he had wished each night that he might never wake again. This wrinkled corner, that drawn bit of skin, they had resulted from those months of despondency when all seemed going against his art, his strength, his love. "You cannot live your life and keep it, Jocelyn," he said. Time was against him and love, and time would probably win.

"When I went away from the first Avice," he continued with whimsical misery, "I had a presentiment that I should ache for it some day. And I am aching – have ached ever since this jade of a Well-Beloved learnt the unconscionable trick of inhabiting one image only."

(*To be continued.*)

CHAPTER XXVI

He Makes a Dash for the Last Incarnation

This desultory courtship of a young girl by an old boy was interrupted by the appearance of Somers and his wife and family on the Budmouth Esplanade. Alfred Somers, once the youthful, picturesque as his own paintings, was now a middle-aged family man with spectacles – spectacles worn, too, with the single object of seeing through them – and a row of daughters tailing off to infancy, who at present added appreciably to the income of the bathing-machine women' established along the sands.

Mrs. Somers – once the intellectual, emancipated Mrs. Pine-Avon – had now retrograded to the petty and timid mental position of her mother and grandmother, keeping sharp, strict regard as to the class of society literature and art that reached the presence of her long perspective of girls. She was another illustration of the sad fact that the succeeding generations of women are seldom marked by cumulative progressiveness, their advance as the girl being lost in their recession as the matron;[2] so that they move up and down the stream of intellectual development like flotsam in a tidal estuary. This, however, not by reason of their faults as individuals, but of their misfortune as child-rearers.

The landscape-painter, now an Academician like Pearston himself – rather popular than distinguished – had given up that peculiar and personal taste in subjects which had marked him in times past, executing instead many pleasing aspects of nature addressed to the furnishing householder through the middling critic, and really very good of their kind. In this way he received many large cheques from persons of wealth in England and America, out of which he built himself a sumptuous studio and an awkward house around it, and paid for the education of the growing maidens.

The vision of Somers's humble position as jackal to this lion of a family[3] and house and studio and social reputation – Somers, to whom strange conceits and wild imaginings were departed joys never to return – led Pearston, as the painter's contemporary, to feel that he ought to be one of the bygones likewise, and to put on an air of unromantic bufferism. He refrained from entering Avice's peninsula for the whole fortnight of Somers's stay in the neighbouring town, although its grey poetical outline – "throned along the sea"[4] – greeted his eyes every morn and eve across the roadstead.

When the painter and his family had gone back from their bathing holiday, he thought that he, too, would leave the neighbourhood. To do so, however, without wishing at least the elder Avice good-bye would be unfriendly, considering the extent of their acquaintance. One evening, therefore, knowing this time of day to suit her best, he took the ten-minutes ride thither by the little railway-train, and arrived at Mrs. Pearston's door just after dark.

A light shone from an upper chamber. On asking for his widowed acquaintance he was informed that she was ill, seriously, though not dangerously. While learning that her daughter was with her, and further particulars, and doubting if he should go in, a message was sent down to ask him to enter. His voice had been heard, and Mrs. Pearston would like to see him.

He could not with any humanity refuse, but there flashed across his mind the recollection that Avice the youngest had never really seen him, had seen nothing more of him than an outline, which might have appertained as easily to a man thirty years his junior as to himself, and a countenance so renovated by faint moonlight as fairly to correspond. It was with misgiving, therefore, that the sculptor ascended the staircase and entered the little upper sitting-room, now arranged as a sick chamber.

Mrs. Pearston reclined on a sofa, her face emaciated to a surprising thinness for the comparatively short interval since her attack. "Come in, Sir," she said, as soon as she saw him, holding out her hand. "Don't let me frighten you."

Avice was seated beside her, reading. The girl jumped up, hardly seeming to recognise him. "O! it's Mr. Pearston," she said in a moment, adding quickly, with evident surprise and off her guard: "I thought Mr. Pearston was"—

What she had thought he was did not pass her lips, and it remained a riddle for Pearston until a new departure in her manner towards him showed that the words "much younger" would have accurately ended the sentence. Had Pearston not now confronted her anew, he might have endured philosophically her changed opinion of him. But he was seeing her again, and the rooted feeling of twenty years was revived.

Pearston now learnt for the first time that the widow had been visited by sudden attacks of this sort not infrequently of late years. They were due to some variety of angina pectoris,[5] the latter paroxysms having been the most severe. She was at the present moment out of pain, though weak, exhausted, and nervous. She would not, however, converse about herself, but took advantage of her daughter's absence from the room to broach the subject most in her thoughts.

"Troubles and sickness change our views, Mr. Pearston," she said. "What I felt no great wish for when you first named it, I have hoped for a good deal since; and I have been so anxious; I am glad indeed that you are come."

"My wanting to marry Avice, you mean, dear Mrs. Pearston?"

"Yes – that's it. I wonder if you are still in the same mind? You are, Sir? Then I wish something could be done – to make her agree to it – so as to get it settled. I feel so anxious as to what will become of her. She is not a practical girl as I was – she would hardly like now to settle down as an islander's wife; and to leave her living here alone would trouble me."

"Nothing will happen to you yet, I hope, my dear old friend."

"Well, it is a risky complaint; and the attacks, when they come, are so agonising that to endure them I ought to get rid of all outside anxieties, folk say. Now – do you want her, Sir?"

"With all my soul! But she doesn't want me."

"I don't think she is so against you as you imagine. I fancy if it were put to her plainly, now I am in this state, it might be done."

From this subject they lapsed into conversation on the early days of their acquaintance, until Mrs. Pearston's daughter re-entered the room.

"Avice," said her mother, when the girl had been with them a few minutes. "About this matter that I have talked over with you so many times since my attack. Here is Mr. Pearston, and he wishes to be your husband. He is much older than you; but, in spite of it, that you will ever get a better husband I don't believe. Now, will you take him, seeing the state I am in, and how naturally anxious I am to see you settled before I die?"

"But you won't die, mother! You are getting better!"

"Just for the present only. Come, he is a good man and a clever man, and a rich man. I want you much to be his wife. I can say no more."

Avice looked appealingly at the sculptor, and then on the floor. "Does he really wish me to?" she asked almost inaudibly, turning as she spoke to Pearston. "He has never quite said so to me."

"My dear one, how can you doubt it?" said Pearston, quickly. "But I won't press you to marry me as a favour, against your feelings."

"I thought Mr. Pearston was younger!" she murmured to her mother.

"That counts for little, when you think how much there is on the other side. Think of our position, and of his – a sculptor, with a studio full of busts and statues that I have dusted in my time, and of the beautiful studies you would be able to take up. Surely the life would just suit you? Your education is wasted down here."

Avice did not care to argue. She was gentle as her grandmother had been, and it was just a question of whether she must or must not. "I think I can agree to marry him," she answered quietly, after some thought. "I see that it would be a wise thing to do, and that you wish it and that Mr. Pearston really does – like me. So – so that"—

Pearston was not backward at this critical juncture, despite unpleasant sensations of his own selfishness. But it was the historic ingredient in this genealogical passion – if its continuity through three generations may be so described – which appealed to his perseverance at the expense of his wisdom. The mother was holding the daughter's hand; she took Pearston's, and laid Avice's in it.

No more was said in argument, and the thing was regarded as determined. Afterwards a noise was heard upon the window-panes, as of fine sand thrown; and, lifting the blind, Pearston saw that the distant lightship winked with a bleared and indistinct eye. A drizzling rain had come on with the night. He had intended to walk the two miles back to the station, but it meant a drenching to do it now. He waited and had supper; and, finding the weather no better, accepted Mrs. Pearston's invitation to stay over the night.

The room he occupied was the one he had been accustomed to sleep in as a boy, before his father had made his fortune, and before his own name had been heard of outside the boundaries of the isle.

He slept but little, and in the first movement of the dawn sat up. Why should he ever live in London or any other fashionable city if this plan of marriage could be carried out? Surely, with this young wife, the island would be the best place for him. It might be possible to rent Dell-i'-th'-rock Castle as he had formerly done – better still to buy it. And if life could offer him anything worth having, it would be a home with Avice there on his native cliffs to the end of his days.

As he sat thus thinking, while the light increased, he discerned, a short distance before him, a movement of something ghostly. His position was facing the window, and he found that by chance the looking-glass had swung itself vertical, so that what he saw was his own shape. The person he appeared, by daylight, being chronologically so far in advance of the person he felt himself to be, Pearston did not care to regard that figure who now confronted him so mockingly. But the question of age being pertinent just now, he could not give the object up, and ultimately got out of bed under the weird fascination of the reflection. Whether he had overwalked himself lately, or what he had done, he knew not; but never had he seemed so aged by a score of years as he was represented in the glass in that cold grey morning light. While his soul was what it was, why should he have been encumbered with that withering carcase, without the ability to shift it off for another, as his ideal Well-Beloved had so frequently done?

By reason of her mother's illness Avice was now living in the house, and, on going downstairs, he found that they were to breakfast *en tête-à-tête*. She was not then in the room, but she entered in the course of a few minutes. Pearston had already heard that the widow felt better this morning, and, elated by the prospect of sitting with Avice at this meal, he went forward to her joyously. As soon as she saw him in the full stroke of day from the window she started; and he then remembered that it was their first meeting under the solar rays.

She was so overcome that she turned and left the room for a moment, as if she had forgotten something; when she re-entered she was visibly pale. Indeed, so much was she affected that he thought she was going to faint. She recovered herself, and apologised. She had been sitting up the night before the last, she said, and was not quite so well as usual.

There may have been some partial truth in this; but Pearston could not assure himself upon it. Avice soon grew friendly enough, and seemed inclined to accept matters as they offered. Jocelyn himself, however, could not get over that first start of hers. He ate scarce any breakfast, and, rising abruptly from the table, said he would take a walk on the cliffs as the morning was fine.

He did so, proceeding along the north-east heights for nearly a mile. Should he give her up? His intention had been to go back to the house in half an hour and pay a morning visit to the invalid; but by not returning the plans of the previous evening might be allowed to lapse silently, as mere *pourparlers* that had come to nothing in the face of Avice's want of love for him. Pearston accordingly went straight along, and in the course of three-quarters of an hour was at Slopeway Well, where he entered the train for Budmouth.

Nothing occurred till the evening to inform him of how his flight had been taken. Then a note arrived from Mrs. Pearston; it was written in pencil, evidently as she lay.

"I am alarmed," she said, "at your going so sudden. Avice seems to think she has offended you. She did not mean to do that, I am sure. It makes me dreadfully anxious! Will you send a line? Surely you will not desert us now – my heart is so set on my child's welfare."

"Back I go!" said Pearston, rising from his chair.

CHAPTER XXVII

He Desperately Clutches the Form

It was the little upper room at Mrs. Pearston's, now fitted up as an invalid's chamber, wherein the widow was still reclining. Though she did not sit up, she was well enough to be left alone, and had been occupying herself in sewing pieces of silk together, to form some fantastic article, suggestive of a bazaar bargain or wedding present. This needlework, however, lay neglected beside her now, while, lost in thought, she gazed out of the window at the long up-Channel view which the situation of the house afforded – not intentionally, but because such a prospect was unavoidable.

A rustling and bustling about, audibly proceeding in a neighbouring chamber, together with the invalid's desertion, denoted that something unusual was afoot, absorbing the whole strength of the domicile. Presently the accents of feminine voices, light and excited, mixed in with the rustling movements; and then the door of Mrs. Pearston's room, which had stood ajar, was pushed open, and Avice appeared before her mother's eyes. She smiled as the matron regarded her, and, placing herself at the foot of the couch, stood passively under scrutiny in a charmingly statuesque pose.

"Yes – it does very well," said the mother. "Not too young – not too old."

Avice was dressed for immediate marriage, and well she looked in the habiliments chosen, which had been of a kind to suit the simple style proposed for the ceremony and the bridegroom's maturity. A walking-dress of dove-coloured silk and a bonnet of somewhat similar shade formed the costume, which, despite its prettiness, was, for a bridal adornment, a cruel toning down of youthful charms that would have done justice to the airiest tissues ever woven by art.

Avice's mother inquired if Mr. Pearston had arrived.

"No. . . . Yes – it is he," murmured Avice, as the noise of a vehicle coming round by the wall of Dell-i'-th'-rock increased till it stopped at the door below. In a few minutes footsteps briskly ascended the stairs, and Pearston, wearing a white waistcoat and flower, was shown into the sick-chamber.

He pressed the fingers of the invalid, the hand she gave being light and diaphanous as a falling leaf, as thin as if cut out in paper. Avice, with a curious access of modesty, had stood somewhat behind the door, and she vented a constrained little laugh when he kissed her on the cheek. There was now only time to speak in business-like tones of the formal matters in hand. Mrs. Pearston declared that she wished to be left by herself, since she was unable to go and give her daughter away; gloves were then put on, and the couple descended the stairs. Below they were joined by a few local friends, and soon Mrs. Pearston heard the bridal party go off to the church on the western cliff.

The house sank into sunny silence, disturbed only by the faint noises of the two servants in the kitchen and the chipping and sawing of the quarrymen afar. Mrs. Pearston timed the party's absence by the clock on the mantel – five minutes to get along the crooked road through East Wake, ten minutes longer going across to the west side of the isle of Forne, where the church stood; the service, with entering, signing, and coming out, half an hour, a quarter returning; about one hour altogether.

She had no compunctions about this marriage. She felt perfectly sure that it was the best thing she could do for her girl. Not a young woman in the island but was envying Avice at that moment, for Pearston was still less than three-score – though, to be sure, not much less – a good-looking man as yet, one whose history was generally known here; also the exact figures of the fortune he had inherited from his father, and the social standing he could claim – a standing which that fortune would not have been large enough to procure unassisted by his reputation in his art.

But Avice had been weak enough, as her mother knew, to indulge in fancies for local youths from time to time; and Mrs. Pearston could not help terrifying herself by the picture of a possible return of the wedding party in consternation, declaring Avice recalcitrant at the last moment, and still no wife. Yet to everyone, except, perhaps, Avice herself, Pearston was the most romantic of lovers. Indeed, was there ever such a romance as that man embodied in his relations to her house? Rejecting the first Avice, the second had rejected him, and to decline upon the third with final achievement was an artistic and tender finish to which it was ungrateful in anybody to be blind.

The widow thought that, after all, the second Avice might not have rejected Pearston if destiny had not arranged that she should be secretly united to another when the proposing moment came.

The sunny pattern of the window-panes on the carpet had moved some way onward; fifty-five minutes had passed; the vehicles could be heard returning, and a little colour came into Mrs. Pearston's pale cheek. If it were all right and done, what a success, upon the whole, her life would have been! She who had begun that life as a homely girl, a small quarry-owner's daughter, had sunk to the position of laundress; had engaged in various menial occupations; had made an unhappy marriage for love, which had, however, in the long run much improved her position; was at last to see her daughter established on a good level of affluence and refinement; and yet not as the wife of a "kimberlin," but of one of their own race and sympathies.

There was a flutter downstairs denoting the entry of the returned personages, and she heard them approaching to ascend. Two people were ascending. In a moment or two they entered the room – Pearston and Avice together. Each came forward and kissed her.

"All was got through easily and satisfactorily, without a single hitch!" cried Pearston. "And here we are, a married couple,¹ hastening up to see you!"

"Have you been no worse all the time, mother?" asked Avice, with an anxious waiving of the chief subject.

Mrs. Pearston said she had been quite easy, and as Avice persisted in keeping away from the event just concluded to talk of her mother's ailments, Jocelyn left them together. When he had gone from the room the widow said, "Now I am contented and thankful, my dear. And I hope you are the same."

"O, I have nothing to say against it!" the girl replied. "I suppose it was necessary, and there's an end of it."

"What – don't you like your husband?"

"Yes – I like him well enough."

"Then have a contented mind."

"I have, mother."

The entry of friends put an end to further conversation of this kind, and there followed the usual accompaniments of a simple country wedding. The present tenants of Dell-i'-th'-rock Castle were among the guests, out of respect for Pearston and liking for their gentle governess. In the afternoon the newly married couple drove over the crest of the island, down the long, steep street of Slopeway Well (where they were recognised by nearly everyone), and onward to the railway station at the foot of the hill, whence they started for London.

Pearston had taken a new red Queen Anne house, of the most approved Kensington pattern,[2] with a studio at the back, in which the only noteworthy feature at present was a rope-ladder for ascending to the upper part. After a brief sojourn in the cathedral cities of the north of England they returned to London in early September, to superintend the fitting and furnishing of this residence.

It was a pleasant, reposeful time to be in town. There was nobody to interrupt them in their proceedings, and, it being out of the season, the largest tradesmen were as attentive to their wants as if those firms had never before been honoured with a single customer whom they really liked. The husband and wife, almost equally inexperienced – for the sculptor had nearly forgotten what knowledge of householding he had acquired earlier in life – could consider and practise thoroughly, in their solitude, a species of skeleton-drill in receiving visitors when the pair should announce themselves at home in the coming winter season.

Avice was charming, even if a little cold. He congratulated himself yet more than other people congratulated him. She was somewhat like her mother, whom he had loved in the flesh, but she was the image of her grandmother, whom he had loved in the spirit – and, for that matter, loved now. Only one criticism had he to pass upon his youthful partner: though in outward semblance her grandame's self, she had not the first Avice's candour of heart, but rather her mother's closeness. He never knew exactly what she was thinking and feeling. Yet he seemed to have such prescriptive rights in women of her blood that her occasional want of confidence did not deeply trouble him.

It was one of those ripe and mellow afternoons that sometimes colour London with their golden light at this time of the year, and produce those marvellous sunset effects which, if they were not known to be made up of kitchen coal-smoke and human and animal exhalations, would be rapturously applauded. Behind the perpendicular, oblique, zigzagged, and curved zinc tubes called "tall-boys," that formed a grey pattern not unlike some early Gothic numerals against the sky, the men and women on the tops of omnibuses saw an irradiation of topaz hues, darkened here and there into richest russet.

Inside Pearston's new studio some gleams of the same light managed to creep. There had been a sharp shower during the afternoon, and Pearston, who had to take care of himself, had worn a pair of goloshes on a short walk in the street. He noiselessly entered the studio, where he knew he should find his wife awaiting him with tea. There she was, seated beside the teapot of brown delf, which, as artists, they affected, her back being towards him. She was holding her handkerchief to her eyes, and then he saw that she was weeping silently.

In another moment he perceived that she was weeping over a book. By this time she had heard him, and came forward. He made it appear that he had not noticed her distress, and they discussed some arrangements of furniture. When he had taken a cup of tea, she went away, leaving the book behind her.

Pearston took it up. The volume was an old school-book; Stièvenard's "Lectures Françaises,"[3] with her name in it as a pupil at Budmouth High School, and date-markings denoting lessons taken at a comparatively recent time, for Avice had been but a novice as governess when he discovered her.

For a school-girl – which she virtually was – to weep over a school-book was strange. Could she have been affected by some subject in the readings? Impossible. Pearston fell to thinking, and the bloom went off the process of furnishing, which he had undertaken so gaily. Somehow, the bloom was disappearing from his marriage also. Yet he loved Avice more and more tenderly; he feared sometimes that in the solicitousness of his affection he was spoiling her by indulging her every whim.

He looked round the large and ambitious apartment, now becoming clouded with shades, out of which the white and cadaverous countenances of his studies, casts, and other lumber peered meditatively at him, as if they were saying, "What are you going to do now, old boy?" They had never looked like that while standing in his past homely workshop, where all the real labours of his life had been carried out. What should a man of his age, who had not for years done anything to speak of – certainly not to add to his reputation as an artist – want with a new place like this? It was all because of the young wife, and she apparently did not want him.

CHAPTER XXVIII

He Possesses it: He Possesses it Not

Pearston did not see Avice again till dinner-time. Then, as he observed her nervously presiding over their limited table, he was tempted to say, "Why are you troubled, my little dearest?" in tones which disclosed that he was as troubled as she.

"Am I troubled?" she said, with a start, turning her gentle hazel eyes upon him. "Yes, I suppose I am. It is because I have received a letter – from an old friend – a person who used to be friendly."

"You didn't show it to me."

"No – I tore it up."

"Why?"

"I didn't care to have it – I didn't like it, so I destroyed it."

Pearston did not press her further on the subject, and she showed no disposition to continue it. Avice retired rather early that evening, and her husband went along the passage to the studio, ostensibly to consider further how the fittings should be arranged. There he remained pacing up and down a long while, musing deeply on many things, not the least being the perception that to wed a woman is by no means the same as to be united with her. His wife's corporeal frame was upstairs: where her spiritual part lurked he could not tell.

At eleven o'clock he ascended also, and softly opened the chamber door. Within he paused a moment. Avice was asleep, and his intent ear caught a sound of a little gasping sigh every now and then between her breathings. When he moved forward his light awoke her; she started up as if from a troublous dream, and regarded him with something in her open eye and large pupils that was not unlike dread. It was so unmistakable that Pearston felt half paralysed, coming, as it did, after thoughts not too assuring; and, placing his candle on the table, he sat down on the couch at the foot of the bed. All of a sudden he felt that he had no moral right to go further.' He had no business there.

He stayed and stayed, sitting there in his dressing-gown till the candle had burnt low; she became conscious of his silence, and said, "You rather startled me when you came in."

"I am sorry," said Pearston, "you looked as if you didn't like my coming."

"Did I? I didn't know that."

"Avice, I am going to tell you something, if you are not too sleepy."

"O, no, I am not sleepy."

"I was once your mother's lover, and wanted to marry her – only she wouldn't, or couldn't, marry me."

"How very strange!" said Avice, now thoroughly awake. "Mother has never told me that. Yet, of course you might have been – you are quite old enough."

"O, yes, quite old enough!" he said grimly. "Almost too old."

"Too old for poor mother?" she said musingly. "How's that?"

"Because I rightly belonged to your grandmother."

"No! How can that be?"

"I was her lover likewise. I should have married her if I had gone straight on instead of round the corner."

"But you couldn't, Jocelyn? You are not old enough? Why, how old are you? – you have never told me."

"I am very old."

"My mother's, and my grandmother's," said she, looking at him no longer as at a husband, or even a friend; but as at a strange fossilised relic in human form. Pearston saw this; but he did not mean to spare himself. In a sudden access of remorse he was determined to pursue this to the bitter end – carried on by a wave of revolt against the curse of never being allowed to grow old.

"Your mother's and your grandmother's lover," he repeated.

"And were you my great-grandmother's too?" she asked, with an expectant interest that had overcome her personal feeling as his wife.

"No; not your great-grandmother's." He winced at that question, unreflectingly as it had been put, perceiving that his information, superadded to her previous sentiments, had already operated damagingly. He went on, however, to repeat with a dogged calm: "But I am very old."

"I did not know it was so much!" she said, in an appalled murmur. "You do not look so, and I thought that what you looked you were."

"No; I am *very* old," he unnecessarily reiterated. "And you – you are very young."

A silence followed, his candle burnt still lower; he was waiting for her to sleep, but she did not. Amid so much difference in their accidents there was much resemblance in their essentials; he was as sympathetically nervous as she, and the mere air itself seemed to bring him the knowledge that she lay in a state of tension which was indescribably more distressing than pain.

He knew that his cause was lost with her by his exaggerating their contrasts. The verge of division, on which they long had trembled, she had at last crossed. Pearston noiselessly arose, took up his candle, and went out of the room. He had an impression that he might never again enter that chamber.

He lay down in an adjoining room, and instead of sleeping tried again to conjecture what had disturbed Avice, and, through her, himself, so much as to drive him to court disaster. There seemed to be something uncanny about London in its effect upon his marriage. He began to hate the grimy city and his new house and his new studio, and to wish he had not re-established himself so elaborately there. The momentary defiance of his matrimonial fate which had led him to speak as he had done in his wife's room now passed away, and he hoped again.

To take her back to his and her own native spot for a few weeks seemed the most promising course for shaking off this nightmare which sat upon them here. Her mother's persuasive powers might reconcile Avice to her new position when nothing else would, notwithstanding the unfortunate indiscretion of which in his despair he had been guilty, that of revealing his past attachments. A good practical reason for their return thither existed in the incomplete condition of their house-furnishing here, and in the still unmending state of his mother-in-law. Dell-i'-th'-rock Castle was now, unfortunately, occupied by a permanent tenant, but there were some lodgings near which he thought he might easily obtain.

When he encountered Avice the next morning there was a trace of surprise in her face, but the distant, apprehensive look had not altogether departed. Yet he would have sacrificed everything – his artistic reputation itself – to give her pleasure. He feared that the conversation of the previous night had established her to regard him as a fearful curiosity; but regrets were too late now. He disclosed his proposition to run down to their old place.

"When?" she asked.

"Soon. Say to-day. I don't like being here among these packing-cases, and the quicker we get away the better."

"I shall be glad to go," she said. "Perhaps mother is not so well, and I should like to be near her."

Whatever had upset her, then, it had nothing to do with locality. Pearston thereupon gave sufficient directions for the further garnishing of his town house, and in the afternoon they set out for the south-west by the familiar railway. Pearston stopped at Budmouth for that night, sending on his wife to her mother's home in the isle, where he promised to join her the next day.

(To be continued.)

It was the first time they had slept under different roofs since their marriage; and when she was gone, and the charm of her personality was idealised by lack of the substance, he felt himself far less able to bear the thought of an estrangement than when her corporeal presence afforded trifling marks for criticism. And yet, concurrently, the conviction grew that, whatever the rights with which the civil law had empowered him, by no law of nature, of reason, had he any right to partnership with Avice against her evident will.

The next day he set out for the island, longing, yet dreading, to see her again. No sooner had he reached the top of the hill and passed the forking of the ways than he discerned in the distance, on the way he had not taken, a form which was unmistakably that of his wife, apparently out on some trifling errand. To go back, take the other road, and join her lest she should miss him, was the obvious thing to do; yet he stood like one enervated, will-bereft, and ashamed. As he stood a man came up, and, noticing his fixity, regarded him with attention.

"A tidy little figure-of-fun that, Sir," said the man.

"Yes. A dainty little creature, like a fairy. . . . Now, would you assert, my friend, that a man has a right to force himself into her presence at all times and seasons, to sit down at her table, to take her hither and thither – all against her liking?"

"No, sure."

"I thought so. And yet a man does it; for he has married her."

"Oh! She's his wife! That's a hoss of another colour. Ha, ha, ha!"

"I don't think it is," said Pearston.

The pedestrian disappeared, and Pearston, still glancing across the quarries at the diverging road, saw that Avice had perceived him, and was standing still, expecting his approach. He climbed over the low side-wall and traversed the open ground to her side. Her young face showed anxiety, and he knew that something had happened.

"I have been looking for you," she said. "I didn't exactly know the time you were coming, or I should have sent somebody to meet the train. Mother has suddenly got so much worse: it seems almost as though my coming had caused it, but it cannot be that, of course, because she is so glad. I am afraid – I am so much afraid she may not live! The change in her has quite shocked me. You would hardly know her. And she has kept it from us that she was not so well, because she would not disturb our happiness. Happiness!"

The last word might have been construed in its relation to her mother or to herself. Pearston was in a mood to suffer anything now, and he did not mind which way she had intended it. They hastened onward together – that is, side by side – with a lineal yard between them, for she was never too ready to take his arm; and soon reached the house at East Wake.

Mrs. Pearston the elder was evidently sinking. The hand she gave him, which had formerly been as thin as a leaf, was now but a cobweb. She was mentally quite at ease, and murmured to him that it was her great comfort and thankfulness to feel that her child was well provided for in the possession of such a good and kind husband.

Avice, her daughter, could not leave the house at night in such circumstances, and, no room being ready for the reception of them as a couple, Pearston left his wife by her mother's side and went out to a lodging near at hand; accident thus making easy of continuance the constraint in their relations which had begun in London.

CHAPTER XXIX

The Elusiveness Continues

Pearston felt that he certainly had tried to be good and kind to the little sylphlike thing he called his wife. He had been uniformly attentive and courteous, had presented her with every pretty trifle and fancy in the shape of art-works, jewellery, clothing, furniture, that money could buy; had anticipated her every wish and whim in other ways. But whether the primal act of marrying her had been goodness and kindness was open to question.

The mother's life was prolonged but a very few days after this; and they buried her[1] not far from the spot where Avice the First had been laid, in that old churchyard over the western cliffs, which was like a miniature forest of oolite, the plethora of freestone in the locality placing a carved memorial within the reach of all. It seemed to Pearston but a season or two earlier that he had stood there in the dusk after the first interment, when the vision of the then daughter appeared, to pull him back to youth anew.

This sad office being performed he hastened up to town, leaving Avice in her mother's late residence, which they now adopted as their own country cottage. She liked remaining there, she said, and, having taken care that she should have every attention, he did not hurry back to her side. A feeling which many people might have called Quixotic was acquiring such strength in him as to make future relations with his charming prize a perplexing problem to a man whose pursuits had taught him to regard impressions and sentiments as more cogent than legal rights,[2] and humours as more cogent than reasons.

It was, therefore, not until nearly a month had passed – during which he had endeavoured to stifle his disappointment at being only the nominal protector of Avice by attending to many long-neglected things – that he found himself one evening at the seaport whence the run into the peninsula was by a short line of railway. Nine o'clock, however, had struck, and the last train had left twenty minutes earlier. He felt stiff and chilly with sitting in the London train so long, and, telegraphing to Avice to expect him late, resolved to walk to her home by the old road, which he had not pursued for many, many years, and which now lay bleached by the moonlight.

His course was over the bridge and through the old town, afterwards skirting the cliffs, till there arose on his left hand, gaunt and bare against the sea, the Tudor castle ruins where he had met his own particular third Avice some time ago, the second Avice earlier; where he would have met the first, and, but for chance, have shaped for himself and the two others a different history. He duly crossed the long framed and braced wooden bridge, its whiteness intensified now by the rays, after which there lay before him the long, featureless road within the pebble barrier that screened it from the outer sea. The bay within lifted and dropped placidly under the moon; the pebble bank ran straight ahead, diminishing in a haze, above which swelled the vast rock that the line of pebbles seemed to tether. It was the place, unchanged almost, that he had traversed in the rain beside the woman whom he had rashly married in his first youth and inexperience.

He had reached about halfway between the island and the main shore when a black spot appeared by the road in front of him, hitherto absolutely deserted. Drawing forward, he found the object to be only the figure of a man sitting upon the bank, his face towards the moonlight. This was strong enough to show Pearston as he passed by that his fellow-pedestrian was a young man of apparently five-and-twenty, with a curly dark moustache. Pearston said "Good-night!" and a reply was returned to him in an accent which was not that of an Englishman. Moreover, the voice was faint and shaken. Pearston halted.

"I hope you are not ill," he said.

"I am unwell," said the foreigner.

"Going my way?"

"Yes."

"Then let me help you onward."

He approached and assisted the stranger, who rose with some difficulty. He was a well-dressed, gentlemanly young fellow, and beside where he had been sitting a white handkerchief lay upon the dry pale pebbles, the handkerchief being stained with what appeared to be blood.

"Have you been coughing?" said Pearston.

"No. I crossed this morning from Havre, and the sea-sickness brought on a slight hæmorrhage. It is not serious."

"I am not so sure about that," said Pearston.

He took the young man's arm, and together they pursued the remainder of the level way to the foot of the isle, where began the little town of Slopeway Well.

"How do you feel now?" Pearston asked. "Can I take you to any house or person?"

"No, no; I thank you," the stranger replied. "I have lodgings here, which I secured by letter; but I missed the train, or I should have been in them by this time. I am much better now, and require no more attention. For that you have given me receive my deepest thanks and courtesies."

"Well, accept my stick, at any rate – you will get along better, if it is only a few steps."

This the young man did, and they parted. There was not a fly left at the station, and, seeing that he would have to walk the remainder of the distance, Pearston entered an inn a few yards up the street to get some simple refreshment by which he might fortify himself for the ascent. When he came out the young man had disappeared.

It was a pleasure indeed to Pearston when, drawing near to the house which was now again his own dear home, he beheld a little figure standing against the door, and presumably awaiting him. Avice, for it was she, dutifully allowed him to kiss her when he reached her side, though her nervousness, only too apparent, was that of a child towards a parent who may prove stern.

While seated indoors at a supper of a more appetising character than the inn had supplied, he became aware that Avice had left the room. Thinking that she had gone upstairs to supervise preparations for his accommodation, he sat on quietly musing and sipping his glass for something like half an hour. Wondering then, for the first time, what had become of her, he rose suddenly and began looking around. She was quite near him, after all; only standing at the front door as she had been doing when he arrived, gazing into the moonlight. But she was agitated now, unmistakably.

"What is it?" he asked.

"I must go and see somebody who is ill – I feel I ought to go! And yet – as you have just come – I suppose you don't approve of my going out."

"Who is the person?"

She did not give any name. "Somebody down that way," she said indefinitely. "I only heard of it just now. It is not very far to the house."

"If you really wish to go, my dear, of course I don't object. I will sit and await your coming back, if you prefer to go alone."

Avice replied by instantly taking advantage of the offer – putting on a hat and cloak and starting forthwith. In leaving him she glanced at him for a moment, as if expecting him to ask a further question. But Pearston refrained.

He continued alone, thinking how entirely her manner was that of one to whom a question of doing anything was merely a question of permission and not of judgment. When she had been gone some little while, he observed that it was getting rather late. How absurd of her, he thought, not to let him accompany her at such an hour! At length, in a state bordering on irritation, he rose, and went out to look for her.

There was no sign of her returning along the road, though he strolled on so far as to the bend round by the north entrance of Dell-i'-th'-rock Castle. Reaching that entrance he stood still under the trees and wall, being unsure by which way to expect her, and the spot commanding the length of the village street or highway.

He was not aware how entirely invisible he had been standing till he perceived two figures – one a man, walking by the aid of a stick, the other a woman, from whom the man also derived some assistance. The place was deserted, and their voices could be heard, though not the words they were saying. The man spoke in a French accent, and he was obviously the young invalid whom Pearston had assisted along the shore.

The woman was weeping. Her accents were so low and the fact was so far from his expectation that Pearston did not at first dream of her being his wife. Then he had a suspicion, and, as they had turned the corner, he felt justified in following them.

They passed at the same slow pace down the lane or gorge leading to the old castle ruins. A heart-sickness had well-nigh prostrated the unhappy Pearston by this time: he was no nearer to the third Avice than he had been to the second and the first.

They reached the corner of the Red King's Castle, where there were some large blocks of loose rock, carved with the initials of natives of past generations. "Do you think it well to go farther?" asked the woman, as if she were anxious that he should return.

"I fear I cannot," he said.

Pearston was now sure that Avice was the young man's companion, and standing under the sheer face of the rock he found that it reflected their words.

"Why did you come, after being away so long? How could I help thinking you had given up all wish to – do what we planned, and had decided to stay in your own country?"

The wind interfered for a moment; then he heard her repeat, like a wounded bird, "Why did you come, Henri, after being absent so long, and bring me and yourself into such trouble as this?"

Her notes of anguish so moved Pearston that he sank his jealousy in pity of her. Whatever had happened, it had been against her will and expectation.

She soon remarked anxiously that she could not stay longer, and begged her companion to seek the rest he needed. Pearston was obliged to remain where he was till they had gone past.

"I am sorry I have no right to offer you shelter in my house," she said. "But it is not because my husband is come that I may not do this. I feel I must not – ought not – even though you are so ill as to make it almost inhuman! O, it is hard for you, Henri: but what can I do!"

"It is not necessary. I have a lodging quite near, where I can stay till tomorrow, and then I can get back to the station; and then – I will see you no more – if it is your command."

"It is – it must be," said she.

They crept slowly back as far as to the north entrance of Dell-i'-th'-rock, where their ways parted.

"Then I sha'n't see you again?" he said, facing her, and leaning on Pearston's stick.

"How can you!"

"I see your reason well enough, but it is no consolation to me. What a blow! Who could expect it? To come so far, and to be so disappointed! You broke an implicit promise, Avice, even if not a verbal one!"

"Don't reproach me, Henri! My poor mother— There, don't let us talk of it. I couldn't have married you, dear. It would have grieved my mother so. There, I am going! Can you really walk back?"

Perhaps he kissed her – more than once; perhaps he did not. There were sniffings and sighings at least, and the young man went along the north road. Avice stood awhile watching his feeble gait; then, as if she could bear it no longer, walked wildly towards her own house.

CHAPTER XXX

He Becomes Retrogressive

Meanwhile, Pearston had entered the gate of the new castle precincts, and, knowing the grounds well, hastened across them inside the wall to the gate opening near their dwelling. He had just time to slip over the way and reach the porch before she arrived round by the regular road.

"Where have you been so long, Avice?" sternly asked the man of nine-and-fifty.

"I will tell you," said Sweet-and-Twenty, with breathless humility. "I have kept you up, haven't I? And you so tired! I could not help it, as you will say when I explain."

She accompanied him indoors, sat down without removing her hat or cloak, and went on to him, as he seated himself opposite. "I have been crying; you can see that, I dare say." While he regarded, she could not repress renewed tears. "It has happened in this way. Just before you arrived, a young man, whom I had not seen for two years, wrote to me saying he was coming to the island to claim me. He – he had been my lover" (here Avice's delicate lip and chin quivered) "when he lived here in England. But I thought – he had deserted me . . . However, he came, not knowing that I – that I – was m–married; not wishing to be seen by anybody till he had found out if I was faithful, he sent a boy with a message; and my name being still Pearston, he did not discover I could not be his, and I had to go out to him and tell him. He had been taken very unwell in crossing, and has not yet recovered, because the sea-sickness caused him some internal bleeding." She continued, sobbing outright: "I wish – he could see a doctor!"

"He shall see a doctor. I'll send one to him at his lodging, if you'll tell me where that is."

"It is at the Green Mermaid."

"How did you get to know this young man originally?" asked Nine-and-Fifty.

"He was the French master at B–B–Budmouth two or three years ago," Twenty replied; "and I learnt of him, and"—

"Fell in love with him."

"I suppose I did. But he did with me – first!"

"And why, in the name of common-sense, didn't you marry him before ever you saw me?"

"We would have married! Only mother thought – she was quite wrong – she thought that as he was penniless and I should have a little money he wanted me on that account. And she didn't like the idea of my marrying a foreigner. Then he went away to his own country to see his friends and get them to help him, so that he might be no poorer than I. They, too, objected to his marrying. He then wrote to say he would not bind me, but if he did get rich and independent he would let me know. As he didn't get richer, he was too honourable to write to me."

"Why did he come back, then?"

"He said he couldn't help it, because he kept thinking of me!" she murmured. "I wish he hadn't come! But I am rightly punished for thinking he could ever forget me! . . . There was not time for me to hinder his coming, and he didn't know how matters were till we stood face to face."

Pearston could not help picturing the scene of the meeting of the two young things and the moment of her sad announcement, under the light of the moon.

"He'll go away to-morrow," she pleaded, "and I shall never see him any more! I hope you'll forgive me, Sir. I am sure not to see him again, because – because, if he reaches home alive, he'll soon die!"

Avice had spoken with great self-command up to this moment, but her firmness gave way, and she burst into a violent fit of weeping.

"I can't – help crying – I know I ought not to – but I loved him very much, and he loved me! And I didn't know he would come again!"

Pearston himself was affected to tears by her utter misery. The results of this marriage were beginning to be bad enough for him; but his was, at worst, a negative grief. To her it was direct and terrible. He took her hand. She had been so frank in her speech, and honourable in her conduct, that he was on her side as against himself.

"I do not blame you at all, dear one," he said. "You would be justified in eloping with him, after such a trial. . . . I wish I could mend all this misery I have caused so unintentionally by my persistence in a cruel blunder."

"I'll try – not to mind, Sir; and I'll do everything I can to forget him – as I ought to do, I know. I could have done it better if he had not been taken ill. O! do you think he'll die?"

"No, no. You must not trouble about that, my child. We'll get the best advice for him if a doctor becomes necessary. I'll go and see him this very night or to-morrow morning. What is he like? Have you a photograph? You have, for certain!"

"I had one; but I destroyed it the day before I married you, because I thought it was not well to keep it."

"Suppose you had never seen me, do you think you would have married him now, since he has come back?"

"O, you can guess well enough – if he had not been too ill! And if he had been too ill I should have nursed him – seeing how he is alone here, without a friend; all because of me!"

"You shall nurse him now. Your having married me need not make any difference at all."

Pearston's sense of his cruelty grew so strong that he could not help kissing her forehead in pure sympathy, as if she were a child under his care. Then he hastily went out – to smoke and think, he told her.

In the open space before the house he walked up and down, the prospect eastward being bounded by the distance-line of the sea; so faintly and delicately drawn, yet the most permanent of features in the prospect. On the other side of him rose the front of his wife's home. There was now a light in her chamber-window, showing that she had retired for the night. The longer he looked the less was he able to escape the conviction that he was the kill-joy of that young life. To any man it would have been an uneasy consideration; to him it was a double and treble gloom of responsibility; for this life was the quintessence of his own past life, the crowning evolution of the idea expressed by the word "Avice," typifying the purest affection it had ever been his lot to experience.

It was certainly an age of barbarism[1] in which he lived; since, whatever were his honest wish to right this ill matter, he could not do it. More, a formal legal ceremony gave him the power at this moment, or at any other, to force his presence upon that suffering girl.

Instead of re-entering Pearston walked along the few hundred yards to the Green Mermaid. A light, too, was in an upper room of the small inn. He wondered if it were Henri's bed-room, and entered the house, though it was on the point of being closed.

To his inquiry of the landlord, a home-come sailor, if a gentleman had taken a room there, an affirmative was returned. "A French gent – Mr. Mons Leverre – him as used to teach in Budmouth. He's badish wi' his stomach, and had to go to bed. We be going to take 'en up a cup of cocoa."

"Will you ask him if he can see me? Tell him I am a friend – that's all."

The sailor went upstairs, and on returning said that Mr. Mons Leverre would be glad to see him. Pearston found his way to the chamber where poor young "Mons" (as he had used to be called in Budmouth, from the appearance of his name on the doorplate) welcomed him feebly from his pillow. A handsome young man with a silken moustache and black curly hair, he seemed little more than Avice's age, though he was probably older, his large anxious eyes and nervous temperament subtracting

somewhat from his years. Having resided in this country with few inter-
ruptions since he was fifteen, his English was nearly as good as Pearston's.

"I come as a friend," said the latter. "We met an hour or two ago, if
you remember. I am the husband of Avice Pearston. Don't start or disturb yourself. I bear you no ill-will, my lad, on that account. I have only
come to inquire how you feel."

The young man confusedly replied that he had felt better since lying
down, and his visitor said that he would send a doctor on the morrow, if
only for his own satisfaction.

"But, Sir: why should you be anxious about me?"

"Never mind that. Now tell me frankly – Did you come from your own
country on purpose to see Avice?"

"Yes; but, Heaven! I didn't know my Avice was a wife! I came to marry
her!" He turned his face away to the wall, and murmured to himself his
regrets.

"Well, don't think too much of that just at present. If you would like to
see her again she shall come with me to-morrow."

"You are very kind!" cried the young man, turning back to Pearston
and seizing his hand. "Let me see her once – once only! I would not wish
to see her but once! I shall be well in a day or two. I shall leave. I will
never inconvenience you or her, Sir, any more afterwards."

Pearston bade him compose himself, ensured that he should be well attended to, and paced back sadly to his own house, where he glanced up at
the window-blind that had been illuminated when he left. It was in darkness now. He strained his eyes back towards the inn: that, too, was dark.
How wrong it was that there should stand a barrier, hard as the stone isle
itself, between a heart in that house and a heart in this!

Having entered he wrote a note to the local surgeon, asking him to call
at the Green Mermaid in the morning, and left it on the hall table with a
direction that it should be delivered early. Then he went softly upstairs,
and listened at the door of her room. She was not asleep, and he heard
her gasp and start when he accidentally brushed against the handle.
Pearston moved onward to the adjoining chamber, and what he sighed to
himself might have been aptly paraphrased by two lines from "Troilus
and Cressida" –

> I had good argument for kissing once,
> But that's no argument for kissing now.[2]

Why should he not play the benign giant to these two dwarfs, as they were in their emotional history, with its one little year of love-tempest to his forty years of the same? Because by that act of charity he would break the laws and ordinances.

(To be continued.)

CHAPTER XXXI

The Magnanimous Thing

It was in the full sunshine of next morning that the mock-married couple walked towards the inn. Avice looked up fearfully at her husband from time to time. She could not understand her lord and master in any other character than that of lording and mastering her. Her father's bearing towards her mother had been only too often of that quality.

When they were reaching the inn-door the surgeon appeared on the threshold, coming out. Pearston said to his wife: "Henri Leverre is to be spoken of as a friend of ours, mind. Nobody will suspect your former relations."

On inquiry the doctor informed them that his patient was restless. The hæmorrhage was from the stomach – the direct result of sea-sickness on predisposing conditions. He would have to be taken care of, and with such care there was no reason why the malady should recur. He could bear removal, and ought to be removed to a quieter place.

The young man was sitting up in bed gazing dreamily through the window at the stretch of quarries and cranes it commanded. At sight of Avice behind Pearston he blushed painfully. Avice blushed with equal distress; and her husband went and looked out of the window.

When he turned his head the sorely tried pair had recovered some apparent equanimity. She had, in fact, whispered to her lover: "My husband knows everything. I told him – I felt bound to do so! He trusts us, assuming that we have no other intention but to part for ever; and we must act up to his expectations."

The conversation of the three was impersonal and flat enough: on the state of France, on the profession of teachers of languages. Yet Pearston could not resist an interest in the young man, which deepened every moment. He was a transparency, a soul so slightly veiled that the outer shaped itself to the inner like a tissue. At one moment he was like the poet Keats, at another like Andrea del Sarto.[1] The latter, indeed, seemed to have returned to earth in him, the same poetry of mien being set amid the same weaknesses.

In a solicitude for Henri Leverre which was almost paternal Jocelyn could well-nigh sink his grief at being denied the affection of Avice. That afternoon he obtained quiet lodgings for the young man in a house across the way, and had him removed thither.

Every day Pearston visited the patient here, sometimes taking Avice with him, though she always shrank from the ordeal. To all outward seeming, Pearston was making a mistake by acting thus; but his conduct, begun in waywardness as a possible remedy by surfeit for the malady of the two unhappy ones, had been continued on other grounds, arising from sympathy with them during the process.

"You think his recovery may now be reckoned on?" he said to the doctor one day.

"Yes – from the hæmorrhage. But mentally he is not at rest. He is unhappy, and that keeps him back. Something worries or grieves him. These foreigners are much given to that. I gather that he has quarrelled with his parents, and the thought of it may depress him."

It suddenly struck Pearston that Avice had begun to look wan and leaden-eyed. He met her only at meals and during walks, on which occasions she always looked up at him with misgiving, as if his plan of never obtruding himself upon her were the illusive beginning of some terrible scheme of vengeance upon her for loving illegally.

He was, in fact, pondering a scheme.

But the scheme which Pearston pondered was of a very different nature from any sultanic determination to bring punishment upon the head of his unhappy bride.

After casting about desperately for relief to his lately awakened natural or moral sense, which began to be oppressed by the present most improper situation ruling between himself and Avice – licensed as it might be by engrossings, fees, stamps and ceremonies – he had come to a conclusion. He could not wean her by surfeit of the sick man; that was obvious. And with the loss of this woman, his third Avice, he had not much left in his life to care for. Pleasant illusions had one by one been dissipated;

he could see the black framework[2] where the flaring jets of the illumination had once dazzled his eyes; and the chief satisfaction remaining to him now was that a man finds in setting his house in order before departure.

Pearston was an artist, not a moralist, and his plan was characteristic of his nature. It was based on the idea of resuscitating his first wife, Marcia, in spirit and seeming, since he had never received definite tidings of her decease. Thirty years of silence had left him and others no moral doubt of her death, but he had never received legal testimony[3] of the event. It was by the channel of escape this offered him that he proposed to restore his Avice, whom he loved better than himself, to approximate happiness. Since his marriage with her was a farce, why not treat it as a farce by playing another to match it?

Coming down to breakfast one morning as usual he found Avice awaiting him with that forlorn and hopeless smile of greeting upon her face which cut his heart like a lash; and he was stimulated to take the first step in her deliverance.

"As our relations are not what – I hoped they might have been," he said as he sat down, "the news I have to tell you will not disturb your mind so much as may be expected by other people. You will remember, of course, how before our marriage we went into the question of my first wife Marcia's existence, and decided that it was quite impossible she should be living, though she was never proved to be dead."

"Yes," murmured Avice. And thereupon a strange light seemed to rise and colour her face, such as sometimes comes over a landscape when there are no direct rays to cause it. O, the quickness of thought! It was the hope of release.

"I have reason to think the probability insufficient. That I ought to ascertain her death beyond shadow of doubt. I am going to send telegrams to the Western States of America and elsewhere, directing search for her by advertisement. I shall probably start thither myself soon – journeying first to Salt Lake City. If I find her I shall never come back – never!"

A pause succeeded, in which the noises of their breakfasting seemed obtrusive.

"If you – don't find her?" said Avice then.

"I shall never come back in that case either."

She gazed up at him.

"In any case I will send you directions what to do. You will go on living here on your own freehold, of course, till you hear from me. Not living alone: I will find some suitable companion for you. . . . And, when you find you are no wife of mine, you must promise me one thing: to marry that lover of yours. He will soon recover, and I will make it worth his while to wed you, in every sense."

"But I may not find I am no"—

"I am certain – from premonitions and other perceptions, which I will not enter into now – I am morally certain that you will find yourself free. What I more precisely wish you to promise is to marry Henri promptly, without delay, immediately that you find yourself free."

"I do promise," she said humbly.

Notwithstanding the wilfully conjectural basis of the proposition Pearston seemed to take it as a definite scheme which would work itself out in fact, and work out well. He seemed to possess, concealed in his mind, certain means of effectuation beyond mere chances.

"Now go and tell the sick man what has been the subject of our talk," he added kindly.

"You will go with me, Sir?"

"No, not this time. You may go alone now."

In about an hour she returned, looking flushed with a startling, dreadful sense of ecstasy. She seemed trying to hide from herself the reason why. What ground had her husband for this sudden conviction? He must have had letters.

He met her at the door, where a fly was standing. "I am going up to town again for a few days," he said. "On my way through Budmouth I will get a quiet young person I know of there to come and stay with you. Good-bye!"

Pearston entered the fly. Opposite the door of Henri's lodgings he stopped and inquired how Mr. Leverre was.

"He's wonderful improved since Mrs. Pearston called. I went up just after, and his face had quite a colour – quite healthy like."

Whether the woman thought it odd that Mrs. Pearston should have been able to come and produce this mental effect, Jocelyn did not care to ascertain, and, re-entering the vehicle, drove on.

CHAPTER XXXII

The Pursuit Abandoned

His return was delayed till eighteen or twenty days had passed, and on his way back over the isle to Avice's house he drew up at Leverre's lodgings as he had done on his departing journey. The young man was in the parlour reading. He appeared bright, and advanced in convalescence. After Pearston's preliminary inquiries the young man with almost childish ingenuousness of motive said, "Have you heard, Sir, of"—

"I have still further evidence that Avice will soon be free."

"A formal decree of nullity will be necessary to complete her freedom?"

"No, no. I think not – in this particular case. I don't go back to her home to live any more. I stay in these lodgings for a day or two, and will have my things sent here. Your landlady has probably told you that I wrote to her, and that she has let to me the parlour opposite to this for the few days I shall be here in the isle before starting for good."

"You have had more specific information, Sir?"

"I have almost indubitable proof that – Avice will be free before long. I shall rejoin my wife as soon as I reach my journey's end. I know, beyond any moral doubt, where she is."

"You do, Sir! Where?"

"I won't say, for certain reasons. But I am going there."

"Salt Lake City?"

"No – not Salt Lake City. . . . You know, Henri," he continued after a pause, and his lower lip quivered as he spoke, "if Avice had loved me, as I foolishly thought she might get to do, I should have – turned up no old stones to hide under. But she loved you, I found; and to me healthy natural instinct is true law, and not an Act of Parliament. So I sheer off."

Leverre looked anxious for clearer explanations, but he did not question further. Pearston – whose worn and dried-up face now fully indexed his age, and indeed more than his age, continued calmly –

"Henri – as I may call you – I wish, as you will believe, above all things that Avice may be happy in spite of this unfortunate marriage with me. She is the outcome of my own emotional life, as I may say. There is no doubt that it is within her power to be so. In addition to her own little competency, a large sum of money – a fortune, in short – has been settled upon her within the last few days, and upon any possible children of hers. With that, and her beauty, she'll soon be snapped up by some worthy man who pities her abnormal position."

"Sir, I love her – I love her dearly. Has she said anything to lead you to think her husband will be other than myself?"

"It depends upon you."

"She will not desert me?"

"If she has promised not to. Haven't you asked her?"

"Not as yet. She would not have listened if I had. She is nominally your wife as yet: and it seems premature – too venturesome, daring, to hope, to think, that this idea you have suggested to us will be borne out by fact. I have never known anything like it – can hardly believe it!"

"You will see," said the now aged man. "Are you afraid to give an undertaking on the contingency? If she becomes free, you will be her husband if she consents?"

"I have said so," he replied fervently.

"You may set about your preparations at once," said Pearston, with forced gaiety. "I go to join my truant wife of thirty years ago."

"O that you may find her!"

"That's right. Express your feelings honestly. I like young men who do so."

That night Pearston sat down and wrote a long letter to the only old friend he had in the world, among so many acquaintances – Alfred Somers, the landscape-painter –

> "My dear Somers –
> "You in your evenly flowing life will be surprised to hear of what has been taking place in my rugged one – inwardly rugged, I mean, which is the true ruggedness."

He thereupon proceeded to give a succinct account of what had happened since his marriage with Avice, of which event Somers was aware, having, in fact, been invited to the ceremony, though he had not found it possible to come. First, the coldness of his young wife, which he had supposed it to be a mere question of time to displace; his lack of any suspicion that in such a remote and quiet existence she had learnt the trick of having a lover before she was eighteen years old; his discovery of his mistake through the return of the young man to claim her, and the whole incidents which followed.

"Now," proceeded Pearston, "some husbands, I suppose, would have sent the young man about his business and put the young woman under lock-and-key till she came to her senses. This was what I could not do. At first I felt it to be a state of things for which there was no remedy. But I considered that to allow everything to remain *in statu quo* was in-animate, unhuman conduct, worthy only of a vegetable. It was not only being indifferent to my own poor scrap of future happiness, which mat-tered little, but to hers. And I soon entered with interest, and even with zest, into an apparently, though not really, wild scheme, which has re-commended itself to me. This is no less than assuming the existence of my wife Marcia, of whose death, as you know, there has never been ab-solute proof, unless you consider that not having heard her voice for more than thirty years to be absolute proof of the death of a termagant spouse. Cases of this kind, if you analyse them, turn on very curious points. My marriage with Avice is valid if I have a reasonable belief in my first wife's death. Now, what man's belief is fixed, and who shall enter into my mind and say what my belief is at any particular time? The moment I have a reasonable belief that Marcia lives Avice is not my wife, it seems to me. I have only therefore to assume that belief and dis-appear, and she is free. That is what I have decided to do.

"Don't attack me for casuistry,' artifice, for contumelious treatment of the laws of my country. A law which, in a particular instance, results in physical cruelty to the innocent deserves to be evaded in that instance if it can be done without injury to anyone. I want the last of the three women, the last embodiment of Avice, to be happy at any cost, and this is the only way of making her so, that I can see. The only detail in my plan that I feel sorry for having been compelled to adopt is the sending of bogus telegrams and advertisements, to prevent my darling's sus-picion of unreality. Poor child! but it is for her good.

"During the last three weeks I have been arranging my affairs, and shall now disappear for ever from England. My life probably will not be long anywhere, it cannot be very long in the nature of things, and it mat-ters very little where I say my *Nunc Dimittis*.

"I shall probably find some kind and simple old nurse body or house-keeper on the other side of the Atlantic, whom I can ask to share my home, and call her Marcia, so as to make it all seem right if any intelligence of my state of existence should be wafted across to this side. To clinch the pious fraud I may think it worth while to send the child Avice a cabinet photograph of this old soul and myself in one picture, in which I appear standing behind her chair with my hand on her shoulder, in the orthodox fashion of the irrevocably united.

"Destroy this document, for Avice's sake.

"My sincere regard and affection to you and all your household.

"J. P."

This was duly posted by himself that evening in the little letter-box in the village square.

He went home to bed. Everything was done, even to the packing of his portmanteau. Nothing remained for him but to depart – to an exile on one of the four quarters of the globe, telegraph that he had found the lost one, and be heard of in this isle no more.

But as he lay he asked himself, did he care for the additional score of years which might, at the outside, be yet owing to him from Nature on such conditions as these? The *tædium vitæ* – formerly such a stranger to him, latterly grown familiar – seemed to intensify to violent disgust. Such an ending to his little drama as he had ostensibly sketched on Avice's behalf – was there not too distinct an attempt in it to save his useless self as well as to save her?

His heaviness endured far into the night, and there was no sign of "joy coming in the morning."[2] At two o'clock he arose and dressed himself. Then, sitting down, he penned a second letter to the same friend.

"My dear Somers –

"When I posted to you the letter I wrote a few hours ago, I assumed that I had the spirit and strength and desire to carry through an ingenious device for human happiness, which I would have entered on with the lightest of hearts forty years ago, or even twenty. But my assumption turns out to be, after all, erroneous. I am no longer spirited: I am weak. My youth, so faithful to me, so enduring, so long regarded as my curse, has incontinently departed within the last few weeks. I do not care for my scheme, which, in my distaste for it, now appears as foolishly artificial as before it seemed simple and effective.

"I abandon it for a better and a grander one – one more worthy of my age, my outlook, and my opportunities. What that is you will know in a few hours.

"J. P."

It was now half-past two. Pearston's next action was to search his pocket and open his card-case; but finding no card therein he wrote his name and address on the first piece of paper that came to hand, and put it in the case. Next, taking out his purse, he emptied some portion of its contents into another piece of paper, which he folded round the money, and placed on the table, directing it to his landlady, with the words, "For rent and small bills." The remainder he rolled up in yet another piece of paper, and directed that to a local charitable institution.

He referred to an almanac, examining the tide-table. From this he gathered that the tide was now at about the half-flow, and it suited him fairly well.

Then he went out of the room, listening at his neighbour's door as he passed. The young man was sleeping peacefully. Pearston descended the stairs and went out, closing the door softly behind him.

The night was not so dark as he had expected it to be, and the unresting and troubled being went along the road without hesitation till he reached a well-known lonely house on the right hand beyond the new castle – the farthest that way. This house contained the form which was the last, most permanent, and sweetest incarnation of the Well-Beloved.

There was no light or sound to be recognised. Pearston paused before the railing with his head bent upon his hand. Time was having his turn of revenge now. Of all the shapes into which the Beloved one had entered she had chosen to remain in this, whose owner was utterly averse to him.

The place and these thoughts quickened his determination; he paused no longer, but turned back by the way he had come, till he reached the point near the north gate of the new castle, where the lane to the ruin of the old castle branched off. This he followed as it wound down the narrow defile spanned by the castle arch, a portion of which defile was, doubtless, the original fosse of the fortress.

The sound of his own footsteps flapped back to him from the vertical faces of the rock. A little farther and he emerged upon the open summit of the lower cliffs, to his right being the sloping pathway leading down to the little creek at their base.

Pearston descended, knowing the place so well that he found it scarcely necessary to guide himself down by touching the vertical face of stone on his right hand. Thus proceeding he arrived at the bottom, and trod the few yards of shingle which here alone could be found on this side of the island. Upon this confined beach there were drawn up two or three fishing-boats and a few skiffs, beside them being a rough slipway for launching. One of the latter he pushed down the slope, floated it, and jumped into it without an oar.

The currents hereabout were strong and complicated. At a specific moment in every flood tide there set in along the shore a reflux contrary to the outer flow, called "the Southern" by the local sailors. It was produced by the peculiar curves of the coast lying east and west of the Beal: these bent southward in two back streams the up-Channel flow on each side of the isle, which two streams united outside the Beal and there met the direct tidal flow, the confluence of the three currents making the surface of the sea at this point to boil like a pot, even in calmest weather. It is called the Race.

Although the outer tide, therefore, was running towards the mainland, the "Southern" ran in full force towards the Beal and the Race beyond. Pearston's boat was caught by it in a few moments, as he had known it would be; and thereupon the grey rocks rising near him, and the grim stone forehead of the isle above, just discernible against the sky, slid away from Pearston northwards.

He lay down in the bottom of the frail craft, gazing at the sky above. The undulations increased in magnitude, and swung him higher and lower. The boat rocked, received a smart slap of the waves now and then, gyrated; so that the lightship, which stolidly winked at him from the quicksand – the single object which told him his bearings – was sometimes on his right hand and sometimes on his left. Nevertheless, he could always discern from it that his course, whether stemwards or sternwards, was steadily south, towards the Race.

The waves seemed to toss him roughly about, though there was really but little lop on the sea. Presently he heard, or fancied he heard, a new murmur from the distance, above the babble of waters immediately about his cockleshell. It was the nearing voice of the Race. "Thank God, I am near my journey's end,"[3] he said.

Yet he was not quite sure about its being the Race. But it did not matter: the Race was sure to come, sooner or later: everything tended thither. He now began to close his eyes. The boat soon shipped larger and larger volumes of spray, and often a pailful came flat upon his face. But he did not mind.

How long this state of jeopardy lasted Pearston hardly knew. It was ended by a sudden crash, which threw him against some hard body, striking his head. He was fully prepared for a liquid death, but a death by concussion was so entirely unanticipated that the shock made him cry out in a fierce resentment at the interruption to his design.

A bright light thereupon shone over him, and some voices shouted out in the island dialect. He knew that the speakers were the lightship men, and felt warm blood running down his head where it had been struck. Then he found himself in the water grasping something; then he was seized in turn, and hauled up. Then he saw faces, and bird-cages, and rabbit-hutches, on a deck – a sort of floating menagerie; and then he remembered no more.

CHAPTER XXXIII

He Becomes Aware of New Conditions

When next Pearston knew that there was such a state as life, and such an attribute of it as perceptiveness, that night of turbulence, spiritual and physical, had a long time passed away. He was lethargically conscious of lying in some soft bed, surrounded by darkness and silence, a warm atmosphere hanging about him, his only trouble being a sense of hugeness as regarded his head, which seemed to be almost the whole of his person, absorbing the rest of his frame into its circumference. Growing more and more conscious of himself, he realised that this enormous head throbbed with a dull pain.

He again lost sense of himself. When he next was cognisant of externals Pearston seemed to hear a whispered conversation going on around him, and the touch of footsteps on a carpet. A dreamy state followed, and a bandage about his head was loosened, and he opened his eyes.

The light in the apartment was so subdued that nothing around him could be seen with any distinctness. A living figure was present, moving about softly. He discerned that it was feminine, and this was all for the time.

He was recalled to his surroundings by a voice murmuring the inquiry: "Does the light try your eyes?"

The tones seemed familiar: they were rich in quality, as if they had once been powerful. Yet he could not attach a personality to them, though he knew they had been spoken by the woman who was nursing him.

Pearston murmured an answer, and tried to understand more of what had happened. Then he felt uneasy, distressed, and stupid again.

Next day he was conscious of a sudden intellectual expansion. For the first time since lying there he seemed to approximate to himself as he had formerly been. Upon the whole, he felt glad that he had not been annihilated by his own act. When he tried to speak he found that he could do so without difficulty, and he said: "Where am I?"

"At your lodgings," the voice of the nurse replied. "At East Wake."

"Was I picked up and brought here?"

"Yes."

That voice – it was known to him absurdly well. Certainly it was. Avice's it was not. As well as his pain would let him, he mentally over-hauled the years of his life. Only one woman in all his experience had ever possessed precisely those tones, and he had assumed her to be dead these thirty years, notwithstanding the sending out of bogus advertise-ments for her to delude Avice into happiness.

Still, that was whose voice it was; and every minute added weight to the conviction that his wife Marcia stood there.

She spoke again about the visit to the surgeon. Yes – it was his wife Marcia.

Pearston was stupefied. Conjecture he could not, would not. It sickened him to enter upon any kind of conjecture whatever. Enough that she was there. As for more, it had always been possible that she should have re-mained alive, and it was therefore not impossible that she should be here.

She evidently did not know that he had recognised her, and spoke on as the nurse merely. To reveal to her his discovery would have begotten ex-planations, and he could not endure the thought of explanations. Thus the two remained. Occasionally others came in – a surgeon, an assistant. A conversation in whispers would follow outside the door. But Marcia seemed always to remain at hand.

His mind had nothing else more prominent to fasten upon, and, the room being still kept almost in darkness, he could not avoid adding her fancied figure to the movements he heard. This process carried him con-siderably backward in his own history. He thought of how he had met this woman on the Pebble Bank, how they had travelled to London to-gether, had hastily married, had repented at leisure; and how thereafter a curtain had dropped between them which had been virtually death, despite a little lifting now. Yes, that very woman[1] was in the room with him, he felt sure.

Since he could not see her, he still continued to imaginatively picture her. The stately, upright figure, the rather high colour, the classical profile, the rather large handsome nose and somewhat prominent though regular teeth, the full dark eye. In short, the queenly – far too queenly – creature who had infatuated him when the first Avice was despised and her successors unknown.

With her comings and goings in the gloom his fancy associated this image so continually that it became not unpleasing to him as an artist in form. The human essence was added when she rendered him the attentions made necessary by his helplessness. But she always kept herself in the remote distance of the room, obviously unaware as yet that he knew her.

"When may I have the daylight let in upon me?" he asked of the doctor.

"Very soon," replied that gentleman. "But the wound is such that you may lose your sight if you are allowed to strain it prematurely."

So he waited, Marcia being always in the background, watchful to tenderness. He hoped she would never attempt to tell him how she came there. He could not endure the thought of having to enter into such details. At present he felt as if he were living in those early days of his marriage with her.

His eyes, having been tested, were deemed able to bear the stress of seeing clearly. Soft daylight was allowed to illuminate the room.

"Nurse," he said. "Let me see you. Why do you always keep behind my head?"

She went to the window, through which the light had only been allowed even now to enter between the blinds. Reaching it, she pulled the blind up a little way, till the outer brightness fell full upon her. An unexpected shock was the result. The face which had been stamped upon his mind-sight by the voice, the face of Marcia forty years ago, vanished utterly. In its place was a wrinkled crone, with a pointed chin, her figure bowed, her hair as white as snow. To this the once handsome face had been brought by the raspings, chisellings, stewings, bakings, and freezings of forty years.[2] The Juno of that day was the Witch of Endor[3] of this.

He must have shuddered at the discovery of what time had done, possibly have uttered a slight gasp; at all events, she knew in some way of the shock of his sensitiveness that her skeleton-figure caused him.

"I am sorry to shock you," she said. "But the moth eats the garment somewhat in five-and-thirty years."

"Yes – yes! . . . I am glad I am become an old man during the last month. For now you have a right to be old also. . . . Don't tell me why you came to me. Still, I wonder why?"

"My life's little measure is nearly danced out. So is yours, apparently. Therefore, when I saw your advertisements for me – proving that you were still living – I thought we might as well make our final bows and exits together. . . . Ah! – who is that?" Somebody had tapped at the door, and she crossed the room and opened it.

"Who was it?" he asked, when the door had closed again.

"Somebody with a telegram for me. Dear me! Curious that it should come just now!"

"What?"

"A telegram to inform me that the declaration of nullity as to the marriage between you and Avice Pearston was pronounced this morning."

"At whose instigation was the petition made?"

"At mine. She asked me what she ought to do."

He put up his hand to tear open his wound, and bring eternal night upon this lurid awakening. "But she is happy," he said. "And, as for me"—

His wife passed by the mantelpiece, over which hung an enlarged photograph of Avice, that he had brought thither when he left the other house, as the single object which he cared to bring. The contrast of the ancient Marcia's aspect, both with this portrait and with her own fine former self, brought into his brain a sudden sense of the grotesqueness of things. His wife was – not Avice, but that parchment-covered skull moving about his room. An irresistible fit of laughter, so violent as to be an agony, seized upon him, and started in him with such momentum that he could not stop it. He laughed and laughed, till he was almost too weak to draw breath.

Marcia hobbled up, frightened. "What's the matter?" she asked; and, turning to a second nurse, "He is weak – hysterical."

"O – no, no! I – I – it is too, too droll – this ending to my would-be romantic history!" Ho-ho-ho!

THE END

THE WELL-BELOVED

A SKETCH
OF A TEMPERAMENT

BY

THOMAS HARDY

WITH AN ETCHING BY
H. MACBETH-RAEBURN
AND A MAP OF WESSEX

'One shape of many names.'
P. B. SHELLEY.

O.　　M.

JAMES R. OSGOOD
McILVAINE & Co.

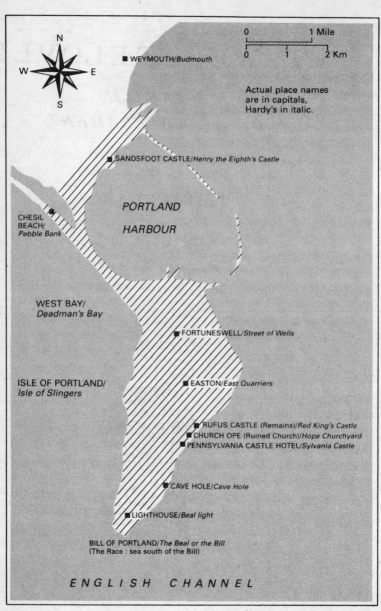

N

W — E

S

0   1 Mile

0   1   2 Km

■ WEYMOUTH/*Budmouth*

Actual place names
are in capitals,
Hardy's in italic.

■ SANDSFOOT CASTLE/*Henry the Eighth's Castle*

PORTLAND

HARBOUR

CHESIL
BEACH/
Pebble Bank

WEST BAY/
Deadman's Bay

■ FORTUNESWELL/*Street of Wells*

ISLE OF PORTLAND/
Isle of Slingers

■ EASTON/*East Quarriers*

■ RUFUS CASTLE (Remains)/*Red King's Castle*
■ CHURCH OPE (Ruined Church)/*Hope Churchyard*
■ PENNSYLVANIA CASTLE HOTEL/*Sylvania Castle*

■ CAVE HOLE/*Cave Hole*

■ LIGHTHOUSE/*Beal light*

BILL OF PORTLAND/*The Beal or the Bill*
(The Race : sea south of the Bill)

E N G L I S H   C H A N N E L

The Isle, as described in the 1897 version

The peninsula[1] carved by Time out of a single stone, whereon most of the following scenes are laid, has been for centuries immemorial the home of a curious and almost distinctive people, cherishing strange beliefs and singular customs, now for the most part obsolescent. Fancies, like certain soft-wooded plants which cannot bear the silent inland frosts, but thrive by the sea in the roughest of weather, seem to grow up naturally here, in particular amongst those natives who have no active concern in the labours of the 'Isle.' Hence it is a spot apt to generate a type of personage like the character imperfectly sketched in these pages – a native of natives – whom some may choose to call a fantast (if they honour him with their consideration so far), but whom others may see only as one that gave objective continuity and a name to a delicate dream which in a vaguer form is more or less common to all men, and is by no means new to Platonic philosophers.[2]

To those who know the rocky coign of England here depicted – overlooking the great Channel Highway with all its suggestiveness, and standing out so far into mid-sea that touches of the Gulf Stream soften the air till February – it is matter of surprise that the place has not been more frequently chosen as the retreat of artists and poets in search of inspiration – for at least a month or two in the year, the tempestuous rather than the fine seasons by preference. To be sure, one nook[3] therein is the retreat, at their country's expense, of other geniuses from a distance; but their presence is hardly discoverable. Yet perhaps it is as well that the artistic visitors do not come, or no more would be heard of little freehold houses being bought and sold there for a couple of hundred pounds – built of solid stone, and dating from the sixteenth century and earlier, with mullions, copings, and corbels complete. These transactions, by the way, are carried out and covenanted, or were till lately, in the parish church, in the face of the congregation, such being the ancient custom of the Isle.

The present is the first publication of this tale in an independent form;

and a few chapters[4] have been rewritten since it was issued in the periodical press in 1892.

January 1897.   T. H.

The peninsula carved by Time out of a single stone, whereon most of the following scenes are laid, has been for centuries immemorial the home of a curious and well-nigh distinct people, cherishing strange beliefs and singular customs, now for the most part obsolescent. Fancies, like certain soft-wooded plants which cannot bear the silent inland frosts, but thrive by the sea in the roughest of weather, seem to grow up naturally here, in particular amongst those natives who have no active concern in the labours of the 'Isle.' Hence it is a spot apt to generate a type of personage like the character imperfectly sketched in these pages – a native of natives – whom some may choose to call a fantast (if they honour him with their consideration so far), but whom others may see only as one that gave objective continuity and a name to a delicate dream which in a vaguer form is more or less common to all men, and is by no means new to Platonic philosophers.

To those who know the rocky coign of England here depicted – overlooking the great Channel Highway with all its suggestiveness, and standing out so far into mid-sea that touches of the Gulf Stream soften the air till February – it is matter of surprise that the place has not been more frequently chosen as the retreat of artists and poets in search of inspiration – for at least a month or two in the year, the tempestuous rather than the fine seasons by preference. To be sure, one nook therein is the retreat, at their country's expense, of other geniuses from a distance; but their presence is hardly discoverable. Yet perhaps it is as well that the artistic visitors do not come, or no more would be heard of little freehold houses being bought and sold there for a couple of hundred pounds – built of solid stone, and dating from the sixteenth century and earlier, with mullions, copings, and corbels complete. These transactions, by the way, are carried out and covenanted, or were till lately, in the parish church, in the face of the congregation, such being the ancient custom of the Isle.

As for the story itself, it may be worth while to remark that, differing from all or most others of the series in that the interest aimed at is of an ideal or subjective nature, and frankly imaginative, verisimilitude in the sequence of events has been subordinated to the said aim.

The first publication of this tale in an independent form was in 1897; but it had appeared in the periodical press in 1892, under the title of 'The Pursuit of the Well-Beloved.' A few chapters of that experimental issue were rewritten for the present and final form of the narrative.

August 1912.   T. H.

CONTENTS

The Well-Beloved

PART FIRST: A YOUNG MAN OF TWENTY

I	*A Supposititious Presentment of Her*	179
II	*The Incarnation is assumed to be True*	182
III	*The Appointment*	187
IV	*A lonely Pedestrian*	189
V	*A Charge*	192
VI	*On the Brink*	197
VII	*Her Earlier Incarnations*	200
VIII	*'Too Like the Lightning'*	204
IX	*Familiar Phenomena in the Distance*	210

PART SECOND: A YOUNG MAN OF FORTY

I	*The Old Phantom becomes Distinct*	217
II	*She Draws Close and Satisfies*	224
III	*She becomes an Inaccessible Ghost*	229
IV	*She Threatens to resume Corporeal Substance*	235
V	*The Resumption takes place*	238
VI	*The Past Shines in the Present*	241
VII	*The New becomes Established*	247
VIII	*His own Soul confronts him*	252
IX	*Juxtapositions*	255
X	*She Fails to Vanish still*	261
XI	*The Image Persists*	265
XII	*A Grille descends between*	270
XIII	*She is Enshrouded from Sight*	277

PART THIRD: A YOUNG MAN TURNED SIXTY

I	*She Returns for the New Season*	283
II	*Misgivings on the Re-embodiment*	290
III	*The Renewed Image burns itself in*	295
IV	*A Dash for the Last Incarnation*	301
V	*On the Verge of Possession*	308
VI	*The Well-Beloved is – Where?*	315
VII	*An Old Tabernacle in a New Aspect*	324
VIII	*'Alas for this Grey Shadow, once a Man!'*	328

PART FIRST

A Young Man of Twenty

—'Now, if Time knows
That Her, whose radiant brows
Weave them a garland of my vows;

Her that dares be
What these lines wish to see:
I seek no further, it is She.'

R. CRASHAW

CHAPTER I

A Supposititious Presentment of Her

A person who differed from the local wayfarers was climbing the steep road which leads through the sea-skirted townlet definable as the Street of Wells, and forms a pass into that Gibraltar of Wessex, the singular peninsula once an island, and still called such, that stretches out like the head of a bird into the English Channel. It is connected with the mainland by a long thin neck of pebbles 'cast up by rages of the se,'[2] and unparalleled in its kind in Europe.

The pedestrian was what he looked like – a young man from London and the cities of the Continent. Nobody could see at present that his urbanism sat upon him only as a garment. He was just recollecting with something of self-reproach that a whole three years and eight months had flown since he paid his last visit to his father at this lonely rock of his birthplace, the intervening time having been spent amid many contrasting societies, peoples, manners, and scenes.

What had seemed usual in the isle when he lived there always looked quaint and odd after his later impressions. More than ever the spot seemed what it was said once to have been, the ancient Vindilia[3] Island, and the Home of the Slingers.[4] The towering rock, the houses above houses, one man's doorstep[5] rising behind his neighbour's chimney, the gardens hung up by one edge to the sky, the vegetables growing on apparently almost vertical planes, the unity of the whole island as a solid and single block of limestone four miles long, were no longer familiar and commonplace ideas. All now stood dazzlingly unique and white against the tinted sea, and the sun flashed on infinitely stratified walls of oolite.

> The melancholy ruins
> Of cancelled cycles, . . .[6]

with a distinctiveness that called the eyes to it as strongly as any spectacle he had beheld afar.

After a laborious clamber he reached the top, and walked along the plateau towards the eastern village. The time being about two o'clock, in the middle of the summer season, the road was glaring and dusty, and drawing near to his father's house he sat down in the sun.

He stretched out his hand upon the rock beside him. It felt warm. That was the island's personal temperature when in its afternoon sleep as now. He listened, and heard sounds: whirr-whirr, saw-saw-saw. Those were the island's snores – the noises of the quarrymen and stone-sawyers.

Opposite to the spot on which he sat was a roomy cottage or homestead. Like the island it was all of stone, not only in walls but in window-frames, roof, chimneys, fence, stile, pig-sty and stable, almost door.

He remembered who had used to live there – and probably lived there now – the Caro family;[7] the 'roan-mare' Caros,[8] as they were called to distinguish them from other branches of the same pedigree, there being but half-a-dozen christian and surnames in the whole island. He crossed the road and looked in at the open doorway. Yes, there they were still.

Mrs. Caro, who had seen him from the window, met him in the entry, and an old-fashioned greeting took place between them. A moment after a door leading from the back rooms was thrown open, and a young girl about seventeen or eighteen came bounding in.

'Why, *'tis* dear Joce!' she burst out joyfully. And running up to the young man, she kissed him.

The demonstration was sweet enough from the owner of such an affectionate pair of bright hazel eyes and brown tresses of hair. But it was so sudden, so unexpected by a man fresh from towns, that he winced for a moment quite involuntarily; and there was some constraint in the manner in which he returned her kiss, and said, 'My pretty little Avice,[9] how do you do after so long?'

For a few seconds her impulsive innocence hardly noticed his start of surprise; but Mrs. Caro, the girl's mother, had observed it instantly. With a pained flush she turned to her daughter.

'Avice – my dear Avice! Why – what are you doing? Don't you know that you've grown up to be a woman since Jocelyn – Mr. Pierston – was last down here? Of course you mustn't do now as you used to do three or four years ago!'

The awkwardness which had arisen was hardly removed by Pierston's assurance that he quite expected her to keep up the practice of her childhood, followed by several minutes of conversation on general subjects. He was vexed from his soul that his unaware movement should so have betrayed him. At his leaving he repeated that if Avice regarded him otherwise than as she used to do he would never forgive her; but though they parted good friends her regret at the incident was visible in her face. Jocelyn passed out into the road and onward to his father's house hard by. The mother and daughter were left alone.

'I was quite amazed at 'ee, my child!' exclaimed the elder. 'A young man from London and foreign cities, used now to the strictest company manners, and ladies who almost think it vulgar to smile broad! How could ye do it, Avice?'

'I – I didn't think about how I was altered!' said the conscience-stricken girl. 'I used to kiss him, and he used to kiss me before he went away.'

'But that was years ago, my dear!'

'O yes, and for the moment I forgot! He seemed just the same to me as he used to be.'

'Well, it can't be helped now. You must be careful in the future. He's got lots of young women, I'll warrant, and has few thoughts left for you. He's what they call a sculptor, and he means to be a great genius in that line some day, they do say.'

'Well, I've done it; and it can't be mended!' moaned the girl.

Meanwhile Jocelyn Pierston, the sculptor of budding fame, had gone onward to the house of his father, an inartistic man of trade and commerce merely, from whom, nevertheless, Jocelyn accepted a yearly allowance pending the famous days to come. But the elder, having received no warning of his son's intended visit, was not at home to receive him. Jocelyn looked round the familiar premises, glanced across the Common at the great yards within which eternal saws were going to and fro upon eternal blocks of stone – the very same saws and the very same blocks that he had seen there when last in the island, so it seemed to him – and then passed through the dwelling into the back garden.

Like all the gardens in the isle it was surrounded by a wall of dry-jointed spawls, and at its further extremity it ran out into a corner, which adjoined the garden of the Caros. He had no sooner reached this spot than he became aware of a murmuring and sobbing on the other side of the wall. The voice he recognized in a moment as Avice's, and she seemed to be confiding her trouble to some young friend of her own sex.

'Oh, what shall I *do*! what *shall* I do!' she was saying bitterly. 'So bold as it was – so shameless! How could I think of such a thing! He will never forgive me – never, never like me again! He'll think me a forward hussy, and yet – and yet I quite forgot how much I had grown. But that he'll never believe!' The accents were those of one who had for the first time become conscious of her womanhood, as an unwonted possession which shamed and frightened her.

'Did he seem angry at it?' inquired the friend.

'O no – not angry! Worse. Cold and haughty. O, he's such a fashionable person now – not at all an island man. But there's no use in talking of it. I wish I was dead!'

Pierston retreated as quickly as he could. He grieved at the incident which had brought such pain to this innocent soul; and yet it was beginning to be a source of vague pleasure to him. He returned to the house, and when his father had come back and welcomed him, and they had shared a meal together, Jocelyn again went out, full of an earnest desire to soothe his young neighbour's sorrow in a way she little expected; though, to tell the truth, his affection for her was rather that of a friend than of a lover, and he felt by no means sure that the migratory, elusive idealization he called his Love who, ever since his boyhood, had flitted from human shell to human shell an indefinite number of times, was going to take up her abode in the body of Avice Caro.

CHAPTER II

The Incarnation is assumed to be True

It was difficult to meet her again, even though on this lump of rock the difficulty lay as a rule rather in avoidance than in meeting. But Avice had been transformed into a very different kind of young woman by the self-consciousness engendered of her impulsive greeting, and, not withstanding their near neighbourhood, he could not encounter her, try as he would. No sooner did he appear an inch beyond his father's door than she was to earth like a fox; she bolted upstairs to her room.

Anxious to soothe her after his unintentional slight he could not stand these evasions long. The manners of the isle were primitive and straightforward, even among the well-to-do, and noting her disappearance one day he followed her into the house and onward to the foot of the stairs.

'Avice!' he called.

'Yes, Mr. Pierston.'

'Why do you run upstairs like that?'

'Oh – only because I wanted to come up for something.'

'Well, if you've got it, can't you come down again?'

'No, I can't very well.'

'Come, *dear* Avice. That's what you are, you know.'

There was no response.

'Well, if you won't, you won't!' he continued. 'I don't want to bother you.' And Pierston went away.

He was stopping to look at the old-fashioned flowers under the garden walls when he heard a voice behind him.

'Mr. Pierston – I wasn't angry with you. When you were gone I thought – you might mistake me, and I felt I could do no less than come and assure you of my friendship still.'

Turning he saw the blushing Avice immediately behind him.

'You are a good, dear girl!' said he, and, seizing her hand, set upon her cheek the kind of kiss that should have been the response to hers on the day of his coming.

'Darling Avice, forgive me for the slight that day! Say you do. Come, now! And then I'll say to you what I have never said to any other woman, living or dead: "Will you have me as your husband?"'

'Ah! – mother says I am only one of many!'

'You are not, dear. You knew me when I was young, and others didn't.'

Somehow or other her objections were got over, and though she did not give an immediate assent, she agreed to meet him later in the afternoon, when she walked with him to the southern point of the island called the Beal, or, by strangers, the Bill, pausing over the treacherous cavern known as Cave Hole, into which the sea roared and splashed now as it had done when they visited it together as children. To steady herself while looking in he offered her his arm, and she took it, for the first time as a woman, for the hundredth time as his companion.

They rambled on to the lighthouse, where they would have lingered longer if Avice had not suddenly remembered an engagement to recite poetry from a platform that very evening at the Street of Wells, the village commanding the entrance to the island – the village that has now advanced to be a town.

'Recite!' said he. 'Who'd have thought anybody or anything could recite down here except the reciter we hear away there – the never speechless sea.'

'O but we are quite intellectual now. In the winter particularly. But, Jocelyn – don't come to the recitation, will you? It would spoil my performance if you were there, and I want to be as good as the rest.'

'I won't if you really wish me not to. But I shall meet you at the door and bring you home.'

'Yes!' she said, looking up into his face. Avice was perfectly happy now; she could never have believed on that mortifying day of his coming that she would be so happy with him. When they reached the east side of the isle they parted, that she might be soon enough to take her place on the platform. Pierston went home, and after dark, when it was about the hour for accompanying her back, he went along the middle road northward to the Street of Wells.

He was full of misgiving. He had known Avice Caro so well of old that his feeling for her now was rather comradeship than love; and what he had said to her in a moment of impulse that morning rather appalled him in its consequences. Not that any of the more sophisticated and accomplished women who had attracted him successively would be likely to rise inconveniently between them. For he had quite disabused his mind of the assumption that the idol of his fancy was an integral part of the personality in which it had sojourned for a long or a short while.

* * * * *

To his Well-Beloved he had always been faithful;[2] but she had had many embodiments. Each individuality known as Lucy, Jane, Flora, Evangeline, or what-not, had been merely a transient condition of her. He did not recognize this as an excuse or as a defence, but as a fact simply. Essentially she was perhaps of no tangible substance; a spirit, a dream, a frenzy, a conception, an aroma, an epitomized sex, a light of the eye, a parting of the lips. God only knew what she really was; Pierston did not. She was indescribable.

Never much considering that she was a subjective phenomenon vivified by the weird influences of his descent and birthplace, the discovery of her ghostliness, of her independence of physical laws and failings, had occasionally given him a sense of fear. He never knew where she next would be, whither she would lead him, having herself instant access to all ranks and classes, to every abode of men. Sometimes at night he dreamt that she was 'the wile-weaving Daughter of high Zeus'[3] in person, bent on tormenting him for his sins against her beauty in his art – the implacable Aphrodite herself indeed.[4] He knew that he loved the masquerading creature wherever he found her, whether with blue eyes, black eyes, or brown; whether presenting herself as tall, fragile, or plump. She was never in two places at once; but hitherto she had never been in one place long.

By making this clear to his mind some time before to-day, he had escaped a good deal of ugly self-reproach. It was simply that she who always attracted him, and led him whither she would as by a silken thread, had not remained the occupant of the same fleshly tabernacle[5] in her career so far. Whether she would ultimately settle down to one he could not say.

Had he felt that she was becoming manifest in Avice, he would have tried to believe that this was the terminal spot of her migrations, and have been content to abide by his words. But did he see the Well-Beloved in Avice at all? The question was somewhat disturbing.

He had reached the brow of the hill, and descended towards the village, where in the long straight Roman street he soon found the lighted hall. The performance was not yet over; and by going round to the side of the building and standing on a mound he could see the interior as far down as the platform level. Avice's turn, or second turn, came on almost immediately. Her pretty embarrassment on facing the audience rather won him away from his doubts. She was, in truth, what is called a 'nice' girl; attractive, certainly, but above all things nice – one of the class with whom the risks of matrimony[6] approximate most nearly to zero. Her intelligent eyes, her broad forehead, her thoughtful carriage, ensured one thing, that of all the girls he had known he had never met one with more charming and solid qualities than Avice Caro's. This was not a mere conjecture – he had known her long and thoroughly; her every mood and temper.

A heavy wagon passing without drowned her small soft voice for him; but the audience were pleased, and she blushed at their applause. He now took his station at the door, and when the people had done pouring out he found her within awaiting him.

They climbed homeward slowly by the Old Road, Pierston dragging himself up the steep by the wayside hand-rail and pulling Avice after him upon his arm. At the top they turned and stood still. To the left of them the sky was streaked like a fan with the lighthouse rays, and under their front, at periods of a quarter of a minute, there arose a deep, hollow stroke like the single beat of a drum, the intervals being filled with a long-drawn rattling, as of bones between huge canine jaws. It came from the vast concave of Deadman's Bay, rising and falling against the pebble dyke.

The evening and night winds here were, to Pierston's mind, charged with a something that did not burden them elsewhere. They brought it up from that sinister Bay to the west, whose movement she and he were hearing now. It was a presence – an imaginary shape or essence from the human multitude lying below: those who had gone down in vessels of war, East Indiamen, barges, brigs, and ships of the Armada – select people, common, and debased, whose interests and hopes had been as wide asunder as the poles, but who had rolled each other to oneness on that restless sea-bed. There could almost be felt the brush of their huge composite ghost as it ran a shapeless figure over the isle, shrieking for some good god who would disunite it again.[7]

The twain wandered a long way that night amid these influences – so far as to the old Hope Churchyard, which lay in a ravine formed by a landslip ages ago. The church had slipped down with the rest of the cliff, and had long been a ruin. It seemed to say that in this last local strong-hold of the Pagan divinities, where Pagan customs lingered yet, Christianity had established itself precariously at best. In that solemn spot Pierston kissed her.[8]

The kiss was by no means on Avice's initiative this time. Her former demonstrativeness seemed to have increased her present reserve.

*　　*　　*　　*　　*

That day was the beginning of a pleasant month passed mainly in each other's society. He found that she could not only recite poetry at intellectual gatherings, but play the piano fairly, and sing to her own accompaniment.

He observed that every aim of those who had brought her up had been to get her away mentally as far as possible from her natural and individual life as an inhabitant of a peculiar island: to make her an exact copy of tens of thousands of other people, in whose circumstances there was nothing special, distinctive, or picturesque; to teach her to forget all the experiences of her ancestors; to drown the local ballads by songs purchased at the Budmouth fashionable music-sellers', and the local vocabulary by a governess-tongue of no country at all. She lived in a house that would have been the fortune of an artist, and learnt to draw London sub-urban villas from printed copies.

Avice had seen all this before he pointed it out, but, with a girl's tract-ability, had acquiesced. By constitution she was local to the bone, but she could not escape the tendency of the age.

The time for Jocelyn's departure drew near, and she looked forward to it sadly, but serenely, their engagement being now a settled thing. Pierston thought of the native custom on such occasions, which had prevailed in his and her family for centuries, both being of the old stock of the isle. The influx of 'kimberlins,' or 'foreigners' (as strangers from the mainland of Wessex were called), had led in a large measure to its discontinuance; but underneath the veneer of Avice's education many an old-fashioned idea lay slumbering, and he wondered if, in her natural melancholy at his leaving, she regretted[9] the changing manners which made unpopular the formal ratification of a betrothal, according to the precedent of their sires and grandsires.

CHAPTER III

The Appointment

'Well,' said he, 'here we are, arrived at the fag-end of my holiday. What a pleasant surprise my old home, which I have not thought worth coming to see for three or four years, had in store for me!'

'You must go to-morrow?' she asked uneasily.

'Yes.'

Something seemed to overweigh them; something more than the nat-ural sadness of a parting which was not to be long; and he decided that instead of leaving in the daytime as he had intended, he would defer his departure till night, and go by the mail-train from Budmouth. This would give him time to look into his father's quarries, and enable her, if she chose, to walk with him along the beach as far as to Henry the Eighth's Castle above the sands, where they could linger and watch the moon rise over the sea. She said she thought she could come.

So after spending the next day with his father in the quarries Jocelyn prepared to leave, and at the time appointed set out from the stone house of his birth in this stone isle to walk to Budmouth-Regis by the path along the beach, Avice having some time earlier gone down to see some friends in the Street of Wells, which was halfway towards the spot of their tryst. The descent soon brought him to the pebble bank, and leaving behind him the last houses of the isle, and the ruins of the village destroyed by the November gale of 1824, he struck out along the narrow thread of land. When he had walked a hundred yards he stopped, turned aside to the pebble ridge which walled out the sea, and sat down to wait for her.

Between him and the lights of the ships riding at anchor in the roadstead two men passed slowly in the direction he intended to pursue. One of them recognized Jocelyn, and bade him good-night, adding, 'Wish you joy, sir, of your choice, and hope the wedden will be soon!'

'Thank you, Seaborn. Well – we shall see what Christmas will do towards bringing it about.'

'My wife opened upon it this mornen: "Please God, I'll up and see that there wedden," says she, "knowing 'em both from their crawling days."'

The men moved on, and when they were out of Pierston's hearing the one who had not spoken said to his friend, 'Who was that young kimberlin? He don't seem one o' we.'

'Oh, he is, though, every inch o' en. He's Mr. Jocelyn Pierston, the stwone-merchant's only son up at East Quarriers. He's to be married to a stylish young body; her mother, a widow woman, carries on the same business as well as she can; but their trade is not a twentieth part of Pierston's. He's worth thousands and thousands, they say, though 'a do live on in the same wold way up in the same wold house. This son is doen great things in London as a' image-carver; and I can mind when, as a boy, 'a first took to carving soldiers out o' bits o' stwone from the soft-bed of his father's quarries; and then 'a made a set o' stwonen chess-men, and so 'a got on. He's quite the gent in London, they tell me; and the wonder is that 'a cared to come back here and pick up little Avice Caro – nice maid as she is notwithstanding. . . . Hullo! there's to be a change in the weather soon.'

Meanwhile the subject of their remarks waited at the appointed place till seven o'clock, the hour named between himself and his affianced, had struck. Almost at the moment he saw a figure coming forward from the last lamp at the bottom of the hill. But the figure speedily resolved itself into that of a boy, who, advancing to Jocelyn, inquired if he were Mr. Pierston, and handed him a note.

CHAPTER IV

A lonely Pedestrian

When the boy had gone Jocelyn retraced his steps to the last lamp, and read, in Avice's hand:

'My Dearest,' – I shall be sorry if I grieve you at all in what I am going to say about our arrangement to meet to-night in the Sandsfoot ruin. But I have fancied that my seeing you again and again lately is in- clining your father to insist, and you as his heir to feel, that we ought to carry out Island Custom in our courting – your people being such old inhabitants in an unbroken line. Truth to say, mother supposes that your father, for natural reasons, may have hinted to you that we ought. Now, the thing is contrary to my feelings: it is nearly left off; and I do not think it good, even where there is property, as in your case, to justify it, in a measure. I would rather trust in Providence.

'On the whole, therefore, it is best that I should not come – if only for appearances – and meet you at a time and place suggesting the custom, to others than ourselves, at least, if known.

'I am sure that this decision will not disturb you much; that you will understand my modern feelings, and think no worse of me for them. And dear, if it were to be done, and we were unfortunate in it, we might both have enough old family feeling to think, like our forefathers, and possibly your father, that we could not marry honourably; and hence we might be made unhappy.

'However, you will come again shortly, will you not, dear Jocelyn? – and then the time will soon draw on when no more good-byes will be required. – Always and ever yours,

'Avice.'

Jocelyn, having read the letter, was surprised at the naïveté it showed, and at Avice and her mother's antiquated simplicity in supposing that to be still a grave and operating principle which was a bygone barbarism to himself and other absentees from the island. His father, as a money-maker, might have practical wishes on the matter of descendants which lent plausibility to the conjecture of Avice and her mother; but to Jocelyn he had never expressed himself in favour of the ancient ways, old-fashioned as he was.

Amused therefore at her regard of herself as modern, Jocelyn was disappointed, and a little vexed, that such an unforeseen reason should have deprived him of her company. How the old ideas survived under the new education!

The reader is asked to remember that the date, though recent in the history of the Isle of Slingers, was more than forty years ago.

* * * * *

Finding that the evening seemed louring, yet indisposed to go back and hire a vehicle, he went on quickly alone. In such an exposed spot the night wind was gusty, and the sea behind the pebble barrier kicked and flounced in complex rhythms, which could be translated equally well as shocks of battle or shouts of thanksgiving.

Presently on the pale road before him he discerned a figure, the figure of a woman. He remembered that a woman passed him while he was reading Avice's letter by the last lamp, and now he was overtaking her.

He did hope for a moment that it might be Avice, with a changed mind. But it was not she, nor anybody like her. It was a taller, squarer form than that of his betrothed, and although the season was only autumn she was wrapped in furs, or in thick and heavy clothing of some kind.

He soon advanced abreast of her, and could get glimpses of her profile against the roadstead lights. It was dignified, arresting, that of a very Juno.[2] Nothing more classical had he ever seen. She walked at a swinging pace, yet with such ease and power that there was but little difference in their rate of speed for several minutes; and during this time he regarded and conjectured. However, he was about to pass her by when she suddenly turned and addressed him.

'Mr. Pierston, I think, of East Quarriers?'

He assented, and could just discern what a handsome, commanding, imperious face it was – quite of a piece with the proud tones of her voice. She was a new type altogether in his experience; and her accent was not so local as Avice's.

'Can you tell me the time, please?'

He looked at his watch by the aid of a light, and in telling her that it was a quarter past seven observed, by the momentary gleam of his match, that her eyes looked a little red and chafed, as if with weeping.

'Mr. Pierston, will you forgive what will appear very strange to you, I dare say? That is, may I ask you to lend me some money for a day or two? I have been so foolish as to leave my purse on the dressing-table.'

It did appear strange: and yet there were features in the young lady's personality which assured him in a moment that she was not an impostor. He yielded to her request, and put his hand in his pocket. Here it remained for a moment. How much did she mean by the words 'some money?' The Junonian quality of her form and manner made him throw himself by an impulse into harmony with her, and he responded regally. He scented a romance. He handed her five pounds.

His munificence caused her no apparent surprise. 'It is quite enough, thank you,' she remarked quietly, as he announced the sum, lest she should be unable to see it for herself.

While overtaking and conversing with her he had not observed that the rising wind, which had proceeded from puffing to growling, and from growling to screeching, with the accustomed suddenness of its changes here, had at length brought what it promised by these vagaries – rain. The drops, which had at first hit their left cheeks like the pellets of a popgun, soon assumed the character of a raking fusillade from the bank adjoining, one shot of which was sufficiently smart to go through Jocelyn's sleeve. The tall girl turned, and seemed to be somewhat concerned at an onset which she had plainly not foreseen before her starting.

'We must take shelter,' said Jocelyn.

'But where?' said she.

To windward was the long, monotonous bank, too obtusely piled to afford a screen, over which they could hear the canine crunching of pebbles by the sea without; on their right stretched the inner bay or roadstead, the distant riding-lights of the ships now dim and glimmering; behind them a faint spark here and there in the lower sky showed where the island rose; before there was nothing definite, and could be nothing, till they reached a precarious wood bridge, a mile further on, Henry the Eighth's Castle being a little further still.

But just within the summit of the bank, whither it had apparently been hauled to be out of the way of the waves, was one of the local boats called lerrets, bottom upwards. As soon as they saw it the pair ran up the pebbly slope towards it by a simultaneous impulse. They then perceived that it had lain there a long time, and were comforted to find it capable of affording more protection than anybody would have expected from a distant view. It formed a shelter or store for the fishermen, the bottom of the lerret being tarred as a roof. By creeping under the bows, which overhung the bank on props to leeward, they made their way within, where, upon some thwarts, oars, and other fragmentary woodwork, lay a mass of dry netting – a whole sein. Upon this they scrambled and sat down, through inability to stand upright.

CHAPTER V

A Charge

The rain fell upon the keel of the old lerret like corn thrown in handfuls by some colossal sower, and darkness set in to its full shade.

They crouched so close to each other that he could feel her furs against him. Neither had spoken since they left the roadway till she said, with attempted unconcern: 'This is unfortunate.'

He admitted that it was, and found, after a few further remarks had passed, that she certainly had been weeping, there being a suppressed gasp of passionateness in her utterance now and then.

'It is more unfortunate for you, perhaps, than for me,' he said, 'and I am very sorry that it should be so.'

She replied nothing to this, and he added that it was rather a desolate place for a woman, alone and afoot. He hoped nothing serious had happened to drag her out at such an untoward time.

At first she seemed not at all disposed to show any candour on her own affairs, and he was left to conjecture as to her history and name, and how she could possibly have known him. But, as the rain gave not the least sign of cessation, he observed: 'I think we shall have to go back.'

'Never!' said she, and the firmness with which she closed her lips was audible in the word.

'Why not?' he inquired.

'There are good reasons.'

'I cannot understand how you should know me, while I have no know-ledge of you.'

'Oh, but you know me – about me, at least.'

'Indeed I don't. How should I? You are a kimberlin.'

'I am not. I am a real islander – or was, rather. . . . Haven't you heard of the Best-Bed Stone Company?'

'I should think so! They tried to ruin my father by getting away his trade – or, at least, the founder of the company did – old Bencomb.'

'He's my father!'

'Indeed. I am sorry I should have spoken so disrespectfully of him, for I never knew him personally. After making over his large business to the company, he retired, I believe, to London?'

'Yes. Our house, or rather his, not mine, is at South Kensington. We have lived there for years. But we have been tenants of Sylvania Castle, on the island here, this season. We took it for a month or two of the owner, who is away.'

'Then I have been staying quite near you, Miss Bencomb. My father's is a comparatively humble residence hard by.'

'But he could afford a much bigger one if he chose.'

'You have heard so? I don't know. He doesn't tell me much of his affairs.'

'My father,' she burst out suddenly, 'is always scolding me for my ex-travagance! And he has been doing it to-day more than ever. He said I go shopping in town to simply a diabolical extent, and exceed my allowance!'

'Was that this evening?'

'Yes. And then it reached such a storm of passion between us that I pretended to retire to my room for the rest of the evening, but I slipped out; and I am never going back home again.'

'What will you do?'

'I shall go first to my aunt in London; and if she won't have me, I'll work for a living. I have left my father for ever! What I should have done if I had not met you I cannot tell – I must have walked all the way to London, I suppose. Now I shall take the train as soon as I reach the mainland.'

'If you ever do in this hurricane.'

'I must sit here till it stops.'

And there on the nets they sat. Pierston knew of old Bencomb as his father's bitterest enemy, who had made a great fortune by swallowing up the small stone-merchants, but had found Jocelyn's sire a trifle too big to digest – the latter being, in fact, the chief rival of the Best-Bed Company to that day. Jocelyn thought it strange that he should be thrown by fate into a position to play the son of the Montagues' to this daughter of the Capulets.

As they talked there was a mutual instinct to drop their voice, and on this account the roar of the storm necessitated their drawing quite close together. Something tender came into their tones as quarter-hour after quarter-hour went on, and they forgot the lapse of time. It was quite late when she started up, alarmed at her position.

'Rain or no rain, I can stay no longer,' she said.

'Do come back,' said he, taking her hand. 'I'll return with you. My train has gone.'

'No; I shall go on, and get a lodging in Budmouth town, if ever I reach it.'

'It is so late that there will be no house open, except a little place near the station where you won't care to stay. However, if you are determined I will show you the way. I cannot leave you. It would be too awkward for you to go there alone.'

She persisted, and they started through the twanging and spinning storm. The sea rolled and rose so high on their left, and was so near them on their right, that it seemed as if they were traversing its bottom like the Children of Israel.[2] Nothing but the frail bank of pebbles divided them from the raging gulf without, and at every bang of the tide against it the ground shook, the shingle clashed, the spray rose vertically, and was blown over their heads. Quantities of sea-water trickled through the pebble wall, and ran in rivulets across their path to join the sea within. The 'Island' was an island still.

They had not realized the force of the elements till now. Pedestrians had often been blown into the sea hereabout, and drowned, owing to a sudden breach in the bank; which, however, had something of a supernatural power in being able to close up and join itself together again after such disruption, like Satan's form when, cut in two by the sword of Michael,

> 'The ethereal substance closed,
> Not long divisible.'[3]

Her clothing offered more resistance to the wind than his, and she was consequently in the greater danger. It was impossible to refuse his proffered aid. First he gave his arm, but the wind tore them apart as easily as coupled cherries. He steadied her bodily by encircling her waist with his arm; and she made no objection.

* * * * *

Somewhere about this time – it might have been sooner, it might have been later – he became conscious of a sensation which, in its incipient and unrecognized form, had lurked within him from some unnoticed moment when he was sitting close to his new friend under the lerret. Though a young man, he was too old a hand not to know what this was, and felt alarmed – even dismayed. It meant a possible migration of the Well-Beloved. The thing had not, however, taken place; and he went on thinking how soft and warm the lady was in her fur covering, as he held her so tightly; the only dry spots in the clothing of either being her left side and his right, where they excluded the rain by their mutual pressure.

As soon as they had crossed the ferry-bridge there was a little more shelter, but he did not relinquish his hold till she requested him. They passed the ruined castle, and having left the island far behind them trod mile after mile till they drew near to the outskirts of the neighbouring watering-place. Into it they plodded without pause, crossing the harbour bridge about midnight, wet to the skin.

He pitied her, and, while he wondered at it, admired her determination. The houses facing the bay now sheltered them completely, and they reached the vicinity of the new railway terminus (which the station was at this date) without difficulty. As he had said, there was only one house open hereabout, a little temperance inn, where the people stayed up for the arrival of the morning mail and passengers from the Channel boats. Their application for admission led to the withdrawal of a bolt, and they stood within the gaslight of the passage.

He could see now that though she was such a fine figure, quite as tall as himself, she was but in the bloom of young womanhood. Her face was certainly striking, though rather by its imperiousness than its beauty; and the beating of the wind and rain and spray had inflamed her cheeks to peony hues.

She persisted in the determination to go on to London by an early morning train, and he therefore offered advice on lesser matters only. 'In that case,' he said, 'you must go up to your room and send down your things, that they may be dried by the fire immediately, or they will not be ready. I will tell the servant to do this, and send you up something to eat.'

She assented to his proposal, without, however, showing any marks of gratitude; and when she had gone Pierston despatched her the light supper promised by the sleepy girl who was 'night porter' at this establishment. He felt ravenously hungry himself, and set about drying his clothes as well as he could, and eating at the same time.

At first he was in doubt what to do, but soon decided to stay where he was till the morrow. By the aid of some temporary wraps, and some slippers from the cupboard, he was contriving to make himself comfortable when the maid-servant came downstairs with a damp armful of woman's raiment.

Pierston withdrew from the fire. The maid-servant knelt down before the blaze and held up with extended arms one of the habiliments of the Juno upstairs, from which a cloud of steam began to rise. As she knelt, the girl nodded forward, recovered herself, and nodded again.

'You are sleepy, my girl,' said Pierston.

'Yes, sir; I have been up a long time. When nobody comes I lie down on the couch in the other room.'

'Then I'll relieve you of that; go and lie down in the other room, just as if we were not here. I'll dry the clothing and put the articles here in a heap, which you can take up to the young lady in the morning.'

The 'night porter' thanked him and left the room, and he soon heard her snoring from the adjoining apartment. Then Jocelyn opened proceedings, overhauling the robes[4] and extending them one by one. As the steam went up he fell into a reverie. He again became conscious of the change which had been initiated during the walk. The Well-Beloved was moving house – had gone over to the wearer of this attire.

In the course of ten minutes he adored her.

And how about little Avice Caro? He did not think of her as before.

He was not sure that he had ever seen the real Beloved in that friend of his youth, solicitous as he was for her welfare. But, loving her or not, he perceived that the spirit, emanation, idealism, which called itself his Love was flitting stealthily from some remoter figure to the near one in the chamber overhead.

Avice had not kept her engagement to meet him in the lonely ruin, fearing her own imaginings. But he, in fact, more than she, had been educated out of the island innocence that had upheld old manners; and this was the strange consequence of Avice's misapprehension.

CHAPTER VI

On the Brink

Miss Bencomb was leaving the hotel for the railway, which was quite near at hand, and had only recently been opened, as if on purpose for this event. At Jocelyn's suggestion she wrote a message to inform her father that she had gone to her aunt's, with a view to allaying anxiety and deterring pursuit. They walked together to the platform and bade each other good-bye; each obtained a ticket independently, and Jocelyn got his luggage from the cloak-room.

On the platform they encountered each other again, and there was a light in their glances at each other which said, as by a flash-telegraph: 'We are bound for the same town, why not enter the same compartment?'

They did.

She took a corner seat, with her back to the engine; he sat opposite. The guard looked in, thought they were lovers, and did not show other travellers into that compartment. They talked on strictly ordinary matters; what she thought he did not know, but at every stopping station he dreaded intrusion. Before they were halfway to London the event he had just begun to realize was a patent fact. The Beloved was again embodied; she filled every fibre and curve of this woman's form.

Drawing near the great London station was like drawing near Doomsday. How should he leave her in the turmoil of a crowded city street? She seemed quite unprepared for the rattle of the scene. He asked her where her aunt lived.

'Bayswater,' said Miss Bencomb.

He called a cab, and proposed that she should share it till they arrived at her aunt's, whose residence lay not much out of the way to his own. Try as he would he could not ascertain if she understood his feelings, but she assented to his offer and entered the vehicle.

'We are old friends,' he said, as they drove onward.

'Indeed, we are,' she answered, without smiling.

'But hereditarily we are mortal enemies, dear Juliet.'[1]

'Yes— What did you say?'

'I said Juliet.'

She laughed in a half-proud way, and murmured: 'Your father is my father's enemy, and my father is mine. Yes, it is so.' And then their eyes caught each other's glance. 'My queenly darling!' he burst out; 'instead of going to your aunt's, will you come and marry me?'

A flush covered her over, which seemed akin to a flush of rage. It was not exactly that, but she was excited. She did not answer, and he feared he had mortally offended her dignity. Perhaps she had only made use of him as a convenient aid to her intentions. However, he went on –

'Your father would not be able to reclaim you then! After all, this is not so precipitate as it seems. You know all about me, my history, my prospects. I know all about you. Our families have been neighbours on that isle for hundreds of years, though you are now such a London product.'

'Will you ever be a Royal Academician?'[2] she asked musingly, her excitement having calmed down.

'I hope to be – I *will* be, if you will be my wife.'

His companion looked at him long.

'Think what a short way out of your difficulty this would be,' he continued. 'No bother about aunts, no fetching home by an angry father.'

It seemed to decide her. She yielded to his embrace.

'How long will it take to marry?' Miss Bencomb asked by-and-by, with obvious self-repression.

'We could do it to-morrow. I could get to Doctors' Commons[3] by noon to-day, and the licence would be ready by to-morrow morning.'

'I won't go to my aunt's, I will be an independent woman! I have been reprimanded as if I were a child of six. I'll be your wife if it is as easy as you say.'

They stopped the cab while they held a consultation. Pierston had rooms and a studio in the neighbourhood of Campden Hill; but it would be hardly desirable to take her thither till they were married. They decided to go to an hotel.

Changing their direction, therefore, they went back to the Strand, and soon ensconced themselves in one of the venerable old taverns of Covent Garden, a precinct which in those days was frequented by West-country people. Jocelyn then left her and proceeded on his errand eastward.

It was about three o'clock when, having arranged all preliminaries necessitated by this sudden change of front, he began strolling slowly back; he felt bewildered, and to walk was a relief. Gazing occasionally into this shop window and that, he called a hansom as by an inspiration, and directed the driver to 'Mellstock Gardens.' Arrived here, he rang the bell of a studio, and in a minute or two it was answered by a young man in shirt-sleeves, about his own age, with a great smeared palette on his left thumb.

'O, you, Pierston! I thought you were in the country. Come in. I'm awfully glad of this. I am here in town finishing off a painting for an American, who wants to take it back with him.'

Pierston followed his friend into the painting-room, where a pretty young woman was sitting sewing. At a signal from the painter she disappeared without speaking.

'I can see from your face you have something to say; so we'll have it all to ourselves. You are in some trouble? What'll you drink?'

'Oh! it doesn't matter what, so that it is alcohol in some shape or form. . . . Now, Somers, you must just listen to me, for I *have* something to tell.'

Pierston had sat down in an arm-chair, and Somers had resumed his painting. When a servant had brought in brandy to soothe Pierston's nerves, and soda to take off the injurious effects of the brandy, and milk to take off the depleting effects of the soda, Jocelyn began his narrative, addressing it rather to Somers's Gothic chimneypiece, and Somers's Gothic clock, and Somers's Gothic rugs, than to Somers himself, who stood at his picture a little behind his friend.

'Before I tell you what has happened to me,' Pierston said, 'I want to let you know the manner of man I am.'

'Lord – I know already.'

'No, you don't. It is a sort of thing one doesn't like to talk of. I lie awake at night thinking about it.'

'No!' said Somers, with more sympathy, seeing that his friend was really troubled.

'I am under a curious curse, or influence. I am posed, puzzled and perplexed by the legerdemain of a creature – a deity rather; by Aphrodite, as a poet would put it, as I should put it myself in marble. . . . But I forget – this is not to be a deprecatory wail, but a defence – a sort of *Apologia pro vitâ meâ*.'[4]

'That's better. Fire away!'

CHAPTER VII

Her Earlier Incarnations

'You, Somers, are not, I know, one of those who continue to indulge in the world-wide, fond superstition that the Beloved One of any man always, or even usually, cares to remain in one corporeal nook or shell for any great length of time, however much he may wish her to do so. If I am wrong, and you do still hold to that ancient error – well, my story will seem rather queer.'

'Suppose you say some men, not any man.'¹

'All right – I'll say one man, this man only, if you are so particular. We are a strange, visionary race down where I come from, and perhaps that accounts for it. The Beloved of this one man, then, has had many incarnations – too many to describe in detail. Each shape, or embodiment, has been a temporary residence only, which she has entered, lived in a while, and made her exit from, leaving the substance, so far as I have been concerned, a corpse, worse luck! Now, there is no spiritualistic nonsense in this – it is simple fact, put in the plain form that the conventional public are afraid of. So much for the principle.'

'Good. Go on.'

'Well; the first embodiment of her occurred, so nearly as I can recollect, when I was about the age of nine. Her vehicle was a little blue-eyed girl of eight or so, one of a family of eleven, with flaxen hair about her shoulders, which attempted to curl, but ignominiously failed, hanging like chimney-crooks only. This defect used rather to trouble me; and was, I believe, one of the main reasons of my Beloved's departure from that tenement. I cannot remember with any exactness when the departure occurred. I know it was after I had kissed my little friend in a garden-seat on a hot noontide, under a blue gingham umbrella, which we had opened over us as we sat, that passers through East Quarriers might not observe our marks of affection, forgetting that our screen must attract more attention than our persons.

'When the whole dream came to an end through her father leaving the island, I thought my Well-Beloved had gone for ever (being then in the unpractised condition of Adam² at sight of the first sunset). But she had not. Laura had gone for ever, but not my Beloved.

'For some months after I had done crying for the flaxen-haired edition of her, my Love did not reappear. Then she came suddenly, unexpectedly, in a situation I should never have predicted. I was standing on the kerbstone of the pavement in Budmouth-Regis, outside the Preparatory School, looking across towards the sea, when a middle-aged gentleman on horseback, and beside him a young lady, also mounted, passed down the street. The girl turned her head, and – possibly because I was gaping at her in awkward admiration, or smiling myself – smiled at me. Having ridden a few paces, she looked round again and smiled.

'It was enough, more than enough, to set me on fire. I understood in a moment the information conveyed to me by my emotion – the Well-Beloved had reappeared. This second form in which it had pleased her to take up her abode was quite a grown young woman's, darker in complexion than the first. Her hair, also worn in a knot, was of an ordinary brown, and so, I think, were her eyes, but the niceties of her features were not to be gathered so cursorily. However, there sat my coveted one, re-embodied; and, bidding my schoolmates a hasty farewell as soon as I could do so without suspicion, I hurried along the Esplanade in the direction she and her father had ridden. But they had put their horses to a canter, and I could not see which way they had gone. In the greatest misery I turned down a side street, but was soon elevated to a state of excitement by seeing the same pair galloping towards me. Flushing up to my hair, I stopped and heroically faced her as she passed. She smiled again, but, alas! upon my Love's cheek there was no blush of passion for me.'

Pierston paused, and drank from his glass, as he lived for a brief moment in the scene he had conjured up. Somers reserved his comments, and Jocelyn continued –

'That afternoon I idled about the streets, looking for her in vain. When I next saw one of the boys who had been with me at her first passing I stealthily reminded him of the incident, and asked if he knew the riders.

'"O yes," he said. "That was Colonel Targe and his daughter Elsie."

'"How old do you think she is?" said I, a sense of disparity in our ages disturbing my mind.

'"O – nineteen, I think they say. She's going to be married the day after to-morrow to Captain Popp, of the 501st, and they are ordered off to India at once."

'The grief which I experienced at this intelligence was such that at dusk I went away to the edge of the harbour, intending to put an end to myself there and then. But I had been told that crabs had been found[3] clinging to the dead faces of persons who had fallen in thereabout, leisurely eating them, and the idea of such an unpleasant contingency deterred me. I should state that the marriage of my Beloved concerned me little; it was her departure that broke my heart. I never saw her again.

'Though I had already learnt that the absence of the corporeal matter did not involve the absence of the informing spirit, I could scarce bring myself to believe that in this case it was possible for her to return to my view without the form she had last inhabited.

'But she did.

'It was not, however, till after a good space of time, during which I passed through that bearish age in boys, their early teens, when girls are their especial contempt. I was about seventeen, and was sitting one evening over a cup of tea in a confectioner's at the very same watering-place, when opposite me a lady took her seat with a little girl. We looked at each other awhile, the child made advances, till I said: "She's a good little thing."

'The lady assented, and made a further remark.

' "She has the soft fine eyes of her mother," said I.

' "Do you think her eyes are good?" asks the lady, as if she had not heard what she had heard most – the last three words of my opinion.

' "Yes – for copies," said I, regarding her.

'After this we got on very well. She informed me that her husband had gone out in a yacht, and I said it was a pity he didn't take her with him for the airing. She gradually disclosed herself in the character of a deserted young wife, and later on I met her in the street without the child. She was going to the landing-stage to meet her husband, so she told me; but she did not know the way.

'I offered to show her, and did so. I will not go into particulars, but I afterwards saw her several times, and soon discovered that the Beloved (as to whose whereabouts I had been at fault so long) lurked here. Though why she had chosen this tantalizing situation of an inaccessible matron's form when so many others offered, it was beyond me to discover. The whole affair ended innocently enough, when the lady left the town with her husband and child: she seemed to regard our acquaintance as a flirtation; yet it was anything but a flirtation for me!

*   *   *   *   *

'Why should I tell the rest of the tantalizing tale! After this, the Well-Beloved put herself in evidence with greater and greater frequency, and it would be impossible for me to give you details of her various incarnations. She came nine times in the course of the two or three ensuing years. Four times she masqueraded as a brunette, twice as a pale-haired creature, and two or three times under a complexion neither light nor dark. Sometimes she was a tall, fine girl, but more often, I think, she preferred to slip into the skin of a lithe airy being, of no great stature. I grew so accustomed to these exits and entrances that I resigned myself to them quite passively, talked to her, kissed her, corresponded with her, ached for her, in each of her several guises. So it went on until a month ago. And then for the first time I was puzzled. She either had, or she had not, entered the person of Avice Caro, a young girl I had known from infancy. Upon the whole, I have decided that, after all, she did not enter the form of Avice Caro, because I retain so great a respect for her still.'

Pierston here gave in brief the history of his revived comradeship with Avice, the verge of the engagement to which they had reached, and its unexpected rupture by him, merely through his meeting with a woman into whom the Well-Beloved unmistakably moved under his very eyes – by name Miss Marcia Bencomb. He described their spontaneous decision to marry offhand; and then he put it to Somers whether he ought to marry or not – her or anybody else – in such circumstances.

'Certainly not,' said Somers. 'Though, if anybody, little Avice. But not even her. You are like other men, only rather worse. Essentially, all men are fickle, like you; but not with such perceptiveness.'

'Surely fickle is not the word? Fickleness means getting weary of a thing while the thing remains the same. But I have always been faithful to the elusive creature whom I have never been able to get a firm hold of, unless I have done so now. And let me tell you that her flitting from each to each individual has been anything but a pleasure for me – certainly not a wanton game of my instigation. To see the creature who has hitherto been perfect, divine, lose under your very gaze the divinity which has informed her, grow commonplace, turn from flame to ashes, from a radiant vitality to a corpse, is anything but a pleasure for any man, and has been nothing less than a racking spectacle to my sight. Each mournful emptied shape stands ever after like the nest of some beautiful bird from which the inhabitant has departed and left it to fill with snow.[4] I have been absolutely miserable when I have looked in a face for her I used to see there, and could see her there no more.'

'You ought not to marry,' repeated Somers.

'Perhaps I oughtn't to! Though poor Marcia will be compromised, I'm afraid, if I don't. . . . Was I not right in saying I am accursed in this thing? Fortunately nobody but myself has suffered on account of it till now. Knowing what to expect, I have seldom ventured on a close acquaintance with any woman, in fear of prematurely driving away the dear one in her; who, however, has in time gone off just the same.'

Pierston soon after took his leave. A friend's advice on such a subject weighs little. He quickly returned to Miss Bencomb.

She was different now. Anxiety had visibly brought her down a notch or two, undone a few degrees of that haughty curl which her lip could occasionally assume. 'How long you have been away!' she said with a show of impatience.

'Never mind, darling. It is all arranged,' said he. 'We shall be able to marry in a few days.'

'Not to-morrow?'

'We can't to-morrow.[5] We have not been here quite long enough.'

'But how did the people at Doctors' Commons know that?'

'Well – I forgot that residence, real or assumed, was necessary, and unfortunately admitted that we had only just arrived.'

'O how stupid! But it can't be helped now. I think, dear, I should have known better, however!'

CHAPTER VIII

'Too Like the Lightning'[1]

They lived on at the hotel some days longer,[2] eyed curiously by the chambermaids, and burst in upon every now and then by the waiters as if accidentally. When they were walking together, mostly in back streets for fear of being recognized, Marcia was often silent, and her imperious face looked gloomy.

'Dummy!' he said playfully, on one of these occasions.

'I am vexed that by your admissions at Doctors' Commons you prevented them giving you the licence at once! It is not nice, my living on like this!'

'But we are going to marry, dear!'

'Yes,' she murmured, and fell into reverie again. 'What a sudden resolve it was of ours!' she continued. 'I wish I could get my father and mother's consent to our marriage. . . . As we can't complete it for another day or two, a letter might be sent to them and their answer received? I have a mind to write.'

Pierston expressed his doubts of the wisdom of this course, which seemed to make her desire it the more, and the result was a tiff between them. 'Since we are obliged to delay it, I won't marry without their consent!' she cried at last passionately.

'Very well then, dear. Write,' he said.

When they were again indoors, she sat down to a note, but after a while threw aside her pen despairingly. 'No: I cannot do it!' she said. 'I can't bend my pride to such a job. Will *you* write for me, Jocelyn?'

'I? I don't see why I should be the one, particularly as I think it premature.'

'But you have not quarrelled with my father as I have done.'

'Well no. But there is a long-standing antagonism, which would make it odd in me to write. Wait till we are married, and then I will write. Not till then.'

'Then I suppose I must. You don't know my father. He might forgive me marrying into any other family without his knowledge, but he thinks so meanly of yours on account of the trade rivalry that he would never pardon till the day of his death my becoming a Pierston secretly. I didn't see it at first.'

This remark caused an unpleasant jar on the mind of Pierston. Despite his independent artistic position in London, he was staunch to the simple old parent who had stubbornly held out for so many years against Bencomb's encroaching trade, and whose money had educated and maintained Jocelyn as an art-student in the best schools. So he begged her to say no more about his family, and she silently resumed her letter, giving an address at a post-office that their quarters might not be discovered, at least just yet.

No reply came by return of post; but, rather ominously, some letters for Marcia that had arrived at her father's since her departure were sent on in silence to the address given. She opened them one by one, till on reading the last, she exclaimed, 'Good gracious!' and burst into laughter.

'What is it?' asked Pierston.

Marcia began to read the letter aloud. It came from a faithful lover of hers, a youthful Jersey gentleman, who stated that he was soon going to start for England to claim his darling, according to her plighted word.

She was half risible, half concerned. 'What shall I do?' she said.

'Do? My dear girl, it seems to me that there is only one thing to do, and that a very obvious thing. Tell him as soon as possible that you are just on the point of marriage.'

Marcia thereupon wrote out a reply to that effect, Jocelyn helping her to shape the phrases as gently as possible.

'I repeat' (her letter concluded) 'that I had quite forgotten! I am deeply sorry; but that is the truth. I have told my intended husband everything, and he is looking over my shoulder as I write.'

Said Jocelyn when he saw this set down: 'You might leave out the last few words. They are rather an extra stab for the poor boy.'

'Stab? It is not that, dear. Why does he want to come bothering me? Jocelyn, you ought to be very proud that I have put you in my letter at all. You said yesterday that I was conceited in declaring I might have married that science-man I told you of. But now you see there was yet another available.'

He, gloomily: 'Well, I don't care to hear about that. To my mind this sort of thing is decidedly unpleasant, though you treat it so lightly.'

'Well,' she pouted, 'I have only done half what you have done!'

'What's that?'

'I have only proved false through forgetfulness, but you have while remembering!'

'O yes; of course you can use Avice Caro as a retort. But don't vex me about her, and make me do such an unexpected thing as regret the falseness.'

She shut her mouth tight, and her face flushed.

The next morning there did come an answer to the letter asking her parents' consent to her union with him; but to Marcia's amazement her father took a line quite other than the one she had expected him to take. Whether she had compromised herself or whether she had not seemed a question for the future rather than the present with him, a native islander, born when old island marriage views prevailed in families; he was fixed in his disapproval of her marriage with a hated Pierston. He did not consent; he would not say more till he could see her: if she had any sense at all she would, if still unmarried, return to the home from which she had evidently been enticed. He would then see what he could do for her in the desperate circumstances she had made for herself; otherwise he would do nothing.

Pierston could not help being sarcastic at her father's evidently low estimate of him and his belongings; and Marcia took umbrage at his sarcasms.

'I am the one deserving of satire if anybody!' she said. 'I begin to feel I was a foolish girl to run away from a father for such a trumpery reason as a little scolding because I had exceeded my allowance.'

'I advised you to go back, Marcie.'

'In a sort of way: not in the right tone. You spoke most contemptuously of my father as a merchant.'

'I couldn't speak otherwise of him than I did, I'm afraid, knowing what—'

'What have you to say against him?'

'Nothing – to you, Marcie, beyond what is matter of common notoriety. Everybody knows that at one time he made it the business of his life to ruin my father; and the way he alludes to me in that letter shows that his enmity still continues.'

'That miser ruined by an open-handed man like my father!' said she. 'It is like your people's misrepresentations to say that!'

Marcia's eyes flashed, and her face burnt with an angry heat, the enhanced beauty which this warmth might have brought being killed by the rectilinear sternness of countenance that came therewith.

'Marcia – this temper is too exasperating! I could give you every step of the proceeding in detail – anybody could – the getting the quarries one by one, and everything, my father only holding his own by the most desperate courage. There is no blinking facts. Our parents' relations are an ugly fact in the circumstances of us two people who want to marry, and we are just beginning to perceive it; and how we are going to get over it I cannot tell.'

She said steadily: 'I don't think we shall get over it at all!'

'We may not – we may not – altogether,' Pierston murmured, as he gazed at the fine picture of scorn presented by his Juno's classical face[3] and dark eyes.

'Unless you beg my pardon for having behaved so!'

Pierston could not quite bring himself to see that he had behaved badly to his too imperious lady, and declined to ask forgiveness for what he had not done.

She thereupon left the room. Later in the day she re-entered and broke a silence by saying bitterly: 'I showed temper just now, as you told me. But things have causes, and it is perhaps a mistake that you should have deserted Avice for me. Instead of wedding Rosaline,[4] Romeo must needs go eloping with Juliet. It was a fortunate thing for the affections of those two Veronese lovers that they died when they did. In a short time the enmity of their families would have proved a fruitful source of dissension; Juliet would have gone back to her people, he to his; the subject would have split them as much as it splits us.'

Pierston laughed a little. But Marcia was painfully serious, as he found at tea-time, when she said that since his refusal to beg her pardon she had been thinking over the matter, and had resolved to go to her aunt's after all – at any rate till her father could be induced to agree to their union. Pierston was as chilled by this resolve of hers as he was surprised at her independence in circumstances which usually make women the reverse. But he put no obstacles in her way, and, with a kiss strangely cold after their recent ardour, the Romeo of the freestone Montagues went out of the hotel, to avoid even the appearance of coercing his Juliet of the rival house. When he returned she was gone.

* * * * *

A correspondence began between these too-hastily pledged ones; and it was carried on in terms of serious reasoning upon their awkward situation on account of the family feud. They saw their recent love as what it was:

> 'Too rash, too unadvised, too sudden;
> Too like the lightning . . .'[5]

They saw it with an eye whose calmness, coldness, and, it must be added, wisdom, did not promise well for their reunion.

Their debates were clinched by a final letter from Marcia, sent from no other place than her recently left home in the Isle. She informed him that her father had appeared suddenly at her aunt's, and had induced her to go home with him. She had told her father all the circumstances of their elopement, and what mere accidents had caused it: he had persuaded her on what she had almost been convinced of by their disagreement; that all thought of their marriage should be at least postponed for the present; any awkwardness and even scandal being better than that they should immediately unite themselves for life on the strength of a two or three days' passion, and be the wretched victims of a situation they could never change.

Pierston saw plainly enough that he owed it to her father being a born islander, with all the ancient island notions of the sexes lying underneath his acquired conventions, that the stone-merchant did not immediately insist upon the usual remedy for a daughter's precipitancy of action, but preferred to await issues.

But the young man still thought that Marcia herself, when her temper had quite cooled, and she was more conscious of her real position, would return to him, in spite of the family hostility. There was no social reason against such a step. In birth the pair were about on one plane; and though Marcia's family had gained a start in the accumulation of wealth, and in the beginnings of social distinction, which lent colour to the feeling that the advantages of the match would be mainly on one side, Pierston was a sculptor who might rise to fame; so that potentially their marriage could not be considered inauspicious for a woman who, beyond being the probable heiress to a considerable fortune, had no exceptional opportunities.

Thus, though disillusioned, he felt bound in honour to remain on call at his London address as long as there was the slightest chance of Marcia's reappearance, or of the arrival of some message requesting him to join her, that they might, after all, go to the altar together. Yet in the night he seemed to hear sardonic voices, and laughter in the wind at this development of his little romance, and during the slow and colourless days he had to sit and behold the mournful departure of his Well-Beloved from the form he had lately cherished, till she had almost vanished away. The exact moment of her complete withdrawal Pierston knew not, but not many lines of her were longer discernible in Marcia's remembered contours, nor many sounds of her in Marcia's recalled accents. Their acquaintance, though so fervid,[6] had been too brief for such lingering.

There came a time when he learnt, through a trustworthy channel, two pieces of news affecting himself. One was the marriage of Avice Caro with her cousin, the other that the Bencombs had started on a tour round the world, which was to include a visit to a relation of Mr. Bencomb's who was a banker in San Francisco. Since retiring from his former large business the stone-merchant had not known what to do with his leisure, and finding that travel benefited his health he had decided to indulge himself thus. Although he was not so informed, Pierston concluded that Marcia had accompanied her parents, and he was more than ever struck with what this signified – her father's obstinate antagonism to her union with one of his blood and name.

CHAPTER IX

Familiar Phenomena in the Distance

By degrees Pierston began to trace again the customary lines of his existence; and his profession occupied him much as of old. The next year or two only once brought him tidings, through some residents at his former home, of the movements of the Bencombs. The extended voyage of Marcia's parents had given them quite a zest for other scenes and countries; and it was said that her father, a man still in vigorous health except at brief intervals, was utilizing the outlook which his cosmopolitanism afforded him by investing capital in foreign undertakings. What he had supposed turned out to be true; Marcia was with them; and thus the separation of himself and his nearly married wife[1] by common consent was likely to be a permanent one.

It seemed as if he would scarce ever again discover the carnate dwelling-place of the haunting minion of his imagination. Having gone so near to matrimony with Marcia as to apply for a licence, he had felt for a long while morally bound to her by the incipient contract, and would not intentionally look about him in search of the vanished Ideality. Thus during the first year of Miss Bencomb's absence, when absolutely bound to keep faith with the elusive one's late incarnation if she should return to claim him, this man of the odd fancy would sometimes tremble at the thought of what would become of his solemn intention if the Phantom were suddenly to disclose herself in an unexpected quarter, and seduce him before he was aware. Once or twice he imagined that he saw her in the distance – at the end of a street, on the far sands of a shore, in a window, in a meadow, at the opposite side of a railway station; but he determinedly turned on his heel, and walked the other way.

During the many uneventful seasons that followed Marcia's stroke of independence (for which he was not without a secret admiration at times), Jocelyn threw into plastic creations that ever-bubbling spring of emotion which, without some conduit into space, will surge upwards and ruin all but the greatest men. It was probably owing to this, certainly not on account of any care or anxiety for such a result, that he was successful in his art, successful by a seemingly sudden spurt, which carried him at one bound over the hindrances of years.

He prospered without effort. He was A.R.A.[2]

But recognitions of this sort, social distinctions, which he had once coveted so keenly, seemed to have no utility for him now. By the accident of being a bachelor, he was floating in society without any soul-anchorage or shrine that he could call his own; and, for want of a domestic centre round which honours might crystallize,[3] they dispersed impalpably without accumulating and adding weight to his material well-being.

He would have gone on working with his chisel with just as much zest if his creations had been doomed to meet no mortal eye but his own. This indifference to the popular reception of his dream-figures lent him a curious artistic *aplomb* that carried him through the gusts of opinion without suffering them to disturb his inherent bias.

The study of beauty was his only joy[4] for years onward. In the streets he would observe a face, or a fraction of a face, which seemed to express to a hair's-breadth in mutable flesh what he was at that moment wishing to express in durable shape. He would dodge and follow the owner like a detective; in omnibus, in cab, in steam-boat, through crowds, into shops, churches, theatres, public-houses, and slums – mostly, when at close quarters, to be disappointed for his pains.

In these professional beauty-chases he sometimes cast his eye across the Thames to the wharves on the south side, and to that particular one whereat his father's tons of freestone were daily landed from the ketches of the south coast. He could occasionally discern the white blocks lying there, vast cubes so persistently nibbled by his parent from his island rock in the English Channel, that it seemed as if in time it would be nibbled all away.

One thing it passed him to understand: on what field of observation the poets and philosophers based their assumption that the passion of love was intensest in youth and burnt lower as maturity advanced. It was possibly because of his utter domestic loneliness that, during the productive interval which followed the first years of Marcia's departure, when he was drifting along from five-and-twenty to eight-and-thirty, Pierston occasionally loved with an ardour – though, it is true, also with a self-control – unknown to him when he was green in judgment.

* * * * *

His whimsical isle-bred fancy had grown to be such an emotion that the Well-Beloved – now again visible – was always existing somewhere near him. For months he would find her on the stage of a theatre: then she would flit away, leaving the poor, empty carcase that had lodged her to mumm on as best it could without her – a sorry lay figure to his eyes, heaped with imperfections and sullied with commonplace. She would reappear, it might be, in an at first unnoticed lady, met at some fashionable evening-party, exhibition, bazaar, or dinner; to flit from her, in turn, after a few months, and stand as a graceful shop-girl at some large drapery warehouse into which he had strayed on an unaccustomed errand. Then she would forsake this figure and redisclose herself in the guise of some popular authoress, piano-player, or fiddleress, at whose shrine he would worship for perhaps a twelvemonth. Once she was a dancing-girl at the Royal Moorish Palace[5] of Varieties, though during her whole continuance at that establishment he never once exchanged a word with her, nor did she first or last ever dream of his existence. He knew that a ten-minutes' conversation in the wings with the substance would send the elusive haunter scurrying fearfully away into some other even less accessible mask-figure.

She was a blonde, a brunette, tall, *petite, svelte,* straight-featured, full, curvilinear. Only one quality remained unalterable: her instability of tenure. In Börne's phrase,[6] nothing was permanent in her but change.

'It is odd,' he said to himself, 'that this experience of mine, or idiosyncrasy, or whatever it is, which would be sheer waste of time for other men, creates sober business for me.' For all these dreams he translated into plaster, and found that by them he was hitting a public taste he had never deliberately aimed at, and mostly despised. He was, in short, in danger of drifting away from a solid artistic reputation to a popularity which might possibly be as brief as it would be brilliant and exciting.

'You will be caught some day, my friend,' Somers would occasionally observe to him. 'I don't mean to say entangled in anything discreditable, for I admit that you are in practice as ideal as in theory. I mean the process will be reversed. Some woman, whose Well-Beloved flits about as yours does now, will catch your eye, and you'll stick to her like a limpet, while she follows her Phantom and leaves you to ache as you will.'

'You may be right; but I think you are wrong,' said Pierston. 'As flesh she dies[7] daily, like the Apostle's corporeal self; because when I grapple with the reality she's no longer in it, so that I cannot stick to one incarnation if I would.'

'Wait till you are older,' said Somers.

PART SECOND

A Young Man of Forty

'Since Love will needs that I shall love,
Of very force I must agree:
And since no chance may it remove,
In wealth and in adversity
I shall alway myself apply
To serve and suffer patiently."

SIR T. WYATT

CHAPTER I

The Old Phantom Becomes Distinct

In the course of these long years Pierston's artistic emotions were abruptly suspended by the news of his father's sudden death[2] at Sandbourne, whither the stone-merchant had gone for a change of air by the advice of his physician.

Mr. Pierston, senior, it must be admitted, had been something miserly in his home life, as Marcia had so rashly reminded his son. But he had never stinted Jocelyn. He had been rather a hard taskmaster, though as a paymaster trustworthy; a ready-money man, just and ungenerous. To every one's surprise, the capital he had accumulated in the stone trade was of large amount for a business so unostentatiously carried on – much larger than Jocelyn had ever regarded as possible. While the son had been modelling and chipping his ephemeral fancies into perennial shapes, the father had been persistently chiselling for half a century at the crude original matter of those shapes, the stern, isolated rock in the Channel; and by the aid of his cranes and pulleys, his trolleys and his boats, had sent off his spoil to all parts of Great Britain. When Jocelyn had wound up everything and disposed of the business, as recommended by his father's will, he found himself enabled to add about eighty thousand pounds to the twelve thousand which he already possessed from professional and other sources.

After arranging for the sale of some freehold properties in the island other than quarries – for he did not intend to reside there – he returned to town. He often wondered what had become of Marcia. He had promised never to trouble her; nor for a whole twenty years had he done so; though he had often sighed for her as a friend of sterling common sense in practical difficulties.

Her parents were, he believed, dead; and she, he knew, had never gone back to the isle. Possibly she had formed some new tie abroad, and had made it next to impossible to discover her by her old name.

A reposeful time ensued. Almost his first entry into society after his father's death occurred one evening, when, for want of knowing what better to do, he responded to an invitation sent by one of the few ladies of rank whom he numbered among his friends, and set out in a cab for the square wherein she lived during three or four months of the year.

The hansom turned the corner, and he obtained a raking view of the houses along the north side, of which hers was one, with the familiar linkman at the door. There were Chinese lanterns, too, on the balcony. He perceived in a moment that the customary 'small and early'[3] reception had resolved itself on this occasion into something very like great and late. He remembered that there had just been a political crisis, which accounted for the enlargement of the Countess of Channelcliffe's assembly;[4] for hers was one of the neutral or non-political houses at which party politics are more freely agitated than at the professedly party gatherings.

There was such a string of carriages that Pierston did not wait to take his turn at the door, but unobtrusively alighted some yards off and walked forward. He had to pause a moment behind the wall of spectators which barred his way, and as he paused some ladies in white cloaks crossed from their carriages to the door on the carpet laid for the purpose. He had not seen their faces, nothing of them but vague forms, and yet he was suddenly seized with a presentiment. Its gist was that he might be going to re-encounter the Well-Beloved that night: after her recent long hiding she meant to reappear and intoxicate him. That liquid sparkle of her eye, that lingual music, that turn of the head, how well he knew it all, despite the many superficial changes, and how instantly he would recognize it under whatever complexion, contour, accent, height, or carriage that it might choose to masquerade!

Pierston's other conjecture, that the night was to be a lively political one, received confirmation as soon as he reached the hall, where a simmer of excitement was perceptible as surplus or overflow from above down the staircase – a feature which he had always noticed to be present when any climax or sensation had been reached in the world of party and faction.

'And where have you been keeping yourself so long, young man?' said his hostess archly, when he had shaken hands with her. (Pierston was always regarded as a young man, though he was now about forty.) 'O yes, of course, I remember,' she added, looking serious in a moment at thought of his loss. The Countess was a woman with a good-natured manner verging on that oft-claimed feminine quality, humour, and was quickly sympathetic.

She then began to tell him of a scandal in the political side to which she nominally belonged, one that had come out of the present crisis; and that, as for herself, she had sworn to abjure politics for ever on account of it, so that he was to regard her forthwith as a more neutral householder than ever. By this time some more people had surged upstairs, and Pierston prepared to move on.

'You are looking for somebody – I can see that,' said she.

'Yes – a lady,' said Pierston.

'Tell me her name, and I'll try to think if she's here.'

'I cannot; I don't know it,' he said.

'Indeed! What is she like?'

'I cannot describe her, not even her complexion or dress.'

Lady Channelcliffe looked a pout, as if she thought he were teasing her, and he moved on in the current. The fact was that, for a moment, Pierston fancied he had made the sensational discovery that the One he was in search of lurked in the person of the very hostess he had conversed with, who was charming always, and particularly charming to-night; he was just feeling an incipient consternation at the possibility of such a jade's trick in his Beloved, who had once before chosen to embody herself as a married woman, though, happily, at that time with no serious results. However, he felt that he had been mistaken, and that the fancy had been solely owing to the highly charged electric condition in which he had arrived by reason of his recent isolation.

The whole set of rooms formed one great utterance of the opinions of the hour. The gods of party were present with their embattled seraphim, but the brilliancy of manner and form in the handling of public questions was only less conspicuous than the paucity of original ideas. No principles of wise government had place in any mind, a blunt and jolly personalism as to the Ins and Outs animating all. But Jocelyn's interest did not run in this stream: he was like a stone in a purling brook, waiting for some peculiar floating object to be brought towards him and to stick upon his mental surface.

Thus looking for the next new version of the fair figure, he did not consider at the moment, though he had done so at other times, that this presentiment of meeting her was, of all presentiments, just the sort of one to work out its own fulfilment.

He looked for her in the knot of persons gathered round a past Prime Minister who was standing in the middle of the largest room discoursing in the genial, almost jovial, manner natural to him at these times. The two or three ladies forming his audience had been joined by another in black and white, and it was on her that Pierston's attention was directed, as well as the great statesman's, whose first sheer gaze at her, expressing 'Who are you?' almost audibly, changed into an interested, listening look as the few words she spoke were uttered – for the Minister differed from many of his standing in being extremely careful not to interrupt a timid speaker, giving way in an instant if anybody else began with him. Nobody knew better than himself that all may learn, and his manner was that of an unconceited man who could catch an idea readily, even if he could not undertake to create one.

The lady told her little story – whatever it was Jocelyn could not hear it – the statesman laughed: 'Haugh-haugh-haugh!'

The lady blushed. Jocelyn, wrought up to a high tension by the afore-said presentiment that his Shelleyan 'One-shape-of-many-names'[5] was about to reappear, paid little heed to the others, watching for a full view of the lady who had won his attention.

That lady remained for the present partially screened by her neigh-bours. A diversion was caused by Lady Channelcliffe bringing up some-body to present to the ex-Minister; the ladies got mixed, and Jocelyn lost sight of the one whom he was beginning to suspect as the stealthily returned absentee.

He looked for her in a kindly young lady of the house,[6] his hostess's relation, who appeared to more advantage that night than she had ever done before – in a sky-blue dress, which had nothing between it and the fair skin of her neck, lending her an unusually soft and sylph-like aspect. She saw him, and they converged. Her look of 'What do you think of me *now*?' was suggested, he knew, by the thought that the last time they met she had appeared under the disadvantage of mourning clothes, on a wet day in a country-house, where everybody was cross.

'I have some new photographs, and I want you to tell me whether they are good,' she said. 'Mind you are to tell me truly, and no favour.'

She produced the pictures from an adjoining drawer, and they sat down together upon an ottoman for the purpose of examination. The portraits, taken by the last fashionable photographer, were very good, and he told her so; but as he spoke and compared them his mind was fixed on something else than the mere judgment. He wondered whether the elusive one were indeed in the frame of this girl.

He looked up at her. To his surprise, her mind, too, was on other things bent than on the pictures. Her eyes were glancing away to distant people, she was apparently considering the effect she was producing upon them by this cosy tête-à-tête with Pierston, and upon one in particular, a man of thirty, of military appearance, whom Pierston did not know. Quite convinced now that no phantom belonging to him was contained in the outlines of the present young lady, he could coolly survey her as he responded. They were both doing the same thing – each was pretending to be deeply interested in what the other was talking about, the attention of the two alike flitting away to other corners of the room even when the very point of their discourse was pending.

No, he had not seen Her yet. He was not going to see her, apparently, to-night; she was scared away by the twanging political atmosphere. But he still moved on searchingly, hardly heeding certain spectral imps other than Aphroditean, who always haunted these places, and jeeringly pointed out that under the white hair of this or that ribanded old man, with a forehead grown wrinkled over treaties which had swayed the fortunes of Europe, with a voice which had numbered sovereigns among its respectful listeners, might be a heart that would go inside a nut-shell; that beneath this or that white rope of pearl and pink bosom, might lie the half-lung which had, by hook or by crook, to sustain its possessor above-ground till the wedding-day.

At that moment he encountered his amiable host, and almost simultaneously caught sight of the lady who had at first attracted him and then had disappeared. Their eyes met, far off as they were from each other. Pierston laughed inwardly: it was only in ticklish excitement as to whether this was to prove a true *trouvaille*, and with no instinct to mirth; for when under the eyes of his Jill-o'-the-Wisp[7] he was more inclined to palpitate like a sheep in a fair.

However, for the minute he had to converse with his host, Lord Channelcliffe, and almost the first thing that friend said to him was: 'Who is that pretty woman in the black dress with the white fluff about it and the pearl necklace?'

'I don't know,' said Jocelyn, with incipient jealousy: 'I was just going to ask the same thing.'

'O, we shall find out presently, I suppose. I daresay my wife knows.' They had parted, when a hand came upon his shoulder. Lord Channelcliffe had turned back for an instant: 'I find she is the granddaughter

of my father's old friend, the last Lord Hengistbury. Her name is Mrs.—
Mrs. Pine-Avon;[8] she lost her husband two or three years ago, very shortly
after their marriage.'

Lord Channelcliffe became absorbed into some adjoining dignitary of
the Church, and Pierston was left to pursue his quest alone. A young
friend of his – the Lady Mabella Buttermead,[9] who appeared in a cloud
of muslin and was going on to a ball – had been brought against him by
the tide. A warm-hearted, emotional girl was Lady Mabella, who laughed
at the humorousness of being alive. She asked him whither he was bent,
and he told her.

'O yes, I know her very well!' said Lady Mabella eagerly. 'She told me
one day that she particularly wished to meet you. Poor thing – so sad –
she lost her husband. Well, it was a long time ago now, certainly. Women
ought not to marry and lay themselves open to such catastrophes, ought
they, Mr. Pierston? *I* never shall. I am determined never to run such a
risk! Now, do you think I shall?'

'Marry? O no; never,' said Pierston drily.

'That's very comforting.' But Mabella was scarcely comfortable under
the answer, even though jestingly returned, and she added: 'But sometimes I think I may, just for the fun of it. . . . Now we'll steer across to her,
and catch her, and I'll introduce you. But we shall never get to her at this
rate!'

'Never, unless we adopt "the ugly rush," like the citizens who follow the
Lord Mayor's Show.'

They talked, and inched towards the desired one, who, as she dis-
coursed with a neighbour, seemed one of those –

'Female forms, whose gestures beam with mind,'[10]

seen by the poet in his Vision of the Golden City of Islam.

Their progress was continually checked. Pierston was as he had sometimes seemed to be in a dream, unable to advance towards the object of
pursuit unless he could have gathered up his feet into the air. After ten
minutes given to a preoccupied regard of shoulder-blades, back hair, glittering headgear, neck-napes, moles, hairpins, pearl-powder,[11] pimples,
minerals cut into facets of many-coloured rays, necklace-clasps, fans,
stays, the seven styles of elbow and arm, the thirteen varieties of ear; and
by using the toes of his dress-boots as coulters with which he ploughed his
way and that of Lady Mabella in the direction they were aiming at, he

drew near to Mrs. Pine-Avon, who was drinking a cup of tea in the back drawing-room.

'My dear Nichola, we thought we should never get to you, because it is worse to-night, owing to these dreadful politics! But we've done it.' And she proceeded to tell her friend of Pierston's existence hard by.

It seemed that the widow really did wish to know him, and that Lady Mabella Buttermead had not indulged in one of the too frequent inventions in that kind. When the youngest of the trio had made the pair acquainted with each other she left them to talk to a younger man than the sculptor.

Mrs. Pine-Avon's black velvets and silks, with their white accompaniments, finely set off the exceeding fairness of her neck and shoulders, which, though unwhitened artificially, were without a speck or blemish of the least degree. The gentle, thoughtful creature she had looked from a distance she now proved herself to be; she held also sound rather than current opinions on the plastic arts, and was the first intellectual woman he had seen there that night, except one or two as aforesaid.

They soon became well acquainted, and at a pause in their conversation noticed the new excitement caused by the arrival of some late comers with more news. The latter had been brought by a rippling, bright-eyed lady in black, who made the men listen to her, whether they would or no.

'I am glad I am an outsider,' said Jocelyn's acquaintance, now seated on a sofa beside which he was standing. 'I wouldn't be like my cousin, over there, for the world. She thinks her husband will be turned out at the next election, and she's quite wild.'

'Yes; it is mostly the women who are the gamesters; the men only the cards. The pity is that politics are looked on as being a game for politicians, just as cricket is a game for cricketers; not as the serious duties of political trustees.'

'How few of us ever think or feel that "the nation of every country dwells in the cottage,"[12] as somebody says!'

'Yes. Though I wonder to hear you quote that.'

'O – I am of no party, though my relations are. There can be only one best course at all times, and the wisdom of the nation should be directed to finding it, instead of zigzagging in two courses, according to the will of the party which happens to have the upper hand.'

Having started thus, they found no difficulty in agreeing on many points. When Pierston went downstairs from that assembly at a quarter to one, and passed under the steaming nostrils of an ambassador's horses to a hansom which waited for him against the railing of the square, he had an impression that the Beloved had re-emerged from the shadows, without any hint or initiative from him – to whom, indeed, such re-emergence was an unquestionably awkward thing.

In this he was aware, however, that though it might be now, as heretofore, the Loved who danced before him, it was the Goddess behind her who pulled the string of that Jumping Jill. He had lately been trying his artist hand again on the Dea's form in every conceivable phase and mood. He had become a one-part man – a presenter of her only. But his efforts had resulted in failures. In her implacable vanity she might be punishing him anew for presenting her so deplorably.[13]

CHAPTER II

She Draws Close and Satisfies

He could not forget Mrs. Pine-Avon's eyes, though he remembered nothing of her other facial details. They were round, inquiring, luminous.[1] How that chestnut hair of hers had shone: it required no tiara to set it off, like that of the dowager he had seen there, who had put ten thousand pounds upon her head to make herself look worse than she would have appeared with the ninepenny muslin cap of a servant woman.

Now the question was, ought he to see her again? He had his doubts. But, unfortunately for discretion, just when he was coming out of the rooms he had encountered an old lady of seventy, his friend Mrs. Brightwalton – the Honourable Mrs. Brightwalton – and she had hastily asked him to dinner for the day after the morrow, stating in the honest way he knew so well that she had heard he was out of town, or she would have asked him two or three weeks ago. Now, of all social things that Pierston liked it was to be asked to dinner off-hand, as a stopgap in place of some bishop, lord, or Under-Secretary who couldn't come, and when the invitation was supplemented by the tidings that the lady who had so impressed him was to be one of the guests, he had promised instantly.

At the dinner, he took down Mrs. Pine-Avon upon his arm, and talked to nobody else during the meal. Afterwards they kept apart awhile in the drawing-room for form's sake; but eventually gravitated together again, and finished the evening in each other's company. When, shortly after eleven, he came away, he felt almost certain that within those luminous grey eyes the One of his eternal fidelity had verily taken lodgings – and for a long lease. But this was not all. At parting, he had, almost involuntarily, given her hand a pressure of a peculiar and indescribable kind; a little response from her, like a mere pulsation, of the same sort, told him that the impression she had made upon him was reciprocated. She was, in a word, willing to go on.

But was he able?

There had not been much harm in the flirtation thus far; but did she know his history, the curse upon his nature? – that he was the Wandering Jew of the love-world,[2] how restlessly ideal his fancies were, how the artist in him had consumed the wooer, how he was in constant dread lest he should wrong some woman twice as good as himself by seeming to mean what he fain would mean but could not, how useless he was likely to be for practical steps towards householding, though he was all the while pining for domestic life. He was now over forty, she was probably thirty; and he dared not make unmeaning love with the careless selfishness of a younger man. It was unfair to go further without telling her, even though, hitherto, such explicitness had not been absolutely demanded.

He determined to call immediately on the New Incarnation.

She lived not far from the long, fashionable Hamptonshire Square, and he went hither with expectations of having a highly emotional time, at least. But somehow the very bell-pull seemed cold, although she had so earnestly asked him to come.

As the house spoke, so spoke the occupant, much to the astonishment of the sculptor. The doors he passed through seemed as if they had not been opened for a month; and, entering the large drawing-room, he beheld, in an easy chair, in the far distance, a lady whom he journeyed across the carpet to reach, and ultimately did reach. To be sure it was Mrs. Nichola Pine-Avon, but frosted over indescribably. Raising her eyes in a slightly inquiring manner from the book she was reading, she leant back in the chair, as if soaking herself in luxurious sensations which had nothing to do with him, and replied to his greeting with a few commonplace words.

The unfortunate Jocelyn, though recuperative to a degree, was at first terribly upset by this reception. He had distinctly begun to love Nichola, and he felt sick and almost resentful. But happily his affection was incipient as yet, and a sudden sense of the ridiculous in his own position carried him to the verge of risibility during the scene. She signified a chair, and began the critical study of some rings she wore.

They talked over the day's news, and then an organ began to grind outside. The tune was a rollicking air he had heard at some music-hall; and, by way of a diversion, he asked her if she knew the composition.

'No, I don't!' she replied.

'Now, I'll tell you all about it,' said he gravely. 'It is based on a sound old melody called "The Jilt's Hornpipe."³ Just as they turn Madeira into port in the space of a single night, so this old air has been taken and doctored, and twisted about, and brought out as a new popular ditty.'

'Indeed!'

'If you are in the habit of going much to the music-halls or the burlesque theatres—'

'Yes?'

'You would find this is often done, with excellent effect.'

She thawed a little, and then they went on to talk about her house, which had been newly painted, and decorated with greenish-blue satin up to the height of a person's head – an arrangement that somewhat improved her slightly faded, though still pretty, face, and was helped by the awnings over the windows.

'Yes; I have had my house some years,' she observed complacently, 'and I like it better every year.'

'Don't you feel lonely in it sometimes?'

'O never!'

However, before he rose she grew friendly to some degree, and when he left, just after the arrival of three opportune young ladies, she seemed regretful. She asked him to come again; and he thought he would tell the truth. 'No: I shall not care to come again,' he answered, in a tone inaudible to the young ladies.

She followed him to the door. 'What an uncivil thing to say!' she murmured in surprise.

'It is rather uncivil. Good-bye,' said Pierston.

As a punishment she did not ring the bell, but left him to find his way out as he could. 'Now what the devil this means I cannot tell,' he said to himself, reflecting stock-still for a moment on the stairs. And yet the meaning was staring him in the face.

Meanwhile one of the three young ladies had said, 'What interesting man was that, with his lovely head of hair? I saw him at Lady Channelcliffe's the other night.'

'Jocelyn Pierston.'

'O, Nichola, that *is* too bad! To let him go in that shabby way, when I would have given anything to know him! I have wanted to know him ever since I found out how much his experiences had dictated his statuary, and I discovered them by seeing in a Jersey paper of the marriage of a person supposed to be his wife, who ran off with him many years ago, don't you know, and then wouldn't marry him, in obedience to some novel social principles she had invented for herself.'

'O! didn't he marry her?' said Mrs. Pine-Avon, with a start. 'Why, I heard only yesterday that he did, though they have lived apart ever since.'

'Quite a mistake,' said the young lady. 'How I wish I could run after him!'

But Jocelyn was receding from the pretty widow's house with long strides. He went out very little during the next few days, but about a week later he kept an engagement to dine with Lady Iris Speedwell, whom he never neglected, because she was the brightest hostess in London.

By some accident he arrived rather early. Lady Iris had left the drawing-room for a moment to see that all was right in the dining-room, and when he was shown in there stood alone in the lamplight Nichola Pine-Avon. She had been the first arrival. He had not in the least expected to meet her there, further than that, in a general sense, at Lady Iris's you expected to meet everybody.

She had just come out of the cloak-room, and was so tender and even apologetic that he had not the heart to be other than friendly. As the other guests dropped in, the pair retreated into a shady corner, and she talked beside him till all moved off for the eating and drinking.

He had not been appointed to take her across to the dining-room, but at the table found her exactly opposite. She looked very charming between the candles, and then suddenly it dawned upon him that her previous manner must have originated in some false report about Marcia, of whose existence he had not heard for years. Anyhow, he was not disposed to resent an inexplicability in womankind, having found that it usually arose independently of fact, reason, probability, or his own deserts.

So he dined on, catching her eyes and the few pretty words she made opportunity to project across the table to him now and then. He was courteously responsive only, but Mrs. Pine-Avon herself distinctly made advances. He re-admired her, while at the same time her conduct in her own house had been enough to check his confidence – enough even to make him doubt if the Well-Beloved really resided within those contours, or had ever been more than the most transitory passenger through that interesting and accomplished soul.

He was pondering this question, yet growing decidedly moved by the playful pathos of her attitude when, by chance, searching his pocket for his handkerchief, something crackled, and he felt there an unopened letter, which had arrived at the moment he was leaving his house, and he had slipped into his coat to read in the cab as he drove along. Pierston drew it sufficiently forth to observe by the post-mark that it came from his natal isle. Having hardly a correspondent in that part of the world now he began to conjecture on the possible sender.

The lady on his right, whom he had brought in, was a leading actress[4] of the town – indeed, of the United Kingdom and America, for that matter – a creature in airy clothing, translucent, like a balsam or sea-anemone, without shadows, and in movement as responsive as some highly lubricated, many-wired machine, which, if one presses a particular spring, flies open and reveals its works. The spring in the present case was the artistic commendation she deserved. At this particular moment she was engaged with the man on her own right, a representative of Family, who talked positively and hollowly, as if shouting down a vista of five hundred years from the Feudal past. The lady on Jocelyn's left, wife of a Lord Justice of Appeal, was in like manner talking to her companion on the outer side; so that, for the time, he was left to himself. He took advantage of the opportunity, drew out his letter, and read it as it lay upon his napkin, nobody observing him, so far as he was aware.

It came from the wife of one of his father's former workmen, and was concerning her son, whom she begged Jocelyn to recommend as candidate for some post in town that she wished him to fill. But the end of the letter was what arrested him –

'You will be sorry to hear, Sir, that dear little Avice Caro, as we used to call her in her maiden days, is dead. She married her cousin, if you do mind, and went away from here for a good-few years, but was left a widow, and came back a twelvemonth ago; since when she faltered and faltered, and now she is gone.'

CHAPTER III

She becomes an Inaccessible Ghost

By imperceptible and slow degrees the scene at the dinner-table receded into the background, behind the vivid presentment of Avice Caro, and the old, old scenes on Isle Vindilia which were inseparable from her personality. The dining-room was real no more, dissolving under the bold stony promontory and the incoming West Sea. The handsome marchioness in geranium-red and diamonds, who was visible to him on his host's right hand opposite, became one of the glowing vermilion sunsets that he had watched so many times over Deadman's Bay, with the form of Avice in the foreground. Between his eyes and the judge who sat next to Nichola, with a chin so raw that he must have shaved every quarter of an hour during the day, intruded the face of Avice, as she had glanced at him in their last parting. The crannied features of the old society lady, who, if she had been a few years older, would have been as old-fashioned as her daughter, shaped themselves to the dusty quarries of his and Avice's parents, down which he had clambered with Avice hundreds of times. The ivy trailing about the table-cloth, the lights in the tall candle-sticks, and the bunches of flowers, were transmuted into the ivies of the cliff-built Castle, the tufts of seaweed, and the lighthouses on the isle. The salt airs of the ocean killed the smell of the viands, and instead of the clatter of voices came the monologue of the tide off the Beal.

More than all, Nichola Pine-Avon lost the blooming radiance which she had latterly acquired; she became a woman of his acquaintance with no distinctive traits; she seemed to grow material, a superficies of flesh and bone merely, a person of lines and surfaces; she was a language in living cipher no more.

When the ladies had withdrawn it was just the same. The soul of Avice – the only woman he had *never* loved of those who had loved him – surrounded him like a firmament. Art drew near to him in the person of one of the most distinguished of portrait painters; but there was only one painter for Jocelyn – his own memory. All that was eminent in European surgery addressed him in the person of that harmless and unassuming fogey whose hands had been inside the bodies of hundreds of living men; but the lily-white corpse of an obscure country-girl chilled the interest of discourse with such a king of operators.

Reaching the drawing-room he talked to his hostess. Though she had entertained twenty guests at her table that night she had known not only what every one of them was saying and doing throughout the repast, but what every one was thinking. So, being an old friend, she said quietly, 'What has been troubling you? Something has, I know. I have been travelling over your face and have seen it there.'

Nothing could less express the meaning his recent news had for him than a statement of its facts. He told of the opening of the letter and the discovery of the death of an old acquaintance.

'The only woman whom I never valued, I may almost say!' he added; 'and therefore the only one I shall ever regret!'

Whether she considered it a sufficient explanation or not the woman of experiences accepted it as such. She was the single lady of his circle whom nothing erratic in his doings could surprise, and he often gave her stray ends of his confidence thus with perfect safety.

He did not go near Mrs. Pine-Avon again; he could not: and on leaving the house walked abstractedly along the streets till he found himself at his own door. In his own room he sat down, and placing his hands behind his head thought his thoughts anew.

At one side of the room stood an escritoire, and from a lower drawer therein he took out a small box tightly nailed down. He forced the cover with the poker. The box contained a variety of odds and ends, which Pierston had thrown into it from time to time in past years for future sorting – an intention that he had never carried out. From the melancholy mass of papers, faded photographs, seals, diaries, withered flowers, and such like, Jocelyn drew a little portrait, one taken on glass' in the primitive days of photography, and framed with tinsel in the commonest way.

It was Avice Caro, as she had appeared during the summer month or two which he had spent with her on the island twenty years before this time, her young lips pursed up, her hands meekly folded. The effect of the glass was to lend to the picture much of the softness characteristic of the original. He remembered when it was taken – during one afternoon they had spent together at a neighbouring watering-place, when he had suggested her sitting to a touring artist on the sands, there being nothing else for them to do. A long contemplation of the likeness completed in his emotions what the letter had begun. He loved the woman dead and inaccessible as he had never loved her in life. He had thought of her but at distant intervals during the twenty years since that parting occurred, and only as somebody he could have wedded. Yet now the times of youthful friendship with her, in which he had learnt every note of her innocent nature, flamed up into a yearning and passionate attachment, embittered by regret beyond words.

That kiss which had offended his dignity, which she had so childishly given him before her consciousness of womanhood had been awakened; what he would have offered to have a quarter of it now!

Pierston was almost angry with himself for his feelings of this night, so unreasonably, motivelessly strong were they towards the lost young play-mate. 'How senseless of me!' he said, as he lay in his lonely bed. She had been another man's wife almost the whole time since he was estranged from her, and now she was a corpse. Yet the absurdity did not make his grief the less: and the consciousness of the intrinsic, almost radiant, purity of this new-sprung affection for a flown spirit forbade him to check it. The flesh was absent altogether; it was love rarefied and refined to its highest attar. He had felt nothing like it before.

The next afternoon he went down to the club; not his large club, where the men hardly spoke to each other, but the homely one where they told stories of an afternoon, and were not ashamed to confess among themselves to personal weaknesses and follies, knowing well that such secrets would go no further. But he could not tell this. So volatile and intangible was the story that to convey it in words would have been as hard as to cage a perfume.

They observed his altered manner, and said he was in love. Pierston admitted that he was; and there it ended. When he reached home he looked out of his bed-room window, and began to consider in what direction from where he stood that darling little figure lay. It was straight across there, under the young pale moon. The symbol signified well. The divinity of the silver bow was not more excellently pure than she, the lost, had been. Under that moon was the island of Ancient Slingers, and on the island a house, framed from mullions to chimney-top like the isle itself, of stone. Inside the window, the moonlight irradiating her winding-sheet, lay Avice, reached only by the faint noises inherent in the isle; the tink-tink of the chisels in the quarries, the surging of the tides in the Bay, and the muffled grumbling of the currents in the never-pacified Race.

He began to divine the truth. Avice, the departed one, though she had come short of inspiring a passion, had yet possessed a ground-quality absent from her rivals, without which it seemed that a fixed and full-rounded constancy to a woman could not flourish in him. Like his own, her family had been islanders for centuries – from Norman, Anglian, Roman, Balearic-British times. Hence in her nature, as in his, was some mysterious ingredient sucked from the isle; otherwise a racial instinct necessary to the absolute unison of a pair. Thus, though he might never love a woman of the island race, for lack in her of the desired refinement, he could not love long a kimberlin – a woman other than of the island race, for her lack of this groundwork of character.

Such was Pierston's view of things. Another fancy of his, an artist's superstition merely, may be mentioned. The Caros, like some other local families, suggested a Roman lineage, more or less grafted on the stock of the Slingers. Their features recalled those of the Italian peasantry to any one as familiar as he was with them; and there were evidences that the Roman colonists had been populous and long-abiding in and near this corner of Britain. Tradition urged that a temple to Venus once stood at the top of the Roman road leading up into the isle; and possibly one to the love-goddess of the Slingers antedated this. What so natural as that the true star of his soul would be found nowhere but in one of the old island breed?[2]

After dinner his old friend Somers came in to smoke, and when they had talked a little while Somers alluded casually to some place at which they would meet on the morrow.

'I shan't be there,' said Pierston.

'But you promised?'

'Yes. But I shall be at the island – looking at a dead woman's grave.' As he spoke his eyes turned, and remained fixed on a table near. Somers followed the direction of his glance to a photograph on a stand.

'Is that she?' he asked.

'Yes.'

'Rather a bygone affair, then?'

Pierston acknowledged it. 'She's the only sweetheart I ever slighted,

Alfred,' he said. 'Because she's the only one I ought to have cared for. That's just the fool I have always been.'

'But if she's dead and buried, you can go to her grave at any time as well as now, to keep up the sentiment.'

'I don't know that she's buried.'

'But to-morrow – the Academy night! Of all days why go then?'

'I don't care about the Academy.'

'Pierston – you are our only inspired sculptor. You are our Praxiteles, or rather our Lysippus.[3] You are almost the only man of this generation who has been able to mould and chisel forms living enough to draw the idle public away from the popular paintings into the usually deserted Lecture-room, and people who have seen your last pieces of stuff say there has been nothing like them since sixteen hundred and – since the sculptors "of the great race" lived and died – whenever that was. Well, then, for the sake of others you ought not to rush off to that God-forgotten sea-rock just when you are wanted in town, all for a woman you last saw a hundred years ago.'

'No – it was only nineteen and three quarters,' replied his friend, with abstracted literalness. He went the next morning.

Since the days of his youth a railway had been constructed along the pebble bank, so that, except when the rails were washed away by the tides, which was rather often, the peninsula was quickly accessible. At two o'clock in the afternoon he was rattled along by this new means of loco-motion, under the familiar monotonous line of bran-coloured stones, and he soon emerged from the station, standing as a strange exotic among the black lerrets, the ruins of the washed-away village, and the white cubes of oolite, just come to view after burial through unreckonable geologic years.

In entering upon the pebble beach the train had passed close to the ruins of Henry the Eighth's or Sandsfoot Castle, whither Avice was to have accompanied him on the night of his departure. Had she appeared the primitive betrothal would probably have taken place; and, as no is-lander had ever been known to break that compact,[4] she would have become his wife.

Ascending the steep incline to where the quarrymen were chipping just as they had formerly done, and within sound of the great stone saws, he looked southward towards the Beal.

The level line of the sea horizon rose above the surface of the isle, a

ruffled patch in mid-distance as usual marking the Race, whence many a
Lycidas had gone

'Visiting the bottom of the monstrous world;'[5]

but had not been blest with a poet as a friend. Against the stretch of
water, where a school of mackerel twinkled in the afternoon light, was
defined, in addition to the distant lighthouse, a church with its tower,
standing about a quarter of a mile off, near the edge of the cliff. The
churchyard gravestones could be seen in profile against the same vast
spread of watery babble and unrest.

Among the graves moved the form of a man clothed in a white sheet,
which the wind blew and flapped sadly every now and then. Near him
moved six men bearing a long box, and two or three persons in black followed. The coffin, with its twelve legs, crawled across the isle, while
around and beneath it the flashing lights from the sea and the school of
mackerel were reflected; a fishing-boat, far out in the Channel, being
momentarily discernible under the coffin also.

The procession wandered round to a particular corner, and halted,
and paused there a long while in the wind, the sea behind them, the surplice of the priest still blowing. Jocelyn stood with his hat off: he was present, though he was a quarter of a mile off; and he seemed to hear the
words that were being said, though nothing but the wind was audible.

He instinctively knew that it was none other than Avice whom he was
seeing interred; *his* Avice, as he now began presumptuously to call her.
Presently the little group withdrew from before the sea-shine, and
disappeared.

He felt himself unable to go further in that direction, and turning aside
went aimlessly across the open land, visiting the various spots that he had
formerly visited with her. But, as if tethered to the churchyard by a cord,
he was still conscious of being at the end of a radius whose pivot was the
grave of Avice Caro; and as the dusk thickened he closed upon his centre
and entered the churchyard gate.

Not a soul was now within the precincts. The grave, newly shaped, was
easily discoverable behind the church, and when the same young moon
arose which he had observed the previous evening from his window in
London he could see the yet fresh foot-marks of the mourners and
bearers. The breeze had fallen to a calm with the setting of the sun: the
lighthouse had opened its glaring eye, and, disinclined to leave a spot sub-

limed both by early association and present regret, he moved back to the church-wall, warm from the afternoon sun, and sat down upon a window-sill facing the grave.

CHAPTER IV

She Threatens to resume Corporeal Substance

The lispings of the sea beneath the cliffs were all the sounds that reached him, for the quarries were silent now. How long he sat here lonely and thinking he did not know. Neither did he know, though he felt drowsy, whether inexpectant sadness – that gentle soporific – lulled him into a short sleep, so that he lost count of time and consciousness of incident. But during some minute or minutes he seemed to see Avice Caro herself, bending over and then withdrawing from her grave in the light of the moon.

She seemed not a year older, not a digit less slender, not a line more angular than when he had parted from her twenty years earlier, in the lane hard by. A renascent reasoning on the impossibility of such a phenomenon as this being more than a dream-fancy roused him with a start from his heaviness.

'I must have been asleep,' he said.

Yet she had seemed so real. Pierston however dismissed the strange impression, arguing that even if the information sent him of Avice's death should be false – a thing incredible – that sweet friend of his youth, despite the transfiguring effects of moonlight, would not now look the same as she had appeared nineteen or twenty years ago. Were what he saw substantial flesh, it must have been some other person than Avice Caro.

Having satisfied his sentiment by coming to the graveside there was nothing more for him to do in the island, and he decided to return to London that night. But some time remaining still on his hands, Jocelyn by a natural instinct turned his feet in the direction of East Quarriers, the village of his birth and of hers. Passing the market-square he pursued the arm of road to 'Sylvania Castle,' a private mansion of comparatively modern date, in whose grounds stood the single plantation of trees of which the isle could boast. The cottages extended close to the walls of the enclosure, and one of the last of these dwellings had been Avice's, in which, as it was her freehold, she possibly had died.

To reach it he passed the gates of 'Sylvania,' and observed above the lawn wall a board announcing that the house was to be let furnished. A few steps further revealed the cottage which, with its quaint and massive stone features of two or three centuries' antiquity, was capable even now of longer resistance to the rasp of Time than ordinary new erections. His attention was drawn to the window, still unblinded, though a lamp lit the room. He stepped back against the wall opposite, and gazed in.

At a table covered with a white cloth a young woman stood putting tea-things away into a corner-cupboard. She was in all respects the Avice he had lost, the girl he had seen in the churchyard and had fancied to be the illusion of a dream. And though there was this time no doubt about her reality, the isolation of her position in the silent house lent her a curiously startling aspect. Divining the explanation he waited for footsteps, and in a few moments a quarryman passed him on his journey home. Pierston inquired of the man concerning the spectacle.

'O yes, sir; that's poor Mrs. Caro's only daughter, and it must be lonely for her there to-night, poor maid! Yes, good-now; she's the very daps of her mother – that's what everybody says.'

'But how does she come to be so lonely?'

'One of her brothers went to sea and was drowned, and t'other is in America.'

'They were quarryowners at one time?'

The quarryman 'pitched his nitch,'[2] and explained to the seeming stranger that there had been three families thereabouts in the stone trade, who had got much involved with each other in the last generation. They were the Bencombs, the Pierstons, and the Caros. The Bencombs strained their utmost to outlift the other two, and partially succeeded. They grew enormously rich, sold out, and disappeared altogether from the island which had been their making. The Pierstons kept a dogged middle course, throve without show or noise, and also retired in their turn. The Caros were pulled completely down in the competition with the other two, and when Widow Caro's daughter married her cousin Jim Caro, he tried to regain for the family its original place in the three-cornered struggle. He took contracts at less than he could profit by, speculated more and more, till at last the crash came; he was sold up, went away, and later on came back to live in this little cottage, which was his wife's by inheritance. There he remained till his death; and now his widow was gone. Hardships had helped on her end.

The quarryman proceeded on his way, and Pierston, deeply remorseful, knocked at the door of the minute freehold. The girl herself opened it, lamp in hand.

'Avice!' he said tenderly; 'Avice Caro!' even now unable to get over the strange feeling that he was twenty years younger, addressing Avice the forsaken.

'Ann, sir,' said she.

'Ah, your name is not the same as your mother's!'

'My second name is.[3] And my surname. Poor mother married her cousin.'

'As everybody does here. . . . Well, Ann or otherwise, you are Avice to me. And you have lost her now?'

'I have, sir.'

She spoke in the very same sweet voice that he had listened to a score of years before, and bent eyes of the same familiar hazel inquiringly upon him.

'I knew your mother at one time,' he said; 'and learning of her death and burial I took the liberty of calling upon you. You will forgive a stranger doing that?'

'Yes,' she said dispassionately, and glancing round the room: 'This was mother's own house, and now it is mine. I am sorry not to be in mourning on the night of her funeral, but I have just been to put some flowers on her grave, and I took it off afore going that the damp mid not spoil the crape. You see, she was bad a long time, and I have to be careful, and do washing and ironing for a living. She hurt her side with wringing up the large sheets she had to wash for the Castle folks here.'

'I hope you won't hurt yourself doing it, my dear.'

'O no, that I sha'n't! There's Charl Woollat, and Sammy Scribben, and Ted Gibsey, and lots o' young chaps; they'll wring anything for me if they happen to come along. But I can hardly trust 'em. Sam Scribben t'other day twisted a linen tablecloth into two pieces, for all the world as if it had been a pipe-light. They never know when to stop in their wringing.'

The voice truly was his Avice's; but Avice the Second was clearly more matter-of-fact, unreflecting, less cultivated than her mother had been.

This Avice would never recite poetry from any platform, local or other, with enthusiastic appreciation of its fire. There was a disappointment in his recognition of this; yet she touched him as few had done: he could not bear to go away. 'How old are you?' he asked.

'Going in nineteen.'

It was about the age of her double, Avice the First, when he and she had strolled together over the cliffs during the engagement. But he was now forty, if a day. She before him was an uneducated laundress, and he was a sculptor and a Royal Academician, with a fortune and a reputation. Yet why was it an unpleasant sensation to him just then to recollect that he was two score?

He could find no further excuse for remaining, and having still half-an-hour to spare he went round by the road to the other or west side of the last-century 'Sylvania Castle,' and came to the furthest house out there on the cliff. It was his early home. Used in the summer as a lodging-house for visitors, it now stood empty and silent, the evening wind swaying the euonymus and tamarisk boughs in the front – the only evergreen shrubs that could weather the whipping salt gales which sped past the walls. Opposite the house, far out at sea, the familiar lightship winked from the sandbank, and all at once there came to him a wild wish – that, instead of having an artist's reputation, he could be living here an illiterate and unknown man, wooing, and in a fair way of winning, the pretty laundress in the cottage hard by.

CHAPTER V

The Resumption takes place

Having returned to London he mechanically resumed his customary life; but he was not really living there. The phantom of Avice, now grown to be warm flesh and blood, held his mind afar. He thought of nothing but the isle, and Avice the Second dwelling therein – inhaling its salt breath, stroked by its singing rains and by the haunted atmosphere of Roman Venus about and around the site of her perished temple there.[1] The very defects in the country girl became charms as viewed from town.

Nothing now pleased him so much as to spend that portion of the afternoon which he devoted to out-door exercise, in haunting the purlieus of the wharves along the Thames, where the stone of his native rock was unshipped from the coasting-craft that had brought it thither. He would pass inside the great gates of these landing-places on the right or left bank, contemplate the white cubes and oblongs, imbibe their associations, call up the *genius loci* whence they came, and almost forget that he was in London.

One afternoon he was walking away from the mud-splashed entrance to one of the wharves, when his attention was drawn to a female form on the opposite side of the way, going towards the spot he had just left. She was somewhat small, slight, and graceful; her attire alone would have been enough to attract him, being simple and countrified to picturesqueness; but he was more than attracted by her strong resemblance to Avice Caro the younger – Ann Avice, as she had said she was called.

Before she had receded a hundred yards he felt certain that it was Avice indeed; and his unifying mood of the afternoon was now so intense that the lost and the found Avice seemed essentially the same person. Their external likeness to each other – probably owing to the cousinship between the elder and her husband – went far to nourish the fantasy. He hastily turned, and rediscovered the girl among the pedestrians. She kept on her way to the wharf, where, looking inquiringly around her for a few seconds, with the manner of one unaccustomed to the locality, she opened the gate and disappeared.

Pierston also went up to the gate and entered. She had crossed to the landing-place, beyond which a lumpy craft lay moored. Drawing nearer, he discovered her to be engaged in conversation with the skipper and an elderly woman – both come straight from the oolitic isle, as was apparent in a moment from their accent. Pierston felt no hesitation in making himself known as a native, the ruptured engagement between Avice's mother and himself twenty years before having been known to few or none now living.

The present embodiment of Avice recognized him, and with the artless candour of her race and years explained the situation, though that was rather his duty as an intruder than hers.

'This is Cap'n Kibbs, sir, a distant relation of father's,' she said. 'And this is Mrs. Kibbs. We've come up from the island wi'en just for a trip, and are going to sail back wi'en Wednesday.'

'O, I see. And where are you staying?'

'Here – on board.'

'What, you live on board entirely?'

'Yes.'

'Lord, sir,' broke in Mrs. Kibbs, 'I should be afeard o' my life to tine my eyes among these here kimberlins at night-time; and even by day, if so be I venture into the streets, I nowhen forget how many turnings to the right and to the left 'tis to get back to Job's vessel – do I, Job?'

The skipper nodded confirmation.

'You are safer ashore than afloat,' said Pierston, 'especially in the Channel, with these winds and those heavy blocks of stone.'

'Well,' said Cap'n Kibbs, after privately clearing something from his mouth, 'as to the winds, there idden much danger in them at this time o' year. 'Tis the ocean-bound steamers that make the risk to craft like ours. If you happen to be in their course, under you go – cut clane in two pieces, and they never lying-to to haul in your carcases, and nobody to tell the tale.'

Pierston turned to Avice, wanting to say much to her, yet not knowing what to say. He lamely remarked at last: 'You go back the same way, Avice?'

'Yes, sir.'

'Well, take care of yourself afloat.'

'O yes.'

'I hope – I may see you again soon – and talk to you.'

'I hope so, sir.'

He could not get further, and after a while Pierston left them, and went away thinking of Avice more than ever.

The next day he mentally timed them down the river, allowing for the pause to take in ballast, and on the Wednesday pictured the sail down the open sea. That night he thought of the little craft under the bows of the huge steam-vessels, powerless to make itself seen or heard, and Avice, now growing inexpressibly dear, sleeping in her little berth at the mercy of a thousand chance catastrophes.

Honest perception had told him that this Avice, fairer than her mother in face and form, was her inferior in soul and understanding. Yet the fervour which the first could never kindle in him was, almost to his alarm, burning up now. He began to have misgivings as to some queer trick that his migratory Beloved was about to play him, or rather the capricious Divinity behind that ideal lady.[2]

A gigantic satire upon the mutations of his nymph[3] during the past twenty years seemed looming in the distance. A forsaking of the accomplished and well-connected Mrs. Pine-Avon for the little laundress, under the traction of some mystic magnet which had nothing to do with reason – surely that was the form of the satire.

But it was recklessly pleasant to leave the suspicion unrecognized as yet, and follow the lead.

In thinking how best to do this Pierston recollected that, as was customary when the summer-time approached, Sylvania Castle had been advertised for letting furnished. A solitary dreamer like himself, whose wants all lay in an artistic and ideal direction, did not require such gaunt accommodation as the aforesaid residence offered; but the spot was all, and the expenses of a few months of tenancy therein he could well afford. A letter to the agent was dispatched that night, and in a few days Jocelyn found himself the temporary possessor of a place which he had never seen the inside of since his childhood, and had then deemed the abode of unpleasant ghosts.

CHAPTER VI

The Past Shines in the Present

It was the evening of Pierston's arrival at Sylvania Castle, an ordinary manor-house on the brink of the cliffs; and he had walked through the rooms, about the lawn, and into the surrounding plantation of elms, which on this island of treeless rock lent a unique character to the enclosure. In name, nature, and accessories the property within the girdling wall formed a complete antithesis to everything in its precincts. To find other trees between Pebble-bank and Beal, it was necessary to recede a little in time – to dig down to a loose stratum of the underlying stone-beds, where a forest of conifers lay as petrifactions, their heads all in one direction, as blown down by a gale in the Secondary geologic epoch.

Dusk had closed in, and he now proceeded with what was, after all, the real business of his sojourn. The two servants who had been left to take care of the house were in their own quarters, and he went out unobserved. Crossing a hollow overhung by the budding boughs he approached an empty garden-house of Elizabethan design, which stood on the outer wall of the grounds, and commanded by a window the fronts of the nearest cottages. Among them was the home of the resuscitated Avice.

He had chosen this moment for his outlook through knowing that the villagers were in no hurry to pull down their blinds at nightfall. And, as he had divined, the inside of the young woman's living-room was visible to him as formerly, illuminated by the rays of its own lamp.

A subdued thumping came every now and then from the apartment. She was ironing linen on a flannel table-cloth, a row of such apparel hanging on a clothes-horse by the fire. Her face had been pale when he encountered her, but now it was warm and pink with her exertions and the heat of the stove. Yet it was in perfect and passionless repose, which imparted a Minerva¹ cast to the profile. When she glanced up, her lineaments seemed to have all the soul and heart that had characterized her mother's, and had been with her a true index of the spirit within. Could it be possible that in this case the manifestation was fictitious? He had met with many such examples of hereditary persistence without the qualities signified by the traits. He unconsciously hoped that it was at least not entirely so here.

The room was less furnished than when he had last beheld it. The 'bo-fet,' or double corner-cupboard, where the china was formerly kept, had disappeared, its place being taken by a plain board. The tall old clock, with its ancient oak carcase, arched brow, and humorous mouth, was also not to be seen, a cheap, white-dialled specimen doing its work. What these displacements might betoken saddened his humanity less than it cheered his primitive instinct in pointing out how her necessities might bring them together.

Having fixed his residence near her for some lengthy time he felt in no hurry to obtrude his presence just now, and went indoors. That this girl's frame was doomed to be a real embodiment of that olden seductive one – that Protean dream-creature, who had never seen fit to irradiate the mother's image till it became a mere memory after dissolution – he doubted less every moment.

There was an uneasiness in recognizing such. There was something abnormal in his present proclivity. A certain sanity had, after all, accompanied his former idealizing passions: the Beloved had seldom informed a personality which, while enrapturing his soul, simultaneously shocked his intellect. A change, perhaps, had come.

It was a fine morning on the morrow. Walking in the grounds towards the gate he saw Avice entering his hired castle with a broad oval wicker-basket covered with a white cloth, which burden she bore round to the back door. Of course, she washed for his own household: he had not thought of that. In the morning sunlight she appeared rather as a sylph than as a washerwoman; and he could not but think that the slightness of her figure was as ill adapted to this occupation as her mother's had been.

But, after all, it was not the washerwoman that he saw now. In front of her, on the surface of her, was shining out that more real, more inter-penetrating being whom he knew so well! The occupation of the subserv-ing minion, the blemishes of the temporary creature who formed the background, were of the same account in the presentation of the in-dispensable one as the supporting posts and framework in a pyrotechnic display.

She left the house and went homeward by a path of which he was not aware, having probably changed her course because she had seen him standing there. It meant nothing, for she had hardly become acquainted with him; yet that she should have avoided him was a new experience. He had no opportunity for a further study of her by distant observation, and hit upon a pretext for bringing her face to face with him. He found fault with his linen, and directed that the laundress should be sent for.

'She is rather young, poor little thing,' said the housemaid apologetic-ally. 'But since her mother's death she has enough to do to keep above water, and we make shift with her. But I'll tell her, sir.'

'I will see her myself. Send her in when she comes,' said Pierston.

One morning, accordingly, when he was answering a spiteful criticism of a late work of his, he was told that she waited his pleasure in the hall. He went out.

'About the washing,' said the sculptor stiffly. 'I am a very particular person, and I wish no preparation of lime to be used.'

'I didn't know folks used it,' replied the maiden, in a scared and re-served tone, without looking at him.

'That's all right. And then, the mangling smashes the buttons.'

'I haven't got a mangle, sir,' she murmured.

'Ah! that's satisfactory. And I object to so much borax in the starch.'

'I don't put any,' Avice returned in the same close way; 'never heard the name o't afore!'

'O I see.'

All this time Pierston was thinking of the girl – or as the scientific might say, Nature was working her plans for the next generation under the cloak of a dialogue on linen. He could not read her individual character, owing to the confusing effect of her likeness to a woman whom he had valued too late. He could not help seeing in her all that he knew of another, and veiling in her all that did not harmonize with his sense of metempsychosis.

The girl seemed to think of nothing but the business in hand. She had answered to the point, and was hardly aware of his sex or of his shape.

'I knew your mother, Avice,' he said. 'You remember my telling you so?'

'Yes.'

'Well – I have taken this house for two or three months, and you will be very useful to me. You still live just outside the wall?'

'Yes, sir,' said the self-contained girl.

Demurely and dispassionately she turned to leave – this pretty creature with features so still. There was something strange in seeing move off thus that form which he knew passing well, she who was once so throbbingly alive to his presence that, not many yards from this spot, she had flung her arms round him and given him a kiss which, despised in its freshness, had revived in him latterly as the dearest kiss of all his life. And now this 'daps' of her mother (as they called her in the dialect here), this perfect copy, why did she turn away?

'Your mother was a refined and well-informed woman, I think I remember?'

'She was, sir; everybody said so.'

'I hope you resemble her.'

She archly shook her head, and drew warily away.

'O! one thing more, Avice. I have not brought much linen, so you must come to the house every day.'

'Very good, sir.'

'You won't forget that?'

'O no.'

Then he let her go. He was a town man, and she an artless islander, yet he had opened himself out like a sea-anemone,[2] without disturbing the epiderm of her nature. It was monstrous that a maiden who had assumed the personality of her of his tenderest memory should be so impervious. Perhaps it was he who was wanting. Avice might be Passion masking as Indifference,[3] because he was so many years older in outward show.

This brought him to the root of it. In his heart he was not a day older than when he had wooed the mother at the daughter's present age. His record moved on with the years, his sentiments stood still.

When he beheld those of his fellows who were defined as buffers and fogeys – imperturbable, matter-of-fact, slightly ridiculous beings, past masters in the art of populating homes, schools, and colleges, and present adepts in the science of giving away brides – how he envied them, assuming them to feel as they appeared to feel, with their commerce and their politics, their glasses and their pipes. They had got past the distracting currents[4] of passionateness, and were in the calm waters of middle-aged philosophy. But he, their contemporary, was tossed like a cork hither and thither upon the crest of every fancy, precisely as he had been tossed when he was half his present age, with the burden now of double pain to himself in his growing vision of all as vanity.

Avice had gone, and he saw her no more that day. Since he could not again call upon her, she was as inaccessible as if she had entered the military citadel on the hill-top beyond them.

In the evening he went out and paced down the lane to the Red King's castle overhanging the cliff, beside whose age the castle he occupied was but a thing of yesterday. Below the castle precipice lay enormous blocks, which had fallen from it, and several of them were carved over with names and initials. He knew the spot and the old trick well, and by searching in the faint moon-rays he found a pair of names which, as a boy, he himself had cut. They were 'AVICE' and 'JOCELYN' – Avice Caro's and his own. The letters were now nearly worn away by the weather and the brine. But close by, in quite fresh letters, stood 'ANN AVICE,' coupled with the name 'ISAAC.'[5] They could not have been there more than two or three years, and the 'Ann Avice' was probably Avice the Second. Who was Isaac? Some boy admirer of her child-time doubtless.

He retraced his steps, and passed the Caros' house towards his own. The revivified Avice animated the dwelling, and the light within the room fell upon the window. She was just inside that blind.

* * * * *

Whenever she unexpectedly came to the castle he started, and lost placidity. It was not at her presence as such, but at the new condition, which seemed to have something sinister in it. On the other hand, the most abrupt encounter with him moved her to no emotion as it had moved her prototype in the old days. She was indifferent to, almost unconscious of, his propinquity. He was no more than a statue to her; she was a growing fire to him.

A sudden Sapphic terror of love[6] would ever and anon come upon the sculptor, when his matured reflecting powers would insist upon informing him of the fearful lapse from reasonableness that lay in this infatuation. It threw him into a sweat. What if now, at last, he were doomed to do penance for his past emotional wanderings (in a material sense) by being chained in fatal fidelity to an object that his intellect despised? One night he dreamt that he saw dimly masking behind that young countenance 'the Weaver of Wiles'[7] herself, 'with all her subtle face laughing aloud.'[8]

However, the Well-Beloved was alive again; had been lost and was found. He was amazed at the change of front in himself. She had worn the guise of strange women; she had been a woman of every class, from the dignified daughter of some ecclesiastic or peer to a Nubian Almeh[9] with her handkerchief, undulating to the beats of the tom-tom; but all these embodiments had been endowed with a certain smartness, either of the flesh or spirit: some with wit, a few with talent, and even genius. But the new impersonation had apparently nothing beyond sex and prettiness. She knew not how to sport a fan or handkerchief, hardly how to pull on a glove.

But her limited life was innocent, and that went far. Poor little Avice! her mother's image: there it all lay. After all, her parentage was as good as his own; it was misfortune that had sent her down to this. Odd as it seemed to him, her limitations were largely what he loved her for. Her rejuvenating power over him had ineffable charm. He felt as he had felt when standing beside her predecessor; but, alas! he was twenty years further onward into the shade.

CHAPTER VII

The New becomes Established

A few mornings later he was looking through an upper back window over a screened part of the garden. The door beneath him opened, and a figure appeared tripping forth. She went round out of sight to where the gardener was at work, and presently returned with a bunch of green stuff fluttering in each hand. It was Avice, her dark hair now braided up snugly under a cap. She sailed on with a rapt and unconscious face, her thoughts a thousand removes from him.

How she had suddenly come to be an inmate of his own house he could not understand, till he recalled the fact that he had given the castle servants a whole holiday to attend a review of the yeomanry in the watering-place over the bay, on their stating that they could provide a temporary substitute to stay in the house. They had evidently called in Avice. To his great pleasure he discovered their opinion of his require-ments to be such a mean one that they had called in no one else.

The Spirit, as she seemed to him, brought his lunch into the room where he was writing, and he beheld her uncover it. She went to the window to adjust a blind which had slipped, and he had a good view of her profile. It was not unlike that of one of the three goddesses in Rubens's 'Judgment of Paris,' and in contour was nigh perfection. But it was in her full face that the vision of her mother was most apparent.

'Did you cook all this, Avice?' he asked, arousing himself.

She turned and half-smiled, merely murmuring, 'Yes, sir.'

Well he knew the arrangement of those white teeth. In the junction of two of the upper ones there was a slight irregularity; no stranger would have noticed it, nor would he, but that he knew of the same mark in her mother's mouth, and looked for it here. Till Avice the Second had re-vealed it this moment by her smile, he had never beheld that mark since the parting from Avice the First, when she had smiled under his kiss as the copy had done now.

Next morning, when dressing, he heard her through the ricketty floor of the building engaged in conversation with the other servants. Having by this time regularly installed herself as the exponent of the Long-pursued – as one who, by no initiative of his own, had been chosen by some superior Power as the vehicle of her next début, she attracted him by the cadences of her voice; she would suddenly drop it to a rich whisper of roguishness, when the slight rural monotony of its narrative speech disappeared, and soul and heart – or what seemed soul and heart – resounded. The charm lay in the intervals, using that word in its musical sense. She would say a few syllables in one note, and end her sentence in a soft modulation upwards, then downwards, then into her own note again. The curve of sound was as artistic as any line of beauty ever struck by his pencil – as satisfying as the curves of her who was the World's Desire.[2]

The subject of her discourse[3] he cared nothing about – it was no more his interest than his concern. He took special pains that in catching her voice he might not comprehend her words. To the tones he had a right, none to the articulations. By degrees he could not exist long without this sound.

On Sunday evening he found that she went to church. He followed behind her over the open road, keeping his eye on the little hat with its bunch of cock's feathers as on a star. When she had passed in Pierston observed her position and took a seat behind her.

Engaged in the study of her ear and the nape of her white neck, he suddenly became aware of the presence of a lady still further ahead in the aisle, whose attire, though of black materials in the quietest form, was of a cut which rather suggested London than this *Ultima Thule*.[4] For the minute he forgot, in his curiosity, that Avice intervened. The lady turned her head somewhat, and, though she was veiled with unusual thickness for the season, he seemed to recognize Nichola Pine-Avon in the form.

Why should Mrs. Pine-Avon be there? Pierston asked himself, if it should, indeed, be she.

The end of the service saw his attention again concentrated on Avice to such a degree that at the critical moment of moving out he forgot the mysterious lady in front of her, and found that she had left the church by the side-door. Supposing it to have been Mrs. Pine-Avon, she would probably be discovered staying at one of the hotels at the watering-place over the bay, and to have come along the Pebble-bank to the island as so many did, for an evening drive. For the present, however, the explanation was not forthcoming; and he did not seek it.

When he emerged from the church the great placid eye of the lighthouse at the Beal Point was open, and he moved thitherward a few steps to escape Nichola, or her double, and the rest of the congregation. Turning at length, he hastened homeward along the now deserted trackway, intending to overtake the revitalized Avice. But he could see nothing of her, and concluded that she had walked too fast for him. Arrived at his own gate he paused a moment, and perceived that Avice's little freehold was still in darkness. She had not come.

He retraced his steps, but could not find her, the only persons on the road being a man and his wife, as he knew them to be though he could not see them, from the words of the man –

'If you had not a'ready married me, you'd cut my acquaintance! That's a pretty thing for a wife to say!'

The remark struck his ear unpleasantly, and by-and-by he went back again. Avice's cottage was now lighted: she must have come round by the other road. Satisfied that she was safely domiciled for the night he opened the gate of Sylvania Castle and retired to his room also.

* * * * *

Eastward from the grounds the cliffs were rugged and the view of the opposite coast picturesque in the extreme. A little door from the lawn gave him immediate access to the rocks and shore on this side. Without the door was a dip-well of pure water, which possibly had supplied the inmates of the adjoining and now ruinous Red King's castle at the time of its erection. On a sunny morning he was meditating here when he discerned a figure on the shore below spreading white linen upon the pebbly strand.

Jocelyn descended. Avice, as he had supposed, had now returned to her own occupation. Her shapely pink arms, though slight, were plump enough to show dimples at the elbows, and were set off by her purple cotton print, which the shore-breeze licked and tantalized. He stood near, without speaking. The wind dragged a shirt-sleeve from the 'popple' or pebble which held it down. Pierston stooped and put a heavier one in its place.

'Thank you,' she said quietly. She turned up her hazel eyes, and seemed gratified to perceive that her assistant was Pierston. She had plainly been so wrapped in her own thoughts – gloomy thoughts, by their signs – that she had not considered him till then.

The young girl continued to converse with him in friendly frankness, showing neither ardour nor shyness. As for love – it was evidently further from her mind than even death and dissolution.

When one of the sheets became intractable Jocelyn said, 'Do you hold it down, and I'll put the popples.'

She acquiesced, and in placing a pebble his hand touched hers.

It was a young hand, rather long and thin, a little damp and coddled from her slopping. In setting down the last stone he laid it, by a pure accident, rather heavily on her fingers.

'I am very, very sorry!' Jocelyn exclaimed. 'O, I have bruised the skin, Avice!' He seized her fingers to examine the damage done.

'No, sir, you haven't!' she cried luminously, allowing him to retain her hand without the least objection. 'Why – that's where I scratched it this morning with a pin. You didn't hurt me a bit with the popple-stone!'

Although her gown was purple, there was a little black crape bow upon each arm. He knew what it meant, and it saddened him. 'Do you ever visit your mother's grave?' he asked.

'Yes, sir, sometimes. I am going there to-night to water the daisies.'

She had now finished here, and they parted. That evening, when the sky was red, he emerged by the garden-door and passed her house. The blinds were not down, and he could see her sewing within. While he paused she sprang up as if she had forgotten the hour, and tossed on her hat. Jocelyn strode ahead and round the corner, and was halfway up the straggling street before he discerned her little figure behind him.

He hastened past the lads and young women with clinking buckets who were drawing water from the fountains by the wayside, and took the direction of the church. With the disappearance of the sun the lighthouse had again set up its flame against the sky, the dark church rising in the foreground. Here he allowed her to overtake him.

'You loved your mother much?' said Jocelyn.

'I did, sir; of course I did,' said the girl, who tripped so lightly that it seemed he might have carried her on his hand.

Pierston wished to say, 'So did I,' but did not like to disclose events which she, apparently, did not guess. Avice fell into thought, and continued –

'Mother had a very sad life for some time when she was about as old as I. I should not like mine to be as hers. Her young man proved false to her because she wouldn't agree to meet him one night, and it grieved mother almost all her life. I wouldn't ha' fretted about him, if I'd been she. She would never name his name, but I think he was a wicked, cruel man; and I hate to think of him.'

After this he could not go into the churchyard with her, and walked onward alone to the south of the isle. He was wretched all night. Yet he would not have stood where he did stand in the ranks of an imaginative profession if he had not been at the mercy of every succubus[5] of the fancy that can beset man. It was in his weaknesses as a citizen and a national-unit that his strength lay as an artist, and he felt it childish to complain of susceptibilities not only innate but cultivated.

But he was paying dearly enough for his Liliths.[6] He saw a terrible vengeance ahead. What had he done to be tormented like this? The Beloved, after flitting from Nichola Pine-Avon to the phantom of a dead woman whom he never adored in her lifetime, had taken up her abode in the living representative of the dead, with a permanence of hold which the absolute indifference of that little brown-eyed representative only seemed to intensify.

Did he really wish to proceed to marriage with this chit of a girl? He did: the wish had come at last. It was true that as he studied her he saw defects in addition to her social insufficiencies. Judgment, hoodwinked as it was, told him that she was colder in nature, commoner in character, than that well-read, bright little woman Avice the First. But twenty years make a difference in ideals, and the added demands of middle-age in physical form are more than balanced by its concessions as to the spiritual content. He looked at himself in the glass, and felt glad at those inner deficiencies in Avice which formerly would have impelled him to reject her.

There was a strange difference in his regard of his present folly and of his love in his youthful time. Now he could be mad with method, knowing it to be madness: then he was compelled to make believe his madness wisdom. In those days any flash of reason upon his loved one's imperfections was blurred over hastily and with fear. Such penetrative vision now did not cool him. He knew he was the creature of a tendency; and passively acquiesced.

To use a practical eye, it appeared that, as he had once thought, this Caro family – though it might not for centuries, or ever, furbish up an individual nature which would exactly, ideally, supplement his own imperfect one and round with it the perfect whole – was yet the only family he had ever met, or was likely to meet, which possessed the materials for her making. It was as if the Caros had found the clay but not the potter, while other families whose daughters might attract him had found the potter but not the clay.[7]

CHAPTER VIII

His own Soul confronts him

From his roomy castle and its grounds and the cliffs hard by he could command every move and aspect of her who was the rejuvenated Spirit of the Past to him – in the effulgence of whom all sordid details were disregarded.

Among other things he observed that she was often anxious when it rained. If, after a wet day, a golden streak appeared in the sky over Deadman's Bay, under a lid of cloud, her manner was joyous and her tread light.

This puzzled him; and he found that if he endeavoured to encounter her at these times she shunned him – stealthily and subtly, but unmistakably. One evening, when she had left her cottage and tripped off in the direction of the under-hill townlet, he set out by the same route, resolved to await her return along the high roadway which stretched between that place and East Quarriers.

He reached the top of the old road where it makes a sudden descent to the townlet, but she did not appear. Turning back, he sauntered along till he had nearly reached his own house again. Then he retraced his steps, and in the dim night he walked backwards and forwards on the bare and lofty convex of the isle; the stars above and around him, the lighthouse on duty at the distant point, the lightship winking from the sandbank, the combing of the pebble-beach by the tide beneath, the church away south-westward, where the island fathers lay.

He walked the wild summit till his legs ached, and his heart ached – till he seemed to hear on the upper wind the stones of the slingers whizzing past, and the voices of the invaders who annihilated them, and married their wives and daughters, and produced Avice as the ultimate flower of the combined stocks.[1] Still she did not come. It was more than foolish to wait, yet he could not help waiting. At length he discerned a dot of a figure, which he knew to be hers rather by its motion than by its shape.

How incomparably the immaterial dream dwarfed the grandest of substantial things, when here, between those three sublimities – the sky, the rock, and the ocean – the minute personality of this washer-girl filled his consciousness to its extremest boundary, and the stupendous in-animate scene shrank to a corner therein.

But all at once the approaching figure had disappeared. He looked about; she had certainly vanished. At one side of the road was a low wall, but she could not have gone behind that without considerable trouble and singular conduct. He looked behind him; she had reappeared further on the road.

Jocelyn Pierston hurried after; and, discerning his movement, Avice stood still. When he came up, she was slily shaking with restrained laughter.

'Well, what does this mean, my dear girl?' he asked.

Her inner mirth escaping in spite of her she turned askance and said: 'When you was following me to Street o' Wells, two hours ago, I looked round and saw you, and huddied behind a stone! You passed and brushed my frock without seeing me. And when, on my way backalong, I saw you waiting hereabout again, I slipped over the wall, and ran past you! If I had not stopped and looked round at 'ee, you would never have catched me!'

'What did you do that for, you elf!'

'That you shouldn't find me.'

'That's not exactly a reason. Give another, dear Avice,' he said, as he turned and walked beside her homeward.

She hesitated. 'Come!' he urged again.

''Twas because I thought you wanted to be my young man,' she answered.

'What a wild thought of yours! Supposing I did, wouldn't you have me?'

'Not now. . . . And not for long, even if it had been sooner than now.'

'Why?'

'If I tell you, you won't laugh at me or let anybody else know?'

'Never.'

'Then I will tell you,' she said quite seriously. ''Tis because I get tired o' my lovers as soon as I get to know them well. What I see in one young man for a while soon leaves him and goes into another yonder, and I follow, and then what I admire fades out of him and springs up some-where else; and so I follow on, and never fix to one. I have loved *fifteen* a'ready! Yes, fifteen, I am almost ashamed to say,' she repeated, laughing. 'I can't help it, sir, I assure you. Of course it is really, to *me*, the same one all through, on'y I can't catch him!' She added anxiously, 'You won't tell anybody o' this in me, will you, sir? Because if it were known I am afraid no man would like me.'

Pierston was surprised into stillness. Here was this obscure and almost illiterate girl engaged in the pursuit of the impossible ideal, just as he had been himself doing for the last twenty years. She was doing it quite involuntarily, by sheer necessity of her organization, puzzled all the while at her own instinct. He suddenly thought of its bearing upon himself, and said, with a sinking heart –

'Am I – one of them?'

She pondered critically.

'You was; for a week; when I first saw you.'

'Only a week?'

'About that.'

'What made the being of your fancy forsake my form and go elsewhere?'

'Well – though you seemed handsome and gentlemanly at first—'

'Yes?'

'I found 'ee too old² soon after.'

'You are a candid young person.'

'But you asked me, sir!' she expostulated.

'I did; and, having been answered, I won't intrude upon you longer. So cut along home as fast as you can. It is getting late.'

When she had passed out of earshot he also followed homewards. This seeking of the Well-Beloved was, then, of the nature of a knife which could cut two ways. To be the seeker was one thing: to be one of the corpses from which the ideal inhabitant had departed was another; and this was what he had become now, in the mockery of new Days.

Drawing near his own gate he smelt tobacco, and could discern two figures in the side lane leading past Avice's door. They did not, however, enter her house, but strolled onward to the narrow pass conducting to Red-King Castle and the sea. He was in momentary heaviness at the thought that they might be Avice with a worthless lover, but a faintly argumentative tone from the man informed him that they were the same married couple going homeward whom he had encountered on a previous occasion.

The next day he gave the servants a half-holiday to get the pretty Avice into the castle again for a few hours, the better to observe her. While she was pulling down the blinds at sunset a whistle of peculiar quality came from some point on the cliffs outside the lawn. He observed that her colour rose slightly, though she bustled about as if she had noticed nothing.

Pierston suddenly suspected that she had not only fifteen past admirers but a current one. Still, he might be mistaken. Stimulated now by ancient memories and present tenderness to use every effort to make her his wife, despite her conventional unfitness, he strung himself up to sift this mystery. If he could only win her – and how could a country girl refuse such an opportunity? – he could pack her off to school for two or three years, marry her, enlarge her mind by a little travel, and take his chance of the rest. As to her want of ardour for him – so sadly in contrast with her sainted mother's affection – a man twenty years older than his bride could expect no better, and he would be well content to put up with it in the pleasure of possessing one in whom seemed to linger as an aroma all the charm of his youth and his early home.

CHAPTER IX

Juxtapositions

It was a sad and leaden afternoon, and Pierston paced up the long, steep pass or street of the Wells. On either side of the road young girls stood with pitchers at the fountains which bubbled there, and behind the houses forming the propylæa of the rock[1] rose the massive forehead of the Isle – crested at this part with its enormous ramparts as with a mural crown.

As you approach the upper end of the street all progress seems about to be checked by the almost vertical face of the escarpment. Into it your track apparently runs point-blank: a confronting mass which, if it were to slip down, would overwhelm the whole town. But in a moment you find that the road, the old Roman highway into the peninsula, turns at a sharp angle when it reaches the base of the scarp, and ascends in the stiffest of inclines to the right. To the left there is also another ascending road, modern, almost as steep as the first, and perfectly straight. This is the road to the forts.

Pierston arrived at the forking of the ways, and paused for breath. Before turning to the right, his proper and picturesque course, he looked up the uninteresting left road to the fortifications. It was new, long, white, regular, tapering to a vanishing point, like a lesson in perspective. About a quarter of the way up a girl was resting beside a basket of white linen: and by the shape of her hat and the nature of her burden he recognized her.

She did not see him, and abandoning the right-hand course he slowly ascended the incline she had taken. He observed that her attention was absorbed by something aloft. He followed the direction of her gaze. Above them towered the green-grey mountain of grassy stone, here levelled at the top by military art. The sky-line was broken every now and then by a little peg-like object – a sentry-box; and near one of these a small red spot kept creeping backwards and forwards monotonously against the heavy sky.

Then he divined that she had a soldier-lover.

She turned her head, saw him, and took up her clothes-basket to continue the ascent. The steepness was such that to climb it unencumbered was a breathless business; the linen made her task a cruelty to her. 'You'll never get to the forts with that weight,' he said. 'Give it to me.'

But she would not, and he stood still, watching her as she panted up the way; for the moment an irradiated being, the epitome of a whole sex: by the beams of his own infatuation

> '. . . . . robed in such exceeding glory
> That he beheld her not;"[2]

beheld her not as she really was, as she was even to himself sometimes. But to the soldier what was she? Smaller and smaller she waned up the rigid mathematical road, still gazing at the soldier aloft, as Pierston gazed at her. He could just discern sentinels, springing up at the different coigns of vantage[3] that she passed, but seeing who she was they did not intercept her; and presently she crossed the drawbridge over the enormous chasm surrounding the forts, passed the sentries there also, and disappeared through the arch into the interior. Pierston could not see the sentry now, and thère occurred to him the hateful idea that this scarlet rival was meeting and talking freely to her, the unprotected orphan girl of his sweet original Avice; perhaps, relieved of duty, escorting her across the interior, carrying her basket, her tender body encircled by his arm.

'What the devil are you staring at, as if you were in a trance?'

Pierston turned his head: and there stood his old friend Somers – still looking the long-leased bachelor that he was.

'I might say what the devil do you do here? if I weren't so glad to see you.'

Somers said that he had come to see what was detaining his friend in such an out-of-the-way place at that time of year, and incidentally to get some fresh air into his own lungs. Pierston made him welcome, and they went towards Sylvania Castle.

'You were staring, as far as I could see, at a pretty little washerwoman with a basket of clothes?' resumed the painter.

'Yes; it was that to you, but not to me. Behind the mere pretty island-girl (to the world) is, in my eye, the Idea, in Platonic phraseology – the essence and epitome of all that is desirable in this existence. . . . I am under a doom, Somers. Yes, I am under a doom. To have been always following a phantom whom I saw in woman after woman while she was at a distance, but vanishing away on close approach, was bad enough; but now the terrible thing is that the phantom does *not* vanish, but stays to tantalize me even when I am near enough to see what it is! That girl holds me, *though* my eyes are open, and *though* I see that I am a fool!'

Somers regarded the visionary look of his friend, which rather intensified than decreased as his years wore on, but made no further remark. When they reached the castle Somers gazed round upon the scenery, and Pierston, signifying the quaint little Elizabethan cottage, said: 'That's where she lives.'

'What a romantic place! – and this island altogether. A man might love a scarecrow or turnip-lantern here.'

'But a woman mightn't. Scenery doesn't impress them, though they pretend it does. This girl is as fickle as—'

'You once were.'

'Exactly – from your point of view. She has told me so – candidly. And it hits me hard.'

Somers stood still in sudden thought. 'Well – that *is* a strange turning of the tables!' he said. 'But you wouldn't really marry her, Pierston?'

'I would – to-morrow. Why shouldn't I? What are fame and name and society to me – a descendant of wreckers and smugglers, like her. Besides, I know what she's made of, my boy, to her innermost fibre; I know the

perfect and pure quarry she was dug from:[4] and that gives a man
confidence.'

'Then you'll win.'

*   *   *   *   *

While they were sitting after dinner that evening their quiet discourse
was interrupted by the long low whistle from the cliffs without. Somers
took no notice, but Pierston marked it. That whistle always occurred at
the same time in the evening when Avice was helping in the house. He
excused himself for a moment to his visitor and went out upon the dark
lawn. A crunching of feet upon the gravel mixed in with the articulation
of the sea – steps light as if they were winged. And he supposed, two
minutes later, that the mouth of some hulking fellow was upon hers,
which he himself hardly ventured to look at, so touching was its young
beauty.

Hearing people about – among others a couple quarrelling, for there
were rough as well as gentle people here in the island – he returned to the
house. Next day Somers roamed abroad to look for scenery for a marine
painting, and, going out to seek him, Pierston met Avice.

'So you have a lover, my lady!' he said severely. She admitted that it was
the fact. 'You won't stick to him,' he continued.

'I think I may *this* one,' said she, in a meaning tone that he failed to
fathom. 'He deserted me once, but he won't again.'

'I suppose he's a wonderful sort of fellow?'

'He's good enough for me.'

'So handsome, no doubt.'

'Handsome enough for me.'

'So refined and respectable.'

'Refined and respectable enough for me.'

He could not disturb her equanimity, and let her pass. The next day
was Sunday, and Somers having chosen his view at the other end of the
island, Pierston determined in the afternoon to see Avice's lover. He
found that she had left her cottage stronghold, and went on towards the
lighthouses at the Beal. Turning back when he had reached the nearest,
he saw on the lonely road between the quarries a young man evidently
connected with the stone trade, with Avice the Second upon his arm.

She looked prettily guilty and blushed a little under his glance. The
man's was one of the typical island physiognomies – his features energetic
and wary in their expression, and half covered with a close, crisp black

beard. Pierston fancied that out of his keen dark eyes there glimmered a dry sense of humour at the situation.

If so, Avice must have told him of Pierston's symptoms of tenderness. This girl, whom, for her dear mother's sake more than for her own unquestionable attractiveness, he would have guarded as the apple of his eye, how could she estimate him so flippantly!

The mortification of having brought himself to this position with the antitype, by his early slight of the type, blinded him for the moment to what struck him a short time after. The man upon whose arm she hung was not a soldier. What, then, became of her entranced gaze at the sentinel? She could hardly have transferred her affections so promptly; or, to give her the benefit of his own theory, her Beloved could scarcely have flitted from frame to frame in so very brief an interval. And which of them had been he who whistled softly in the dusk to her?

Without further attempt to find Alfred Somers Pierston walked homeward, moodily thinking that the desire to make reparation to the original woman by wedding and enriching the copy – which lent such an unprecedented permanence to his new love – was thwarted, as if by set intention of his destiny.

At the door of the grounds about the castle there stood a carriage. He observed that it was not one of the homely flys from the under-hill town, but apparently from the fashionable town across the bay. Wondering why the visitor had not driven in he entered, to find in the drawing-room Nichola Pine-Avon.

At his first glance upon her, fashionably dressed and graceful in movement, she seemed beautiful; at the second, when he observed that her face was pale and agitated, she seemed pathetic likewise. Altogether, she was now a very different figure from her who, sitting in her chair with such finished composure, had snubbed him in her drawing-room in Hamptonshire Square.

'You are surprised at this? Of course you are!' she said, in a low, pleading voice, languidly lifting her heavy eyelids, while he was holding her hand. 'But I couldn't help it! I know I have done something to offend you – have I not? O! what can it be, that you have come away to this outlandish rock, to live with barbarians in the midst of the London season?'

'You have not offended me, dear Mrs. Pine-Avon,' he said. 'How sorry I am that you should have supposed it! Yet I am glad, too, that your fancy should have done me the good turn of bringing you here to see me.'

'I am staying at Budmouth-Regis,' she explained.

'Then I did see you at a church-service here a little while back?'

She blushed faintly upon her pallor, and she sighed. Their eyes met. 'Well,' she said at last, 'I don't know why I shouldn't show the virtue of candour. You know what it means. I was the stronger once; now I am the weaker. Whatever pain I may have given you in the ups and downs of our acquaintance I am sorry for, and would willingly repair all errors of the past by – being amenable to reason in the future.'

It was impossible that Jocelyn should not feel a tender impulsion towards this attractive and once independent woman, who from every worldly point of view was an excellent match for him – a superior match, indeed, except in money. He took her hand again and held it awhile, and a faint wave of gladness seemed to flow through her. But no – he could go no further. That island girl, in her coquettish Sunday frock and little hat with its bunch of cock's feathers held him as by strands of Manila rope. He dropped Nichola's hand.

'I am leaving Budmouth to-morrow,' she said. 'That was why I felt I must call. You did not know I had been there all through the Whitsun holidays?'

'I did not, indeed; or I should have come to see you.'

'I didn't like to write. I wish I had, now!'

'I wish you had, too, dear Mrs. Pine-Avon.'

But it was 'Nichola' that she wanted to be. As they reached the landau he told her that he should be back in town himself again soon, and would call immediately. At the moment of his words Avice Caro, now alone, passed close along by the carriage on the other side, towards her house hard at hand. She did not turn head or eye to the pair: they seemed to be in her view objects of indifference.

Pierston became cold as a stone. The chill towards Nichola that the presence of the girl, – sprite, witch, troll that she was – brought with it came like a doom. He knew what a fool he was, as he had said. But he was powerless in the grasp of the idealizing passion. He cared more for Avice's finger-tips than for Mrs. Pine-Avon's whole personality.

Perhaps Nichola saw it, for she said mournfully: 'Now I have done all I could! I felt that the only counterpoise to my cruelty to you in my drawing-room would be to come as a suppliant to yours.'

'It is most handsome and noble of you, my very dear friend!' said he, with an emotion of courtesy rather than of enthusiasm.

Then adieux were spoken, and she drove away. But Pierston saw only the retreating Avice, and knew that he was helpless in her hands. The church of the island had risen near the foundations of the Pagan temple, and a Christian emanation from the former might be wrathfully torturing him through the very false gods to whom he had devoted himself both in his craft, like Demetrius of Ephesus,[5] and in his heart.[6] Perhaps Divine punishment for his idolatries had come.

CHAPTER X

She Fails to Vanish still

Pierston had not turned far back towards the castle when he was over-taken by Somers and the man who carried his painting lumber. They paced together to the door; the man deposited the articles and went away, and the two walked up and down before entering.

'I met an extremely interesting woman in the road out there,' said the painter.

'Ah, she is! A sprite, a sylph; Psyche' indeed!'

'I was struck with her.'

'It shows how beauty will out through the homeliest guise.'

'Yes, it will; though not always. And this case doesn't prove it, for the lady's attire was in the latest and most approved taste.'

'Oh, you mean the lady who was driving?'

'Of course. What, were you thinking of the pretty little cottage-girl outside here? I did meet her, but what's she? Very well for one's picture, though hardly for one's fireside. This lady—'

'Is Mrs. Pine-Avon. A kind, proud woman, who'll do what people with no pride would not condescend to think of. She is leaving Budmouth to-morrow, and she drove across to see me. You know how things seemed to be going with us at one time? But I am no good to any woman. She's been very generous towards me, which I've not been to her. . . . She'll ultim-ately throw herself away upon some wretch unworthy of her, no doubt.'

'Do you think so?' murmured Somers. After a while he said abruptly, 'I'll marry her myself, if she'll have me. I like the look of her.'

261

'I wish you would, Alfred, or rather could! She has long had an idea of slipping out of the world of fashion into the world of art. She is a woman of individuality and earnest instincts. I am in real trouble about her. I won't say she can be won – it would be ungenerous of me to say that. But try. I can bring you together easily.'

'I'll marry her, if she's willing!' With the phlegmatic dogmatism that was part of him, Somers added: 'When you have decided to marry, take the first nice woman you meet. They are all alike.'

'Well – you don't know her yet,' replied Jocelyn, who could give praise where he could not give love.

'But you do, and I'll take her on the strength of your judgment. Is she really handsome? – I had but the merest glance. But I know she is, or she wouldn't have caught your discriminating eye.'

'You may take my word for it; she looks as well at hand as afar.'

'What colour are her eyes?'

'Her eyes? I don't go much into colour, being professionally sworn to form. But, let me see – grey; and her hair rather light than dark brown.'

'I wanted something darker,' said Somers airily. 'There are so many fair models among native Englishwomen. Still, blondes are useful property! . . . Well, well; this is flippancy. But I liked the look of her.'

* * * * *

Somers had gone back to town. It was a wet day on the little peninsula: but Pierston walked out as far as the garden-house of his hired castle, where he sat down and smoked. This erection being on the boundary-wall of his property his ear could now and then catch the tones of Avice's voice from her open-doored cottage in the lane which skirted his fence; and he noticed that there were no modulations in it. He knew why that was. She wished to go out, and could not. He had observed before that when she was planning an outing a particular note would come into her voice during the preceding hours: a dove's roundness of sound; no doubt the effect upon her voice of her thoughts of her lover, or lovers. Yet the latter it could not be. She was pure and single-hearted: half an eye could see that. Whence, then, the two men? Possibly the quarrier was a relation.

There seemed reason in this when, going out into the lane, he en-countered one of the red-jackets he had been thinking of. Soldiers were seldom seen in this outer part of the isle: their beat from the forts, when on pleasure, was in the opposite direction, and this man must have had a special reason for coming hither. Pierston surveyed him. He was a round-faced, good-humoured fellow to look at, having two little pieces of moustache on his upper lip, like a pair of minnows rampant, and small black eyes, over which the Glengarry cap straddled flat. It was a hateful idea that her tender cheek should be kissed by the lips of this heavy young man, who had never been sublimed by a single battle, even with defenceless savages.

The soldier went before her house, looked at the door, and moved on down the crooked way to the cliffs, where there was a path back to the forts. But he did not adopt it, returning by the way he had come. This showed his wish to pass the house again. She gave no sign, however, and the soldier disappeared.

Pierston could not be satisfied that Avice was in the house, and he crossed over to the front of her little freehold and tapped at the door, which stood ajar.

Nobody came: hearing a slight movement within he crossed the threshold. Avice was there alone, sitting on a low stool in a dark corner, as though she wished to be unobserved by any casual passer-by. She looked up at him without emotion or apparent surprise; but he could then see that she was crying. The view, for the first time, of distress in an unprotected young girl towards whom he felt drawn by ties of extraordinary delicacy and tenderness, moved Pierston beyond measure. He entered without ceremony.

'Avice, my dear girl!' he said. 'Something is the matter!'

She looked assent, and he went on: 'Now tell me all about it. Perhaps I can help you. Come, tell me.'

'I can't!' she murmured. 'Grammer Stockwool is upstairs, and she'll hear!' Mrs. Stockwool was the old woman who had come to live with the girl for company since her mother's death.

'Then come into my garden opposite. There we shall be quite private.'

She rose, put on her hat, and accompanied him to the door. Here she asked him if the lane were empty, and on his assuring her that it was she crossed over and entered with him through the garden-wall.

The place was a shady and secluded one, though through the boughs the sea could be seen quite near at hand, its moanings being distinctly audible. A water-drop from a tree fell here and there, but the rain was not enough to hurt them.

'Now let me hear it,' he said soothingly. 'You may tell me with the greatest freedom. I was a friend of your mother's, you know. That is, I knew her; and I'll be a friend of yours.'

The statement was risky, if he wished her not to suspect him of being her mother's false one. But that lover's name appeared to be unknown to the present Avice.

'I can't tell you, sir,' she replied unwillingly; 'except that it has to do with my own changeableness. The rest is the secret of somebody else.'

'I am sorry for that,' said he.

'I am getting to care for one I ought not to think of, and it means ruin. I ought to get away!'

'You mean from the island?'

'Yes.'

Pierston reflected. His presence in London had been desired for some time; yet he had delayed going because of his new solicitudes here. But to go and take her with him would afford him opportunity of watching over her, tending her mind, and developing it; while it might remove her from some looming danger. It was a somewhat awkward guardianship for him, as a lonely man, to carry out; still, it could be done. He asked her abruptly if she would really like to go away for a while.

'I like best to stay here,' she answered. 'Still, I should not mind going somewhere, because I think I ought to.'

'Would you like London?'

Avice's face lost its weeping shape. 'How could that be?' she said.

'I have been thinking that you could come to my house and make yourself useful in some way. I rent just now one of those new places called flats,[2] which you may have heard of; and I have a studio at the back.'

'I haven't heard of 'em,' she said without interest.

'Well, I have two servants there, and as my man has a holiday you can help them for a month or two.'

'Would polishing furniture be any good? I can do that.'

'I haven't much furniture that requires polishing. But you can clear away plaster and clay messes in the studio, and chippings of stone, and help me in modelling, and dust all my Venus failures,[3] and hands and heads and feet and bones, and other objects.'

She was startled, yet attracted by the novelty of the proposal.

'Only for a time?' she said.

'Only for a time. As short as you like, and as long.'

The deliberate manner in which, after the first surprise, Avice discussed the arrangements that he suggested, might have told him how far was any feeling for himself beyond friendship, and possibly gratitude, from agitating her breast. Yet there was nothing extravagant in the discrepancy between their ages, and he hoped, after shaping her to himself, to win her. What had grieved her to tears she would not more particularly tell.

She had naturally not much need of preparation, but she made even less preparation than he would have expected her to require. She seemed eager to be off immediately, and not a soul was to know of her departure. Why, if she were in love and at first averse to leave the island, she should be so precipitate now he failed to understand.

But he took great care to compromise in no way a girl in whom his interest was as protective as it was passionate. He accordingly left her to get out of the island alone, awaiting her at a station a few miles up the railway, where, discovering himself to her through the carriage-window, he entered the next compartment, his frame pervaded by a glow which was almost joy at having for the first time in his charge one who inherited the flesh and bore the name so early associated with his own, and at the prospect of putting things right which had been wrong through many years.

CHAPTER XI

The Image Persists

It was dark when the four-wheeled cab wherein he had brought Avice from the station stood at the entrance to the pile of flats of which Pierston occupied one floor – rarer then as residences in London than they are now. Leaving Avice to alight and get the luggage taken in by the porter Pierston went upstairs. To his surprise his floor was silent, and on entering with a latchkey the rooms were all in darkness. He descended to the hall, where Avice was standing helpless beside the luggage, while the porter was outside with the cabman.

'Do you know what has become of my servants?' asked Jocelyn.

'What – and ain't they there, saur? Ah, then my belief is that what I suspected is thrue! You didn't leave your wine-cellar unlocked, did you, saur, by no mistake?'

Pierston considered. He thought he might have left the key with his elder servant, whom he had believed he could trust, especially as the cellar was not well stocked.

'Ah, then it was so! She's been very queer, saur, this last week or two. O yes, sending messages down the spakin'-tube which were like madness itself, and ordering us this and that, till we would take no notice at all. I see them both go out last night, and possibly they went for a holiday not expecting ye, or maybe for good! Shure, if ye'd written, saur, I'd ha' got the place ready, ye being out of a man, too, though it's not me duty at all!'

When Pierston got to his floor again he found that the cellar door was open; some bottles were standing empty that had been full, and many abstracted altogether. All other articles in the house, however, appeared to be intact. His letter to his housekeeper lay in the box as the postman had left it.

By this time the luggage had been sent up in the lift; and Avice, like so much more luggage, stood at the door, the hall-porter behind offering his assistance.

'Come here, Avice,' said the sculptor. 'What shall we do now? Here's a pretty state of affairs!'

Avice could suggest nothing, till she was struck with the bright thought that she should light a fire.

'Light a fire? – ah, yes. . . . I wonder if we could manage. This is an odd coincidence – and awkward!' he murmured. 'Very well, light a fire.'

'Is this the kitchen, sir, all mixed up with the parlours?'

'Yes.'

'Then I think I can do all that's wanted here for a bit; at any rate, till you can get help, sir. At least, I could if I could find the fuel-house. 'Tis no such big place as I thought!'

'That's right: take courage!' said he with a tender smile. 'Now, I'll dine out this evening, and leave the place for you to arrange as best you can with the help of the porter's wife downstairs.'

This Pierston accordingly did, and so their common residence began. Feeling more and more strongly that some danger awaited her in her native island he determined not to send her back till the lover or lovers who seemed to trouble her should have cooled off. He was quite willing to take the risk of his action thus far in his solicitous regard for her.

* * * * *

It was a dual solitude, indeed; for, though Pierston and Avice were the only two people in the flat, they did not keep each other company, the former being as scrupulously fearful of going near her now that he had the opportunity as he had been prompt to seek her when he had none. They lived in silence, his messages to her being frequently written on scraps of paper deposited where she could see them. It was not without a pang that he noted her unconsciousness of their isolated position – a position to which, had she experienced any reciprocity of sentiment, she would readily have been alive.

Considering that, though not profound, she was hardly a matter-of-fact girl as that phrase is commonly understood, she was exasperating in the matter-of-fact quality of her responses to the friendly remarks which would escape him in spite of himself, as well as in her general conduct. Whenever he formed some culinary excuse for walking across the few yards of tessellated hall which separated his room from the kitchen, and spoke through the doorway to her, she answered, 'Yes, sir,' or 'No, sir,' without turning her eyes from the particular work that she was engaged in.

In the usual course he would have obtained a couple of properly qualified servants immediately; but he lived on with the one, or rather the less than one, that this cottage-girl afforded. It had been his almost invariable custom to dine at one of his clubs. Now he sat at home over the miserable chop or steak to which he limited himself in dread lest she should complain of there being too much work for one person, and demand to be sent home. A charwoman came every two or three days, effecting an extraordinary consumption of food and alcoholic liquids: yet it was not for this that Pierston dreaded her presence, but lest, in conversing with Avice, she should open the girl's eyes to the oddity of her situation. Avice could see for herself that there must have been two or three servants in the flat during his former residence there: but his reasons for doing without them seemed never to strike her.

His intention had been to keep her occupied exclusively at the studio, but accident had modified this. However, he sent her round one morning, and entering himself shortly after found her engaged in wiping the layers of dust from the casts and models.

The colour of the dust never ceased to amaze her. 'It is like the hold of a Budmouth collier,' she said, 'and the beautiful faces of these clay people are quite spoilt by it.'

'I suppose you'll marry some day, Avice?' remarked Pierston, as he regarded her thoughtfully.

'Some do and some don't,' she said, with a reserved smile, still attending to the casts.

'You are very offhand,' said he.

She archly weighed that remark without further speech. It was tantalizing conduct in the face of his instinct to cherish her; especially when he regarded the charm of her bending profile; the well-characterized though softly lined nose, the round chin with, as it were, a second leap in its curve to the throat, and the sweep of the eyelashes over the rosy cheek during the sedulously lowered glance. How futilely he had laboured to express the character of that face in clay, and, while catching it in substance, had yet lost something that was essential!

That evening at dusk, in the stress of writing letters, he sent her out for stamps. She had been absent some quarter of an hour when, suddenly drawing himself up from over his writing-table, it flashed upon him that he had absolutely forgotten her total ignorance of London.

The head post-office, to which he had sent her because it was late, was two or three streets off, and he had made his request in the most general manner, which she had acceded to with alacrity enough. How could he have done such an unreflecting thing?

Pierston went to the window. It was about nine o'clock, and owing to her absence the blinds were not down. He opened the casement and stepped out upon the balcony. The green shade of his lamp screened its rays from the gloom without. Over the opposite square the moon hung, and to the right there stretched a long street, filled with a diminishing array of lamps, some single, some in clusters, among them an occasional blue or red one. From a corner came the notes of a piano-organ strumming out a stirring march of Rossini's.[1] The shadowy black figures of pedestrians moved up, down, and across the embrowned roadway. Above the roofs was a bank of livid mist, and higher a greenish-blue sky, in which stars were visible, though its lower part was still pale with daylight, against which rose chimney-pots in the form of elbows, prongs, and fists.

From the whole scene proceeded a ground rumble, miles in extent, upon which individual rattles, voices, a tin whistle, the bark of a dog, rode like bubbles on a sea. The whole noise impressed him with the sense that no one in its enormous mass ever required rest.

In this illimitable ocean of humanity there was a unit of existence, his Avice, wandering alone.

Pierston looked at his watch. She had been gone half an hour. It was impossible to distinguish her at this distance, even if she approached. He came inside, and putting on his hat determined to go out and seek her. He reached the end of the street, and there was nothing of her to be seen. She had the option of two or three routes from this point to the post-office; yet he plunged at random into one, till he reached the office to find it quite deserted. Almost distracted now by his anxiety for her he retreated as rapidly as he had come, regaining home only to find that she had not returned.

He recollected telling her that if she should ever lose her way she must call a cab and drive home. It occurred to him that this was what she would do now. He again went out upon the balcony; the dignified street in which he lived was almost vacant, and the lamps stood like placed sentinels awaiting some procession which tarried long. At a point under him where the road was torn up there stood a red light, and at the corner two men were talking in leisurely repose, as if sunning themselves at noonday. Lovers of a feline disposition, who were never seen by daylight, joked and darted at each other in and out of area gates.

His attention was fixed on the cabs, and he held his breath as the hollow clap of each horse's hoofs drew near the front of the house, only to go onward into the square. The two lamps of each vehicle afar dilated with its near approach, and seemed to swerve towards him. It was Avice surely? No, it passed by.

Almost frantic he again descended and let himself out of the house, moving towards a more central part, where the roar still continued. Before emerging into the noisy thoroughfare he observed a small figure approaching leisurely along the opposite side, and hastened across to find it was she.

CHAPTER XII

A Grille descends between

'O Avice!' he cried, with the tenderly subdued scolding of a mother. 'What is this you have done to alarm me so!'

She seemed unconscious of having done anything, and was altogether surprised at his anxiety. In his relief he did not speak further till he asked her suddenly if she would take his arm since she must be tired.

'O no, sir!' she assured him, 'I am not a bit tired, and I don't require any help at all, thank you.'

They went upstairs without using the lift, and he let her and himself in with his latchkey. She entered the kitchen, and he, following, sat down in a chair there.

'Where have you been?' he said, with almost angered concern on his face. 'You ought not to have been absent more than ten minutes.'

'I knew there was nothing for me to do, and thought I should like to see a little of London,' she replied naïvely. 'So when I had got the stamps I went on into the fashionable streets, where folks are all walking about just as if it were daytime! 'Twas for all the world like coming home by night from Martinmas Fair¹ at the Street o' Wells, only more genteel.'

'O Avice, Avice, you must not go out like this! Don't you know that I am responsible for your safety? I am your – well, guardian, in fact, and am bound by law and morals, and I don't know what-all, to deliver you up to your native island without a scratch or blemish. And yet you indulge in such a midnight vagary as this!'

'But I am sure, sir, the people in the street were more respectable than they are anywhere at home! They were dressed in the latest fashion, and would have scorned to do me any harm; and as to their love-making, I never heard anything so polite before.'

'Well, you must not do it again. I'll tell you some day why. What's that you have in your hand?'

'A mouse-trap. There are lots of mice in this kitchen – sooty mice, not clean like ours – and I thought I'd try to catch them. That was what I went so far to buy, as there were no shops open just about here. I'll set it now.'

She proceeded at once to do so, and Pierston remained in his seat regarding the operation, which seemed entirely to engross her. It was extraordinary, indeed, to observe how she wilfully limited her interests; with what content she received the ordinary things that life offered, and persistently refused to behold what an infinitely extended life lay open to her through him. If she had only said the word he would have got a licence and married her the next morning. Was it possible that she did not perceive this tendency in him? She could hardly be a woman if she did not; and in her airy, elusive, offhand demeanour she was very much of a woman indeed.

'It only holds one mouse,' he said absently.

'But I shall hear it throw in the night, and set it again.'

He sighed, and left her to her own resources and retired to rest, though he felt no tendency to sleep. At some small hour of the darkness, owing, possibly, to some intervening door being left open, he heard the mouse-trap click. Another light sleeper must have heard it too, for almost immediately after the pit-pat of naked feet, accompanied by the brushing of drapery, was audible along the passage towards the kitchen. After her absence in that apartment long enough to reset the trap, he was startled by a scream from the same quarter. Pierston sprang out of bed, jumped into his dressing-gown, and hastened in the direction of the cry.

Avice, barefooted and wrapped in a shawl, was standing in a chair; the mouse-trap lay on the floor, the mouse running round and round in its neighbourhood.

'I was trying to take en out,' said she excitedly, 'and he got away from me!'

Pierston secured the mouse while she remained standing on the chair. Then, having set the trap anew, his feeling burst out petulantly –

'A girl like you to throw yourself away upon such a commonplace fellow as that quarryman! Why do you do it!'

Her mind was so intently fixed upon the matter in hand that it was some moments before she caught his irrelevant subject. 'Because I am a foolish girl,' she said quietly.

'What! Don't you love him?' said Jocelyn, with a surprised stare up at her as she stood, in her concern appearing the very Avice who had kissed him twenty years earlier.

'It is not much use to talk about that,' said she.

'Then, is it the soldier?'

'Yes, though I have never spoken to him.'

'Never spoken to the soldier?'

'Never.'

'Has either one treated you badly – deceived you?'

'No. Certainly not.'

'Well, I can't make you out; and I don't wish to know more than you choose to tell me. Come, Avice, why not tell me exactly how things are?'

'Not now, sir!' she said, her pretty pink face and brown eyes turned in simple appeal to him from her pedestal. 'I will tell you all to-morrow; an that I will!'

He retreated to his own room and lay down meditating. Some quarter of an hour after she had retreated to hers the mouse-trap clicked again, and Pierston raised himself on his elbow to listen. The place was so still and the jerry-built door-panels so thin that he could hear the mouse jumping about inside the wires of the trap. But he heard no footstep this time. As he was wakeful and restless he again arose, proceeded to the kitchen with a light, and removing the mouse reset the trap. Returning he listened once more. He could see in the far distance the door of Avice's room; but that thoughtful housewife had not heard the second capture. From the room came a soft breathing like that of an infant.

He entered his own chamber and reclined himself gloomily enough. Her lack of all consciousness of him, the aspect of the deserted kitchen, the cold grate, impressed him with a deeper sense of loneliness than he had ever felt before.

Foolish he was, indeed, to be so devoted to this young woman. Her defencelessness, her freedom from the least thought that there lurked a danger in their propinquity, were in fact secondary safeguards, not much less strong than that of her being her mother's image, against risk to her from him. Yet it was out of this that his depression came.

At sight of her the next morning Pierston felt that he must put an end to such a state of things. He sent Avice off to the studio, wrote to an agent for a couple of servants, and then went round to his work. Avice was busy righting all that she was allowed to touch. It was the girl's delight to be occupied among the models and casts, which for the first time she regarded with the wistful interest of a soul struggling to receive ideas of beauty vaguely discerned yet ever eluding her. That brightness in her mother's mind which might have descended to the second Avice with the maternal face and form, had been dimmed by admixture with the mediocrity of her father's, and by one who remembered like Pierston the dual organization the opposites could be often seen wrestling internally.

They were alone in the studio, and his feelings found vent. Putting his arms round her he said, 'My darling, sweet little Avice! I want to ask you something – surely you guess what? I want to know this: will you be married to me, and live here with me always and ever?'

'O, Mr. Pierston, what nonsense!'

'Nonsense?' said he, shrinking somewhat.

'Yes, sir.'

'Well, why? Am I too old? Surely there's no serious difference?'

'O no – I should not mind that if it came to marrying. The difference is not much for husband and wife, though it is rather much for keeping company.'

She struggled to get free, and when in the movement she knocked down the Empress Faustina's head[2] he did not try to retain her. He saw that she was not only surprised but a little alarmed.

'You haven't said why it is nonsense!' he remarked tartly.

'Why, I didn't know you was thinking of me like that. I hadn't any thought of it! And all alone here! What shall I do?'

'Say yes, my pretty Avice! We'll then go out and be married at once, and nobody be any the wiser.'

She shook her head. 'I couldn't, sir.'

'It would be well for you. You don't like me, perhaps?'

'Yes I do – very much. But not in that sort of way – quite. Still, I might have got to love you in time, if—'

'Well, then, try,' he said warmly. 'Your mother did!'

No sooner had the words slipped out than Pierston would have recalled them. He had felt in a moment that they jeopardized his cause.

'Mother loved you?' said Avice, incredulously gazing at him.

'Yes,' he murmured.

'You were not her false young man, surely? That one who—'

'Yes, yes! Say no more about it.'

'Who ran away from her?'

'Almost.'

'Then I can *never, never* like you again! I didn't know it was a gentleman – I – I thought—'

'It wasn't a gentleman, then.'

'O, sir, please go away! I can't bear the sight of 'ee at this moment! Perhaps I shall get to – to like you as I did; but—'

'No; I'm d—d if I'll go away!' said Pierston, thoroughly irritated. 'I have been candid with you; you ought to be the same with me!'

'What do you want me to tell?'

'Enough to make it clear to me why you don't accept this offer. Everything you have said yet is a reason for the reverse. Now, my dear, I am not angry.'

'Yes you are.'

'No I'm not. Now what is your reason?'

'The name of it is Isaac Pierston, down home.'

'How?'

'I mean he courted me, and led me on to island custom,[3] and then I went to chapel one morning and married him in secret, because mother didn't care about him; and I didn't either by that time. And then he quarrelled with me; and just before you and I came to London he went away to Guernsey.[4] Then I saw a soldier; I never knew his name, but I fell in love with him because I am so quick at that! Still, as it was wrong, I tried not to think of him, and wouldn't look at him when he passed. But it made me cry very much that I mustn't. I was then very miserable, and you asked me to come to London. I didn't care what I did with myself, and I came.'

'Heaven above us!' said Pierston, his pale and distressed face showing with what a shock this announcement had come. 'Why have you done such extraordinary things? Or, rather, why didn't you tell me of this before? Then, at the present moment you are the wife of a man who is in Guernsey, whom you do not love at all; but instead of him love a soldier whom you have never spoken to; while I have nearly brought scandal upon us both by your letting me love you. Really, you are a very wicked woman!'

'No, I am not!' she pouted.

Still, Avice looked pale and rather frightened, and did not lift her eyes from the floor. 'I said it was nonsense in you to want to have me!' she went on, 'and, even if I hadn't been married to that horrid Isaac Pierston, I couldn't have married you after you told me that you was the man who ran away from my mother.'

'I have paid the penalty!' he said sadly. 'Men of my sort always get the worst of it somehow. Now, Avice – I'll call you dear Avice for your mother's sake and not for your own – I must see what I can do to help you out of the difficulty that unquestionably you are in. Why can't you love your husband now you have married him?'

Avice looked aside at the statuary as if the subtleties of her organization were not very easy to define.

'Was he that black-bearded typical local character I saw you walking with one Sunday? The same surname as mine; though, of course, you don't notice that in a place where there are only half-a-dozen surnames?'

'Yes, that was Ike. It was that evening we disagreed. He scolded me again, and I answered him, and the next day he went away.'

'Well, as I say, I must consider what it will be best to do for you in this. The first thing, it seems to me, will be to get your husband home.'

She impatiently shrugged her shoulders. 'I don't like him!'

'Then why did you marry him?'

'I was obliged to, after we'd proved each other.'

'You shouldn't have thought of such a thing. It is ridiculous and out of date nowadays.'

'Ah, he's so old-fashioned in his notions that he doesn't think like that. However, he's gone.'

'Ah – it is only a tiff between you, I dare say. I'll start him in business if he'll come. . . . Is the cottage at home still in your hands?'

'Yes, it is my freehold. Grammer Stockwool is taking care o' it for me.'

'Good. And back there you go straightway, my pretty madam, and wait till your husband comes to make it up with you.'

'I won't go! – I don't want him to come!' she sobbed. 'I want to stay here, or anywhere, except where he can come!'

'You will get over that. Now, go back to the flat, there's a dear Avice, and be ready in one hour, waiting in the hall for me.'

'I don't want to!'

'But I say you shall!'

She found it was no use to disobey. Precisely at the moment appointed he met her there himself, burdened only with a valise and umbrella, she with a box and other things. Directing the porter to put Avice and her belongings into a four-wheeled cab for the railway-station, he walked out of the door, and kept looking behind till he saw the cab approaching. He then entered beside the astonished girl, and onward they went together.

They sat opposite each other in an empty compartment, and the tedious railway journey began. Regarding her closely now by the light of her revelation he wondered at himself for never divining her secret. Whenever he looked at her the girl's eyes grew rebellious, and at last she wept.

'I don't want to go to him!' she sobbed in a repressed voice.

Pierston was almost as much distressed as she. 'Why did you put yourself and me in such a position?' he said bitterly. 'It is no use to regret it now! And I can't say that I do. It affords me a way out of a trying position. Even if you had not been married to him you would not have married me!'

'Yes, I would, sir.'

'What! You would? You said you wouldn't not long ago.'

'I like you better now! I like you more and more!'

Pierston sighed, for emotionally he was not much older than she. That hitch in his development, rendering him the most lopsided of God's creatures, was his standing misfortune. A proposal to her which crossed his mind was dismissed as disloyalty, particularly to an inexperienced fellow-islander and one who was by race and traditions almost a kinswoman.

Little more passed between the twain on that wretched, never-to-be-forgotten day. Aphrodite, Ashtaroth, Freyja,[5] or whoever the love-queen of his isle might have been, was punishing him sharply, as she knew but too well how to punish her votaries when they reverted from the ephemeral to the stable mood. When was it to end – this curse of his heart not ageing while his frame moved naturally onward? Perhaps only with life.

His first act the day after depositing her in her own house was to go to the chapel where, by her statement, the marriage had been solemnized, and make sure of the fact. Perhaps he felt an illogical hope that she might be free, even then, in the tarnished condition which such freedom would have involved. However, there stood the words distinctly: Isaac Pierston, Ann Avice Caro, son and daughter of So-and-so, married on such a day, signed by the contracting parties, the officiating minister, and the two witnesses.

CHAPTER XIII

She is Enshrouded from Sight

One evening in early winter, when the air was dry and gusty, the dark little lane which divided the grounds of Sylvania Castle from the cottage of Avice, and led down to the adjoining ruin of Red-King Castle, was paced by a solitary man. The cottage was the centre of his beat; its western limit being the gates of the former residence, its eastern the drawbridge of the ruin. The few other cottages thereabout – all as if carved from the solid rock – were in darkness, but from the upper window of Avice's tiny freehold glimmered a light. Its rays were repeated from the far-distant sea by the lightship lying moored over the mysterious Shambles quicksand, which brought tamelessness and domesticity into due position as balanced opposites.

The sea moaned – more than moaned – among the boulders below the ruins, a throe of its tide being timed to regular intervals. These sounds were accompanied by an equally periodic moan from the interior of the cottage chamber; so that the articulate heave of water and the articulate heave of life seemed but differing utterances of the selfsame troubled terrestrial Being – which in one sense they were.

Pierston – for the man in the lane was he – would look from lightship to cottage window; then back again, as he waited there between the travail of the sea without, and the travail of the woman within. Soon an infant's wail of the very feeblest was also audible in the house. He started from his easy pacing, and went again westward, standing at the elbow of the lane a long time. Then the peace of the sleeping village which lay that way was broken by light wheels and the trot of a horse. Pierston went back to the cottage gate and awaited the arrival of the vehicle.

It was a light cart, and a man jumped down as it stopped. He was in a broad-brimmed hat, under which no more of him could be perceived than that he wore a black beard clipped like a yew fence – a typical aspect in the island.

'You are Avice's husband?' asked the sculptor quickly.

The man replied that he was, in the local accent. 'I've just come in by to-day's boat,' he added. 'I couldn't git here avore. I had contracted for the job at Peter-Port, and had to see to't to the end.'

'Well,' said Pierston, 'your coming means that you are willing to make it up with her?'

'Ay, I don't know but I be,' said the man. 'Mid so well do that as anything else!'

'If you do, thoroughly, a good business in your old line awaits you here in the island.'

'Wi' all my heart, then,' said the man. His voice was energetic, and, though slightly touchy, it showed, on the whole, a disposition to set things right.

The driver of the trap was paid off, and Jocelyn and Isaac Pierston – undoubtedly scions of a common stock in this isle of intermarriages, though they had no proof of it – entered the house. Nobody was in the ground-floor room, in the centre of which stood a square table, in the centre of the table a little wool mat, and in the centre of the mat a lamp, the apartment having the appearance of being rigidly swept and set in order for an event of interest.

The woman who lived in the house with Avice now came downstairs, and to the inquiry of the comers she replied that matters were progressing favourably, but that nobody could be allowed to go upstairs just then. After placing chairs and viands for them she retreated, and they sat down, the lamp between them – the lover of the sufferer above, who had no right to her, and the man who had every right to her, but did not love her. Engaging in desultory and fragmentary conversation they listened to the trampling of feet on the floor-boards overhead – Pierston full of anxiety and attentiveness, Ike awaiting the course of nature calmly.

Soon they heard the feeble bleats repeated, and then the local practitioner descended and entered the room.

'How is she now?' said Pierston, the more taciturn Ike looking up with him for the answer that he felt would serve for two as well as for one.

'Doing well, remarkably well,' replied the professional gentleman, with a manner of having said it in other places; and his vehicle not being at the door he sat down and shared some refreshment with the others. When he had departed Mrs. Stockwool again stepped down, and informed them that Ike's presence had been made known to his wife.

The truant quarrier seemed rather inclined to stay where he was and finish the mug of ale, but Pierston quickened him, and he ascended the staircase. As soon as the lower room was empty Pierston leant with his elbows on the table, and covered his face with his hands.

Ike was absent no great time. Descending with a proprietary mien that had been lacking before, he invited Jocelyn to ascend likewise, since she had stated that she would like to see him. Jocelyn went up the crooked old steps, the husband remaining below.

Avice, though white as the sheets, looked brighter and happier than he had expected to find her, and was apparently very much fortified by the pink little lump at her side. She held out her hand to him.

'I just wanted to tell 'ee,' she said, striving against her feebleness, 'I thought it would be no harm to see you, though 'tis rather soon – to tell 'ee how very much I thank you for getting me settled again with Ike. He is very glad to come home again, too, he says. Yes, you've done a good many kind things for me, sir.'

Whether she were really glad, or whether the words were expressed as a matter of duty, Pierston did not attempt to learn.

He merely said that he valued her thanks. 'Now, Avice,' he added tenderly, 'I resign my guardianship of you. I hope to see your husband in a sound little business here in a very short time.'

'I hope so – for baby's sake,' she said, with a bright sigh. 'Would you – like to see her, sir?'

'The baby? O yes . . . *your* baby! You must christen her Avice.'

'Yes – so I will!' she murmured readily, and disclosed the infant with some timidity. 'I hope you forgive me, sir, for concealing my thoughtless marriage!'

'If you forgive me for making love to you.'

'Yes. How were you to know! I wish –'

Pierston bade her good-bye, kissing her hand; turned from her and the incipient being whom he was to meet again under very altered conditions, and left the bed-chamber with a tear in his eye.

'Here endeth that dream!' said he.

*　　*　　*　　*　　*

Hymen, in secret or overt guise, seemed to haunt Pierston just at this time with undignified mockery which savoured rather of Harlequin[1] than of the torch-bearer. Two days after parting in a lone island from the girl he had so disinterestedly loved he met in Piccadilly his friend Somers, wonderfully spruced up, and hastening along with a preoccupied face.

'My dear fellow,' said Somers, 'what do you think! I was charged not to tell you, but, hang it! I may just as well make a clean breast of it now as later.'

'What – you are not going to . . .' began Pierston, with divination.

'Yes. What I said on impulse six months back I am about to carry out in cold blood. Nichola and I began in jest and ended in earnest. We are going to take one another next month for good and all.'

PART THIRD

A Young Man Turned Sixty

'In me thou seest the glowing of such fire,
That on the ashes of his youth doth lie
As the death-bed whereon it must expire,
Consumed with that which it was nourished by.'

W. SHAKESPEARE

CHAPTER I

She Returns for the New Season

Twenty years had spread their films over the events which wound up with the reunion of the second Avice and her husband; and the hoary peninsula called an island looked just the same as before; though many who had formerly projected their daily shadows upon its unrelieved summer whiteness ceased now to disturb the colourless sunlight there.

The general change, nevertheless, was small. The silent ships came and went from the wharf, the chisels clinked in the quarries; file after file of whitey-brown horses, in strings of eight or ten, painfully dragged down the hill the square blocks of stone on the antediluvian wooden wheels just as usual. The lightship winked every night from the quicksands to the Beal Lantern, and the Beal Lantern glared through its eye-glass on the ship. The canine gnawing audible on the Pebble-bank had been repeated ever since at each tide, but the pebbles remained undevoured.

Men drank, smoked, and spat in the inns with only a little more adulteration in their refreshments and a trifle less dialect in their speech than of yore. But one figure had never been seen on the Channel rock in the interval, the form of Pierston the sculptor, whose first use of the chisel that rock had instigated.

He had lived abroad a great deal, and, in fact, at this very date he was staying at an hotel in Rome. Though he had not once set eyes on Avice since parting from her in the room with her firstborn, he had managed to obtain tidings of her from time to time during the interval. In this way Pierston learnt that, shortly after their resumption of a common life in her house, Ike had ill-used her, till fortunately, the business to which Jocelyn had assisted him chancing to prosper, he became immersed in its details, and allowed Avice to pursue her household courses without interference, initiating that kind of domestic reconciliation which is so calm and durable, having as its chief ingredient neither hate nor love, but an all-embracing indifference.

At first Pierston had sent her sums of money privately, fearing lest her husband should deny her material comforts; but he soon found, to his great relief, that such help was unnecessary, social ambition prompting

Ike to set up as quite a gentleman-islander, and to allow Avice a scope for show which he would never have allowed in mere kindness.

Being in Rome, as aforesaid, Pierston returned one evening to his hotel to dine, after spending the afternoon among the busts in the long gallery of the Vatican. The unconscious habit, common to so many people, of tracing likes in unlikes had often led him to discern, or to fancy he discerned, in the Roman atmosphere, in its lights and shades, and particularly in its reflected or secondary lights, something resembling the atmosphere of his native promontory. Perhaps it was that in each case the eye was mostly resting on stone – that the quarries of ruins in the Eternal City reminded him of the quarries of maiden rock at home.[2]

This being in his mind when he sat down to dinner at the common table, he was surprised to hear an American gentleman, who sat opposite, mention the name of Pierston's birthplace. The American was talking to a friend about a lady – an English widow, whose acquaintance they had renewed somewhere in the Channel Islands during a recent tour, after having known her as a young woman who came to San Francisco with her father and mother many years before. Her father was then a rich man just retired from the business of a stone-merchant in England;[3] but he had engaged in large speculations, and had lost nearly all his fortune. Jocelyn further gathered that the widowed daughter's name was Mrs. Leverre; that she had a step-son, her husband having been a Jersey gentleman, a widower; and that the step-son seemed to be a promising and interesting young man.

Pierston was instantly struck with the perception that these and other allusions, though general, were in accord with the history of his long-lost Marcia.[4] He hardly felt any desire to hunt her up after nearly two score years of separation, but he was impressed enough to resolve to exchange a word with the strangers as soon as he could get opportunity.

He could not well attract their attention through the plants upon the wide table, and even if he had been able he was disinclined to ask questions in public. He waited on till dinner was over, and when the strangers withdrew Pierston withdrew in their rear.

They were not in the drawing-room, and he found that they had gone out. There was no chance of overtaking them, but Pierston, waked to restlessness by their remarks, wandered up and down the adjoining Piazza di Spagna, thinking they might return. The streets below were immersed in shade, the front of the church at the top[5] was flooded with orange light, the gloom of evening gradually intensifying upon the broad, long flight of steps, which foot-passengers incessantly ascended and descended with the insignificance of ants; the dusk wrapped up the house to the left, in which Shelley had lived, and that to the right, in which Keats had died.

Getting back to the hotel he learnt that the Americans had only dropped in to dine, and were staying elsewhere. He saw no more of them; and on reflection he was not deeply concerned, for what earthly woman, going off in a freak as Marcia had done, and keeping silence so long, would care for a belated friendship with him now in the sere, even if he were to take the trouble to discover her.

*   *   *   *   *

Thus much Marcia.[6] The other thread of his connection with the ancient Isle of Slingers was stirred by a letter he received from Avice a little after this date, in which she stated that her husband Ike had been killed[7] in his own quarry by an accident within the past year; that she herself had been ill, and though well again, and left amply provided for, she would like to see him if he ever came that way.

As she had not communicated for several long years, her expressed wish to see him now was likely to be prompted by something more, something newer, than memories of him. Yet the manner of her writing precluded all suspicion that she was thinking of him as an old lover whose suit events had now made practicable. He told her he was sorry to hear that she had been ill, and that he would certainly take an early opportunity of going down to her home on his next visit to England.

He did more. Her request had revived thoughts of his old home and its associations, and instead of awaiting other reasons for a return he made her the operating one. About a week later he stood once again at the foot of the familiar steep whereon the houses at the entrance to the Isle were perched like grey pigeons on a roof-side.

At Top-o'-Hill – as the summit of the rock was mostly called – he stood looking at the busy doings in the quarries beyond, where the numerous black hoisting-cranes scattered over the central plateau had the appearance of a swarm of crane-flies resting there. He went a little further, made some general inquiries about the accident which had carried off Avice's husband in the previous year, and learnt that though now a widow, she had plenty of friends and sympathizers about her, which rendered any immediate attention to her on his part unnecessary.

Considering, therefore, that there was no great reason why he should call on her so soon, and without warning, he turned back. Perhaps after all her request had been dictated by a momentary feeling only, and a considerable strangeness to each other must naturally be the result of a score of dividing years. Descending to the bottom he took his seat in the train on the shore, which soon carried him along the Bank, and round to the watering-place five miles off, at which he had taken up his quarters for a few days.

Here, as he stayed on, his local interests revived. Whenever he went out he could see the island that was once his home lying like a great snail upon the sea across the bay. It was the spring of the year; local steamers had begun to run, and he was never tired of standing on the thinly occupied deck of one of these as it skirted the island and revealed to him on the cliffs far up its height the ruins of Red-King Castle, behind which the little village of East Quarriers lay.

Thus matters went on, if they did not rather stand still, for several days before Pierston redeemed his vague promise to seek Avice out. And in the meantime he was surprised by the arrival of another letter from her by a roundabout route. She had heard, she said, that he had been on the island, and imagined him therefore to be staying somewhere near. Why did he not call as he had told her he would do? She was always thinking of him, and wishing to see him.

Her tone was anxious, and there was no doubt that she really had something to say which she did not wish to write. He wondered what it could be, and started the same afternoon.

Avice, who had been little in his mind of late years, began to renew for herself a distinct position therein. He was fully aware that since his earlier manhood a change had come over his regard of womankind. Once the individual had been nothing more to him than the temporary abiding-place of the typical or ideal; now his heart showed its bent to be a growing fidelity to the specimen, with all her pathetic flaws of detail; which flaws, so far from sending him further, increased his tenderness. This maturer feeling, if finer and higher, was less convenient than the old. Ardours of passion could be felt as in youth without the recuperative intervals which had accompanied evanescence.

The first sensation was to find that she had long ceased to live in the little freehold cottage she had occupied of old. In answer to his inquiries he was directed along the road to the west of the modern castle, past the entrance on that side, and onward to the very house that had once been his own home. There it stood as of yore, facing up the Channel, a comfortable roomy structure, the euonymus and other shrubs, which alone would stand in the teeth of the salt wind, living on at about the same stature in front of it; but the paint-work much renewed. A thriving man had resided there of late, evidently.

The widow in mourning who received him in the front parlour was, alas! but the sorry shadow of Avice the Second. How could he have fancied otherwise after twenty years? Yet he had been led to fancy otherwise, almost without knowing it, by feeling himself unaltered. Indeed, curiously enough, nearly the first words she said to him were: 'Why – you are just the same!'

'Just the same. Yes, I am, Avice,' he answered sadly; for this inability to ossify with the rest of his generation threw him out of proportion with the time. Moreover, while wearing the aspect of comedy, it was of the nature of tragedy.

'It is well to be you, sir,' she went on. 'I have had troubles to take the bloom off me!'

'Yes; I have been sorry for you.'

She continued to regard him curiously, with humorous interest; and he knew what was passing in her mind: that this man, to whom she had formerly looked up as to a person far in advance of her along the lane of life, seemed now to be a well-adjusted contemporary, the pair of them observing the world with fairly level eyes.

He had come to her with warmth for a vision which, on reaching her, he found to have departed; and, though fairly weaned by the natural reality, he was so far staunch as to linger hankeringly. They talked of past days, his old attachment, which she had then despised, being now far more absorbing and present to her than to himself.

She unmistakably won upon him as he sat on. A curious closeness between them had been produced in his imagination by the discovery that she was passing her life within the house of his own childhood. Her similar surname meant little here; but it was also his, and, added to the identity of domicile, lent a strong suggestiveness to the accident.

'This is where I used to sit when my parents occupied the house,' he said, placing himself beside that corner of the fireplace which commanded a view through the window. 'I could see a bough of tamarisk wave outside at that time, and, beyond the bough, the same abrupt grassy waste towards the sea, and at night the same old lightship blinking far out there. Place yourself on the spot, to please me.'

She set her chair where he indicated, and Pierston stood close beside her, directing her gaze to the familiar objects he had regarded thence as a boy. Her head and face – the latter thoughtful and worn enough, poor thing, to suggest a married life none too comfortable – were close to his breast, and, with a few inches further incline, would have touched it.

'And now you are the inhabitant; I the visitor,' he said. 'I am glad to see you here – so glad, Avice! You are fairly well provided for – I think I may assume that?' He looked round the room at the solid mahogany furniture, and at the modern piano and show bookcase.

'Yes, Ike left me comfortable. 'Twas he who thought of moving from my cottage to this larger house. He bought it, and I can live here as long as I choose to.'

Apart from the decline of his adoration to friendship, there seemed to be a general convergence of positions which suggested that he might make amends for the original desertion by proposing to this Avice when a meet time should arrive. If he did not love her as he had done when she was a slim thing catching mice in his rooms in London, he could surely be content at his age with comradeship. After all she was only forty to his sixty. The feeling that he really could be thus content was so convincing that he almost believed the luxury of getting old and reposeful was coming to his restless, wandering heart at last.

'Well, you have come at last, sir,' she went on; 'and I am grateful to you. I did not like writing, and yet I wanted to be straightforward. Have you guessed[8] at all why I wished to see you so much that I could not help sending twice to you?'

'I have tried, but cannot.'

'Try again. It is a pretty reason, which I hope you'll forgive.'

'I am sure I sha'n't unriddle it. But I'll say this on my own account before you tell me. I have always taken a lingering interest in you, which you must value for what it is worth. It originated, so far as it concerns you personally, with the sight of you in that cottage round the corner, nineteen or twenty years ago, when I became tenant of the castle opposite. But that was not the very beginning. The very beginning was a score of years before that, when I, a young fellow of one-and-twenty, coming home here, from London, to see my father, encountered a tender woman as like you as your double; was much attracted by her as I saw her day after day flit past this window; till I made it my business to accompany her in her walks awhile. I, as you know, was not a staunch fellow, and it all ended badly. But, at any rate, her daughter and I are friends.'

'Ah! there she is!' suddenly exclaimed Avice, whose attention had wandered somewhat from his retrospective discourse. She was looking from the window towards the cliffs, where, upon the open ground quite near at hand, a slender female form was seen rambling along. 'She is out for a walk,' Avice continued. 'I wonder if she is going to call here this afternoon? She is living at the castle opposite as governess.'

'O, she's—'

'Yes. Her education was very thorough – better even than her grandmother's. I was the neglected one, and Isaac and myself both vowed that there should be no complaint on that score about her. We christened her Avice, to keep up the name, as you requested. I wish you could speak to her – I am sure you would like her.'

'Is that the baby?' faltered Jocelyn.

'Yes, the baby.'

The person signified, now much nearer, was a still more modernized, up-to-date edition of the two Avices of that blood with whom he had been involved more or less for the last forty years. A ladylike creature was she – almost elegant. She was altogether finer in figure than her mother or grandmother had ever been, which made her more of a woman in appearance than in years. She wore a large-disked sun-hat, with a brim like a wheel whose spokes were radiating folds of muslin lining the brim, a black margin beyond the muslin being the felloe. Beneath this brim her hair was massed low upon her brow, the colour of the thick tresses being obviously, from her complexion, repeated in the irises of her large, deep eyes. Her rather nervous lips were thin and closed, so that they only appeared as a delicate red line. A changeable temperament was shown by that mouth – quick transitions from affection to aversion, from a pout to a smile.

It was Avice the Third.

Jocelyn and the second Avice continued to gaze ardently at her.

'Ah! she is not coming in now; she hasn't time,' murmured the mother, with some disappointment. 'Perhaps she means to run across in the evening.'

The tall girl, in fact, went past and on till she was out of sight. Pierston stood as in a dream. It was the very she, in all essential particulars, and with an intensification of general charm, who had kissed him forty years before. When he turned his head from the window his eyes fell again upon the intermediate Avice at his side. Before but the relic of the Well-Beloved, she had now become its empty shrine. Warm friendship, indeed, he felt for her; but whatever that might have done towards the instauration of a former dream was now hopelessly barred by the rivalry of the thing itself in the guise of a lineal successor.

CHAPTER II

Misgivings on the Re-embodiment

Pierston had been about to leave, but he sat down again on being asked if he would stay and have a cup of tea. He hardly knew for a moment what he did; a dim thought that Avice – the renewed Avice – might come into the house made his reseating himself an act of spontaneity.

He forgot that twenty years earlier he had called the now Mrs. Pierston an elf, a witch; and that lapse of time had probably not diminished the subtleties implied by those epithets. He did not know that she had noted every impression that her daughter had made upon him.

How he contrived to attenuate and disperse the rather tender personalities he had opened up with the new Avice's mother, Pierston never exactly defined. Perhaps she saw more than he thought she saw – read something in his face – knew that about his nature which he gave her no credit for knowing. Anyhow, the conversation took the form of a friendly gossip from that minute, his remarks being often given while his mind was turned elsewhere.

But a chill passed through Jocelyn when there had been time for reflection. The renewed study of his art in Rome without any counterbalancing practical pursuit had nourished and developed his natural responsiveness to impressions; he now felt that his old trouble, his doom – his curse, indeed, he had sometimes called it – was come back again. His divinity[1] was not yet propitiated for that original sin against her image in the person of Avice the First, and now, at the age of one-and-sixty, he was urged on and on like the Jew Ahasuerus[2] – or, in the phrase of the island-ers themselves, like a blind ram.

The Goddess, an abstraction to the general,[3] was a fairly real person-age to Pierston. He had watched the marble images of her which stood in his working-room, under all changes of light and shade – in the brighten-ing of morning, in the blackening of eve, in moonlight, in lamplight. Every line and curve of her body none, naturally, knew better than he; and, though not a belief, it was, as has been stated, a formula, a supersti-tion, that the three Avices were interpenetrated with her essence.

'And the next Avice – your daughter,' he said stumblingly; 'she is, you say, a governess at the castle opposite?'

Mrs. Pierston reaffirmed the fact, adding that the girl often slept at home because she, her mother, was so lonely. She often thought she would like to keep her daughter at home altogether.

'She plays that instrument, I suppose?' said Pierston, regarding the piano.

'Yes, she plays beautifully; she had the best instruction that masters could give her. She was educated at Sandbourne.'

'Which room does she call hers when at home?' he asked curiously.

'The little one over this.'

It had been his own. 'Strange,' he murmured.

He finished tea, and sat after tea, but the youthful Avice did not arrive. With the Avice present he conversed as the old friend – no more. At last it grew dusk, and Pierston could not find an excuse for staying longer.

'I hope to make the acquaintance – of your daughter,' he said in leav-ing, knowing that he might have added with predestinate truth, 'of my new tenderly-beloved.'

'I hope you will,' she answered. 'This evening she evidently has gone for a walk instead of coming here.'

'And, by-the-bye, you have not told me what you especially wanted to see me for?'

'Ah, no. I will put it off.'

'Very well. I don't pretend to guess.'

'I must tell you another time.'

'If it is any little business in connection with your late husband's affairs, do command me. I'll do anything I can.'

'Thank you. And I shall see you again soon?'

'Certainly. Quite soon.'

When he was gone she looked reflectively at the spot where he had been standing, and said: 'Best hold my tongue. It will work of itself, without my telling.'

Jocelyn went from the house, but as the white road passed under his feet he felt in no mood to get back to his lodgings in the town on the mainland. He lingered about upon the undulating ground[4] for a long while, thinking of the extraordinary reproduction of the original girl in this new form he had seen, and of himself as of a foolish dreamer in being so suddenly fascinated by the renewed image in a personality not one-third his age. As a physical fact, no doubt, the preservation of the likeness was no uncommon thing here, but it helped the dream.

Passing round the walls of the new castle he deviated from his homeward track by turning down the familiar little lane which led to the ruined castle of the Red King. It took him past the cottage in which the new Avice was born, from whose precincts he had heard her first infantine cry. Pausing he saw near the west behind him the new moon growing distinct upon the glow.

He was subject to gigantic fantasies still. In spite of himself, the sight of the new moon, as representing one who, by her so-called inconstancy, acted up to his own idea of a migratory Well-Beloved, made him feel as if his wraith in a changed sex[5] had suddenly looked over the horizon at him. In a crowd secretly, or in solitude boldly, he had often bowed the knee three times to this sisterly divinity on her first appearance monthly, and directed a kiss towards her shining shape. The curse of his qualities (if it were not a blessing) was far from having spent itself yet.

In the other direction the castle ruins rose square and dusky against the sea. He went on towards these, around which he had played as a boy, and stood by the walls at the edge of the cliff pondering. There was no wind and but little tide, and he thought he could hear from years ago a voice that he knew. It certainly was a voice, but it came from the rocks beneath the castle ruin.

'Mrs. Atway!'

A silence followed, and nobody came. The voice spoke again; 'John Stoney!'

Neither was this summons attended to. The cry continued, with more entreaty: 'William Scribben!'

The voice was that of a Pierston – there could be no doubt of it – young Avice's, surely? Something or other seemed to be detaining her down there against her will. A sloping path beneath the beetling cliff and the castle walls rising sheer from its summit, led down to the lower level whence the voice proceeded. Pierston followed the pathway, and soon beheld a girl in light clothing – the same he had seen through the window – standing upon one of the rocks, apparently unable to move. Pierston hastened across to her.

'O, thank you for coming!' she murmured with some timidity. 'I have met with an awkward mishap. I live near here, and am not frightened really. My foot has become jammed in a crevice of the rock, and I cannot get it out, try how I will. What *shall* I do!'

Jocelyn stooped and examined the cause of discomfiture. 'I think if you can take your boot off,' he said, 'your foot might slip out, leaving the boot behind.'

She tried to act upon this advice, but could not do so effectually. Pierston then experimented by slipping his hand into the crevice till he could just reach the buttons of her boot, which, however, he could not un-fasten any more than she. Taking his penknife from his pocket he tried again, and cut off the buttons one by one. The boot unfastened, and out slipped the foot.

'O, how glad I am!' she cried joyfully. 'I was fearing I should have to stay here all night. How can I thank you enough?'

He was tugging to withdraw the boot, but no force that he could exer-cise would move it. At last she said: 'Don't try any longer. It is not far to the house. I can walk in my stocking.'

'I'll assist you in,' he said.

She said she did not want help, nevertheless allowed him to help her on the unshod side. As they moved on she explained that she had come out through the garden door; had been standing on the boulders to look at something out at sea just discernible in the evening light as assisted by the moon, and, in jumping down, had wedged her foot as he had found it.

Whatever Pierston's years might have made him look by day, in the dusk of evening he was fairly presentable as a pleasing man of no marked antiquity, his outline differing but little from what it had been when he was half his years. He was well preserved, still upright, trimly shaven, agile in movement; wore a tightly buttoned suit which set off a naturally slight figure; in brief, he might have been of any age as he appeared to her at this moment. She talked to him with the co-equality of one who assumed him to be not far ahead of her own generation; and, as the growing darkness obscured him more and more, he adopted her assumption of his age with increasing boldness of tone.

The flippant, harmless freedom of the watering-place Miss, which Avice had plainly acquired during her sojourn at the Sandbourne school, helped Pierston greatly in this rôle of *jeune premier*[6] which he was not unready to play. Not a word did he say about being a native of the island; still more carefully did he conceal the fact of his having courted her grandmother, and engaged himself to marry that attractive lady.

He found that she had come out upon the rocks through the same little private door from the lawn of the modern castle which had frequently afforded him egress to the same spot in years long past. Pierston accompanied her across the grounds almost to the entrance of the mansion – the place being now far better kept and planted than when he had rented it as a lonely tenant; almost, indeed, restored to the order and neatness which had characterized it when he was a boy.

Like her granny[7] she was too inexperienced to be reserved, and during this little climb, leaning upon his arm, there was time for a great deal of confidence. When he had bidden her farewell, and she had entered, leaving him in the dark, a rush of sadness through Pierston's soul swept down all the temporary pleasure he had found in the charming girl's company. Had Mephistopheles sprung from the ground there and then with an offer to Jocelyn of restoration to youth on the usual terms of his firm,[8] the sculptor might have consented to sell a part of himself which he felt less immediate need of than of a ruddy lip and cheek and an unploughed brow.

But what could only have been treated as a folly by outsiders was almost a sorrow for him. Why was he born with such a temperament? And this concatenated interest could hardly have arisen, even with Pierston, but for a conflux of circumstances only possible here. The three Avices, the second something like the first, the third a glorification of the first, at all events externally, were the outcome of the immemorial island customs of intermarriage and of prenuptial union, under which conditions the type of feature was almost uniform from parent to child through generations: so that, till quite latterly, to have seen one native man and woman was to have seen the whole population of that isolated rock, so nearly cut off from the mainland. His own predisposition and the sense of his early faithlessness did all the rest.

He turned gloomily away, and let himself out of the precincts. Before walking along the couple of miles of road which would conduct him to the little station on the shore, he redescended to the rocks whereon he had found her, and searched about for the fissure which had made a prisoner of this terribly belated edition of the Beloved. Kneeling down beside the spot he inserted his hand, and ultimately, by much wriggling, withdrew the little boot.[9] He mused over it for a moment, put it in his pocket, and followed the stony route to the Street of Wells.

CHAPTER III

The Renewed Image burns itself in

There was nothing to hinder Pierston in calling upon the new Avice's mother as often as he should choose, beyond the five miles of intervening railway and additional mile or two of clambering over the heights of the island. Two days later, therefore, he repeated his journey and knocked about tea-time at the widow's door.

As he had feared, the daughter was not at home. He sat down beside the old sweetheart who, having eclipsed her mother in past days, had now eclipsed herself in her child. Jocelyn produced the girl's boot from his pocket.

'Then, 'tis *you* who helped Avice out of her predicament?' said Mrs. Pierston, with surprise.

'Yes, my dear friend; and perhaps I shall ask you to help me out of mine before I have done. But never mind that now. What did she tell you about the adventure?'

Mrs. Pierston was looking thoughtfully upon him. 'Well, 'tis rather strange it should have been you, sir,' she replied. She seemed to be a good deal interested. 'I thought it might have been a younger man – a much younger man.'

'It might have been as far as feelings were concerned.' . . . Now, Avice, I'll to the point at once. Virtually I have known your daughter any number of years. When I talk to her I can anticipate every turn of her thought, every sentiment, every act, so long did I study those things in your mother and in you. Therefore I do not require to learn her; she was learnt by me in her previous existences. Now, don't be shocked: I am willing to marry her – I should be overjoyed to do it, if there would be nothing preposterous about it, or that would seem like a man making himself too much of a fool, and so degrading her in consenting. I can make her comparatively rich, as you know, and I would indulge her every whim. There is the idea, bluntly put. It would set right something in my mind that has been wrong for forty years. After my death she would have plenty of freedom and plenty of means to enjoy it.'

Mrs. Isaac Pierston seemed only a little surprised; certainly not shocked.

'Well, if I didn't think you might be a bit taken with her!' she said with an arch simplicity which could hardly be called unaffected. 'Knowing the set of your mind, from my little time with you years ago, nothing you could do in this way would astonish me.'

'But you don't think badly of me for it?'

'Not at all. . . . By-the-bye, did you ever guess why I asked you to come? . . . But never mind it now: the matter is past. . . . Of course, it would depend upon what Avice felt. . . . Perhaps she would rather marry a younger man.'

'And suppose a satisfactory younger man should not appear?'

Mrs. Pierston showed in her face that she fully recognized the difference between a rich bird in hand and a young bird in the bush. She looked him curiously up and down.

'I know you would make anybody a very nice husband,' she said. 'I know that you would be nicer than many men half your age; and, though there is a great deal of difference between you and her, there have been more unequal marriages, that's true. Speaking as her mother, I can say that I shouldn't object to you, sir, for her, provided she liked you. That is where the difficulty will lie.'

'I wish you would help me to get over that difficulty,' he said gently. 'Remember, I brought back a truant husband to you twenty years ago.'

'Yes, you did,' she assented; 'and, though I may say no great things as to happiness came of it, I've always seen that your intentions towards me were none the less noble on that account. I would do for you what I would do for no other man, and there is one reason in particular which inclines me to help you with Avice – that I should feel absolutely certain I was helping her to a kind husband.'

'Well, that would remain to be seen. I would, at any rate, try to be worthy of your opinion. Come, Avice, for old times' sake, you must help me. You never felt anything but friendship in those days, you know, and that makes it easy and proper for you to do me a good turn now.'

After a little more conversation his old friend promised that she really would do everything that lay in her power. She did not say how simple she thought him[2] not to perceive that she had already, by writing to him, been doing everything that lay in her power; had created the feeling which prompted his entreaty. And to show her good faith in this promise she asked him to wait till later in the evening, when Avice might possibly run across to see her.

Pierston, who fancied he had won the younger Avice's interest, at least, by the part he had played upon the rocks the week before, had a dread of encountering her in full light till he should have advanced a little further in her regard. He accordingly was perplexed at this proposal, and, seeing his hesitation, Mrs. Pierston suggested that they should walk together in the direction whence Avice would come, if she came at all.

He welcomed the idea, and in a few minutes they started, strolling along under the now strong moonlight, and when they reached the gates of Sylvania Castle turning back again towards the house. After two or three such walks up and down the gate of the castle grounds clicked, and a form came forth which proved to be the expected one.

As soon as they met the girl recognized in her mother's companion the gentleman who had helped her on the shore; and she seemed really glad to find that her chivalrous assistant was claimed by her parent as an old friend. She remembered hearing at divers times about this worthy London man of talent and position, whose ancestry were people of her own isle, and possibly, from the name, of a common stock with her own.

'And you have actually lived in Sylvania Castle yourself, Mr. Pierston?' asked Avice the daughter, with her innocent young voice. 'Was it long ago?'

'Yes, it was some time ago,' replied the sculptor, with a sinking at his heart lest she should say how long.

'It must have been when I was away – or when I was very little?'

'I don't think you were away.'

'But I don't think I could have been here?'

'No, perhaps you couldn't have been here.'

'I think she was hiding herself in the parsley-bed,' said Avice's mother blandly.

They talked in this general way till they reached Mrs. Pierston's house; but Jocelyn resisted both the widow's invitation and the desire of his own heart, and went away without entering. To risk, by visibly confronting her, the advantage that he had already gained, or fancied he had gained, with the re-incarnate Avice required more courage than he could claim in his present mood.

* * * * *

Such evening promenades as these were frequent during the waxing of that summer moon. On one occasion, as they were all good walkers, it was arranged that they should meet halfway between the island and the town in which Pierston had lodgings. It was impossible that by this time the pretty young governess should not have guessed the ultimate reason of these rambles to be a matrimonial intention; but she inclined to the belief that the widow rather than herself was the object of Pierston's regard; though why this educated and apparently wealthy man should be attracted by her mother – whose homeliness was apparent enough to the girl's more modern training – she could not comprehend.

They met accordingly in the middle of the Pebble-bank, Pierston coming from the mainland, and the women from the peninsular rock. Crossing the wooden bridge which connected the bank with the shore proper they moved in the direction of Henry the Eighth's Castle, on the verge of the rag-stone cliff. Like the Red King's Castle on the island, the interior was open to the sky, and when they entered and the full moon streamed down upon them over the edge of the enclosing masonry, the whole present reality faded from Jocelyn's mind under the press of memories. Neither of his companions guessed what Pierston was thinking of. It was in this very spot that he was to have met the grandmother of the girl at his side, and in which he would have met her had she chosen to keep the appointment, a meeting which might – nay, must – have changed the whole current of his life.

Instead of that, forty years had passed – forty years of severance from Avice, till a secondly renewed copy of his sweetheart had arisen to fill her place. But he, alas, was not renewed. And of all this the pretty young thing at his side knew nothing.

Taking advantage of the younger woman's retreat to view the sea through an opening of the walls, Pierston appealed to her mother in a whisper: 'Have you ever given her a hint of what my meaning is? No? Then I think you might, if you really have no objection.'

Mrs. Pierston, as the widow, was far from being so coldly disposed in her own person towards her friend as in the days when he wanted to marry her. Had she now been the object of his wishes he would not have needed to ask her twice. But like a good mother she stifled all this, and said she would sound Avice there and then.

'Avice, my dear,' she said, advancing to where the girl mused in the window-gap, 'what do you think of Mr. Pierston paying his addresses to you – coming courting, as *I* call it in my old-fashioned way. Supposing he were to, would you encourage him?'

'To *me*, mother?' said Avice, with an inquiring laugh. 'I thought – he meant you!'

'O no, he doesn't mean me,' said her mother hastily. 'He is nothing more than my friend.'

'I don't want any addresses,' said the daughter.

'He is a man in society, and would take you to an elegant house in London suited to your education, instead of leaving you to mope here.'

'I should like that well enough,' replied Avice carelessly.

'Then give him some encouragement.'

'I don't care enough about him to do any encouraging. It is his business, I should think, to do all.'

She spoke in her lightest vein; but the result was that when Pierston, who had discreetly withdrawn, returned to them, she walked docilely, though perhaps gloomily, beside him, her mother dropping to the rear. They came to a rugged descent, and Pierston took her hand to help her. She allowed him to retain it when they arrived on level ground.

Altogether it was not an unsuccessful evening for the man with the unanchored heart, though possibly initial success meant worse for him in the long run than initial failure. There was nothing marvellous in the fact of her tractability thus far. In his modern dress and style, under the rays of the moon, he looked a very presentable gentleman indeed, while his knowledge of art and his travelled manners were not without their attractions for a girl who with one hand touched the educated middle-class and with the other the rude and simple inhabitants of the isle. Her intensely modern sympathies were quickened by her peculiar outlook.

Pierston would have regarded his interest in her as overmuch selfish if there had not existed a redeeming quality in the substratum of old pathetic memory by which such love had been created – which still permeated it, rendering it the tenderest, most anxious, most protective instinct he had ever known. It may have had in its composition too much of the boyish fervour that had characterized such affection when he was cherry-cheeked, and light in the foot as a girl; but, if it was all this feeling of youth, it was more.

Mrs. Pierston, in fearing to be frank, lest she might seem to be angling[3] for his fortune, did not fully divine his cheerful readiness to offer it, if by so doing he could make amends for his infidelity to her family forty years back in the past. Time had not made him mercenary, and it had quenched his ambitions; and though his wish to wed Avice was not entirely a wish to enrich her, the knowledge that she would be enriched beyond anything that she could have anticipated was what allowed him to indulge his love.

He was not exactly old he said to himself the next morning as he beheld his face in the glass.[4] And he looked considerably younger than he was. But there was history in his face – distinct chapters of it; his brow was not that blank page it once had been. He knew the origin of that line in his forehead; it had been traced in the course of a month or two by past troubles. He remembered the coming of this pale wiry hair; it had been brought by the illness in Rome, when he had wished each night that he might never wake again. This wrinkled corner, that drawn bit of skin, they had resulted from those months of despondency when all seemed going against his art, his strength, his happiness. 'You cannot live your life and keep it, Jocelyn,' he said. Time was against him and love, and time would probably win.

'When I went away from the first Avice,' he continued with whimsical misery, 'I had a presentiment that I should ache for it some day. And I am aching – have ached ever since this jade of an Ideal learnt the unconscionable trick of inhabiting one image only.'

Upon the whole he was not without a bodement that it would be folly to press on.[5]

CHAPTER IV

A Dash for the Last Incarnation

This desultory courtship of a young girl which had been brought about by her mother's contrivance was interrupted by the appearance of Somers and his wife and family on the Budmouth Esplanade. Alfred Somers, once the youthful, picturesque as his own paintings, was now a middle-aged family man with spectacles – spectacles worn, too, with the single object of seeing through them – and a row of daughters tailing off to infancy, who at present added appreciably to the income of the bathing-machine women' established along the sands.

Mrs. Somers – once the intellectual, emancipated Mrs. Pine-Avon – had now retrograded to the petty and timid mental position of her mother and grandmother, giving sharp, strict regard to the current literature and art that reached the innocent presence of her long perspective of girls, with the view of hiding every skull and skeleton of life from their dear eyes. She was another illustration of the rule that succeeding generations of women are seldom marked by cumulative progress, their advance as girls being lost in their recession as matrons;[2] so that they move up and down the stream of intellectual development like flotsam in a tidal estuary. And this perhaps not by reason of their faults as individuals, but of their misfortune as child-rearers.

The landscape-painter, now an Academician like Pierston himself – rather popular than distinguished – had given up that peculiar and personal taste in subjects which had marked him in times past, executing instead many pleasing aspects of nature addressed to the furnishing householder through the middling critic, and really very good of their kind. In this way he received many large cheques from persons of wealth in England and America, out of which he built himself a sumptuous studio and an awkward house around it, and paid for the education of the growing maidens.

The vision of Somers's humble position as jackal to this lion[3] of a family and house and studio and social reputation – Somers, to whom strange conceits and wild imaginings were departed joys never to return – led Pierston, as the painter's contemporary, to feel that he ought to be one

301

of the bygones likewise, and to put on an air of unromantic bufferism. He refrained from entering Avice's peninsula for the whole fortnight of Somers's stay in the neighbouring town, although its grey poetical outline – 'throned along the sea'[4] – greeted his eyes every morn and eve across the roadstead.

When the painter and his family had gone back from their bathing holiday, he thought that he, too, would leave the neighbourhood. To do so, however, without wishing at least the elder Avice good-bye would be unfriendly, considering the extent of their acquaintance. One evening, knowing this time of day to suit her best, he took the few-minutes' journey to the rock along the thin connecting string of junction, and arrived at Mrs. Pierston's door just after dark.

A light shone from an upper chamber. On asking for his widowed acquaintance he was informed that she was ill, seriously, though not dangerously. While learning that her daughter was with her, and further particulars, and doubting if he should go in, a message was sent down to ask him to enter. His voice had been heard, and Mrs. Pierston would like to see him.

He could not with any humanity refuse, but there flashed across his mind the recollection that Avice the youngest had never yet really seen him, had seen nothing more of him than an outline, which might have appertained as easily to a man thirty years his junior as to himself, and a countenance so renovated by faint moonlight as to fairly correspond. It was with misgiving, therefore, that the sculptor ascended the staircase and entered the little upper sitting-room, now arranged as a sick-chamber.

Mrs. Pierston reclined on a sofa, her face emaciated to a surprising thinness for the comparatively short interval since her attack. 'Come in, sir,' she said, as soon as she saw him, holding out her hand. 'Don't let me frighten you.'

Avice was seated beside her, reading. The girl jumped up, hardly seeming to recognize him. 'O! it's Mr. Pierston,' she said in a moment, adding quickly, with evident surprise and off her guard: 'I thought Mr. Pierston was—'

What she had thought he was did not pass her lips, and it remained a riddle for Jocelyn until a new departure in her manner towards him showed that the words 'much younger' would have accurately ended the sentence. Had Pierston not now confronted her anew, he might have endured philosophically her changed opinion of him. But he was seeing her again, and a rooted feeling was revived.

Pierston now learnt for the first time that the widow had been visited by sudden attacks of this sort not infrequently of late years. They were said to be due to angina pectoris,[5] the latter paroxysms having been the most severe. She was at the present moment out of pain, though weak, exhausted, and nervous. She would not, however, converse about herself, but took advantage of her daughter's absence from the room to broach the subject most in her thoughts.

No compunctions had stirred her as they had her visitor on the expediency of his suit in view of his years. Her fever of anxiety lest after all he should not come to see Avice again had been not without an effect upon her health; and it made her more candid than she had intended to be.

'Troubles and sickness raise all sorts of fears, Mr. Pierston,' she said. 'What I felt only a wish for, when you first named it, I have hoped for a good deal since; and I have been so anxious that – that it should come to something! I am glad indeed that you are come.'

'My wanting to marry Avice, you mean, dear Mrs. Pierston?'

'Yes – that's it. I wonder if you are still in the same mind? You are? Then I wish something could be done – to make her agree to it – so as to get it settled. I dread otherwise what will become of her. She is not a practical girl as I was – she would hardly like now to settle down as an islander's wife; and to leave her living here alone would trouble me.'

'Nothing will happen to you yet, I hope, my dear old friend.'

'Well, it is a risky complaint; and the attacks, when they come, are so agonizing that to endure them I ought to get rid of all outside anxieties, folk say. Now – do you want her, sir?'

'With all my soul! But she doesn't want me.'

'I don't think she is so against you as you imagine. I fancy if it were put to her plainly, now I am in this state, it might be done.'

They lapsed into conversation on the early days of their acquaintance, until Mrs. Pierston's daughter re-entered the room.

'Avice,' said her mother, when the girl had been with them a few minutes. 'About this matter that I have talked over with you so many times since my attack. Here is Mr. Pierston, and he wishes to be your husband. He is much older than you; but, in spite of it, that you will ever get a better husband I don't believe. Now, will you take him, seeing the state I am in, and how naturally anxious I am to see you settled before I die?'

'But you won't die, mother! You are getting better!'

'Just for the present only. Come, he is a good man and a clever man, and a rich man. I want you, O so much, to be his wife! I can say no more.'

Avice looked appealingly at the sculptor, and then on the floor. 'Does he really wish me to?' she asked almost inaudibly, turning as she spoke to Pierston. 'He has never quite said so to me.'

'My dear one, how can you doubt it?' said Jocelyn quickly. 'But I won't press you to marry me as a favour, against your feelings.'

'I thought Mr. Pierston was younger!' she murmured to her mother.

'That counts for little, when you think how much there is on the other side. Think of our position, and of his – a sculptor, with a mansion, and a studio full of busts and statues that I have dusted in my time, and of the beautiful studies you would be able to take up. Surely the life would just suit you? Your expensive education is wasted down here!'

Avice did not care to argue. She was outwardly gentle as her grand-mother had been, and it seemed just a question with her of whether she must or must not. 'Very well – I feel I ought to agree to marry him, since you tell me to,' she answered quietly, after some thought. 'I see that it would be a wise thing to do, and that you wish it, and that Mr. Pierston really does – like me. So – so that—'

Pierston was not backward at this critical juncture, despite unpleasant sensations. But it was the historic ingredient in this genealogical passion – if its continuity through three generations may be so described – which appealed to his perseverance at the expense of his wisdom. The mother was holding the daughter's hand; she took Pierston's, and laid Avice's in it.

No more was said in argument, and the thing was regarded as deter-mined. Afterwards a noise was heard upon the window-panes, as of fine sand thrown; and, lifting the blind, Pierston saw that the distant lightship winked with a bleared and indistinct eye. A drizzling rain had come on with the dark, and it was striking the window in handfuls. He had in-tended to walk the two miles back to the station, but it meant a drenching to do it now. He waited and had supper; and, finding the weather no better, accepted Mrs. Pierston's invitation to stay over the night.

Thus it fell out that again he lodged in the house he had been accus-tomed to live in as a boy, before his father had made his fortune, and before his own name had been heard of outside the boundaries of the isle.

He slept but little, and in the first movement of the dawn sat up in bed. Why should he ever live in London or any other fashionable city if this plan of marriage could be carried out? Surely, with this young wife, the island would be the best place for him. It might be possible to rent Sylvania Castle as he had formerly done – better still to buy it. If life could offer him anything worth having it would be a home with Avice there on his native cliffs to the end of his days.

As he sat thus thinking, and the daylight increased, he discerned, a short distance before him, a movement of something ghostly. His position was facing the window, and he found that by chance the looking-glass had swung itself vertical, so that what he saw was his own shape. The recognition startled him. The person he appeared was too grievously far, chronologically, in advance of the person he felt himself to be. Pierston did not care to regard the figure confronting him so mockingly. Its voice seemed to say 'There's tragedy hanging on to this!'[6] But the question of age being pertinent he could not give the spectre up, and ultimately got out of bed under the weird fascination of the reflection. Whether he had overwalked himself lately, or what he had done, he knew not; but never had he seemed so aged by a score of years as he was represented in the glass in that cold grey morning light. While his soul was what it was, why should he have been encumbered with that withering carcase, without the ability to shift it off for another, as his ideal Beloved had so frequently done?

By reason of her mother's illness Avice was now living in the house, and, on going downstairs, he found that they were to breakfast *en tête-à-tête*. She was not then in the room, but she entered in the course of a few minutes. Pierston had already heard that the widow felt better this morning, and elated by the prospect of sitting with Avice at this meal he went forward to her joyously. As soon as she saw him in the full stroke of day from the window she started; and he then remembered that it was their first meeting under the solar rays.

She was so overcome that she turned and left the room as if she had forgotten something; when she re-entered she was visibly pale. She recovered herself, and apologized. She had been sitting up the night before the last, she said, and was not quite so well as usual.

There may have been some truth in this; but Pierston could not get over that first scared look of hers. It was enough to give daytime stability to his night views of a possible tragedy lurking in this wedding project. He determined that, at any cost to his heart, there should be no misapprehension about him from this moment.[7]

'Miss Pierston,' he said as they sat down, 'since it is well you should know all the truth before we go any further, that there may be no awkward discoveries afterwards, I am going to tell you something about myself – if you are not too distressed to hear it?'

'No – let me hear it.'

'I was once the lover of your mother, and wanted to marry her; only she wouldn't, or rather couldn't, marry me.'

'O how strange!' said the girl, looking from him to the breakfast things, and from the breakfast things to him. 'Mother has never told me that. Yet of course, you might have been. I mean, you are old enough.'

He took the remark as a satire she had not intended. 'O yes – quite old enough,' he said grimly. 'Almost too old.'

'Too old for mother? How's that?'

'Because I belonged to your grandmother.'

'No? How can that be?'

'I was her lover likewise. I should have married her if I had gone straight on instead of round the corner.'

'But you couldn't have been, Mr. Pierston! You are not old enough? Why, how old are you? – you have never told me.'

'I am very old.'

'My mother's, and my grandmother's,' said she, looking at him no longer as at a possible husband, but as a strange fossilized relic in human form. Pierston saw it, but meaning to give up the game he did not care to spare himself.

'Your mother's and your grandmother's young man,' he repeated.

'And were you my great-grandmother's too?' she asked, with an expectant interest in his case as a drama that overcame her personal considerations for a moment.

'No – not your great-grandmother's. Your imagination beats even my confessions! . . . But I am *very* old, as you see.'

'I did not know it!' said she in an appalled murmur. 'You do not look so; and I thought that what you looked you were.'

'And you – you are very young,' he continued.

A stillness followed, during which she sat in a troubled constraint, regarding him now and then with something in her open eyes and large pupils that might have been sympathy or nervousness. Pierston ate scarce any breakfast, and rising abruptly from the table said he would take a walk on the cliffs as the morning was fine.

He did so, proceeding along the north-east heights for nearly a mile. He had virtually given Avice up, but not formally. His intention had been to go back to the house in half-an-hour and pay a morning visit to the invalid; but by not returning the plans of the previous evening might be allowed to lapse silently, as mere *pourparlers* that had come to nothing in the face of Avice's want of love for him. Pierston accordingly went straight along, and in the course of an hour was at his Budmouth lodgings.

Nothing occurred till the evening to inform him how his absence had been taken. Then a note arrived from Mrs. Pierston; it was written in pencil, evidently as she lay.

'I am alarmed,' she said, 'at your going so suddenly. Avice seems to think she has offended you. She did not mean to do that, I am sure. It makes me dreadfully anxious! Will you send a line? Surely you will not desert us now – my heart is so set on my child's welfare!'

'Desert you I won't,' said Jocelyn. 'It is too much like the original case. But I must let her desert me!'

On his return, with no other object than that of wishing Mrs. Pierston good-bye, he found her painfully agitated. She clasped his hand and wetted it with her tears.

'O don't be offended with her!' she cried. 'She's young. We are one people – don't marry a kimberlin! It will break my heart if you forsake her now! Avice!'

The girl came. 'My manner was hasty and thoughtless this morning,' she said in a low voice. 'Please pardon me. I wish to abide by my promise.'

Her mother, still tearful, again joined their hands; and the engagement stood as before.[8]

Pierston went back to Budmouth, but dimly seeing how curiously, through his being a rich suitor, ideas of beneficence and reparation were retaining him in the course arranged by her mother, and urged by his own desire in the face of his understanding.

CHAPTER V

On the Verge of Possession

In anticipation of his marriage Pierston had taken a new red house of the approved Kensington pattern,[1] with a new studio at the back as large as a mediæval barn. Hither, in collusion with the elder Avice – whose health had mended somewhat – he invited mother and daughter to spend a week or two with him, thinking thereby to exercise on the latter's imagination an influence which was not practicable while he was a guest at their house; and by interesting his betrothed in the fitting and furnishing of this residence to create in her an ambition to be its mistress.

It was a pleasant, reposeful time to be in town. There was nobody to interrupt them in their proceedings, and, it being out of the season, the largest tradesmen were as attentive to their wants as if those firms had never before been honoured with a single customer whom they really liked. Pierston and his guests, almost equally inexperienced – for the sculptor had nearly forgotten what knowledge of householding he had acquired earlier in life – could consider and practise thoroughly a species of skeleton-drill in receiving visitors when the pair should announce themselves as married and at home in the coming winter season.

Avice was charming, even if a little cold. He congratulated himself yet again that time should have reserved for him this final chance for one of the line. She was somewhat like her mother, whom he had loved in the flesh, but she had the soul of her grandmother, whom he had loved in the spirit – and, for that matter, loved now. Only one criticism had he to pass upon his choice: though in outward semblance her grandam idealized, she had not the first Avice's candour, but rather her mother's closeness. He never knew exactly what she was thinking and feeling. Yet he seemed to have such prescriptive rights in women of her blood that her occasional want of confidence did not deeply trouble him.

It was one of those ripe and mellow afternoons that sometimes colour London with their golden light at this time of the year, and produce those marvellous sunset effects which, if they were not known to be made up of kitchen coal-smoke and animal exhalations, would be rapturously applauded. Behind the perpendicular, oblique, zigzagged, and curved zinc 'tall-boys,' that formed a grey pattern not unlike early Gothic numerals against the sky, the men and women on the tops of omnibuses saw an irradiation of topaz hues, darkened here and there into richest russet.

There had been a sharp shower during the afternoon, and Pierston – who had to take care of himself – had worn a pair of goloshes on his short walk in the street. He noiselessly entered the studio, inside which some gleams of the same mellow light had managed to creep, and where he guessed he should find his prospective wife and mother-in law awaiting him with tea. But only Avice was there, seated beside the teapot of brown delf, which, as artists, they affected, her back being toward him. She was holding her handkerchief to her eyes, and he saw that she was weeping silently.

In another moment he perceived that she was weeping over a book. By this time she had heard him, and came forward. He made it appear that he had not noticed her distress, and they discussed some arrangements of furniture. When he had taken a cup of tea she went away, leaving the book behind her.

Pierston took it up. The volume was an old school-book; Stièvenard's 'Lectures Françaises,'[2] with her name in it as a pupil at Sandbourne High School, and date-markings denoting lessons taken at a comparatively recent time, for Avice had been but a novice as governess when he discovered her.

For a school-girl – which she virtually was – to weep over a school-book was strange. Could she have been affected by some subject in the readings? Impossible. Pierston fell to thinking, and zest died for the process of furnishing, which he had undertaken so gaily. Somehow, the bloom was again disappearing from his approaching marriage. Yet he loved Avice more and more tenderly; he feared sometimes that in the solicitousness of his affection he was spoiling her by indulging her every whim.

He looked round the large and ambitious apartment, now becoming clouded with shades, out of which the white and cadaverous countenances of his studies, casts, and other lumber peered meditatively at him, as if they were saying, 'What are you going to do now, old boy?' They had never looked like that while standing in his past homely workshop, where all the real labours of his life had been carried out. What should a man of his age, who had not for years done anything to speak of – certainly not to add to his reputation as an artist – want with a new place like this? It was all because of the elect lady, and she apparently did not want him.

Pierston did not observe anything further in Avice to cause him misgiving till one dinner-time, a week later, towards the end of the visit. Then, as he sat himself between her and her mother at their limited table, he was struck with her nervousness, and was tempted to say, 'Why are you troubled, my little dearest?' in tones which disclosed that he was as troubled as she.

'Am I troubled?' she said with a start, turning her gentle hazel eyes upon him. 'Yes, I suppose I am. It is because I have received a letter – from an old friend.'

'You didn't show it to me,' said her mother.

'No – I tore it up.'

'Why?'

'It was not necessary to keep it, so I destroyed it.'

Mrs. Pierston did not press her further on the subject, and Avice showed no disposition to continue it. They retired rather early,[3] as they always did, but Pierston remained pacing about his studio a long while, musing on many things, not the least being the perception that to wed a woman may be by no means the same thing as to be united with her. The 'old friend' of Avice's remark had sounded very much like 'lover.' Otherwise why should the letter have so greatly disturbed her?

There seemed to be something uncanny, after all, about London, in its relation to his contemplated marriage. When she had first come up she was easier with him than now. And yet his bringing her there had helped his cause; the house had decidedly impressed her – almost overawed her, and though he owned that by no law of nature or reason had her mother or himself any right to urge on Avice partnership with him against her inclination, he resolved to make the most of having her under his influence by getting the wedding details settled before she and her mother left.

The next morning he proceeded to do this. When he encountered Avice there was a trace of apprehension on her face; but he set that down to a fear that she had offended him the night before by her taciturnity. Directly he requested her mother, in Avice's presence, to get her to fix the day quite early, Mrs. Pierston became brighter and brisker. She, too, plainly had doubts about the wisdom of delay, and turning to her daughter said, 'Now, my dear, do you hear?'

It was ultimately agreed that the widow and her daughter should go back in a day or two, to await Pierston's arrival on the wedding-eve, immediately after their return.

*   *   *   *   *

In pursuance of the arrangement Pierston found himself on the south shore of England in the gloom of the aforesaid evening, the isle, as he looked across at it with his approach, being just discernible as a moping countenance, a creature sullen with a sense that he was about to withdraw from its keeping the rarest object it had ever owned. He had come alone, not to embarrass them, and had intended to halt a couple of hours in the neighbouring seaport to give some orders relating to the wedding, but the little railway train being in waiting to take him on, he proceeded with a natural impatience, resolving to do his business here by messenger from the isle.

He passed the ruins of the Tudor castle and the long featureless rib of grinding pebbles that screened off the outer sea, which could be heard lifting and dipping rhythmically in the wide vagueness of the Bay. At the under-hill island townlet of the Wells there were no flys, and leaving his things to be brought on, as he often did, he climbed the eminence on foot.

Half-way up the steepest part of the pass he saw in the dusk a figure pausing – the single person on the incline. Though it was too dark to identify faces, Pierston gathered from the way in which the halting stranger was supporting himself by the handrail, which here bordered the road to assist climbers, that the person was exhausted.

'Anything the matter?'[4] he said.

'O no – not much,' was returned by the other. 'But it is steep just here.'

The accent was not quite that of an Englishman, and struck him as hailing from one of the Channel Islands. 'Can't I help you up to the top?' he said, for the voice, though that of a young man, seemed faint and shaken.

'No, thank you. I have been ill; but I thought I was all right again; and as the night was fine I walked into the island by the road. It turned out to be rather too much for me, as there is some weakness left still; and this stiff incline brought it out.'

'Naturally. You'd better take hold of my arm – at any rate to the brow here.'

Thus pressed the stranger did so, and they went on towards the ridge, till, reaching the lime-kiln standing there the stranger abandoned his hold, saying: 'Thank you for your assistance, sir. Good-night.'

'I don't think I recognize your voice as a native's?'

'No, it is not. I am a Jersey man. Good-night, sir.'

'Good-night, if you are sure you can get on. Here, take this stick – it is no use to me.' Saying which, Pierston put his walking-stick into the young man's hand.

'Thank you again. I shall be quite recovered when I have rested a minute or two. Don't let me detain you, please.'

The stranger as he spoke turned his face towards the south, where the Beal light had just come into view, and stood regarding it with an obstinate fixity. As he evidently wished to be left to himself Jocelyn went on, and troubled no more about him, though the desire of the young man to be rid of his company, after accepting his walking-stick and his arm, had come with a suddenness that was almost emotional; and impressionable as Jocelyn was, no less now than in youth, he was saddened for a minute by the sense that there were people in the world who did not like even his sympathy.

However, a pleasure which obliterated all this arose when Pierston drew near to the house that was likely to be his dear home on all future visits to the isle, perhaps even his permanent home as he grew older and the associations of his youth re-asserted themselves. It had been, too, his father's house, the house in which he was born, and he amused his fancy with plans for its enlargement under the supervision of Avice and himself. It was a still greater pleasure to behold a tall and shapely figure standing against the light of the open door and presumably awaiting him.

Avice, who it was, gave a little jump when she recognized him, but dutifully allowed him to kiss her when he reached her side; though her nervousness was only too apparent, and was like a child's towards a parent who may prove stern.

'How dear of you to guess that I might come on at once instead of later!' says Jocelyn. 'Well, if I had stayed in the town to go to the shops and so on, I could not have got here till the last train. How is mother?[5] – our mother, as I shall call her soon.'

Avice said that her mother had not been so well – she feared not nearly so well since her return from London, so that she was obliged to keep her room. The visit had perhaps been too much for her. 'But she will not acknowledge that she is much weaker, because she will not disturb my happiness.'

Jocelyn was in a mood to let trifles of manner pass, and he took no notice of the effort which had accompanied the last word. They went upstairs to Mrs. Pierston, whose obvious relief and thankfulness at sight of him was grateful to her visitor.

'I am so, O so glad you are come!' she said huskily, as she held out her thin hand and stifled a sob. 'I have been so—'

She could get no further for a moment, and Avice turned away weeping, and abruptly left the room.

'I have so set my heart on this,' Mrs. Pierston went on, 'that I have not been able to sleep of late, for I have feared I might drop off suddenly before she is yours, and lose the comfort of seeing you actually united. Your being so kind to me in old times has made me so sure that she will find a good husband in you, that I am over anxious, I know. Indeed, I have not liked to let her know quite how anxious I am.'

Thus they talked till Jocelyn bade her good-night, it being noticeable that Mrs. Pierston, chastened by her illnesses, maintained no longer any reserve on her gladness to acquire him as her son-in-law; and her feelings destroyed any remaining scruples he might have had from perceiving that Avice's consent was rather an obedience than a desire. As he went downstairs, and found Avice awaiting his descent, he wondered if anything had occurred here during his absence to give Mrs. Pierston new uneasiness about the marriage, but it was an inquiry he could not address to a girl whose actions could alone be the cause of such uneasiness.

He looked round for her as he supped, but though she had come into the room with him she was not there now. He remembered her telling him that she had had supper with her mother, and Jocelyn sat on quietly musing and sipping his wine for something near half-an-hour. Wondering then for the first time what had become of her, he rose and went to the door. Avice was quite near him after all – only standing at the front door as she had been doing when he came, looking into the light of the full moon, which had risen since his arrival. His sudden opening of the dining-room door seemed to agitate her.

'What is it, dear?' he asked.

'As mother is much better and doesn't want me, I ought to go and see somebody I promised to take a parcel to – I feel I ought. And yet, as you have just come to see me – I suppose you don't approve of my going out while you are here?'

'Who is the person?'

'Somebody down that way,' she said indefinitely. 'It is not very far off. I am not afraid – I go out often by myself at night hereabout.'

He reassured her good-humouredly. 'If you really wish to go, my dear, of course I don't object. I have no authority to do that till to-morrow, and you know that if I had it I shouldn't use it.'

'O but you have! Mother being an invalid, you are in her place, apart from – to-morrow.'

'Nonsense, darling. Run across to your friend's house by all means if you want to.'

'And you'll be here when I come in?'

'No, I am going down to the inn to see if my things are brought up.'

'But hasn't mother asked you to stay here? The spare room was got ready for you. . . . Dear me, I am afraid I ought to have told you.'

'She did ask me. But I have some things coming, directed to the inn, and I had better be there. So I'll wish you good-night, though it is not late. I will come in quite early to-morrow, to inquire how your mother is going on, and to wish you good-morning. You will be back again quickly this evening?'

'O yes.'

'And I needn't go with you for company?'

'O no, thank you. It is no distance.'

Pierston then departed, thinking how entirely her manner was that of one to whom a question of doing anything was a question of permission and not of judgment. He had no sooner gone than Avice took a parcel from a cupboard, put on her hat and cloak, and following by the way he had taken till she reached the entrance to Sylvania Castle, there stood still. She could hear Pierston's footsteps passing down East Quarriers to the inn; but she went no further in that direction. Turning into the lane on the right, of which mention has so often been made, she went quickly past the last cottage, and having entered the gorge beyond she clambered into the ruin of the Red King's or Bow-and-Arrow Castle, standing as a square black mass against the moonlit, indefinite sea.

CHAPTER VI

The Well-Beloved is – Where?

Mrs. Pierston passed a restless night, but this she let nobody know; nor, what was painfully evident to herself, that her prostration was increased by anxiety and suspense about the wedding on which she had too much set her heart.

During the very brief space in which she dozed Avice came into her room. As it was not infrequent for her daughter to look in upon her thus she took little notice, merely saying to assure the girl: 'I am better, dear. Don't come in again. Get to sleep yourself.'

The mother, however, went thinking anew. She had no apprehensions about this marriage. She felt perfectly sure that it was the best thing she could do for her girl. Not a young woman on the island but was envying Avice at that moment; for Jocelyn was absurdly young for three score, a good-looking man, one whose history was generally known here; as also were the exact figures of the fortune he had inherited from his father, and the social standing he could claim – a standing, however, which that fortune would not have been large enough to procure unassisted by his reputation in his art.

But Avice had been weak enough, as her mother knew, to indulge in fancies for local youths from time to time, and Mrs. Pierston could not help congratulating herself that her daughter had been so docile in the circumstances. Yet to every one except, perhaps, Avice herself, Jocelyn was the most romantic of lovers. Indeed was there ever such a romance as that man embodied in his relations to her house? Rejecting the first Avice, the second had rejected him, and to rally to the third with final achievement was an artistic and tender finish to which it was ungrateful in anybody to be blind.

The widow thought that the second Avice might probably not have rejected Pierston on that occasion in the London studio so many years ago if destiny had not arranged that she should have been secretly united to another when the proposing moment came.

But what had come was best. 'My God,' she said at times that night, 'to think my aim in writing to him should be fulfilling itself like this!'

When all was right and done, what a success upon the whole her life would have been. She who had begun her career as a cottage-girl, a small quarry-owner's daughter, had sunk so low as to the position of laundress, had engaged in various menial occupations, had made an unhappy marriage for love which had, however, in the long run, thanks to Jocelyn's management, much improved her position, was at last to see her daughter secure what she herself had just missed securing, and established in a home of affluence and refinement.

Thus the sick woman excited herself as the hours went on. At last, in her tenseness it seemed to her that the time had already come at which the household was stirring, and she fancied she heard conversation in her daughter's room. But she found that it was only five o'clock, and not yet daylight. Her state was such that she could see the hangings of the bed tremble with her tremors. She had declared overnight that she did not require any one to sit up with her, but she now rang a little hand-bell, and in a few minutes a nurse appeared; Ruth Stockwool, an island woman and a neighbour, whom Mrs. Pierston knew well, and who knew all Mrs. Pierston's history.

'I am so nervous that I can't stay by myself,' said the widow. 'And I thought I heard Becky dressing Miss Avice in her wedding things.'

'O no – not yet, ma'am. There's nobody up. But I'll get you something.'

When Mrs. Pierston had taken a little nourishment she went on: 'I can't help frightening myself with thoughts that she won't marry him. You see he is older than Avice.'

'Yes, he is,' said her neighbour. 'But I don't see how anything can hender the wedden now.'

'Avice, you know, had fancies; at least one fancy for another man; a young fellow of five-and-twenty. And she's been very secret and odd about it. I wish she had raved and cried and had it out; but she's been quite the other way. I know she's fond of him still.'

'What – that young Frenchman, Mr. Leverre o' Sandbourne? I've heard a little of it. But I should say there wadden much between 'em.'

'I don't think there was. But I've a sort of conviction that she saw him last night. I believe it was only to bid him good-bye, and return him some books he had given her; but I wish she had never known him; he is rather an excitable, impulsive young man, and he might make mischief. He isn't a Frenchman, though he has lived in France. His father was a Jersey gentleman, and on his becoming a widower he married as his second wife a native of this very island. That's mainly why the young man is so at home in these parts.'

'Ah – now I follow 'ee. She was a Bencomb, his stepmother: I heard something about her years ago.'

'Yes; her father had the biggest stone-trade on the island at one time; but the name is forgotten here now. He retired years before I was born. However, mother used to tell me that she was a handsome young woman, who tried to catch Mr. Pierston when he was a young man, and scandalized herself a bit with him. She went off abroad with her father, who had made a fortune here; but when he got over there he lost it nearly all in some way. Years after she married this Jerseyman, Mr. Leverre, who had been fond of her as a girl, and she brought up his child as her own.'

Mrs. Pierston paused, but as Ruth did not ask any question she presently resumed her self-relieving murmur:

'How Miss Avice got to know the young man was in this way. When Mrs. Leverre's husband died she came from Jersey to live at Sandbourne; and made it her business one day to cross over to this place to make inquiries about Mr. Jocelyn Pierston. As my name was Pierston she called upon me with her son, and so Avice and he got acquainted. When she went back to Sandbourne to the finishing school they kept up the acquaintance in secret. He taught French somewhere there, and does still, I believe.'

'Well, I hope she'll forget en. He idden good enough.'

'I hope so – I hope so. . . . Now I'll try to get a little nap.'

Ruth Stockwool went back to her room, where, finding it would not be necessary to get up for another hour, she lay down again and soon slept. Her bed was close to the staircase, from which it was divided by a lath partition only, and her consciousness either was or seemed to be aroused by light brushing touches on the outside of the partition, as of fingers feeling the way downstairs in the dark. The slight noise passed, and in a few seconds she dreamt or fancied she could hear the unfastening of the back door.

She had nearly sunk into another sound sleep when precisely the same phenomena were repeated; fingers brushing along the wall close to her head, down, downward, the soft opening of the door, its close, and silence again.

She now became clearly awake. The repetition of the process had made the whole matter a singular one. Early as it was the first sounds might have been those of the housemaid descending, though why she should have come down so stealthily and in the dark did not make itself clear. But the second performance was inexplicable. Ruth got out of bed and lifted her blind. The dawn was hardly yet pink, and the light from the sandbank was not yet extinguished. But the bushes of euonymus against the white palings of the front garden could be seen, also the light surface of the road winding away like a riband to the north entrance of Sylvania Castle, thence round to the village, the cliffs, and the Cove behind. Upon the road two dark figures could just be discerned, one a little way behind the other, but overtaking and joining the foremost as Ruth looked. After all they might be quarriers or lighthouse-keepers from the south of the island, or fishermen just landed from a night's work. There being nothing to connect them with the noises she had heard indoors she dismissed the whole subject, and went to bed again.

*　　*　　*　　*　　*

Jocelyn had promised to pay an early visit to ascertain the state of Mrs. Pierston's health after her night's rest, her precarious condition being more obvious to him than to Avice, and making him a little anxious. Subsequent events caused him to remember that while he was dressing he casually observed two or three boatmen standing near the cliff beyond the village, and apparently watching with deep interest what seemed to be a boat far away towards the opposite shore of South Wessex. At half-past eight he came from the door of the inn and went straight to Mrs. Pierston's. On approaching he discovered that a strange expression which seemed to hang about the house-front that morning was more than a fancy, the gate, door, and two windows being open, though the blinds of other windows were not drawn up, the whole lending a vacant, dazed look to the domicile, as of a person gaping in sudden stultification. Nobody answered his knock, and walking into the dining-room he found that no breakfast had been laid. His flashing thought was, 'Mrs. Pierston is dead.'

While standing in the room somebody came downstairs, and Jocelyn encountered Ruth Stockwool, an open letter fluttering in her hand.

'O Mr. Pierston, Mr. Pierston! The Lord-a-Lord!'

'What? Mrs. Pierston—'

'No, no! Miss Avice! She is gone!' – yes – gone! Read ye this, sir. It was left in her bedroom, and we be fairly gallied out of our senses!'

He took the letter[2] and confusedly beheld that it was in two handwritings, the first section being in Avice's:

'My dear Mother, – How ever will you forgive me for what I have done! So deceitful as it seems. And yet till this night I had no idea of deceiving either you or Mr. Pierston.

'Last night at ten o'clock I went out, as you may have guessed, to see Mr. Leverre for the last time, and to give him back his books, letters, and little presents to me. I went only a few steps – to Bow-and-Arrow Castle, where we met as we had agreed to do, since he could not call. When I reached the place I found him there waiting, but quite ill. He had been unwell at his mother's house for some days, and had been obliged to stay in bed, but he had got up on purpose to come and bid me good-bye. The over-exertion of the journey upset him, and though we stayed and stayed till twelve o'clock he felt quite unable to go back home – unable, indeed, to move more than a few yards. I had tried so hard not to love him any longer, but I loved him so now that I could not desert him and leave him out there to catch his death. So I helped him – nearly carrying him – on and on to our door, and then round to the back. Here he got a little better, and as he could not stay there, and everybody was now asleep, I helped him upstairs into the room we had prepared for Mr. Pierston if he should have wanted one. I got him into bed, and then fetched some brandy and a little of your tonic. Did you see me come into your room for it, or were you asleep?

'I sat by him all night. He improved slowly, and we talked over what we had better do. I felt that, though I had intended to give him up, I could not now becomingly marry any other man, and that I ought to marry him. We decided to do it at once, before anybody could hinder us. So we came down before it was light, and have gone away to get the ceremony solemnized.

'Tell Mr. Pierston it was not premeditated, but the result of an accident. I am sincerely sorry to have treated him with what he will think unfairness, but though I did not love him I meant to obey you and marry him. But God sent this necessity of my having to give shelter to my Love, to prevent, I think, my doing what I am now convinced would have been wrong. – Ever your loving daughter,

'Avice.'

The second was in a man's hand:

'Dear Mother (as you will soon be to me), – Avice has clearly explained above how it happened that I have not been able to give her up to Mr. Pierston. I think I should have died if I had not accepted the hospitality of a room in your house this night, and your daughter's tender nursing through the dark dreary hours. We love each other beyond expression, and it is obvious that, if we are human, we cannot resist marrying now, in spite of friends' wishes. Will you please send the note lying beside this to my mother. It is merely to explain what I have done. – Yours with warmest regard,

'*Henri Leverre.*'

Jocelyn turned away and looked out of the window.

'Mrs. Pierston thought she heard some talking in the night, but of course she put it down to fancy. And she remembers Miss Avice coming into her room at one o'clock in the morning, and going to the table where the medicine was standing. A sly girl – all the time her young man within a yard or two, in the very room, and a using the very clean sheets that you, sir, were to have used! They are our best linen ones, got up beautiful, and a kept wi' rosemary. Really, sir, one would say you stayed out o' your chammer o' purpose to oblige the young man with a bed!'

'Don't blame them, don't blame them!' said Jocelyn in an even and characterless voice. 'Don't blame her, particularly. She didn't make the circumstances. I did. . . . It was how I served her grandmother. . . . Well, she's gone! You needn't make a mystery of it. Tell it to all the island: say that a man came to marry a wife, and didn't find her at home. Tell everybody that she's run away. It must be known sooner or later.'

One of the servants said, after waiting a few moments: 'We shan't do that, sir.'

'Oh – Why won't you?'

'We liked her too well, with all her faults.'

'Ah – did you,' said he; and he sighed. He perceived that the younger maids were secretly on Avice's side.

'How does her mother bear it?' Jocelyn asked. 'Is she awake?'

Mrs. Pierston had hardly slept, and, having learnt the tidings inadvertently, became so distracted and incoherent as to be like a person in a delirium; till, a few moments before he arrived, all her excitement ceased, and she lay in a weak, quiet silence.

'Let me go up,' Pierston said. 'And send for the doctor.'

Passing Avice's chamber he perceived that the little bed had not been slept on. At the door of the spare room he looked in. In one corner stood a walking-stick – his own.

'Where did that come from?'

'We found it there, sir.'

'Ah yes – I gave it to him. 'Tis like me to play another's game!'

It was the last spurt of bitterness that Jocelyn let escape him. He went on towards Mrs. Pierston's room, preceded by the servant.

'Mr. Pierston has come, ma'am,' he heard her say to the invalid. But as the latter took no notice the woman rushed forward to the bed, 'What has happened to her, Mr. Pierston? O what do it mean?'

Avice the Second was lying placidly in the position in which the nurse had left her; but no breath came from her lips, and a rigidity of feature was accompanied by the precise expression which had characterized her face when Pierston had her as a girl in his studio. He saw that it was death,[3] though she appeared to have breathed her last only a few moments before.

Ruth Stockwool's composure deserted her. ''Tis the shock of finding Miss Avice gone that has done it!' she cried. 'She has killed her mother!'

'Don't say such a terrible thing!' exclaimed Jocelyn.

'But she ought to have obeyed her mother – a good mother as she was! How she had set her heart upon the wedding, poor soul; and we couldn't help her knowing what had happened! O how ungrateful young folk be! That girl will rue this morning's work!'

'We must get the doctor,' said Pierston, mechanically, hastening from the room.

When the local practitioner came he merely confirmed their own verdict, and thought her death had undoubtedly been hastened by the shock of the ill news upon a feeble heart, following a long strain of anxiety about the wedding. He did not consider that an inquest would be necessary.

* * * * * *

The two shadowy figures seen through the grey gauzes of the morning by Ruth, five hours before this time, had gone on to the open place by the north entrance of Sylvania Castle, where the lane to the ruins of the old castle branched off. A listener would not have gathered that a single word passed between them. The man walked with difficulty, supported by the woman. At this spot they stopped and kissed each other a long while.

'We ought to walk all the way to Budmouth, if we wish not to be discovered,' he said sadly. 'And I can't even get across the island, even by your help, darling. It is two miles to the foot of the hill.'

She, who was trembling, tried to speak consolingly:

'If you could walk we should have to go down the Street of Wells, where perhaps somebody would know me? Now if we get below here to the Cove, can't we push off one of the little boats I saw there last night, and paddle along close to the shore till we get to the north side? Then we can walk across to the station very well. It is quite calm, and as the tide sets in that direction, it will take us along of itself, without much rowing. I've often got round in a boat that way.'

This seemed to be the only plan that offered, and abandoning the straight road they wound down the defile spanned further on by the old castle arch, and forming the original fosse of the fortress.

The stroke of their own footsteps, lightly as these fell, was flapped back to them with impertinent gratuitousness by the vertical faces of the rock, so still was everything around. A little further, and they emerged upon the open ledge of the lower tier of cliffs, to the right being the sloping pathway leading down to the secluded creek at their base – the single practicable spot of exit from or entrance to the isle on this side by a seagoing craft; once an active wharf, whence many a fine public building had sailed – including Saint Paul's Cathedral.

The timorous shadowy shapes descended the footway, one at least of them knowing the place so well that she found it scarcely necessary to guide herself down by touching the natural wall of stone on her right hand, as her companion did. Thus, with quick suspensive breathings they arrived at the bottom, and trod the few yards of shingle which, on the forbidding shore hereabout, could be found at this spot alone. It was so solitary as to be unvisited often for four-and-twenty hours by a living soul. Upon the confined beach were drawn up two or three fishing-lerrets, and a couple of smaller ones, beside them being a rough slipway for launching, and a boathouse of tarred boards. The two lovers united their strength to push the smallest of the boats down the slope, and floating it they scrambled in.

The girl broke the silence by asking, 'Where are the oars?'

He felt about the boat, but could find none. 'I forgot to look for the oars!' he said.

'They are locked in the boathouse, I suppose. Now we can only steer and trust to the current!'

The currents here were of a complicated kind. It was true, as the girl had said, that the tide ran round to the north, but at a special moment in every flood there set in along the shore a narrow reflux contrary to the general outer flow, called 'The Southern' by the local sailors. It was produced by the peculiar curves of coast lying east and west of the Beal; these bent southward in two back streams the up-Channel flow on each side of the peninsula, which two streams united outside the Beal, and there met the direct tidal flow, the confluence of the three currents making the surface of the sea at this point to boil like a pot, even in calmest weather. The disturbed area, as is well known, is called the Race.

Thus although the outer sea was now running northward to the roadstead and the mainland of Wessex, 'The Southern' ran in full force towards the Beal and the Race beyond. It caught the lovers' hapless boat in a few moments, and, unable to row across it – mere river's width that it was – they beheld the grey rocks near them, and the grim wrinkled forehead of the isle above, sliding away northwards.

They gazed helplessly at each other, though, in the long-living faith of youth, without distinct fear. The undulations increased in magnitude, and swung them higher and lower. The boat rocked, received a smart slap of the waves now and then, and wheeled round, so that the lightship which stolidly winked at them from the quicksand, the single object which told them of their bearings, was sometimes on their right hand and sometimes on their left. Nevertheless they could always discern from it that their course, whether stemwards or sternwards, was steadily south.[4]

A bright idea occurred to the young man. He pulled out his handkerchief and, striking a light, set it on fire. She gave him hers, and he made that flare up also. The only available fuel left was the small umbrella the girl had brought; this was also kindled in an opened state, and he held it up by the stem till it was consumed.

The lightship had loomed quite large by this time, and a few minutes after they had burnt the handkerchiefs and umbrella a coloured flame replied to them from the vessel. They flung their arms round each other.

'I knew we shouldn't be drowned!' said Avice hysterically.

'I thought we shouldn't too,' said he.

With the appearance of day a boat put off to their assistance, and they were towed towards the heavy red hulk with the large white letters on its side.

CHAPTER VII

An Old Tabernacle in a New Aspect

The October day thickened into dusk, and Jocelyn sat musing beside the corpse of Mrs. Pierston. Avice having gone away nobody knew whither, he had acted as the nearest friend of the family, and attended as well as he could to the sombre duties necessitated by her mother's decease. It was doubtful, indeed, if anybody else were in a position to do so. Of Avice the Second's two brothers, one had been drowned at sea, and the other had emigrated, while her only child besides the present Avice had died in infancy. As for her friends, she had become so absorbed in her ambitious and nearly accomplished design of marrying her daughter to Jocelyn, that she had gradually completed that estrangement between herself and the other islanders which had been begun so long ago as when, a young woman, she had herself been asked by Pierston to marry him. On her tantalizing inability to accept the honour offered, she and her husband had been set up in a matter-of-fact business in the stone trade by her patron, but that unforgettable request in the London studio had made her feel ever since a refined kinship with sculpture, and a proportionate aloofness from mere quarrying, which was, perhaps, no more than a venial weakness in Avice the Second. Her daughter's objection to Jocelyn she could never understand. To her own eye he was no older than when he had proposed to her.

As he sat darkling here the ghostly outlines of former shapes taken by his Love came round their sister the unconscious corpse, confronting him from the wall in sad array, like the pictured Trojan women beheld by Æneas[1] on the walls of Carthage. Many of them he had idealized in bust and in figure from time to time, but it was not as such that he remembered and reanimated them now; rather was it in all their natural circumstances, weaknesses, and stains.[2] And then as he came to himself their voices grew fainter; they had all gone off on their different careers, and he was left here alone.

The probable ridicule that would result to him from the events of the day he did not mind in itself at all. But he would fain have removed the misapprehensions on which it would be based. That, however, was impossible. Nobody would ever know the truth about him; *what* it was he had sought that had so eluded, tantalized, and escaped him; what it was that had led him such a dance, and had at last, as he believed just now in the freshness of his loss, been discovered in the girl who had left him. It was not the flesh; he had never knelt low to that. Not a woman in the world had been wrecked by him, though he had been impassioned by so many. Nobody would guess the further sentiment – the cordial loving-kindness – which had lain behind what had seemed to him the enraptured fulfilment of a pleasing destiny postponed for forty years. His attraction to the third Avice would be regarded by the world as the selfish designs of an elderly man on a maid.

His life seemed no longer a professional man's experience, but a ghost story; and he would fain have vanished from his haunts on this critical afternoon, as the rest had done. He desired to sleep away his tendencies, to make something happen which would put an end to his bondage to beauty in the ideal.[3]

So he sat on till it was quite dark, and a light was brought. There was a chilly wind blowing outside, and the lightship on the quicksand afar looked harassed and forlorn. The haggard solitude was broken by a ring at the door.

Pierston heard a voice below, the accents of a woman. They had a ground quality of familiarity, a superficial articulation of strangeness. Only one person in all his experience had ever possessed precisely those tones; rich, as if they had once been powerful. Explanations seemed to be asked for and given, and in a minute he was informed that a lady was downstairs whom perhaps he would like to see.

'Who is the lady?' Jocelyn asked.

The servant hesitated a little. 'Mrs. Leverre – the mother of the – young gentleman Miss Avice has run off with.'

'Yes – I'll see her,' said Pierston.

He covered the face of the dead Avice, and descended. 'Leverre,' he said to himself. His ears had known that name before to-day. It was the name those travelling Americans he had met in Rome gave the woman he supposed might be Marcia Bencomb.

A sudden adjusting light burst upon many familiar things at that moment. He found the visitor in the drawing-room, standing up veiled, the carriage which had brought her being in waiting at the door. By the dim light he could see nothing of her features in such circumstances.

'Mr. Pierston?'

'I am Mr. Pierston.'

'You represent the late Mrs. Pierston?'

'I do – though I am not one of the family.'

'I know it. . . . I am Marcia[4] – after forty years.'[5]

'I was divining as much, Marcia. May the lines have fallen to you in pleasant places[6] since we last met! But, of all moments of my life, why do you choose to hunt me up now?'

'Why – I am the step-mother and only relation of the young man your bride eloped with this morning.'

'I was just guessing that, too, as I came downstairs. But—'

'And I am naturally making inquiries.'

'Yes. Let us take it quietly, and shut the door.'

Marcia sat down. And he learnt that the conjunction of old things and new was no accident. What Mrs. Pierston had discussed with her nurse and neighbour as vague intelligence, was now revealed to Jocelyn at first hand by Marcia herself; how, many years after their separation, and when she was left poor by the death of her impoverished father, she had become the the wife of that bygone Jersey lover of hers, who wanted a tender nurse and mother for the infant left him by his first wife recently deceased; how he had died a few years later, leaving her with the boy, whom she had brought up at St. Heliers and in Paris, educating him as well as she could with her limited means, till he became the French master at a school in Sandbourne; and how, a year ago, she and her son had got to know Mrs. Pierston and her daughter on their visit to the island, 'to ascertain,' she added, more deliberately, 'not entirely for sentimental reasons, what had become of the man with whom I eloped in the first flush of my young womanhood, and only missed marrying by my own will.'

Pierston bowed.

'Well, that was how the acquaintance between the children began, and their passionate attachment to each other.' She detailed how Avice had induced her mother to let her take lessons in French of young Leverre, rendering their meetings easy. Marcia had never thought of hindering their intimacy, for in her recent years of affliction she had acquired a new interest in the name she had refused to take in her purse-proud young womanhood; and it was not until she knew how determined Mrs. Pierston was to make her daughter Jocelyn's wife that she had objected to her son's acquaintance with Avice. But it was too late to hinder what had been begun. He had lately been ill, and she had been frightened by his not returning home the night before. The note she had received from him that day had only informed her that Avice and himself had gone to be married immediately – whither she did not know.

'What do you mean to do?' she asked.

'I do nothing: there is nothing to be done. . . . It is how I served her grandmother – one of Time's revenges.'[7]

'Served her so for me.'

'Yes. Now she me for your son.'

Marcia paused a long while thinking that over, till arousing herself she resumed: 'But can't we inquire which way they went out of the island, or gather some particulars about them?'

'Aye – yes. We will.'

And Pierston found himself as in a dream walking beside Marcia along the road in their common quest. He discovered that almost every one of the neighbouring inhabitants knew more about the lovers than he did himself.

At the corner some men were engaged in conversation on the occurrence. It was allusive only, but knowing the dialect, Pierston and Marcia gathered its import easily. As soon as it had got light that morning one of the boats was discovered missing from the creek below, and when the flight of the lovers was made known it was inferred that they were the culprits.

Unconsciously Pierston turned in the direction of the creek, without regarding whether Marcia followed him, and though it was darker than when Avice and Leverre had descended in the morning he pursued his way down the incline till he reached the water-side.

'Is that you, Jocelyn?'

The inquiry came from Marcia. She was behind him, about half-way down.

'Yes,' he said, noticing that it was the first time she had called him by his Christian name.

'I can't see where you are, and I am afraid to follow.'

Afraid to follow. How strangely that altered his conception of her. Till this moment she had stood in his mind as the imperious, invincible Marcia of old. There was a strange pathos in this revelation. He went back and felt for her hand. 'I'll lead you down,' he said. And he did so.

They looked out upon the sea, and the lightship shining as if it had quite forgotten all about the fugitives. 'I am so uneasy,' said Marcia. 'Do you think they got safely to land?'

'Yes,' replied some one other than Jocelyn. It was a boatman smoking in the shadow of the boathouse. He informed her that they were picked up by the lightship men, and afterwards, at their request, taken across to the opposite shore, where they landed, proceeding thence on foot to the nearest railway station and entering the train for London. This intelligence had reached the island about an hour before.

'They'll be married to-morrow morning!' said Marcia.

'So much the better. Don't regret it, Marcia. He shall not lose by it. I have no relation in the world except some twentieth cousins in this isle, of whom her father was one, and I'll take steps at once to make her a good match for him. As for me . . . I have lived a day too long.'

CHAPTER VIII

'Alas for this Grey Shadow, Once a Man!'[1]

In the month of November which followed, Pierston was lying dangerously ill of a fever[2] at his house in London.

The funeral of the second Avice had happened to be on one of those drenching afternoons of the autumn, when the raw rain flies level as the missiles of the ancient inhabitants across the beaked promontory which has formed the scene of this narrative, scarcely alighting except against the upright sides of things sturdy enough to stand erect. One person only followed the corpse into the church as chief mourner, Jocelyn Pierston – fickle lover in the brief, faithful friend in the long run. No means had been found of communicating with Avice before the interment, though the death had been advertised in the local and other papers in the hope that it might catch her eye.

So, when the pathetic procession came out of the porch and moved round into the graveyard, a hired vehicle from Budmouth was seen coming at great speed along the open road from Top-o'-Hill. It stopped at the churchyard gate, and a young man and woman alighted and entered, the vehicle waiting. They glided along the path and reached Pierston's side just as the body was deposited by the grave.

He did not turn his head. He knew it was Avice, with Henri Leverre – by this time, he supposed, her husband. Her remorseful grief, though silent, seemed to impregnate the atmosphere with its heaviness. Perceiving that they had not expected him to be there Pierston edged back; and when the service was over he kept still further aloof, an act of considerateness which she seemed to appreciate.

Thus, by his own contrivance, neither Avice nor the young man held communication with Jocelyn by word or by sign. After the burial they returned as they had come.

It was supposed that his exposure that day in the bleakest churchyard in Wessex, telling upon a distracted mental and bodily condition, had thrown Pierston into the chill and fever which held him swaying for weeks between life and death shortly after his return to town. When he had passed the crisis, and began to know again that there was such a state as mental equilibrium and physical calm, he heard a whispered conversation going on around him, and the touch of footsteps on the carpet. The light in the chamber was so subdued that nothing around him could be seen with any distinctness. Two living figures were present, a nurse moving about softly, and a visitor. He discerned that the latter was feminine, and for the time this was all.

He was recalled to his surroundings by a voice murmuring the inquiry: 'Does the light try your eyes?'

The tones seemed familiar: they were spoken by the woman who was visiting him. He recollected them to be Marcia's, and everything that had happened before he fell ill came back to his mind.

'Are you helping to nurse me, Marcia?' he asked.

'Yes. I have come up to stay here till you are better, as you seem to have no other woman friend who cares whether you are dead or alive. I am living quite near. I am glad you have got round the corner. We have been very anxious.'

'How good you are! . . . And – have you heard of the others?'

'They are married. They have been here to see you, and are very sorry. She sat by you, but you did not know her. She was broken down when she discovered her mother's death, which had never once occurred to her as being imminent. They have gone away again. I thought it best she should leave, now that you are out of danger. Now you must be quiet till I come and talk again.'

Pierston was conscious of a singular change in himself, which had been revealed by this slight discourse. He was no longer the same man that he had hitherto been. The malignant fever, or his experiences, or both, had taken away something from him, and put something else in its place.

During the next days, with further intellectual expansion, he became clearly aware of what this was. The artistic sense had left him, and he could no longer attach a definite sentiment to images of beauty recalled from the past. His appreciativeness was capable of exercising itself only on utilitarian matters, and recollection of Avice's good qualities alone had any effect on his mind; of her appearance none at all.

At first he was appalled; and then he said 'Thank God!'

Marcia, who, with something of her old absolutism, came to his house continually to inquire and give orders, and to his room to see him every afternoon, found out for herself in the course of his convalescence this strange death of the sensuous side of Jocelyn's nature. She had said that Avice was getting extraordinarily handsome, and that she did not wonder her stepson lost his heart to her – an inadvertent remark which she immediately regretted, in fear lest it should agitate him. He merely answered, however, 'Yes; I suppose she is handsome. She's more – a wise girl who will make a good housewife in time. . . . I wish you were not handsome, Marcia.'

'Why?'

'I don't quite know why. Well – it seems a stupid quality to me. I can't understand what it is good for any more.'

'O – I as a woman think there's good in it.'

'Is there? Then I have lost all conception of it. I don't know what has happened to me. I only know I don't regret it. Robinson Crusoe lost a day[3] in his illness: I have lost a faculty, for which loss Heaven be praised!'

There was something pathetic in this announcement, and Marcia sighed as she said, 'Perhaps when you get strong it will come back to you.'

Pierston shook his head. It then occurred to him that never since the reappearance of Marcia had he seen her in full daylight, or without a bonnet and veil, which she always retained on these frequent visits, and that he had been unconsciously regarding her as the Marcia of their early time, a fancy which the small change in her voice well sustained. The stately figure, the good colour, the classical profile, the rather large handsome nose and somewhat prominent, regular teeth, the full dark eye, formed still the Marcia of his imagination; the queenly creature who had infatuated him when the first Avice was despised and her successors unknown. It was this old idea which, in his revolt from beauty, had led to his words on her handsomeness. He began wondering now how much remained of that presentation after forty years.

'Why don't you ever let me see you, Marcia?' he asked.

'O, I don't know. You mean without my bonnet? You have never asked me to, and I am obliged to wrap up my face with this wool veil because I suffer so from aches in these cold winter winds, though a thick veil is awkward for any one whose sight is not so good as it was.'

The impregnable Marcia's sight not so good as it was, and her face in the aching stage of life: these simple things came as sermons to Jocelyn.

'But certainly I will gratify your curiosity,' she resumed good-naturedly. 'It is really a compliment that you should still take that sort of interest in me.'

She had moved round from the dark side of the room to the lamp – for the daylight had gone – and she now suddenly took off the bonnet, veil and all. She stood revealed to his eyes as remarkably good-looking, considering the lapse of years.

'I am – vexed!' he said, turning his head aside impatiently. 'You are fair and five-and-thirty – not a day more. You still suggest beauty. *You* won't do as a chastisement, Marcia!'

'Ah, but I may! To think that you know woman no better after all this time!'

'How?'

'To be so easily deceived. Think: it is lamplight; and your sight is weak at present; and . . . Well, I have no reason for being anything but candid now, God knows! So I will tell you. . . . My husband was younger than myself; and he had an absurd wish to make people think he had married a young and fresh-looking woman. To fall in with his vanity I tried to look it. We were often in Paris, and I became as skilled in beautifying artifices as any *passée* wife of the Faubourg St. Germain.[4] Since his death I have kept up the practice, partly because the vice is almost ineradicable, and partly because I found that it helped me with men in bringing up his boy on small means. At this moment I am frightfully made up. But I can cure that. I'll come in to-morrow morning, if it is bright, just as I really am;

you'll find that Time has not disappointed you. Remember I am as old as yourself; and I look it.'

The morrow came, and with it Marcia, quite early, as she had promised. It happened to be sunny, and shutting the bedroom door she went round to the window, where she uncovered immediately, in his full view, and said, 'See if I am satisfactory now – to you who think beauty vain. The rest of me – and it is a good deal – lies on my dressing-table[5] at home. I shall never put it on again – never!'

But she was a woman; and her lips quivered, and there was a tear in her eye, as she exposed the ruthless treatment to which she had subjected herself. The cruel morning rays – as with Jocelyn under Avice's scrutiny – showed in their full bareness, unenriched by addition, undisguised by the arts of colour and shade, the thin remains of what had once been Marcia's majestic bloom. She stood the image and superscription of Age – an old woman, pale and shrivelled, her forehead ploughed, her cheek hollow, her hair white as snow. To this the face he once kissed had been brought by the raspings, chisellings, scourgings, bakings, freezings of forty invidious years – by the thinkings of more than half a lifetime.

'I am sorry if I shock you,' she went on huskily but firmly, as he did not speak. 'But the moth eats[6] the garment somewhat in such an interval.'

'Yes – yes! . . . Marcia, you are a brave woman. You have the courage of the great women of history. I can no longer love; but I admire you from my soul!'

'Don't say I am great. Say I have begun to be passably honest. It is more than enough.'

'Well – I'll say nothing then, more than how wonderful it is that a woman should have been able to put back the clock of Time thirty years!'

'It shames me now, Jocelyn. I shall never do it any more!'

* * * * *

As soon as he was strong enough he got her to take him round to his studio in a carriage. The place had been kept aired, but the shutters were shut, and they opened them themselves. He looked round upon the familiar objects – some complete and matured, the main of them seedlings, grafts, and scions of beauty, waiting for a mind to grow to perfection in.

'No – I don't like them!' he said, turning away. 'They are as ugliness to me! I don't feel a single touch of kin with or interest in any one of them whatever.'

'Jocelyn – this is sad.'

'No – not at all.' He went again towards the door. 'Now let me look round.' He looked back, Marcia remaining silent. 'The Aphrodites – how I insulted her fair form by those failures! – the Freyjas, the Nymphs and Fauns, Eves, Avices, and other innumerable Well-Beloveds – I want to see them never any more! . . . "Instead of sweet smell there shall be stink, and there shall be burning instead of beauty,"[7] said the prophet.'

And they came away. On another afternoon they went to the National Gallery, to test his taste in paintings, which had formerly been good. As she had expected, it was just the same with him there. He saw no more to move him, he declared, in the time-defying presentations of Perugino, Titian, Sebastiano,[8] and other statuesque creators than in the work of the pavement artist they had passed on their way.

'It is strange!' said she.

'I don't regret it. I have lost a faculty which has, after all, brought me my greatest sorrows, if a few little pleasures. Let us be gone.'

He was now so well advanced in convalescence that it was deemed a most desirable thing to take him down into his native air. Marcia agreed to accompany him. 'I don't see why I shouldn't,' said she. 'An old friendless woman like me, and you an old friendless man.'

'Yes. Thank Heaven I am old at last. The curse is removed.'

It may be shortly stated here that after his departure for the isle Pierston never again saw his studio or its contents. He had been down there but a brief while when, finding his sense of beauty in art and nature absolutely extinct, he directed his agent in town to disperse the whole collection; which was done. His lease of the building was sold, and in the course of time another sculptor won admiration there from those who knew not Joseph.[9] The next year his name figured on the retired list of Academicians.

* * * * *

As time went on he grew as well as one of his age could expect to be after such a blasting illness, but remained on the isle, in the only house he now possessed, a comparatively small one at the top of the Street of Wells. A growing sense of friendship which it would be foolish to interrupt led him to take a somewhat similar house for Marcia quite near, and remove her furniture thither from Sandbourne. Whenever the afternoon was fine he would call for her, and they would take a stroll together towards the Beal, or the ancient Castle, seldom going the whole way, his sciatica and her rheumatism[10] effectually preventing them, except in the driest atmospheres. He had now changed his style of dress entirely, appearing always in a homely suit of local make, and of the fashion of thirty years before, the achievement of a tailoress at East Quarriers. He also let his iron-grey beard grow as it would, and what little hair he had left from the baldness which had followed the fever. And thus, numbering in years but two-and-sixty, he might have passed for seventy-five.

Though their early adventure as lovers had happened so long ago, its history had become known in the isle with mysterious rapidity and fulness of detail. The gossip to which its bearing on their present friendship gave rise was the subject of their conversation on one of these walks along the cliffs.

'It is extraordinary what an interest our neighbours take in our affairs,' he observed. 'They say "those old folk ought to marry; better late than never." That's how people are – wanting to round off other people's histories in the best machine-made conventional manner.'

'Yes. They keep on about it to me, too, indirectly.'

'Do they! I believe a deputation will wait upon us some morning, requesting in the interests of matchmaking that we will please to get married as soon as possible. . . . How near we were to doing it forty years ago, only you were so independent! I thought you would have come back, and was much surprised that you didn't.'

'My independent ideas were not blameworthy in me, as an islander, though as a kimberlin young lady perhaps they would have been. There was simply no reason from an islander's point of view why I should come back; and I didn't. My father kept that view before me, and I bowed to his judgment.'

'And so the island ruled our destinies, though we were not on it. Yes – we are in hands not our own. . . . Did you ever tell your husband?'

'No.'

'Did he ever hear anything?'

'Not that I am aware.'

Calling upon her one day, he found her in a state of great discomfort. In certain gusty winds the chimneys of the little house she had taken here smoked intolerably, and one of these winds was blowing then. Her drawing-room fire could not be kept burning, and rather than let a woman who suffered from rheumatism shiver fireless he asked her to come round and lunch with him as she had often done before. As they went he thought, not for the first time, how needless it was that she should be put to this inconvenience by their occupying two houses, when one would better suit their now constant companionship, and disembarrass her of the objectionable chimneys. Moreover, by marrying Marcia, and establishing a parental relation with the young people, the rather delicate business of his making them a regular allowance would become a natural proceeding.

And so the zealous wishes of the neighbours to give a geometrical shape to their story were fulfilled almost in spite of the chief parties themselves. When he put the question to her distinctly, Marcia admitted that she had always regretted the imperious decision of her youth; and she made no ado about accepting him.

'I have no love to give, you know, Marcia,' he said. 'But such friendship as I am capable of is yours till the end.'

'It is nearly the same with me – perhaps not quite. But, like the other people, I have somehow felt, and you will understand why, that I ought to be your wife before I die.'

It chanced that a day or two before the ceremony, which was fixed to take place very shortly after the foregoing conversation, Marcia's rheumatism suddenly became acute. The attack promised, however, to be only temporary, owing to some accidental exposure of herself in making preparations for removal, and as they thought it undesirable to postpone their union for such a reason, Marcia, after being well wrapped up, was wheeled into the church in a chair.

* * * * *

A month thereafter, when they were sitting at breakfast one morning, Marcia exclaimed 'Well – good heavens!' while reading a letter she had just received from Avice, who was living with her husband in a house Pierston had bought for them at Sandbourne.

Jocelyn looked up.

'Why – Avice says she wants to be separated from Henri!' Did you ever hear of such a thing! She's coming here about it to-day.'

'Separated? What does the child mean!' Pierston read the letter. 'Ridiculous nonsense!' he continued. 'She doesn't know what she wants. I say she sha'n't be separated! Tell her so, and there's an end of it. Why – how long have they been married? Not twelve months. What will she say when they have been married twenty years!'

Marcia remained reflecting. 'I think that remorseful feeling she unluckily has at times, of having disobeyed her mother, and caused her death, makes her irritable,' she murmured. 'Poor child!'

Lunch-time had hardly come when Avice arrived, looking very tearful and excited. Marcia took her into an inner room, had a conversation with her, and they came out together.

'O it's nothing,' said Marcia. 'I tell her she must go back directly she has had some luncheon.'

'Ah, that's all very well!' sobbed Avice. 'B-b-but if you two had been m-married so long as I have, y-you wouldn't say go back like that!'

'What is it all about?' inquired Pierston.

'He said that if he were to die I – I – should be looking out for somebody with fair hair and grey eyes, just – just to spite him in his grave, because he's dark, and he's quite sure I don't like dark people! And then he said – But I won't be so treacherous as to tell any more about him! I wish—'

'Avice, your mother did this very thing. And she went back. Now you are to do the same. Let me see; there's a train—'

'She must have something to eat first. Sit down, dear.'

The question was settled by the arrival of Henri himself at the end of luncheon, with a very anxious and pale face. Pierston went off to a business meeting, and left the young couple to adjust their differences in their own way.

His business was, among kindred undertakings which followed the extinction of the Well-Beloved and other ideals, to advance a scheme for the closing of the old natural fountains in the Street of Wells, because of their possible contamination, and supplying the townlet with water from pipes, a scheme that was carried out at his expense, as is well known. He was also engaged in acquiring some old moss-grown, mullioned Elizabethan cottages, for the purpose of pulling them down because they were damp; which he afterwards did, and built new ones with hollow walls, and full of ventilators.[12]

At present he is sometimes mentioned as 'the late Mr. Pierston' by gourd-like young art-critics; and his productions are alluded to as those of a man not without genius, whose powers were insufficiently recognized in his lifetime.

NOTES

The Pursuit of the Well-Beloved
(1892)

I have made grateful use of previous editions by J. Hillis Miller and E. Mendelson (1975); and by Tom Hetherington (1986). The beginning of each of the twelve weekly instalments in the *Illustrated London News* is marked below by the insertion of the appropriate date. For Shakespeare I refer to Peter Alexander (ed.) *The Tudor Edition of William Shakespeare, the Complete Works* (London and Glasgow: Collins, 1951).

1 October 1892

PART FIRST: A YOUNG MAN OF TWENTY

CHAPTER I
Relics

This chapter is omitted in 1897.

1. *for a transient time*: the recurring idea that the beloved migrates from woman to woman owes much to Shelley (1792–1822) whose *Epipsychidion* deals with a similar theme of fugitive love: 'In many mortal forms I rashly sought/The shadow of that idol of my thought' (lines 267–8). Hardy himself several times refers to it as 'Platonic'. He did so defensively in a letter to Edmund Gosse (1849–1928) written in reaction to a hostile review (March 1897): 'the tale was sketched many years ago, when I was virtually a young man & interested in the Platonic Idea' (*Collected Letters* II p. 156).

CHAPTER II
A Supposititious Presentment of Her

1. *called an island*: Portland, which is linked to the mainland by a causeway. Uniquely in Hardy's novels, the obsessive description of this rocky formation and the sea around it replaces rural Wessex. In September 1890 Hardy visited Portland with Edmund Gosse and later wrote: 'I wish you wd buy a little house on the "Isle" ' (*Collected Letters* II p. 152).
2. *one man's doorstep*: a similar description of Portland is found in *The Trumpet-Major*: 'The pleasant peculiarity of one man's doorstep being behind his neighbour's chimney' (chapter 34).

3. *The melancholy ruins* . . . : from Act IV of Shelley's *Prometheus Unbound*, part of a cosmic coda sung by Panthea (IV.288–9). The fossilized rocks are 'cancelled cycles' of history, a possible reference to the triple frustration of Pearston with the three Avices.

4. *Caro*: Hardy in the *Life* declares that ' "Caro" (like all the other surnames) is an imitation of a local name . . . this particular modification having been adopted because of its resemblance to the Italian for "dear" ' (p. 304). A hostile reviewer pointed out another possible origin: '*Caro, carnis* [flesh] is the noun with the declension of which Mr. Hardy is perpetually and everlastingly preoccupied in his new book' (*The World* 1897.13).

5. *roan-mare Caros*: since a roan mare is one whose predominant colour is mixed with others, these Caros are perhaps said to be less inbred than others. The text emphasizes repeatedly the intermarriage between islanders generally and even within extended families.

6. *Avice*: in the *Life* (p. 10) Hardy explains this as a name taken from a seventeenth-century member of the Talbot family, neighbours of his forbears. It was the original name for Eustacia Vye used in the manuscript of *The Return of the Native*.

CHAPTER III
The Incarnation is Assumed to be a True One

1. *destroying the letters*: this scene is deleted from 1897 and with it the detailing of names of Jocelyn's many previous beloveds.

2. *I am – only one – in a long, long row*: compare Tess Durbeyfield's wish not to know more about her heredity: 'what's the use of learning that I am one of a long row only' (chapter 19).

3. *To his intrinsic Well-Beloved*: this echoes *Epipsychidion* on the many 'mortal forms of beauty': 'And some were fair – but beauty dies away:/Others were wise – but honeyed words betray:/And One was true . . .' (lines 269–71).

4. *Protean creature*: Proteus, a sea god who had the power of assuming different shapes. Hardy has a poem 'A Protean Maiden' beginning 'This single girl is two girls' (*Poems* III p. 125).

5. *fleshly tabernacle*: a phrase used by Milton in *Paradise Regained* (IV. 599) to refer to Christ.

6. *the risks of matrimony approximate most nearly to nil*: the first of many attacks on the institution of marriage made almost casually.

7. *local custom*: the custom of premarital intercourse to test or 'prove' a woman's fertility. In this text he wonders whether Avice 'expects' it. In 1897 he thinks she may 'regret' the loss of the practice. See chapter XII note 3.

CHAPTER IV
The Lonely Pedestrian

1. *conform to the custom*: this discussion of the island custom is omitted from 1897.

8 October 1892

2. *cannot agree*: in 1897 the letter is altered to one in which she explains her absence as caused by other people's views and hints about the island custom.

3. *a very Juno*: the current meaning was 'a woman of stately beauty'. Juno was the wife of Jupiter and goddess of fertility and power. It is recurrently used of Marcia. See also chapter VIII note 3. She resembles the 'fine dark-eyed' Arabella in *Jude the Obscure*, that 'complete and substantial female animal' (Book 1 chapter 6).

CHAPTER V
A Charge

1. *son of the Montagues to this daughter of the Capulets*: the idea of Pearston as Romeo to Marcia's Juliet is suggested by the trade hostility between their fathers. The running references to the parallel become increasingly ironic as their relationship deteriorates. See also chapter VI note 1 and chapter VIII note 4. In the *Life* (March 1884) Hardy writes: 'Write a novel entitled "Time against Two", in which the antagonism of the parents of a Romeo and Juliet *does* succeed in separating the couple and stamping out their love, – alas, a more probable development than the other!' (p. 171).

2. *children of Israel*: God divided the waters of the Red Sea so that his chosen people the Israelites could pass safely through them (Exodus 14:21–31).

3. *the fair white linen*: a similar scene occurs in *Jude the Obscure* where Jude dries Sue Bridehead's clothes. Sue denies the sexual implications of the clothes evident here, saying they are 'sexless cloth and linen' (Book 3 chapter 3). 1897 omits the details of Marcia's lacy underclothes.

CHAPTER VI
On the Brink

1. *Juliet*: see note 1 to chapter V above.

2. *Royal Academician*: member of the Royal Academy of Arts. Marcia evidently asks the question in an attempt to assess his social and financial prospects. See also chapter IX note 3 below.

3. *Doctors' Commons*: up to 1858 this was a centre for some lawyers dealing with marriage, divorce and probate. Pearston intends to procure a marriage licence.

4. *Apologia pro vitâ meâ*: explanation of my course of life. An allusion to J. H. Newman's *Apologia pro Vita Sua* (1864). Hardy has several passages from Newman in his *Notebooks*. The parallel seems farcical: Newman was explaining his then shocking conversion to Roman Catholicism, not a series of romantic entanglements.

CHAPTER VII
Her Earlier Incarnations

1. *unpractised condition of Adam*: who assumed that the first setting sun he saw had gone for ever. See also *Desperate Remedies* chapter 2.

15 October 1892

2. *crabs had been found clinging*: an image used to describe the face of the disillusioned husband who drowns himself in Hardy's poem 'The Newcomer's Wife': 'they searched, and at the deepest place / Found him with crabs upon his face' (*Poems* II p. 79).

3. *to fill with snow*: the image of a snow-filled nest is taken from Wordsworth's sonnet 'Why art thou silent?' where it is used to evoke a lover's emptiness after being rejected.

4. *It is all arranged*: the hasty marriage resembles that of Jude to Arabella after two or three months because he believes her pregnant.

CHAPTER VIII
A Miscalculation

1. *had been married*: in 1897 there is no marriage, merely a brief affair. In this text the marriage lasts for four years.

2. *City of Flowers*: Florence.

3. *Juno-wife's face*: see chapter IV note 3.

4. *Rosaline*: Romeo's first love who precedes Juliet in Shakespeare's play. See chapter V note 1.

5. *A legal marriage it was*: the first explicit questioning of the institution found also at the end of the novel. See chapter XXVIII. The topic is a main strand in *Jude the Obscure* and Hardy wrote in 1895 that a 'bad marriage' is 'one of the direst things on earth and one of the cruellest' (*Collected Letters* II p. 98).

6. *despite her Quos egos*: despite her arbitrary and obstinate judgements.

CHAPTER IX
Familiar Phenomena in the Distance

1. *make our own matrimonial laws*: this is what Arabella does in *Jude the Obscure* when she marries bigamously in Australia. As she says to the startled Jude: 'Crime! Pooh. They don't think much of such as that over there! Lots of 'em do it . . . He was very fond of me, and we lived honourable enough, and as respectable as any married couple' (Book 3 chapter 9).

2. *Parthian fling*: Marcia is attempting what the Parthians were skilled at: shooting backwards while retreating.

3. *A.R.A.*: Associate of the Royal Academy of Arts. See chapter VI note 2.

4. *round which honours might crystallize*: a strange chemical metaphor referring to the formation of crystals around a nucleus.

5. *The study of beauty was his only joy*: In the early part of the nineteenth century 'Ideal Works' of sculpture were regarded (W. M. Rossetti (1829–1919), brother of D. G. Rossetti, said) as '. . . the highest attempts to which the sculptor can gird himself and not to be meddled with at all save by the fewest' (B. Read, *Victorian Sculpture* (New Haven and London: Yale University Press, 1982), p. 199). By the 1880s a phase had developed in British sculpture which treated the human form in a naturalistic and detailed way (see Read p. 289 on 'The New Sculpture'). So Pearston belongs to a fading school of artists given to idealized nudes, often with classical subjects.

6. *he was green in judgment*: this reverses Cleopatra's view that in her 'salad days' she was also 'cold in blood' (*Antony and Cleopatra* I.v.73–4). Pearston's ardour grows stronger as he ages.

7. *Royal Moorish Palace*: Alhambra Music Hall.

8. *Börne's phrase*: 'Nothing is permanent but change'. In a speech in 1910 Hardy quotes this as the assertion of 'a German author' (*Life* p. 380). Ludwig Börne (1786–1837).

9. *As flesh she dies daily*: this reference to St Paul's First Epistle to the Corinthians (15: 31–44) parodies his idea that to die 'in the flesh' is to be raised in spiritual glory.

CHAPTER X
The Old Phantom Becomes Distinct

1. *small and early*: a small evening party not meant to last long. They were not popular. Disraeli (1880) writes, 'How I hate a small and early'; and Henry James in *Partial Portraits* (1888) refers to the 'late and suffocating "small and early"'. This seems to be the point here of the party turning into something 'large and late' and therefore suffocatingly crowded.

2. *the Countess of Channelcliffe's assembly*: according to Millgate, the original of

Lady Channelcliffe was Lady Portsmouth, a fact which must have been 'recognizable at least to those most immediately concerned' (*Biography* p. 329). See also notes 4, 6 and 7 below.

3. *his Shelleyan 'One-shape-of-many-names'*: This reference to *The Revolt of Islam* became the epigraph for 1897. In Shelley's poem it is however the 'spirit of evil' that takes many shapes: 'the Spirit of evil, / One Power of many shapes which none may know, / One Shape of many names' (I.xxvii.361–3). Hardy's copy of the poem which he owned from 1866 has many underlinings.

22 October 1892

4. *the young lady of the house*: according to Millgate, the original was recognizable as Lady Gwendolen Margaret Wallop, Lady Portsmouth's daughter. See note 2 above.

5. *Jill-o'-the Wisp*: a joking variation on 'Will o' the Wisp', an elusive sprite; Gill Flirt or Jill Flirt was a traditional name for a wanton woman.

6. *Mrs. Pine-Avon*: identified by Millgate as based on Mrs Rosamund Tomson (*Biography* p. 329). She was a poet and writer with whom Hardy had some correspondence. See note 2 above.

7. *Lady Mabella Buttermead*: Millgate thinks the original was Lady Winifred Burghclere (née Herbert), niece of Lady Portsmouth (*Biography* p. 329). See note 2 above.

8. *Female forms . . .*: from Shelley's *The Revolt of Islam*: 'Some, female forms, whose gestures beamed with mind' are amongst 'The Great, who had departed from mankind' (I.liv.605–8). The last clause is underlined in Hardy's copy. See also the description of Elizabeth Jane at the end of *The Mayor of Casterbridge* as having 'the serene Minerva-eyes of one "whose gestures beamed with mind"' (chapter 45).

9. *pearl-powder*: a cosmetic used to whiten the skin. The whole list is an ironic reference to the artifices mingled with genuine beauty in the fashionable crowd.

10. *the nation of every country dwells in the cottage*: this unexpectedly democratic comment from Nichola Pine-Avon is from a speech of John Bright in 1858 urging more social equity.

CHAPTER XI
She Draws Close, and Satisfies

1. *round, inquiring, luminous*: taken from the description of Lady Milnes-Gaskell's 'Round luminous enquiring eyes' (*Personal Notebooks* pp. 228–9).

2. *his Aphrodite*: the Greek goddess of love and beauty. See also chapters xv note 6, xvi notes 1 and 6, xxi note 4, xxiv notes 1 and 5.

3. *of his wife*: not in 1897.

4. *Calder Fair*: 1897 'The Jilt's Hornpipe'.

5. *a leading actress*: based on a reference for 1891 in the *Life*: 'Presently Ellen Terry arrived – diaphanous – a sort of balsam or sea-anemone, without shadow ... like a machine in which, if you press a spring, all the works fly open' (p. 244).

CHAPTER XII

She Becomes an Inaccessible Ghost

1. *taken on glass in the more primitive days*: glass plates, made by the photographer to support photographic salts, were first used in 1851.

2. *our Praxiteles*: a renowned Greek sculptor (born *c.* 390 BC). His work includes a famous naked figure of Aphrodite of Cnidus.

3. *that compact*: premarital sex. See chapter III note 7.

29 October 1892

PART SECOND: A YOUNG MAN OF FORTY

CHAPTER XIII

She Threatens to Resume Corporeal Substance

1. *pitched his nitch*: put down his bundle and (evidently) prepared to gossip.

2. *Both my names*: in 1897 she tells him she is called Ann Avice. In the *Life* (February 1889) Hardy writes that 'The story of a face which goes through three generations or more, would make a fine novel or poem of the passage of Time. The differences in personality to be ignored' (p. 226). The idea is used with a different significance in the poem 'Heredity': 'I am the family face; / Flesh perishes, I live on, / Projecting trait and trace / Through times to times anon, / And leaping from place to place / Over oblivion' (*Poems* II, pp. 166–7). See also the Introduction on his erasing of the individual identity of the Avices.

CHAPTER XIV

The Resumption Takes Place

1. *nympholepsy* (see Glossary): 'ecstasy or frenzy especially one inspired by the unattainable'. 1897: *nymph*. A small instance of the less overtly sexual nature of the later text.

CHAPTER XV

The Past Shines in the Present

1. *Minerva*: goddess of trades and crafts, a classical gloss on her work as a washerwoman.

2. *this girl's frame was doomed to be a real embodiment of that olden, seductive one*: in Hardy's poem 'The Well-Beloved' the poet meets this essence on the way to his bride. But she vanishes saying 'Thou lovest what thou dreamest her; / I am thy very dream!' (*Poems* I p. 170).

3. *Venus masking as Minerva*: the (Roman) goddess of love masquerading as the goddess of trades.

4. *past the distracting currents of passionateness*: the theme of passion outliving the ageing of the body is one treated seriously in several of Hardy's poems. See chapter xxv notes 1 and 2.

5. *Sapphic terror of love*: Sappho's poem number 31 (quoted by Longinus in *On the Sublime*) refers to her overpowering and confused emotions for young girls which have an element of terror because the girls will leave her for marriage.

6. *the white implacable Aphrodite*: the reference is unclear but may allude to a passage in *The Iliad* III.412 where Aphrodite intervenes after Helen of Troy has refused to go to bed with Paris. The goddess is there referred to in a phrase that could be translated as 'the bright, wrathful Aphrodite'. For other references to Aphrodite see chapters xi note 2, xvi notes 1 and 6, xxi note 4, xxiv notes 1 and 5.

7. *Nubian Almeh*: Egyptian dancing girl.

CHAPTER XVI

The New Becomes Established

1. *Rubens's 'Judgment of Paris'*: a reference to the three Avices. Rubens's late painting now in the National Gallery shows Paris choosing the most beautiful of three goddesses, Hera, Athena and Aphrodite.

2. *the world's desire*: Aphrodite.

3. *The subject of her discourse he cared nothing about*: see Introduction on the significance of his ignoring Avice the second's distinguishing characteristics.

4. *Ultima Thule*: 'remotest Thule'. This was a northern land noticed in the fourth century and never certainly identified. The phrase became a cliché for a place remote from civilization.

5 November 1892

5. *island custom*: see chapter iii note 7.

6. *the cruel Aphrodite*: though primarily the goddess of love, she was also a god-

NOTES

dess of war. See also chapters XI note 2, XV note 6, XXI note 4, XXIV notes 1 and 5.

7. *mad with method*: he sees himself as Polonius sees Hamlet (II.ii.203–4), acting apparently irrationally for a purpose which has reason in it. For the significance of his self-deceiving glosses on his conduct, see Introduction.

[CHAPTER XVII]
[*His Own Soul Confronts Him*]

CHAPTER XVIII
Juxtapostions

1. *robed in such exceeding glory* . . .: from Shelley's *Epipsychidion* (lines 199–200), referring to the eternal image of Beauty for whom he searches in many women. A sharp contrast is provided by its application here to a washerwoman.

2. *coigns of vantage*: projecting viewing places. An echo of Banquo's innocently ironic description of Macbeth's castle as a place of peace (I.vi.7).

12 November 1892

CHAPTER XIX
She Fails to Vanish when Closely Confronted

1. *Psyche*: another strikingly inappropriate account of Avice the second. Psyche was so beautiful that even Aphrodite was jealous of her; and she is the heroine of a legend often interpreted as an allegory of the soul.

2. *new places called flats*: flats were originally working-class housing but by the 1880s they were beginning to be built for the middle classes in places like Kensington.

CHAPTER XX
A Homely Medium does not Dull the Image

1. *Donizetti's*: Gaetano Donizetti (1797–1848), one of the composers noticed by Hardy in his early days in London (1862–3) as writing the 'foreign-operas' which were then in vogue (*Life* p. 45).

CHAPTER XXI
A Grille Descends Between the Vision and Him

1. *Martinmas Fair*: 11 November, feast of St Martin, a time for hiring-fairs for servants and labourers in country districts.

347

2. *Faustina's head*: a Roman empress said by ancient writers to be faithless, a possible reference to Avice's imminent revelation of her marriage.

19 November 1892

3. *island custom*: see chapter III note 7.
4. *Aphrodite was punishing him*: see chapter XV note 6. Pearston sees himself, ironically, as *too* faithful. See also chapters XI note 2, XV note 6, XVI notes 1 and 6, XXIV notes 1 and 5.

CHAPTER XXII
She is Finally Enshrouded from Sight

1. *Hymen . . . Harlequin*: Hymen, carrying torch and veil, was the god who presided over weddings. Here he behaves more like the comic figure of Harlequin who vies with a clown for the love of Columbine. Avice, her husband and Pearston make up the analogous trio.

PART THIRD: A YOUNG MAN OF FIFTY-NINE

CHAPTER XXIII
She Returns for the New Season

1. *like the quarries of maiden rock at home*: an instance of Pearston's obsession with life on Portland to which everything is made to relate.
2. *long-lost wife*: this and immediately following references to Marcia as his wife are not in 1897 since in that text there is no marriage.
3. *He pursued his inquiries*: his only attempt to satisfy the due inquiries for the whereabouts of a missing spouse in order to presume death after seven years of absence. See chapter XXIX note 2. Arabella in *Jude the Obscure* (Book 3 chapter 9) makes none. She simply contracts a bigamous second marriage in Australia on the grounds that she has no intention of coming back to England where her first husband Jude is living.

26 November 1892

CHAPTER XXIV
Misgivings on this Unexpected Re-embodiment

1. *Aphrodite*: see also chapters XI note 2, XV note 6, XVI notes 1 and 6, XXI note 4, and note 5 below.

2. *Ahasuerus*: the Wandering Jew who in legend was fated to roam the world for ever as punishment for urging Christ when carrying his cross to walk faster.

3. *to the general*: to the mass of people. An allusion to Hamlet's reference to a play that 'pleas'd not the million; 'twas caviare to the general' (II.ii.431–2).

4. *her so-called inconstancy*: one of Pearston's agile reworkings of his own conduct: he is only inconstant as the moon is. Her waxing and waning is, he claims, a model of constancy like him in his flitting from one woman to another.

5. *He feared Aphrodite, but Selene he cherished*: he fears the goddess of love but worships the moon goddess. Aphrodite strikes at random; Selene (as he reads her) is constant. For other Aphrodite references see note 1 above.

6. *jeune premier*: juvenile lead in a theatrical performance. The concealment of his age is seen as farcical not poignant, unlike the treatment of ageing love in Hardy's poems.

7. *Mephistopheles . . . usual terms of his firm*: if the devil had offered him youth in return for his soul.

CHAPTER XXV
The Renewed Image Burns Itself In

1. *It might have been, as far as feelings were concerned*: in Hardy's poem 'I Look into my Glass' the ageing speaker laments that Time, by not weakening his passions, still 'shakes this fragile frame at eve / With throbbings of noontide' (*Poems* I p. 106).

2. *as he regarded his face in the glass*: with this and chapter XXVI compare Hardy's poem 'I look into my glass, / And view my wasting skin, / And say, "Would God it came to pass / My heart had shrunk as thin!"' ' (*Poems* I p. 106).

3 December 1892

CHAPTER XXVI
He Makes a Dash for the Last Incarnation

1. *bathing-machine women*: attendants on small wheeled huts for sea-side bathers. The huts were pushed a short way into the sea and could be used for dressing and undressing and for bathing in privacy. Queen Victoria had one and thought it delightful.

2. *their recession as the matron*: a similar idea is expressed in *Jude the Obscure* with reference to the girls in a Training School for Teachers: 'They formed a pretty, suggestive, pathetic sight, of whose pathos and beauty they were themselves unconscious, and would not discover till, amid the storms and strains of afteryears, with their injustice, loneliness, child-bearing, and bereavement, their minds would revert to this experience as to something . . . insufficiently regarded' (Book 3 chapter 3).

3. *jackal to this lion of a family*: a clever twisting of the idea of an 'artistic lion' turned into a financial predator to support his handsome wife and daughters who now rule him.

4. *throned along the sea*: 'grim Dundagel thron'd along the sea', from a poem 'The Quest of the Sangraal' (1863) by R. S. Hawker, referring to Tintagel as the starting point of the quest for the Holy Grail. Hawker (1803–75) was the vicar of Morwenstow, Cornwall. He knew the Reverend Holder with whom Emma Gifford, Hardy's first wife, was staying when he met her. The quotation is used also in *A Pair of Blue Eyes*, chapter 21, in the famous cliff scene where Elfride rescues Knight.

5. *angina pectoris*: chest pains symptomatic of heart disease.

CHAPTER XXVII
He Desperately Clutches the Form

1. *a married couple*: in 1897 this marriage does not take place.

2. *of the most approved Kensington pattern*: from the 1860s on, an increase in red brick in this area caused some controversy, as over the building of the Albert Hall (completed 1872). So Pearston is keeping up with a fashion.

3. *Stièvenard's 'Lectures Françaises'*: a text-book by Leonce Stièvenard, a teacher at King's College London, where, Hardy says, he studied French 'for a term or two' in the 1860s (*Life* p. 52).

CHAPTER XXVIII
He Possesses it: He Possesses it Not

1. *he had no moral right to go further*: Avice's dread at waking to find her husband Pearston in the bedroom is an anticipation of the scene between Phillotson and his wife Sue in *Jude the Obscure*. After 'starting up half awake, staring wildly' Sue throws herself from the window to avoid him (Book 4 chapter 4).

10 December 1892

CHAPTER XXIX
The Elusiveness Continues

1. *they buried her*: in 1897 Avice's mother does not of course die after the marriage of her daughter to Pearston, but from the shock of her premarital elopement.

2. *more cogent than legal rights*: an idea also expressed in *Jude the Obscure* (1895). As late as 1912 Hardy wrote a piece entitled 'Laws the Cause of Misery' in which he says, 'I can only suppose, in a general way, that a marriage should be dissolv-

able at the wish of either party, if that party prove it to be a cruelty to him or her' (*Nash's Magazine* V.6.683).

CHAPTER XXX

He Becomes Retrogressive

1. *an age of barbarism*: this view of marriage is echoed in a passage in the manuscript of *Jude the Obscure* omitted from the printed version: 'When men of a later age look back upon the barbarism, cruelty, and superstition of the times in which we have the unhappiness to live, it will appear more clearly to them than it does to us that the irksomeness of life is less owing to its natural conditions . . . than to those artificial compulsions arranged for our well being' (p. 427).

2. *I had good argument for kissing once . . . now*: *Troilus and Cressida* IV.v.26–7. The first line is spoken by Helen's Greek husband Menelaus whom she deserted for the Trojan Paris; the second by Patroclus as a jibe against him when the other Greeks are kissing Cressida in welcome.

17 December 1892

CHAPTER XXXI

The Magnanimous Thing

1. *like the poet Keats . . . like Andrea del Sarto*: the suggestion seems to be that he has a Keatsian sensibility and possibly, if Hardy has Browning's 'Andrea del Sarto' (*Men and Women* 1855) in mind, a love for Avice which is morally debilitating.

2. *black framework*: Pearston compares his life after the loss of the third Avice to the framework left behind after a firework display.

3. *he had never received legal testimony*: he has in fact made only the most casual attempts to trace his wife. See chapter XXIII note 3.

CHAPTER XXXII

The Pursuit Abandoned

1. *Don't attack me for casuistry*: his argument is not so much casuistry as a willingness to disregard statutory law in favour of what he regards as Natural Law: 'The moment I have a reasonable belief that Marcia lives Avice is not my wife, it seems to me'. These outrageous views disappear from 1897.

2. *joy coming in the morning*: Psalms 30:5.

3. *I am near my journey's end*: the details of Pearston's attempted suicide are used in the description of the premarital elopement of Avice the second and Leverre in 1897.

CHAPTER XXXIII
He Becomes Aware of New Conditions

1. *that very woman*: Marcia (not his wife) returns in 1897 after the elopement of her stepson Henri Leverre with Pierston's bride-to-be and nurses him through an illness caught while attending the funeral of the second Avice. He marries her later out of pity when she is confined to a wheel-chair.

2. *the raspings, chisellings . . . of forty years*: see the reference in 'The Revisitation' (*Poems* I p. 241) to the work of 'Time's transforming chisel' on the face of a once-loved beautiful woman.

3. *the Witch of Endor*: or 'pythoness', who in I Samuel 28:7–13 raises the spirit of Samuel for Saul. Traditionally she was a hag. The reference suggests a malign power in Marcia.

The Well-Beloved, A Sketch of a Temperament
(1897)

1. *One shape of many names*: from *The Revolt of Islam* by Shelley (1792–1822) I.xxvii.363 and VIII.ix.3276. However, Shelley uses this phrase for the spirit of evil.

PREFACE

1. *The peninsula*: Portland. This Preface lays a new stress on Portland, reinforced throughout 1897 by added references to how the place strangely shapes the character of its natives and their destinies.

2. *by no means new to Platonic philosophers*: to Plato Beauty was an abstraction or 'Idea', which did not exist in the world of the senses, though it had some relation to things seen. Jocelyn's pursuit of the 'Well-Beloved' is a vulgarized version of this idea. In writing about this book version of the text in the *Life*, Hardy later said, 'The theory on which this fantastic tale of subjective idea was constructed is explained in the Preface . . . the theory of the transmigration of the ideal beloved one, who only exists in the lover, from material woman to material woman – as exemplified also by Proust (1871–1922) many years later'. This was a response to critics of 1892 who 'affected to find unmentionable moral atrocities in its pages' (*Life* p. 303).

3. *one nook*: Portland prison.

4. *a few chapters*: in practice this 1897 version created a different novel minus the two marriages (one bigamous) and Jocelyn's attempted suicide, which are all found in 1892. See Introduction.

In the 1912 Preface the last paragraph is omitted and two new ones added which are defensive in tone and refer to the 1892 version as 'experimental'.

PART FIRST: A YOUNG MAN OF TWENTY

CHAPTER I
A Supposititious Presentment of Her

1. *Now, if Time knows . . . it is She*: from the last few stanzas of 'Wishes to his (supposed) Mistresse' by Richard Crashaw (1612–49), a poem about the impossibility of finding a woman so full of the perfections he describes. The newly inserted epigraphs are part of an increased 'literariness' in 1897, which accompanies the toning down of sexual reference and new allusion to some obscure form of destiny at work amongst Islanders.

2. *cast up by rages of the se*: an addition in 1897; from a sixteenth-century description of Chesil Beach, Portland, in *The Itinerary of John Leland in or about the years 1535–43* ed. L. T. Smith (London, George Bell, 1907, III p. 251): 'a causey al of pible and sand cast up by the rages of the se'.

3. *Vindilia*: added in 1897, the Roman name for Portland.

4. *the Slingers*: new in 1897. A reference to the ability of the natives to defend themselves by slinging stones. See Leland p. 252.

5. *one man's doorstep*: see 1892, chapter II note 2.

6. *The melancholy ruins / Of cancelled cycles*: see 1892, chapter II note 3.

7. *Caro family*: see 1892, chapter II note 4.

8. *roan-mare Caros*: see 1892, chapter II note 5.

9. *Avice*: see 1892, chapter II note 6.

CHAPTER II
The Incarnation is assumed to be True

1. *I am only one of many*: see 1892, chapter III note 2.

2. *he had always been faithful*: see 1892, chapter III note 3.

3. *the 'wile-weaving Daughter of high Zeus'*: an addition in 1897 which connects the object of Pierston's pursuit with the most powerful of the gods and also links his obsession with his art. 'Wile-weaving' is a phrase used for Aphrodite only in a poem by Sappho. It adds to the suggestion that Pierston is hapless at the mercy of the manipulative goddess. See also below Part Second, chapter VI notes 7 and 8.

4. *Never much considering . . . Aphrodite herself indeed*: added in 1897. One of several additions which make Pierston's pursuit of women less earthy and less controllable.

5. *fleshly tabernacle*: see 1892, chapter III note 5.

6. *the risks of matrimony*: see 1892, chapter III note 6.

7. *The evening . . . disunite it again*: this paragraph is added in 1897. Like Portland itself, the sea is, in this text, endowed with an ability to influence the natives of the place powerfully (though vaguely). It seems to be malign. 'The Souls of the Slain' (1900) (*Poems* I pp. 124–7) describes a similar vision seen off Portland Bill of the spirits of those slain in battle. In the poem some spirits finally plunge into the sea off Portland Bill:

> And towering to seaward in legions,
>   They paused at a spot
>   Overbending the Race –
> That engulphing, ghast, sinister place –
> Whither headlong they plunged, to the fathomless regions
>   Of myriads forgot (*Poems* I p. 127).

8. *It seemed to say . . . Pierston kissed her*: added in 1897, the reference to paganism links with the idea of Portland as a powerfully disturbing place.

9. *if . . . she regretted*: 1892 reads 'if she expected', in keeping with a plot in which he asks her to conform to the 'island custom' of premarital sex. See 1892, chapter III note 7.

CHAPTER III
The Appointment

CHAPTER IV
A Lonely Pedestrian

1. *My dearest*: the letter is changed from 1892 where she refuses to conform to *his* request.

2. *Juno*: see 1892, chapter IV note 3.

CHAPTER V
A Charge

1. *son of the Montagues*: see 1892, chapter V note 1.

2. *Children of Israel*: see 1892, chapter V note 2.

3. *like Satan's form . . . divisible*: the quotation, added in 1897, is from Milton's *Paradise Lost* VI.330–1. Another equation of the malign forces surrounding Portland with undefined evil.

4. *overhauling the robes*: see 1892, chapter V note 3 for comparison of the scene there which is more specific. There his reverie is fed by the details of Marcia's lacy underclothes.

CHAPTER VI
On the Brink

1. *Juliet*: see 1892, chapter VI note 1.
2. *Royal Academician*: see 1892, chapter VI note 2.
3. *Doctors' Commons*: see 1892, chapter VI note 3.
4. *Apologia pro vitâ meâ*: see 1892, chapter VI note 4.

CHAPTER VII
Her Earlier Incarnations

1. *Suppose you say some men*: 1912 changes this to 'suppose you say the Beloved of some men'.
2. *unpractised condition of Adam*: see 1892, chapter VII note 1.
3. *crabs had been found*: see 1892, chapter VII note 2.
4. *left it to fill with snow*: see 1892, chapter VII note 3.
5. *We can't to-morrow*: this is a lie told because of his uncertainty about marrying her. It is not in 1892 where he does marry Marcia.

CHAPTER VIII
'Too Like the Lightning'

1. *Too Like the Lightning*: a new title in 1897. From *Romeo and Juliet* II.ii.119 where Juliet tells Romeo that their love is 'Too like the lightning, which doth cease to be'.
2. *some days longer*: in 1892 they live together after marriage for four years.
3. *Juno's classical face*: see 1892, chapter IV note 3.
4. *Rosaline*: see 1892, chapter VIII note 4.
5. *Too rash . . . too like the lightning . . .*: added in 1897. See note 1 above.
6. *though so fervid*: this implies that the affair was consummated.

CHAPTER IX
Familiar Phenomena in the Distance

1. *nearly married wife*: see 1892, chapter VIII note 1.
2. *A.R.A.*: see 1892, chapter VI note 2.
3. *round which honours might crystallize*: see 1892, chapter IX note 4.
4. *The study of beauty was his only joy*: see 1892, chapter IX note 5.
5. *Royal Moorish Palace*: see 1892, chapter IX note 7.
6. *Börne's phrase*: see 1892, chapter IX note 8.
7. *As flesh she dies*: see 1892, chapter IX note 9.

PART SECOND: A YOUNG MAN OF FORTY

CHAPTER I
The Old Phantom becomes Distinct

1. *Since Love will needs . . . suffer patiently*: the addition in 1897 of this self-explanatory epigraph from 'The lover determineth to serve faithfully' lines 1–6 by Sir Thomas Wyatt (*c.* 1503–42) continues the rehabilitation of Jocelyn as compared with 1892. It stresses his helplessness at the hands of fate rather than showing an obsession (with a strong sexual element) for which *he* is responsible. See also 1897 Part First, chapter I note 1.

2. *his father's sudden death*: in 1892 this death takes place within Part First, which ends with the death of the first Avice and so gives her greater prominence in the earlier text.

3. *small and early*: see 1892, chapter X note 1.

4. *Countess of Channelcliffe's assembly*: see 1892, chapter X note 2.

5. *his Shelleyan 'One-shape-of-many-names'*: see 1892, chapter X note 3, and above, Title Page note 1.

6. *a kindly young lady of the house*: see 1892, chapter X note 4.

7. *Jill-o'-the-Wisp*: see 1892, chapter X note 5.

8. *Mrs. Pine-Avon*: see 1892, chapter X note 6.

9. *Lady Mabella Buttermead*: see 1892, chapter X note 7.

10. *Female forms . . . beam with mind*: see 1892, chapter X note 8.

11. *pearl-powder*: see 1892, chapter X note 9.

12. *the nation of every country dwells in the cottage*: see 1892, chapter X note 10.

13. *In this he was aware . . . deplorably*: added in 1897, a further instance of the link made in this text between his pursuit of women and his pursuit of the ideal feminine in art.

CHAPTER II
She Draws Close and Satisfies

1. *round, inquiring, luminous*: see 1892, chapter XI note 1.

2. *the Wandering Jew of the love-world*: replaces a more specific account of his history in 1892. See also below Part Third, chapter II note 2.

3. *The Jilt's Hornpipe*: replaces 1892 'Calder Fair'.

4. *a leading actress*: see 1892, chapter XI note 5.

CHAPTER III
She Becomes an Inaccessible Ghost

1. *taken on glass*: see 1892, chapter XII note 1.

2. *He began to divine . . . the old island breed*: a significant addition to 1892. It emphasizes again the importance of the fact that Jocelyn and Avice are natives of this ancient place and links his obsession with Venus–Aphrodite who is now given a putative temple there.

3. *our Lysippus*: added to the Praxiteles of 1892, this is a reference to another Greek sculptor renowned for his realism – inapt for Pierston.

4. *that compact*: see 1892, chapter III note 7.

5. *many a Lycidas . . . world*: an addition in 1897. Lycidas in Milton's elegy of that name figures his drowned friend Edward King. This convoluted reference to line 158 of the poem presumably alludes to those drowned who die unmourned.

CHAPTER IV
She Threatens to resume Corporeal Substance

1. *Sylvania Castle*: in 1892 this is Dell-i-th'-rock and in reality it is Pensylvania Castle (Hotel).

2. *pitched his nitch*: see 1892, chapter XIII note 1.

3. *My second name is*: here she is Ann Avice; in 1892 merely Avice. Hence his erasure of her identity is more obvious in 1892. See Introduction.

CHAPTER V
The Resumption takes place

1. *He thought of nothing . . . temple there*: added in 1897. See above Part Second, chapter III note 2.

2. *or rather the capricious Divinity behind that ideal lady*: added in 1897, stressing Jocelyn's blamelessness.

3. *nymph*: for 1892's nympholepsy, 'ecstasy/frenzy especially one inspired by the unattainable'. A change of emphasis from Jocelyn's frenzy to a more harmless-sounding object of pursuit.

CHAPTER VI
The Past Shines in the Present

1. *Minerva*: see 1892, chapter XV note 1.

2. *like a sea-anemone*: added in 1897, suggesting his vulnerability.

3. *Passion masking as Indifference*: replaces 1892 'Venus masking as Minerva'. A less overtly sexual reference.

4. *past the distracting currents*: see 1892, chapter XV note 4.

5. *Isaac*: replaces 1892 'George'.

6. *Sapphic terror of love*: see 1892, chapter XV note 5.

7. *Weaver of Wiles*: added in 1897. See also above, Part First, chapter II note 3.

8. *with all her subtle face laughing aloud*: in Sappho's poem, where Aphrodite is referred to as 'wile-weaving' (Book I.i.12–13), she is laughing in amusement at Sappho's amorous predicament.

9. *Nubian Almeh*: see 1892, chapter xv note 7.

CHAPTER VII

The New becomes Established

1. *Rubens's 'Judgment of Paris'*: see 1892, chapter xvi note 1.

2. *the World's Desire*: see 1892, chapter xvi note 2.

3. *The subject of her discourse*: see 1892, chapter xvi note 3.

4. *Ultima Thule*: see 1892, chapter xvi note 4.

5. *succubus*: replaces 1892 'sentiment of fancy'. Like other changes, it removes agency from Pierston, since a 'succubus' is a demon in female form supposed to have carnal relations with men in their sleep. In 1912 it is replaced by the more neutral word 'haunting'.

6. *paying dearly enough for his Liliths*: for his previous infatuations. The reference is added in 1897. Lilith in legend was Adam's first wife and became a demon.

7. *To use a practical eye . . . not the clay*: an elaboration added in 1897, stressing some destined connection between the Caros and Pierston because of their heredity. The mismatch with a girl twenty years his junior is thus romanticized by him.

CHAPTER VIII

His own Soul confronts him

1. *he seemed to hear . . . combined stocks*: added in 1897. Another allusion to the pressure of the past (particularly the Isle) upon the present found in this version.

2. *found 'ee too old*: 1912 changes "ee' to 'you'.

CHAPTER IX

Juxtapositions

1. *forming the propylæa of the rock*: the propylæa were the great roofed gateway and entrance to the Acropolis at Athens. Another reference added in 1897 increasing the suggestion of the Isle's grandeur and status.

2. *robed in such exceeding glory . . . not*: see 1892, chapter xviii note 1.

3. *coigns of vantage*: see 1892, chapter xviii note 2.

4. *What are fame and name . . . I know the perfect and pure quarry she was dug from*: a significant addition in 1897. The equation of the second Avice with the rock of the Isle itself is part of the new explanatory account of Pierston's strange obsession with the Caro women.

5. *Demetrius of Ephesus*: from Acts 19:23–41. Demetrius was a silversmith who made statues of Diana of the Ephesians and who stirred up riots against St Paul for preaching that the gods such as Diana were mere idols. Pierston now regards himself as a worshipper of Aphrodite, both as a man and as a sculptor.
6. *The church of the island . . . heart*: another 1897 addition suggesting a mixture of pagan and Christian fate haunting the place and Pierston.

CHAPTER X
She Fails to Vanish still

1. *Psyche*: see 1892, chapter XIX note 1.
2. *new places called flats*: see 1892, chapter XIX note 2.
3. *all my Venus failures*: added 1897.

CHAPTER XI
The Image Persists

1. *Rossini's*: Gioacchino Rossini (1792–1868). This is changed from a reference to Donizetti (1892, chapter XX note 1). Both composers are mentioned in the *Life* p. 45.

CHAPTER XII
A Grille descends between

1. *Martinmas Fair*: see 1892, chapter XXI note 1.
2. *Empress Faustina's head*: see 1892, chapter XXI note 2.
3. *island custom*: see 1892, chapter III note 7.
4. *to Guernsey*: in 1892 it was Australia.
5. *Aphrodite, Ashtaroth, Freyja*: the last two names added in 1897. Ashtaroth is Astarte, goddess of fertility (Judges 2:13); Freyja is the Norse goddess of love and beauty. The new mythological references, like the epigraphs, increase the overt literariness of this text.

CHAPTER XIII
She is Enshrouded from Sight

1. *Hymen . . . Harlequin*: see 1892, chapter XXII note 1.

PART THIRD: A YOUNG MAN TURNED SIXTY

CHAPTER I
She Returns for the New Season

1. *In me thou seest . . . was nourished by*: the third quatrain of Shakespeare's sonnet LXXIII: 'That time of year thou mayst in me behold'. The epigraph, added in 1897, suggests a new dignity in the man of sixty. See also 1897, Part First, chapter I note 1.

2. *the quarries of maiden rock at home*: see 1892, chapter XXIII note 1.

3. *in England*: changed in 1912 to 'in the Isle of Slingers'.

4. *his long-lost Marcia*: replaces 1892's 'long-lost wife'.

5. *the church at the top*: becomes the 'Church of the Trinita dei Monti' in 1912.

6. *Thus much Marcia*: this incident is abbreviated from 1892, since the question of presuming the death of a missing spouse does not arise. See 1892, chapter XXIII note 3.

7. *Ike had been killed*: in 1892 this news reaches him only after his return to the Isle.

8. *Have you guessed*: the first of several allusions, added in 1897, to the second Avice's premeditated plan to marry him to her daughter. Another device removing agency from Pierston.

CHAPTER II
Misgivings on the Re-embodiment

1. *His divinity*: replaces 1892 Aphrodite. The removal of this and some other Aphrodite references is perhaps part of an attempt to make sexual passion less obtrusive than in 1892.

2. *Ahasuerus*: see above, Part Second, chapter II note 2.

3. *to the general*: see 1892, chapter XXIV note 3.

4. *the undulating ground*: this changed in 1912 to 'the rugged ground'.

5. *his wraith in a changed sex*: replaces 1892 'his sweetheart in the flesh'. In the same paragraph references to Aphrodite and Selene are removed. See 1892, chapter XXIV note 5; and note 1 above.

6. *jeune premier*: see 1892, chapter XXIV note 6.

7. *Like her granny*: added in 1897.

8. *Mephistopheles . . . terms of his firm*: see 1892, chapter XXIV note 7.

9. *little boot*: changed to 'pretty boot' in 1912.

CHAPTER III
The Renewed Image burns itself in

1. *as far as feelings were concerned*: see 1892, chapter XXV note 1.
2. *She did not say how simple she thought him*: another reference to her having planned this. See above, Part Third, chapter 1 note 8.
3. *lest she might seem to be angling*: see above Part Third, chapter 1 note 8.
4. *as he beheld his face in the glass*: see 1892, chapter XXV note 2. The theme of physical ageing dominates Part Third in 1897 by being more detailed than in 1892.
5. *Upon the whole . . . press on*: this sentence of foreboding was added in 1897.

CHAPTER IV
A Dash for the Last Incarnation

1. *bathing-machine women*: see 1892, chapter XXVI note 1.
2. *their recession as matrons*: see 1892, chapter XXVI note 2.
3. *jackal to this lion*: see 1892, chapter XXVI note 3.
4. *throned along the sea*: see 1892, chapter XXVI note 4.
5. *angina pectoris*: see 1892, chapter XXVI note 5.
6. *Its voice . . . 'There's tragedy hanging on this!'*: added in 1897.
7. *It was enough . . . from this moment*: added in 1897 to lead into his confession to Avice that he courted her mother and her grandmother. In 1892 this is not told to her till after their wedding. See 1892, chapter XXVIII.
8. *the engagement stood as before*: in this text Jocelyn returns, unmarried but engaged, to Kensington. It diverges radically at this point from 1892 where he takes his new wife Avice the third back to London. Now Avice and her mother merely visit him there.

CHAPTER V
On the Verge of Possession

1. *of the approved Kensington pattern*: see 1892, chapter XXVII note 2.
2. *Stiévenard's 'Lectures Françaises'*: see 1892, chapter XXVII note 3.
3. *They retired rather early*: at this point in 1892 (chapter XXVIII) Jocelyn makes his unwelcome visit to his wife's bedroom and is then prompted to tell her of his love for her mother and grandmother. Avice's frightened reaction to his entering the bedroom is reminiscent of the more extreme scene in *Jude the Obscure* (Book 4 chapter 4) where Sue Bridehead leaps from a window to escape her husband Phillotson. At this point in 1892 Avice returns to the Isle ahead of him.
4. *Anything the matter?*: in 1892 the meeting with Leverre does not occur immediately on Jocelyn's return to the Isle but when they do meet he gets to know the young man well.

5. *How is mother?*: at this point in the narrative in 1892 the third Avice's mother dies and Jocelyn goes back to London. Much is omitted in 1897.

CHAPTER VI
The Well-Beloved is – Where?

1. *She is gone!*: the episode of Avice's elopement with Leverre is new in 1897. In 1892 it is Pearston who slips out at night in a small boat to attempt suicide.

2. *He took the letter*: this letter from the third Avice is new in 1897 and replaces Pearston's note to his friend Somers in 1892 (chapter XXXII) about his own disappearance, meant to facilitate his wife's marriage to Leverre.

3. *He saw that it was death*: in 1892 Avice's mother dies peacefully (chapter XXIX) when the girl is already married to Pearston. The revised version blames Avice for her mother's death since it is caused by the shock of her elopement with Leverre at a time when she is engaged to Pierston.

4. *A little further . . . steadily south*: the lovers' descent to the beach and departure in the boat draws upon the 1892 description of Pearston's attempt to drown himself which it replaces (see 1892, chapter XXXII).

CHAPTER VII
An Old Tabernacle in a New Aspect

1. *the pictured Trojan women beheld by Æneas*: another new literary addition in 1897. A reference to Virgil's *Aeneid* I where Aeneas sees depicted on the walls of a temple Trojan women pleading in vain with the goddess Pallas Athena for mercy on the city of Troy. Pierston's past loves are now seen by him as piteous creatures that he rejected as the goddess did the women.

2. *rather it was in all their natural circumstances, weaknesses, and stains*: a new reference in 1897 to his recognition that he fictionalized the real women.

3. *The October day thickened . . . in the ideal*: this long reverie, an addition in 1897, gives a new meditative and elegiac tone to the conclusion, compared with the abrupt ending of 1892.

4. *I am Marcia*: in 1892 his encounter with Marcia occurs when he wakes up from his near-drowning to find her nursing him. The episode takes up a single short chapter and ends the novel with her revelation that her apparent beauty is a delusion and that she too is old and withered.

5. *after forty years*: see 'The Man who Forgot' (*Poems* II p. 286) in which the poet searches for a woman only to realize suddenly that 'Forty years' frost and flower/Had fleeted since I'd used to come/To meet her in that bower'.

6. *May the lines have fallen to you in pleasant places*: an allusion to Psalms 16:6, meaning 'I hope your life has been fortunate and happy'.

7. *one of Time's revenges*: the clown in *Twelfth Night* referring to the overthrow of the arrogant Malvolio, says that 'thus the whirligig of time brings in his revenges' (V.i.376–7).

Most of this chapter is new in 1897.

1. *Alas for this grey shadow, once a man!*: new in 1897; from 'Tithonus', line 11, by Tennyson (1809–92). In Greek myth the goddess of dawn Eos procured for her lover Tithonus the gift of immortality but forgot to ask also for eternal youth. The poem thus highlights the physical process of ageing by dealing with it in an extreme way.

2. *dangerously ill of a fever*: this illness caused by catching cold at the second Avice's funeral replaces the one caused by near-drowning in 1892. Here, as there, Marcia nurses him.

3. *Robinson Crusoe lost a day*: a reference not found in 1892. Crusoe slept for two days and thought it was one. Pierston makes the strained comparison to underline his loss of interest in female beauty and because possibly he thinks of himself as metaphorically shipwrecked.

4. *Faubourg St. Germain*: a high-class suburb of Paris indicating that Marcia and her husband were well-to-do.

5. *The rest of me . . . lies on my dressing-table*: in 1892 it is merely the absence of daylight that deceives Jocelyn about Marcia's appearance. Here it is because she has used 'beautifying artifices' now left off. The added detail is part of the extra emphasis in 1897 on the physical processes of ageing.

6. *the moth eats*: becomes in 1912 'the moth frets'.

7. *Instead of sweet smell there shall be stink . . . beauty*: Isaiah 3:24. New in 1897. This predicts the same fate for Pierston's artistic creations and the women he has loved as Isaiah prophesied for the daughters of Zion who 'are haughty, and walk with stretched forth necks and wanton eyes' (3:16).

8. *the time-defying presentations of Perugino, Titian, Sebastiano*: this reference (new in 1897) to three great painters of the Italian Renaissance (Pietro Perugino (1446–1524), Tiziano Vecellio (*c.* 1487–1576) and Sebastiano Luciani (*c.* 1485–1547)) makes Pierston's denigration of his own work ambiguous. He now claims to have lost all artistic judgement and not to be able to distinguish works of genius from those of pavement artists. Like much of the other new material in this Part, it diminishes him.

9. *those who knew not Joseph*: an ambiguous comment. Exodus 1:8 speaks, after Joseph's death, of 'a new king over Egypt, which knew not Joseph'. This suggests that a great man is soon forgotten.

10. *his sciatica and her rheumatism*: the detailed account of their physical ills is new in 1897.

11. *Avice says she wants to be separated from Henri!*: this new incident in 1897 seems to start up the cycle of changing affections seen in Jocelyn and also in the second Avice who claimed to have loved fifteen men already. See 1897, Part Second, chapter VIII.

12. *His business was . . . ventilators*: this paragraph, added in 1897, has been read as a metaphor for Pierston's impotence.

A Note on the Illustrations to The Pursuit of the Well-Beloved

The Pursuit of the Well-Beloved was serialized in the *Illustrated London News* (1 October – 17 December 1892). It appeared in twelve weekly parts each with an identical headpiece and two illustrations by Walter Paget (1863–1935). The illustration of serial fiction (first when issued in parts and later when published in periodical magazines) had become hugely popular in the nineteenth century. As George du Maurier (illustrator of *The Hand of Ethelberta* and *A Laodicean*) wrote in 1880: 'Evidently the illustrated book is a "felt want". The majority of civilised human nature like to read, and a majority of that majority likes to have its book (even its newspaper!) full of little pictures.'[1]

In fact by the time that Hardy wrote his novels, prior publication, serially in periodicals and with illustrations, was a common way to introduce new fiction to a wider public piecemeal and cheaply before it appeared in a more expensive volume form. As a struggling beginner, Hardy did not achieve this for his first two novels, *Desperate Remedies* (1871) and *Under the Greenwood Tree* (1872), but all his later works except *Two on a Tower* (1882) and *The Woodlanders* (1887) were serialized and illustrated in this way. In the case of *Far from the Madding Crowd* (1874) and *The Hand of Ethelberta* (1876) some illustrations were also used in the first volume edition. Only with *A Pair of Blue Eyes*, *Far from the Madding Crowd*, *The Return of the Native* and *The Trumpet-Major* did Hardy intervene with the artist, largely to discuss the accuracy of details to be included in the drawings.[2] With the other novels, like *The Pursuit of the Well-Beloved*, the periodical chose the artist and Hardy had no hand in the illustrations. In this case, as in others, the determinants were the type of magazine and the intended readership. It would seem likely that Hardy, now at the peak of his success, was content to leave the pictures to the artist.

So it is distinctly significant to Paget's illustrations that he was providing them for the *Illustrated London News*. This was not a general cultural magazine but a weekly, founded in 1842, as the first of a successful type where the primary purpose was the illustration of current events, 'subordinating in a manner its letterpress to its pictures'.[3] An attraction of this up-market picture magazine was its supposed ability to provide, like today's television, on-the-spot detail from inaccessible places: 'Not only on the battlefield is the artist indispensable, but the royal wedding, the royal christening, the public funeral in the Abbey, and a thousand other functions dear to the heart of the public, belong to him alone.'[4] The illustration of actualities was what the *Illustrated London News* originally provided for its readership and continued to do so even after the introduction of more cultural matter and then of serialized fiction in July 1883. The issue in which the first instalment of *The Pursuit* appeared, for instance, included illustrated news items on a cholera outbreak at Hamburg, the centenary of the French Republic, an obituary of the Duke of Sutherland, as well as an article on Napoleon's horse Marengo with a photograph of its skeleton. Fiction never took the primary place in the *Illustrated London News*. Advertisements were confined to the back pages, reportage set the tone and the high quality of the illustrations was maintained. They persisted also after the introduction of photographs which, by the end of the century, were more numerous than the drawings.

The influx of photographs, which began as early as the mid-century, allowed what appeared to be 'a magical transcription from life into art'.[5] It suggested a different way of looking at visual detail from an earlier emblematic or symbolic mode, in which one thing symbolized another. This iconographic tradition had largely faded by the 1890s and, instead of competing with photography on its own terms, the artist could now sometimes create more generally 'atmospheric' pictures indicating the imaginative impact of a scene or character in the text upon him or her.

Paget himself was a figure painter as well as a book and periodical illustrator. As a book illustrator of *Robinson Crusoe* in 1896 he was praised as an 'excellent figure draughtsman . . . [with a] strong poetic feeling for landscape' and 'consummate' accuracy of detail in 'costumes and accessory'.[6] Clearly in what was considered a cut above mere periodical illustration he brought to bear all his professional skills in these highly regarded wood engravings. The accuracy of detail would have been practised in his time as a war correspondent for the *Illustrated London News* during the Gordon Relief Expedition, and also with General Gerald Graham's army in the Sudan (1884–5). The drawings of 'The War in the Sudan', attributed to 'our special artist Mr Walter Paget', were numerous. Though the battle scenes are 'atmospheric' in their emphasis on imperial bravery and dash, they are also minutely detailed. So, by the time that he illustrated

The Pursuit, Walter Paget was an experienced graphic illustrator in the literalist/reportage tradition but with some skill in figure drawing and 'poetic landscape'. Hardy's strange novel presented a peculiar challenge to such talents.

The decorative headpiece, which was to be repeated on the first page of each of the twelve instalments, is an attempt to capture the pursuit of the title in a fanciful emblematic form alien to Paget. To the left is a crudely drawn half-draped and blindfolded male figure stretching out feebly towards at least five disembodied female heads disappearing off the right-hand side of the page. The symbolism is laboured: love is blind, Pearston (presumably the half-nude male) is pursuing a Platonic ideal. His passion for a succession of different women is non-physical – there are no female bodies – and somehow mythological. The visual incoherence of the composition indicates Paget's unease with this high-flown gloss on the title.

Since Paget had to satisfy only the editors of the *Illustrated London News*, who already knew his work, what his illustrations offer is the first contemporary interpretation of the text. And what the readers of this first novel took in was a composite text in which the words were accompanied by idiosyncratic visual pointers to its meaning. One aspect of illustration which Hardy had earlier shown himself to believe significant was the relative visual importance of the characters. He had spelled out to Arthur Hopkins,[7] then illustrating *The Return of the Native*, his own ranking of the characters in that novel, putting Clym Yeobright first and Eustacia Vye second. For Paget in *The Pursuit of the Well-Beloved* clearly Pearston was not only the most important character but overwhelmingly so. He appears in twenty-three of the twenty-four pictures and he is, with the exception of the second Avice pictured as washerwoman, the only character seen alone. He is seen burning his love letters, sitting near the first Avice's grave, looking at a quarry where the second Avice's husband Isaac has been killed, sitting on his bed with his packed portmanteau, and standing in the oarless skiff in which he attempts suicide. This is the melodramatic scene which forms the last picture, instead of the final compellingly ironic scene in the text in which an aged Pearston finds himself nursed back from near-death by drowning by a shrivelled and wrinkled Marcia of sixty.

The emphasis on Pearston as a hero figure is in keeping with a novel which plays ironically on the notion of male dominance and in which the man in question is self- rather than other-obsessed, despite his protestations about pursuing a feminine ideal. The women become almost figments of his imagination as he refigures them to himself. Paget captures this subordination of women, amongst whom only the second Avice and Marcia are given a degree of prominence. The former appears tête-à-tête with Pearston no fewer than six times. The most striking of these is her first lamplit confrontation with him, an epiphanic scene sometimes used to illustrate Hardy's first meeting with his wife-to-be, Emma, at the rectory at St Juliot's. Less focused in their impact are the pictures of her on the sea-shore with Pearston, dusting the studio in his Kensington flat watched by him, and in a train returning to the Isle after admitting that she is married. In middle age she is shown in the churchyard with Pearston discussing her daughter's future, and lying ill on her sofa pressing the girl to marry him. In pictorial terms the other two Avices are marginalized even further. The first Avice is seen only in an early illustration standing on a cliff edge with Pearston. Though the third Avice is pictured four times, in one of these she is the third figure in a group with her mother and Pearston. For the rest she is seen with Pearston in his Kensington flat, and with Leverre on the Isle. She is only centre stage when Pearston, at their first meeting, helps to release her foot from a crack in the rocks on the sea-shore.

Marcia, on the other hand, though rarely present, is strikingly depicted three times as a dark Junoesque beauty in scenes which all convey a strong sense of tension. The first shows her scrutinized by the light which Pearston has lit when they meet by chance at night. The confrontation is close and her simple dark figure and illuminated face make one of the most effective illustrations to the novel. The second scene pictures her at a desk writing a letter to a discarded lover while Pearston stands disapprovingly behind her. Their relative positions allow her to appear dominant and almost to be spurning him; and her figure is characterized by a determination the other women lack. The final picture is one in which the smouldering beauty hurls one of his own statuettes at him before leaving him.

The remaining object of Pearston's wandering affection, Nichola Pine-Avon, is given one weirdly static depiction when she visits Pearston in his drawing room after he has lost interest in her. The picture is half-comic in its combination of a grim-faced woman scorned and the ornate elaboration of her fashionable clothes.

In all these scenes, particularly the interiors, Paget fills in much mundane detail. This is no longer emblematic but obviously aims at the literal accuracy of the reporter/war artist. Nichola Pine-Avon for instance is not only dressed in a flowered hat, drooping scarf and layered dress, with gloves in one hand, but has the other hand resting on a flounced, fabric-covered piece of furniture topped with small pictures and statuettes. This concern with detail is persistent whether the scene is a train or a quarry. In such drawings the careful eye of the illustrator of actualities is seen at work anchoring Pearston's private obsessions in the cumbersome trappings of the real world in which he lives. The pseudo-Platonic fantasy of 'the Well-Beloved' sits uneasily with this unbeautiful and sometimes ludicrous clutter.

The aspect of the novel which lends imaginative force to Pearston's pursuit of an ideal beauty or lover is the description of the Isle itself with which he himself connects it. The suggestion of a terrible inhuman beauty is captured by Hardy in recurrent descriptions of the rocky peninsula and especially its sounds as the sea and wind roar against it. It is as full of sounds as Prospero's isle and can be read as more prominent than any character. This is not how Paget reads it. Only seven illustrations include the rocks, cliffs or sea-shore, five of them in the latter half of the text. In these drawings Paget produces less detailed and more 'atmospheric' scenes, coloured always with a sense of menace. Two such illustrations frame the text: the one depicting Pearston with the first Avice on a vertiginous cliff's edge and the last with him alone in the oarless skiff with the dark cliffs looming behind him. The blunt contrast between the literalism of detail in the Victorian setting and the romantically atmospheric scenery is true to the strange dichotomy of the text. It captures the written insistence on the non-physical and high-minded nature of Pearston's pursuit of women, contrasting with the reality of his role in the unromantic and cluttered world to which he fails to relate. Seen even through Paget's unromantic eye, the text was evidently as ambivalent then as it seems today.

The 1897 volume edition of *The Well-Beloved* has only one illustration (in addition to a map of Wessex): an etched frontispiece by Henry Macbeth Raeburn, 'The "Isle" of the Story'. It is no longer a composite text and the pictorial absence of Pierston by chance mirrors his subordination to the women in the second text. In the Wessex Edition of 1912 (volume XIII) a photograph of the Isle of Slingers (Portland) finally replaces any drawn illustration and marks Hardy's determination to emphasize the reality of 'Wessex' generally.

Notes

1. George du Maurier, 'The Illustrating of Books From the Serious Artist's Point of View', *Magazine of Art* (1890), 349.
2. Arlene M. Jackson, *Illustration and the Novels of Thomas Hardy* (Totowa, N.J.: Rowman and Littlefield, 1981), pp. 30–39.
3. C. K. Shorter, 'Illustrated Journalism', *Contemporary Review*, no. 400 (1899), 485.
4. Shorter, 487.
5. A. Hopkinson, *Julia Margaret Cameron* (London: Virago Press, 1986), p. 10.
6. M. H. Spielman, 'The New *Robinson Crusoe*', *Magazine of Art* (December 1891), 51.
7. Jackson, p. 43.

GLOSSARY

ABBREVIATIONS

adj.	adjective	advb.	adverb
pa.t.	past tense	pr.p.	present participle
pr.t.	present tense	p.p.	past participle
prep.	preposition	pron.	pronoun
sb.	substantive	sb.pl.	substantive plural
vb.	verb		

a', pron.	he.
afore, advb.	formerly.
afore, prep.	before.
ashlar, sb.	dressed hewn stone.
avore, advb.	beforehand.
backalong, advb.	back.
beer-blown, adj.	fat from beer swilling.
beetling, adj.	overhanging.
bo-fet, sb.	corner display cupboard for china and glass.
chammer, sb.	room.
chimney-crooks, sb.pl.	hooks for cooking.
clane, advb.	completely.
clothes-horse, sb.	drying frame.
coddled, adj.	water-sodden.
coigns, sb.	projecting viewing points.
collier, sb.	coal-barge.
copings, sb.pl.	courses of stone or brick.
corbels, sb.pl.	supporting projections.
coulter, sb.	blade of a plough-share.
daps, sb.	copy.
delf, sb.	Delft glazed pottery.
dummy, sb.	blockhead, idiot.
elf, sb.	tricksy creature (esp. child).
'en/ 'n, pron.	him.
epiderm, sb.	surface.
fag-end, sb.	last remnant.
fainéans, sb.pl.	idlers.

fantast, sb.	a person given to fantasies.
felloe, sb.	exterior rim of a wheel or part of it.
fly, sb.	fast horse-drawn carriage let out for hire.
gallied, adj.	frightened.
geologic, adj.	geological.
git, vb.	get.
grammer, sb.	grandmother.
half-risible, adj.	half-laughing.
huddied, vb.pa.t.	hid.
instauration, sb.	renewal.
jade, sb.	hussy, minx, coquette.
kimberlins, sb.pl.	strangers, aliens.
landau, sb.	four-wheeled carriage.
lerret, sb.	boat suitable for heavy seas, used around Portland.
lingual, adj.	pertaining to language.
linkman, sb.	man employed to carry a torch.
mask-figure, sb.	masquerader, one wearing a mask.
masking, adj.	disguised.
metempsychosis, sb.	passage of the soul from one body to the other.
mid, vb.	might.
mullions, sb.pl.	vertical bars.
mumm, vb.	act in dumb show, mime.
nitch, sb.	threw down his bundle.
(in phr. pitched his nitch)	
nympholepsy, sb.	ecstasy or frenzy.
opened (up), vb.pa.t.	disclosed.
organisation, sb.	physical and mental constitution.
ossify, vb.	harden (fig.).
petite, adj.	slight, small.
petrifications, sb.pl.	fossils.
pipe-light, sb.	twist of paper, spill.
popple-stone, sb.	pebble.
pourparlers, sb.pl.	informal discussions.
quatrefoils, sb.pl.	four-leaved shapes.
rasp, sb.	erosion.
risibility, sb.	inclination to laugh.
scarp, sb.	steep face of a hill.
shure, advb.	indeed.
slopping, sb.	splashing.
spaking-tube, sb.	speaking tube.
spawls, sb.pl.	chips of stone.
squatted, p.p.	crushed.

stonen, adj.   stone.

sublimed, adj.   elevated, refined, purified.

subserving, adj.   subservient.

sultanic, adj.   despotic.

svelte, adj.   graceful, slender.

thrue, adj.   true.

tine, vb.   close.

trouvaille, sb.   lucky find, windfall.

wadden, vb.   was not.

wedden, sb.   wedding.

well, adj.   lucky.
   (in phr. well to be you)

wold, adj.   old.

READ MORE IN PENGUIN

In every corner of the world, on every subject under the sun, Penguin represents quality and variety – the very best in publishing today.

For complete information about books available from Penguin – including Puffins, Penguin Classics and Arkana – and how to order them, write to us at the appropriate address below. Please note that for copyright reasons the selection of books varies from country to country.

In the United Kingdom: Please write to *Dept. EP, Penguin Books Ltd, Bath Road, Harmondsworth, West Drayton, Middlesex UB7 0DA*

In the United States: Please write to *Consumer Sales, Penguin Putnam Inc., P.O. Box 999, Dept. 17109, Bergenfield, New Jersey 07621-0120.* VISA and MasterCard holders call 1-800-253-6476 to order Penguin titles

In Canada: Please write to *Penguin Books Canada Ltd, 10 Alcorn Avenue, Suite 300, Toronto, Ontario M4V 3B2*

In Australia: Please write to *Penguin Books Australia Ltd, P.O. Box 257, Ringwood, Victoria 3134*

In New Zealand: Please write to *Penguin Books (NZ) Ltd, Private Bag 102902, North Shore Mail Centre, Auckland 10*

In India: Please write to *Penguin Books India Pvt Ltd, 210 Chiranjiv Tower, 43 Nehru Place, New Delhi 110 019*

In the Netherlands: Please write to *Penguin Books Netherlands bv, Postbus 3507, NL-1001 AH Amsterdam*

In Germany: Please write to *Penguin Books Deutschland GmbH, Metzlerstrasse 26, 60594 Frankfurt am Main*

In Spain: Please write to *Penguin Books S. A., Bravo Murillo 19, 1° B, 28015 Madrid*

In Italy: Please write to *Penguin Italia s.r.l., Via Benedetto Croce 2, 20094 Corsico, Milano*

In France: Please write to *Penguin France, Le Carré Wilson, 62 rue Benjamin Baillaud, 31500 Toulouse*

In Japan: Please write to *Penguin Books Japan Ltd, Kaneko Building, 2-3-25 Koraku, Bunkyo-Ku, Tokyo 112*

In South Africa: Please write to *Penguin Books South Africa (Pty) Ltd, Private Bag X14, Parkview, 2122 Johannesburg*

READ MORE IN PENGUIN

THOMAS HARDY

'Hardy is one of the relatively few writers who produced, by common consent, both major fiction and major poetry' – Martin Seymour-Smith

Tess of the D'Urbervilles
'An extraordinarily beautiful book ... Perhaps this is another way of saying that *Tess* is a poetic novel' – A. Alvarez

Far From the Madding Crowd
'The novel which announced Hardy's arrival as a great writer' – Ronald Blythe

Jude the Obscure
'The characters ... are built up not merely against the background of the huge and now changing Wessex, but out of it. It is this which makes the novel the completion of an oeuvre' – C. H. Sisson

The Woodlanders
'In no other novel does Hardy seem more confidently in control of what he has to say, more assured of the tone in which to say it' – Ian Gregor

The Return of the Native
'It came to embody more faithfully than any other book the quintessence of all that Wessex already represented in Hardy's mind' – George Woodcock

The Mayor of Casterbridge
In depicting a man who overreaches the limits, Hardy once again demonstrates his uncanny psychological grasp and his deeply rooted knowledge of mid-nineteenth-century Dorset.

and

The Trumpet-Major
A Pair of Blue Eyes
Under the Greenwood Tree
The Hand of Ethelberta
The Well-Beloved
Two on a Tower

The Distracted Preacher
  and Other Tales
Selected Poetry
A Laodicean
Desperate Remedies